1973

Singh -

Rita

THE MINOTAUR GARDEN

THE MINOTAUR GARDEN

Lewis Hosegood

HEINEMANN : LONDON

William Heinemann Ltd
15 Queen Street, Mayfair, London W1X 8BE
LONDON   MELBOURNE   TORONTO
JOHANNESBURG   AUCKLAND

First published 1972
© Lewis Hosegood 1972
434 34850 3

The quotation from *The Leopard* (*Il Gattopardo*) by Giuseppe di Lampedusa, translated by Archibald Colquhoun, is reprinted by kind permission of the publishers, Collins & Harvill.

Printed in Great Britain by
Northumberland Press Ltd., Gateshead

Für Elise

I have been here before,
But when or how I cannot tell ..
        Dante Gabriel Rossetti
           (Sudden Light)

'Eh, miss ... *baby*....' The male voice with the foreign inflexion was hoarse, imploring attention.

The girl in the pale-blue Levis, frayed and colour-drained from constant washing and overnight drying because she carried so little in the way of personal belongings on this trip, sat astride her motor-bike for a few seconds longer, gazing deliberately at the oily intensity of the lake with its little flashes of scintillating light— a crucible of heavy molten bronze waiting to be poured, it seemed —and contemplated the rocky island tiered into terrace gardens vivid with azaleas and surmounted by a Palladian villa. Beyond the island the juniper-blue mountains faded eventually in the distance into milky, washed-out colourlessness like her trousers.

Then as the heat of the sun beat down swelteringly into her leather jacket, intolerable after the exhilarating ride down from Vezzano, through the Sarca valley and along the tree-lined east side of the lake skirting Monte Baldo, she unbuckled it and took it off. Underneath she wore a voile shirt through whose gossamer the sun penetrated to her skin, burning her back but with a kindlier touch, less humid, less oppressive than the airless heat inside the jacket and tempered a little by the warm roadside breeze smelling of exhaust petrol, *espresso* coffee and the strong scent of smartly coiffeured bourgeoise Italian ladies walking arm-in-arm with their attentive husbands.

After a moment or two the plastic seat of the Honda had become stickily unbearable and the girl stood up, unstraddled the machine, swinging her leg over, and, with her jacket over the handlebars, pushed it along to a vacant space in the parking strip overlooking the water, ran it up on to its stand and locked it.

Here, avoiding the importunate men in lavender suits eating ice cream round a humming kiosk, she leaned against a magnolia on the promenade growing almost out of the lapping water's edge, and under its cool shade gazed again at the hump of land called so oddly Isola Malcontenta, rising from the surface a little way out.

The island, though it may have been such at one time, was in fact now a promontory, being joined to the shore and the lakeside highway behind her, lively with fast motor traffic, by a causeway some two hundred metres in length built up from solid blocks of stone sunk directly into the lake bed where it was shallow. At the island end, just in front of great arched iron gates which were now closed, it widened out to form a bay for about six cars, no more, but farther round on a strip facing the village there was a jetty where a succession of motor boats, whirring like mad clocks whose pendulums had been removed, crossed and re-crossed the strait to discharge a few passengers, perhaps twenty at a time, and bring back a similar number. Evidently the island, or the villa, was a showplace, open to visitors. But not indiscriminately like the most famous stately English homes, to massed coach loads. The filigree wrought iron gates remained closed at the private end of the road. Flanked on either side by a massive curved pinkish-grey wall surmounted by classical urns and dramatically gesticulating statuary, it looked solid enough to repel the unwanted. She knew the name of the island from her map. The village adjacent was called Pianezze—there had been a sign just up the road. She wondered what the name of the villa was. Only the upper storey could be seen above the terrace walk—buff-coloured stone, fluted Venetian red tiles, a colonnaded portico rising to a shallow peak, and from the roof at every corner more statuary, draped and undraped marble figures gazing out coolly over the lake and village, and on the apex of the central dome a great spread-winged eagle looking as if it had just alighted there from the Giudicarian Alps barely visible to the north-west, balancing itself for a moment before folding its pinions.

Lost in this distant contemplation she gradually became aware that she too was the object of interest for somebody else—three of the ice-cream gallants had detached themselves from the group and were hemming her in, approaching her stealthily with broad, sunny smiles and musical whistles.

'Hello there, baby!' said one in rich American-English, savoury as *spaghetti bolognese*. 'You alone? You wanna drink, maybe?' The three grinned at each other, and at her. They were harmless but persistent, like children begging; local boys, she guessed, not *capelloni* from Milan. She smiled and shook her head. How did they know she was English? Then she realized—of course they'd seen the GB plate on the Honda.

'C'mon, baby—you like a drink?' His suit was pink with brown stripes. 'Nice cool.' He parted his expressive hands vertically, miming its length and satisfaction. He was able to make it seem almost sexual.

'No, thank you.' Still smiling, she shook her head again and turned away, towards the lake.

They surrounded her, edging round to lean on the rail, gazing at her, smiling, admiring, searching her blouse with their dark liquid eyes.

She folded her arms casually, hoping to eliminate temptation without appearing offhand. They were not really offensive—just running true to Italian male form. Why did they all, street gangsters and city gentlemen alike, assume that an English girl would open her legs for them at the drop of a hat? It was all those illustrated articles in the glossy magazines, she supposed—swinging Londra and the *vita permissiva*—which so fascinated a predominantly strait-laced, conventional Catholic society still aligned to a peasant morality. For that matter, of course, we were just as bad; we continued to enjoy the same sort of myth about the Swedes.

'No, thanks,' she said again gently. She had no wish to offend; they were bucolic, but very charming and happy, chewing their gum, eating her with their eyes. Then, hoping to deter them, she added: 'I'm waiting for my husband.'

She had her left hand hidden under the other folded arm but she knew they didn't believe her. One of them touched her back, tentatively, exploratively, running his hand down and across in curiosity, perhaps out of interest as to what, if anything, she had underneath. She made an attempt to slip her leather jacket on again, but it was her undoing. Half way into it she realized the movement had probably revealed too much. They closed in on her like wasps round a jar of honey.

'He's very big,' she added, smiling, without raising her voice, trying to keep it all friendly and light-hearted. 'Six foot four. An American ... From Texas ...' They didn't believe a word of it. They could see now that the only ring on her finger was a jade scarab from Paraphernalia, Carnaby Street.

'You always riding the *motocicletta*?'

'What is your-a name?'

'You like to go riding in my car?' The questions were simultaneous and from all sides. 'Listen, I tell you. This evening we go to

Garda. I show you. Cabaret. Very good dancing.' He mimed a vigorous style of rock some five or ten years out of date by London standards. 'Nice place. Good to eata. Very beautiful. You like it. Nice big. Not dirty little place. Nice cooking. You eata by the lake. Very beautiful ... Scampi. Valpolicella ... Film stars. Monica Vitti. All big people ...'

She continued to shake her head, to smile, to decline her firm thanks which they in their turn continued to ignore. Her good humour, engendered by the beautiful day and cerulean sky and the softness of the air, began to dissipate. She felt the first twinge of annoyance. How did one shake off this kind of pestering? Call for help? The local passers-by looked at her hostilely, as though she had only herself to blame, in that immodest gear, if she now found herself in difficulties; the *poliziotto* leaning against the floral lamp-standard as if his feet were hot did not look any more sympathetic —the gallants, he would say, were only behaving as one would expect young men to behave. And anyway she wasn't sure of the correct mode of address; her Italian was very weak. '*Per favore, vuol' aiutarmi?*' Then what?

All at once she saw her escape route. Not far away at the floating duck-boarded pontoon which formed a jetty, decked with tubs of scarlet salvias, another motor boat was filling up. One umber-skinned man in a khaki drill shirt was bending over the inboard engine, another was preparing to cast off with a boat hook. Ducking quickly under the rail, she turned towards the three youths. '*Mi rincresce, ma non posso proprio trattenermi di più!*' she said, hoping that was right, and then ran along the narrow strip of slaty rubble between the rail and the lake edge, leaping on to the pontoon and thence, by way of a pair of mounting steps, on to the hot smooth gunwale of the *barchetta*. A hand came up to help her, supporting her firmly under the elbow, and she was down in the swaying launch.

'*Grazie!*'

'*Prego, signorina. All' isola?*'

'*Si, permesso.*'

He cast off and the boat's engine jogged to life, rattling the housing. The launch headed out over the water. Looking back she saw the landing stage, the café, the road, and the crowd with the three young men in it, receding and dwindling in importance. The sun beat down. There was a waft of hot petrol fumes and lubricating oil. She let her arm drop, dangling her hand childishly over the side to feel the cool swirl of water over her fingers. Her mind went back in a flash of association to Frogmore Creek and the cottage, the school holidays, her mother, now dead, and her brother Nicholas; then she was instantly in the present again.

Approaching the island jetty, swinging wide to circumnavigate it and make the landing on the other side, the boat turned. She could see now the reason for the boatman's question—it was but the first stage in a longer journey. A previous launch was leaving the jetty to go on, presumably across the lake to a small town (Campione?) faintly visible through the haze on the other side, and then perhaps farther still, to Riva maybe, all round the northern shore, criss-crossing from village to village. She could get off at the island, take a look at whatever was to be seen there, and then return to Pianezze on the next launch. She didn't want to leave her motor-bike too long. True it was locked, and so were the panniers, but they contained all her belongings—clothes, documents, travellers' cheques, her passport. Not that she worried particularly. She had got by so far these last six weeks without spending much. She had been able to do casual work, earning money as a waitress, a market gardener in Alsace hoeing lettuces, a courier meeting homeward-bound school-journey trains at Basle at the end of the Easter rush period, washing up dishes in Innsbruck. And she could have earned a lot more if she hadn't discouraged the attention of so many, more important than the three village oafs but persistent like them. She didn't want to get involved again with anybody yet. She had had her spell with Tom. It had been more than enough. Now she wanted to forget it, to forget him completely and be free. It was part of the plan. Not getting involved was part of the adventure. She was not afraid of being alone. She was twenty. When she was thirty, then she would be afraid, but not yet. She adored company, but she was not afraid of going it alone.

As they neared the island—Isola Malcontenta of the peculiar name—she saw the villa more clearly from the other side for it had obviously been designed to face out over the lake. The terraces were all landscaped in that direction, a series of shallow levels with glimpses of curving paths, arbours, pergolas, a colonnaded summerhouse like a little temple with a green cupola, a flight of steps flanked by more statuary, at water level a boathouse resembling a Renaissance tomb and trailing over with some vine-like tentacles; and above it all, on the skyline, the villa itself, the central part square with flanking wings of lesser proportions, and outbuildings all in the same matching Palladian style, including a flat-topped campanile, the whole thing impressively elegant rather than big. In the shimmering, reflected light, and with the milky blue mountains behind it, framing it, their tops bare and crenellated, the intervening hills forested with pines or chalk-smudged with cherry woods (or were they pear orchards?), it did not look malcontented. It seemed to be sitting there, peacefully quiet, withdrawn from contemporary vulgarity, a little remote perhaps, but with an air of antiquity, gracious manners, elegance, wisdom. One could have termed it both idyllic and civilized.

She stepped off the launch with several others, on to a stone quay with a wooden upright spar, painted red, with a lantern cage on the top like those she associated with pictures of Venice. Following the rest of the group, who appeared to be German, she climbed a flight of shallow, wide stone steps, weeping with overhanging trees, and found herself on the first terrace, a broad walk to right and left laid out geometrically with ornamental flower beds—primulas, auriculas, geraniums and red-and-silver-foliaged ones whose name she did not know, and towering above it the great retaining wall which supported the next. She soon lost the Germans—they went to the right so she chose the left—and though she passed through several little knots of sauntering visitors less purposeful than herself she did not hear any English spoken. Italian, French, something that might have been Dutch, but no English. Not even any Americans. She didn't mind this, she discovered, which struck her at once as being unusual. Her nature was not to shun company; she needed it as a rule. She loved hearing people talk, and laugh, and she liked men and men's admiration. It was odd therefore that she should deliberately turn her back on all that and choose to walk alone here at this end of the promenade, avoiding people.

She made some interesting discoveries. A plantation of lemon trees grew under the wall, almost leaning out from it, their roots anchored beneath the foundations, the leaves dark green and glossy and with little dried lemons, last year's, the size of walnuts drooping from them. A pungent smell of eucalyptus halted her. This terrace was an arboretum, and at the base of each tree was a little leaden tag with the Latin name identifying it. Stooping, she discovered the source and then, crushing a leaf between her fingers, confirmed it. Like the water cascading over her hand, it took her back to her childhood. Colds. Something her mother had rubbed on her chest ages ago, before she had even gone to school. She looked up. There were name tags even on the shrubs growing out of the crannies of the wall. Capers. *Capparis spinosa.* Aloes.

The end of the walk brought her to the foot of the house. An enormous iron gate, padlocked, seemed to lead into a basement like a dungeon, all mossed tiles and dripping walls enclosed from the sun and from which sprouted valerian and hanging stonecrops. There was a wooden notice attached to the gate, the white paint old and flaked, the lettering indistinct. She had to go up close to make it out. It read: *Proprietá privata. Divieto d'ingresso.* Farther down in one corner there was a name. It looked like d'Anza.

Returning the way she had come she walked as far as the other extremity, a blank wall smothered with an apricot tree. She then climbed another flight of steps, one of a matching pair, curved, with stone balustrades, and came out on to a wide upper terrace with huge quarried flagstones underfoot. From here, leaning on one of the low walls, she could make out the village, the flash of cars in the sunlight, the wake of another motor boat scratching the mirror surface of the lake. Sitting on the parapet she lit a cigarette, whiling away another ten minutes. A green lizard basked on the wall near her hand, throbbing as it breathed. When she made a movement, putting the cigarette to her mouth, it suddenly scuttled away. Then she wandered on, discovering more intriguing things—water gardens, fountains, statues everywhere, an overgrown bower with apparently two naked lovers half reclining in it, startling her for a moment, but it turned out to be Cupid and Psyche in white marble slightly browned by the weather. Oleanders. Yuccas. Tall fragrant laurels. Once she thought she heard the sound of peacocks and following yet another flight of steps, guided by the ear-splitting screams emitted at intervals, she emerged upon a level grass sward where three white birds strutted and a few people were trying to take photographs. Suddenly one of the peacocks spread its tail in a great fan of erotic display and there was a clicking of cameras, a little burst of laughter and triumphant exclamations in French and German.

Philippa Rowantree watched, and then smiled. It was extraordinary this feeling of content which had come over her. Something to do with the place? Some atmosphere of quiet romantic melancholy amounting to happiness? How odd—she wasn't that sort of person. It was just because everything was slightly overgrown. Swinging her leather battledress tunic from one hand she moved on. There were more surprises—a grotto made of shells, thousands of them; a young gardener singing at his work, full operatic tenor, E *lucevan le stelle*. He was very good; even the Puccini sob was there.

Finally she came to another arched gate, whose stiff iron handle she managed to turn and pushed open. It trundled heavily back with a scream of unlubricated metal and she stepped down into a sunken garden with palms, clipped lavender, box hedges and a rose pergola like an enclosed avenue. It was so quiet. Bees zoomed past her and butterflies oscillated their wings in great orgasmic throbs on the hanging buddleias. Sheltered, it was almost unbearably hot and deserted. She walked through to the other end of the garden, mounted the corresponding steps there and came up to another gate. Three or four metres behind this was yet another, the space between being shadowed by walls of cypress so that it made a little corridor of no-man's-land, plain gravel, like a buffer strip between two frontier posts. On this second gate, which was surmounted by a strand of barbed wire, was another notice, more legible this time, the letters in red. *Pericolo! Corrente ad alta tensione! Divieto d'ingresso.* This was evidently the end of the public gardens. Beyond lay those of the house, wherein they had no intention evidently of allowing anyone to trespass. *I contravventori saranno puniti a termine di legge!* It sounded like a papal excommunication.

The girl, being young, modern and independent, did not take kindly to such injunctions. She opened the first gate, with some difficulty, and stepped into the rectangular no-man's-land. Having come this far she wanted to see what lay beyond, to catch a glimpse of the front of the house perhaps. However, she had no intention of being hurled back by an electric shock—she would merely go up to the other gate and stand there before it, observing what she could through the interstices.

Suddenly, half way there, she heard a raised voice behind her, a sharp incomprehensible sentence which made her turn round immediately. In the centre path of the sunken garden a man was standing, facing her. He was tall, thin, about sixty, in a light grey suit with a panama hat and carried a walking stick. He had an open-necked cream shirt with a dark blue silk neckerchief loosely tied and tucked in. From under the panama, at the sides, iron grey hair. Striding quickly but easily towards her, scarcely using the stick to feel the ground, he continued, with an urgency in his voice that suggested some kind of a warning, to speak in a tongue which she not only did not understand but whose origin she didn't even recognize.

She stared at him. He was distinguished-looking and upright, quite tall for an Italian, if that's what he was, with a brown lined face. Many years ago, as a young man, he must have been handsome. He looked as if he might have been a soldier. His lips, which were full and rather moist, were the only unprepossessing feature. Otherwise he was dominant, every inch an aristocrat. As he approached, climbing the old terra cotta brick steps, he spoke again, a drumming of rolled r's like bursts of machine gun fire. Some of his sentences went up at the ends as if they might have been questions, and he was frowning at her. Faced with this kind of emergency, she forgot all her Italian—every scrap of it went out of her head—and answered, simply, in English: 'I'm sorry. Am I trespassing?'

The man drew up precipitately, raising his head—like a horse, she thought, shying at the last minute at a hedge. He seemed as surprised as she had just now been. Then he said, in good English, with scarcely any noticeable accent: 'I beg your pardon. Forgive me, signorina—I took you to be one of the Hungarian touring party who are officially visiting the island. It was a foolish but perhaps not unnatural mistake. They are members of the State Ballet. You have, if I may say so, something of that appearance.' He was looking at her critically but appreciatively, thoughtful, unsmiling, professional, as she had seen photographers look. She took it as a compliment. 'I was unaware that you were English, you understand,' he added. It sounded as if it might have been an apology but he was staring at her haughtily and his expression was still grim. His eyes, which were intensely steady and disconcerting, were brown and wrinkled around with crow's feet.

'I'm sorry,' she repeated. She thought it best to be demurely patient; it usually paid off.

'The villa itself is out of bounds,' he explained.

'Yes, of course. I understand.'

'It was just that I was afraid that you would suffer hurt to yourself. I was trying to warn you. That gate is electrified during the daytime, during the permitted hours of visiting the gardens.'

'Rather drastic, isn't it? Do you get many casualties?'

He said nothing for a moment, looking at her gravely with that penetrating frown. Then he continued: 'It is necessary. There are many valuable things within, you understand. Paintings, ceramics, gold and silverware. Also we get a great many undesirable people —snoopers, journalists ... We Italians are jealous of our privacy; perhaps even more than you, the British ... It is difficult to explain.'

She looked up at him. 'I could be a journalist,' she said.

He considered this. 'A very young one,' he said. Then he rejected the idea. 'You have no camera, no notebook. I think not. I think you have just lost your way and are looking for the exit.'

She noted the polite subtlety of the suggestion, and acted upon it. 'Yes,' she agreed. 'Thank you.'

She stepped towards him and he closed the outer gate behind her. Then he walked with her, down the steps, through the sultry garden, the reverse way she had entered it. She was conscious of his dignified presence at her side, escorting her the trespasser in her old casual jeans frayed at the bottoms and smudged with oil, firmly but courteously away from the house and his privacy. There was something tremendously impressive about him. He walked like a king. Perhaps he was the owner of the villa.

At the peacock terrace he bowed stiffly and handed her over to the rest of the public. He waved a hand to the right. 'You will find the steps to the landing stage in that direction,' he assured her. '*Arrivederci, signorina!*'

'*Arriveder La, signore*,' she answered politely, and then, still in slow schoolgirl Italian, she added, because the man intrigued her: 'Tell me, please, have I the honour of addressing ...' And then she stopped, searching for the right words. She didn't know his name. She wanted to discover if she was correct in thinking he was the occupier of the villa and the island. 'The owner of the *palazzo*?' she began. 'Tell me—'

With a yellowish hand he raised his old-fashioned panama. 'D'Anza,' he informed her, curtly and yet diffidently, as though forced to admit something. It was a moment before she realized it was a surname. When she looked up again he was almost gone, moving away briskly but somehow gracefully between the little knots of sightseers. Presently he was out of sight.

She glanced at her wrist watch. She had been on the island nearly an hour. The village gallants had probably disbanded by now, she thought. She decided to go down and catch the next ferry back to Pianezze. It was cooler now. Waiting at the jetty she put on her tunic but left it unzipped. She could see the café with its little red and white tables and the ice-cream kiosk and the parked cars. By narrowing her eyes and squinting through her lashes she even thought she could distinguish the Honda. Leaning against the picturesque and slightly theatrical mooring pole, waiting for the *barchetta*, she made plans for her accommodation that night. There was a camping site farther along the lake, according to her map; or failing that no doubt she could find a cheap pension in Malcesine. And a meal. She had to conserve her dwindling *lire*.

She hadn't long to wait; soon she was heading back to the village in a boat, more graceful than the previous one, called *Leda*. Stepping off the launch, she first checked that her motor-cycle was still there and then went to a table for a *cappuccino* and another cigarette. The three youths had gone, and she ignored the stout middle-aged man in glasses at the next table who showed interest in her. She didn't think he was likely to cause any trouble. At the desk, fluttering in the slight breeze, she noticed an arcade of glossy postcards and local guides, bright gaudy unnatural colours, and getting up she went over and studied them, thinking perhaps to find one of the villa and gardens for her collection, to remind her of the afternoon. She was successful. Several cards showed the front of what must have been the house whose view she'd been unable to discover. The same picture occurred on the garishly illustrated pamphlet of local attractions—well-proportioned house, winged curving steps, double colonnade, roof-top statuary, the outstretched eagle. She read the explanatory matter, in three languages.

'Isola Malcontenta, reached by frequent motor boat service, is the picturesque site of the Villa Franceschini now d'Anza, designed and partly built by Muttoni in the late XVIIIth Century in the Palladian style. The extensive public gardens, open from 10.30 to 18.00 hours 1st April—31st Oct., contain for the visitor many interesting features, including an arboretum founded in 1889 by the explorer and naturalist Dr Maurizio d'Anza, then a member of the family. It contains among other rare specimens, a banyan tree, said to be the only one existent in Europe. The white peacocks are also an attraction, rivalling those at Isola Bella, Lake Maggiore. The house itself, whose present owner is the Count Raffaele Alesssandro d'Anza-Pianezze, is not open to the public, nor is the legendary Minotaur Garden which may be viewed only by appointment ...'

Having paid for her coffee and bought some more cigarettes, she unlocked her Honda, wheeled it round and sat astride it, zipping up her jacket and then fishing in one of the panniers for her white crash helmet. Putting it on she tucked her hair in, fastened the flap under her chin and pushed off, into the flow of traffic. She smelt the fumes of exhaust again. A great articulated lorry trundled in front of her, carrying marble chippings. She eased out to the left and overtook it. The sun, reflected from the bald road, dazzled her with heat, making her frown. Motor horns blared constantly in her ear. Skilfully she weaved in and out of the bunched vehicles, all going south.

Suddenly at the junction which led to the causeway and the Villa Franceschini a green Opel Ascona saloon pulled out sharply into the road alongside her, forcing her over to the centre. She braked and heard the squeal of tyres behind her, and at the same time she saw the gigantic petrol tanker ahead, on the crown of the road because of a parked car, bearing down on her. She had time to see the driver's horrified look, perched high, eyes round with alarm; then she swerved to avoid it, back towards the Ascona, the articulated truck somewhere behind her. She felt the Opel strike her handlebar. A judder up her arm from the wrist. She swerved again and braked. She felt the back wheel skid round on the greasy road, her body heeling over, losing balance. She was coming off. The bike was flattening, becoming horizontal, but still moving under its momentum in a straight line. She was between the Ascona and the petrol tanker. She was going to hit the road. This was it, something said inside her head. This was an accident. She was going to get hurt. Crushed between the enormous wheels of the tanker, the wings of the green saloon and the articulated truck screaming behind her, all in the narrowing space of road now flying towards her. This was serious, perhaps final. And there was nothing she could do about it. She had no time to feel afraid, to recognize the terror of death; she only knew that it was stupid and unnecessary.

The ground suddenly hit her, then a series of metal bars flogging her. A great blow on the back of her helmet. An agonizing pain between her shoulders, the position difficult to define. Noise. Screeching. Petrol fumes. Dirt in her mouth, gritty between her teeth. Her hair round her face. How had it come undone? A hot wind. Still moving. If only she could anchor herself to the ground before she slid under something and got crushed!

And then, suddenly, stillness.

Everything had stopped. Voices. Shouting. A diesel engine running, mechanically vibrating, a raucous knocking sound, pulsating like red double heart beats. Rapid Italian voices, excited, from invisible sources on all sides. *Che cosa è successo? ... Mandi a chiamare un medico! ... Telefoni all'ambulanza!* So she was still alive.

Then someone was lifting her. Pressure under her armpits. Disembodied voices round her head. The excruciating pain again, just under the left shoulder blade at the back. Sky, buildings, faces began to reel. She was in a great vortex of sickness, her bowels loose, being sucked down in a whirl like bath-water. There was too great a darkness over everything, closing in upon her. The sky was going black. It was very peaceful; she didn't care....

* * *

It was with a kind of fascinated disgust that Philippa Rowantree, twenty last birthday, and shivering a little on the edge of the small handful of unemotional mourners, watched the symbolic spadefuls of soil being thrown down into the grave. She heard the stuff, kept dry for the occasion by the blue plastic tarpaulin, rattle down on to the invisible coffin below like a shower of sleet, accompanied by the words of the man in the windswept surplice with his little book. It was all so unreal, so repellent. It was so unnatural, and therefore to Pippa unworthy, that her mother should be lying there on her back and the gravel jettisoned on to her face, or at least on to the thin board that imprisoned her face, separating it from the world, or the world that mattered. It was unnatural and barbaric, disgusting. She edged back a step, her body taut with nerves, as though she felt she might be drawn in over the edge with the nausea of it, as she sometimes felt when standing on the edge of a cliff. The cliffs at Bolt Head; do you remember, Nicholas? Or the old house in Putney. (Why had that flashed into her mind?) If this was what was known as Christian burial it revolted her—the leaden sky and the uncomfortable wind, everyone standing about, distant relations one had never seen before, embarrassed with the solemnity of it all, trying not to fidget, trying not to look at one another, at her, the orphan. That must be—

what's her name?—Philippa? One can't see her face, she keeps her head down, under that rather charming hat. What will she do now, do you suppose? Stay on in the house? I don't even know what she does, do you? I mean I suppose she's got a job somewhere. There's a brother too, of course, isn't there? Isn't he here today? Where does he live?

Pippa frowned at her feet, stared at the rough builders' boards protecting the edge of the grave. How long was this going on for?

It must have rained during the night for there were pools of yellowish water on the gravel paths, and the dead winter grass everywhere was wet and the soil saturated, but it was over now and in the air at least only a dampness remained, raw and dull, cold (but not yet cold enough for snow), sunless, gloomed with a chill haze of smoke, a typical urban English January. It was the time of year when the day never seems to grow truly light, a sort of promise of dawn and then the afternoon is upon us, the lights are turned on again indoors. In the offices and schools they would be on all day. Beyond the bare trees and the railings at the perimeter of the cemetery Pippa, looking up now, could see the lights in the great complex of new rectangular factories which surrounded this new estate and new town. They were unnaturally white, strips of dazzling moonlight, magnesium flares to pierce the sombre greyness of the day and to photograph it for her in her memory. They had the effect of making the archaic words of the man in the rippling surplice seem even more remote and meaningless as he intoned them. They confirmed her atheism. *I am the resurrection and the life, saith the Lord: he that believeth in me, though he were dead, yet shall he live.* She felt she was rowing a very small boat in a very large ocean.

We commit her body to the ground; earth to earth, ashes to ashes, dust to dust. The raw east wind tugged at her scarf. The body of her mother might be in the first process of turning to dust but it had arrived by a different biological synthesis, more impressive to Pippa, because more truthful, than the metaphysics of all that dreary peroration. A jet transport plane roared, circling for Heathrow, and the noise drowned the words of the speaker, temporarily at any rate gagging his outflow of religious consolation.

Why couldn't they have left her at the hospital? They could have disposed of the body just how they liked as far as she was concerned. Burnt it up, that would have been the best way. She didn't want to think of that awful process of decay and putrescence, started in the hospital, continuing underground like an obscene mycelium until there was nothing left but a black sticky mass of bones and hair. Her mother was gone. She had lived and now she was gone. Never to return. That was the end of it. She had spent her allocation of life, a shorter one than most, but it was final, it was complete. No one ought to expect immortality. *We brought nothing into this world and it is certain we can carry nothing out ...*

Pippa heard them turning away, a succession of diminishing shuffles on the wet gravel, and she realized she was alone. Her feet were cold from standing, her legs chilled. She missed her ubiquitous Levis.

Feeling a touch on her arm she turned and looked up. It was Uncle George being solicitous. 'Come along, my dear,' he said in a low voice. 'All over now.'

He meant well but she despised his sympathy which was all part of the convention. It presupposed that she was a poor waif from his own generation, World War II, tearful and unable to cope. But not wishing to hurt him she smiled her acknowledgement gently, and she could see immediately he was affected. 'My God, she's turned out to be a proper little charmer! Splendid girl! A real brick!'—some such phraseology of a bygone age. He would quite enjoy telling Auntie Mavis all about it afterwards. 'I took her by the elbow, she was looking so forlorn, y'know, and she smiled at me brave as you like!' But her aunt would not encourage him. 'Looked smashing in black.' She would receive the description coldly because she was less of a sentimentalist than he was; she was more like Pippa. Despite the generation gap she understood. And she was not deceived by Pippa's large melting eyes nor her look of apparent helplessness. She was a woman and recognized one of her own sort, tough, sceptical, heartless. After all they two were the blood relations. Pippa's father had been Mavis's brother.

When they got back home Pippa stayed long enough to see that everyone was being catered for, with Jean—Mrs Morgan from next door—in attendance, and then, unable to bear the company of people like Uncle George and Auntie Mavis any longer, she went upstairs to her room and played all her pop records. She turned up the central heating and put on the electric fire and, kicking her shoes off, lay on her back on the divan bed and played a stack of them, record after record, automatically changing themselves with hardly a pause between while she stared at the ceiling with her head pillowed in her arms, her eyes wide and still and scarcely blinking.

Why hadn't Nicholas been there? Why couldn't he be here now?

Of course there was the cable, she knew all about that. It was impossible for him to get there from Canada at a day's notice, just like that, and he was on his way, flying, and he'd be here on Friday—she understood all this. She was adult and not unreasonable. But it was somehow typical of her brother to be absent when she needed him, to let her down by his absence whether he could help it or not. She wanted him. When he eventually turned up, full of quiet male efficiency and unconscious unexpressed superiority, he would irritate her, as he always had. But she wanted him, his superiority, *now*. She leaned over and found a cigarette.

Downstairs they would be glancing up from time to time at the thumping ceiling with embarrassed excuses, and Uncle George, twisting his sherry, would mumble: 'Poor kid, she's taking it hard, y'know.' And she wasn't doing anything of the sort. It was simply that she was trying to wash herself clean of all that burial service. *When thou with rebukes doth chasten man for sin, thou makest his beauty to consume away, like as it were a moth fretting a garment.* The living force of her favourite pop group, her favourite singers, her favourite numbers, the blaze of youth, the language of her contemporaries—all this was systematically rinsing away from her body the horror of the old world's deification of death. Her purpose, the role of mankind as she understood and believed it, was to live and to love, freely—not to maunder on about sin and redemption.

Her mother was gone. And that was another thing she needed to cleanse herself of—the stench of cancer, permeating the ward like a neglected pigsty, inevitable, ineradicable, inexorable as the passage of time. Death. Her mother's stomach becoming livid and then swelling up and going black, and her body stinking. There had never been any great love between herself and her mother but she was the only parent she had, or knew about, and now she was dead. No longer there. She didn't exist.

Pippa had no idea where her father was, nor indeed if he was alive either. There had been a divorce, years ago. She could barely remember him. He had gone abroad somewhere, with his woman. Nicholas, four years older than her, could remember him. They used to talk about him sometimes, in the old days, cleaning out the boat or sharing clandestine cigarettes in the toolshed at home, their old home at Putney, before they sold up and came here. She'd often contemplated the strange condition of having a father, what it must be like. All the other girls at school had had fathers —some of them father fixations. Since she was three she had never had any means of knowing. There had been uncles. Mother had had a man or two in the house from time to time, temporary lovers she supposed. And there were real uncles. Uncle George. Uncle Barney, now dead ... She remembered Uncle Barney with something like nostalgic affection. Really he was her great-uncle. He had been very generous at Christmas time, arriving in his battered old Wolseley with a margarine box full of presents done up in old-fashioned plain brown paper. He had had a white moustache. It must always have been white, she thought. And he was old enough to have fought in the First World War. But she couldn't really remember her father. They had moved here from Putney when her mother had got her managerial post with Acetylan Ltd, coming in at the most propitious moment in the development of this synthetic wonder fibre, which had, it seemed, every characteristic of natural wool except shrinking and felting. Terry Macdonald was downstairs now, representing the firm, very tall and expensively suited and trying not to look middle-aged. There had probably been no need for her mother to go on working these last five years. There was all that financial interest tied up in the business when it moved premises out here, all those lovely increasing dividends. She could have retired to Bexhill or wherever it was she fancied. Not to the farm cottage at South Pool which they'd first rented, then bought, for holidays—that would have been too remote from London. Mummy liked her comforts. Which in her case, being a child of the 'thirties, meant sophistication and the West End theatre. But she'd continued to work for other reasons. She knew about the cancer, and she wanted to forget it. It was probably wise—better than going off to Devon and brooding about it by calor gas like Joan Crawford in some hoary old film. Drive to the office every day. Think up new sales-promotion ideas. Organize people. Mummy had been very good at bossing people about, getting the best out of them. Now she was dead.

There was a tap at the bedroom door which Pippa scarcely heard for the music, but at the end of the record when it was repeated she sat up and said: 'Come in!'

It was George with a cup of tea.

'I've brought you a cup of tea,' he said obviously. He was staring at the large wall poster of Che Guevara behind her.

'Thank you,' she said. She switched off the record player on the floor beside her. This was Mavis's husband; she was downstairs with the rest of the watchful group now eyeing one another warily over their teacups and sherry glasses. He wasn't even a close relative. He might have been a complete stranger; she'd only met him twice before. But it was he who had brought her the peace offering. 'Won't you come down, eh? Philippa? Mm? ... Can't spend all your time up here, you know. Won't do at all.' He had put two lumps of sugar in the saucer, not knowing whether she took it or not. She looked up at him, appreciating his kindness and trying to like him, but he was so unknown, as remote as a passer-by. She wasn't capable of liking him. 'Realize you're upset, my dear,' he was saying. From the angle from which she saw him he looked enormously polished and round-shouldered, with a florid face, well cared-for and featureless. 'It's been a blow for you.'

It hadn't been a blow at all. It had dragged itself on miserably for too long, and now it was over. She had once had a cat which had been hit by a passing car which did not stop. Dying, it had crawled fifty yards to the gate where she found it. Here, its eyes told her as it lay exhausted, will be comfort and security and all will be made well. And she had picked up the mess of blood and fur and run in with it and put it in a cardboard box, where it had tried to wash itself and then died. Her mother's dying was over. No more pain, no more pleading, no more agonized passing of time, the long crawl to the sanctuary of the gate, just the dead cat in a box, the body to be got rid of.

She wasn't upset; it was just that she wanted all those hawks downstairs to hurry up and go away, so that life could get back to normal and perhaps when Nicholas came home the day after tomorrow they could have a party, invite a few of their current friends, people who spoke her language.

'What do you plan to do now?' George said. She thought for a moment that he was inquiring if she meant to go on sitting there indefinitely listening to records, but he continued: 'You could come and live with us, you know. You'd be very welcome. Your aunt and I would be pleased to give you a home with us if you wanted one.'

'It's very kind of you,' she said automatically, staring at him.

What an extraordinary idea, and how typical of his severed generation that he should continue to think that she, two years over her majority and a woman for longer than that, should want a home of the sort that they could offer. They lived on a superior estate just outside Sheffield. She had been there once on a visit with her mother. All open-plan boxes with misty views of distant hills scarred by verticals, chimneys, pylons. All the men came home from work at the same time, polished their cars at the same time, and trimmed their back lawns on a Sunday. Looking out of the bedroom window one could see all the gleamingly polished heads busy over their tasks. She was capable of making her own home. Not here; but somewhere. Nothing would be polished in it. Nothing ever again would be neat and orthodox. She might even throw out the picture of Che if it proved to be too conventional. 'It's very kind of you,' she said, 'but I have plans for working in London. I shall be all right.'

'Well, don't be in too great a hurry to do anything immediately. Talk it over with Nicholas when he comes.'

'Thank you, George. I'll do that.' She never called him Uncle George nowadays and she thought he appreciated it. He seemed to expand. With Mavis it always narrowed her.

'Now don't stop up here on your own, my dear. Come on down. They want to see you downstairs. The Macdonalds and Mrs Joliffe and Elsie have all gone; there's only the family left.'

Nevertheless a family she had rarely seen. An odd sort of ceremony, she thought, where both the nearest relatives were absent—her father because he didn't know, or maybe he wouldn't have cared anyway, or possibly he was dead too; and Nicholas because he was unavoidably tied up somewhere in Alberta. She put her teacup down on the bedside table, trying to make room for it among the two overflowing ashtrays, the paperbacks and the stacked copies of *Honey*, but George took it from her.

'All right,' she said. 'I'll come.' She was aware that she had to get this duty over.

She wanted Nicky. She knew that if he walked in now she would make a fool of herself, she was in a mood to throw herself at him and weep. On Friday when he arrived she would be more herself, and they would be quarrelling within the hour as they always did.

* * *

She was not conscious of the house's emptiness. It had been empty for some time now, ever since her mother had gone into hospital, and Pippa was not afraid of the emptiness, only bored by it, just as she was frequently bored by people when she had company. Anyway she had to go to work so she was out of the house all day. She hated the secretarial job her mother had got her with the firm but she'd been determined to leave school and, since she wasn't prepared to go to university either or knew what else she wanted to do, this had seemed the only alternative, and she'd drifted into it as inevitably and purposelessly as a stick in a backwater. At least it was better than St Helen's and St Catherine's, the place she'd been sent to at considerable expense where the girls all walked around happily in boaters and regulation uniforms and regaled each other after the holidays with lurid and surely imaginary stories of orgies they had undergone in that time with the most fabulous men. At least she was free. To some extent she was free, she immediately qualified it. She was free from five o'clock until the alarm went next morning, beside her ear.

She was having a bath with the door open, since there was nobody in the house, and listening for the telephone. She had been expecting it all the evening. Even so when it came it made her jump. She had been soaking for half an hour, reading a paperback, her head on a sponge. Springing up, sluicing water, she wrapped herself quickly in a hot bathtowel and padded wetly to her mother's room where the extension phone was and, sitting on the bed, picked up the receiver. She heard the sound of a push button being operated in a public callbox, and she knew immediately who it was, before he spoke.

'Hello, Pip.'

'Nicky?'

'Yes, I'm at the station. Just got in. How are you?'

'I'll get the car out. Just give me time to dress. I'm having a bath. Wet and getting rapidly colder. Be with you in ten minutes—no, seven. Go and have a drink while you're waiting. Or take a taxi, if you'd rather.'

'It's all right, I'll hang on for you. Everything all right?'

She put the phone down before he could continue a pointless conversation.

On her arrival at the station, leaving the Singer in the precinct, she found her brother standing waiting with his hand luggage in the foyer, reading the *Evening Standard*.

'Hello,' she said. After eighteen months' absence and having anticipated this homecoming so often and with such pleasure she couldn't, when it came to it, think of anything else to say. Instead she reached up and kissed him lightly on the cheek. The action seemed to embarrass him a little, temporarily, and he flickered a glance sideways round the entrance hall, but it was a place used to such greetings and partings; no one took any notice.

His first words too were typical. 'You're smoking too much.'

He hadn't changed at all, she thought. A bit more weathered, if anything; not quite such a boy, not so gangling. Tallish, he had a long nose, a big mouth, not really handsome. Following her to the car he flung his two pieces of baggage on the back seat and then turned to face her. 'Well?' he prompted. 'Tell me about it then.'

'The funeral? God, it was awful!'

'I meant about Mother.'

She didn't answer. Concentrating on the traffic she whipped the big car neatly out on to the main road, the windscreen wipers softly clearing the drizzle. 'That was awful too. I'll talk about it sometime. Not now.'

Driving fast through the wintry, deserted town centre, the road surface agleam with reflected shop lights, she could feel his critical eyes on the speedometer. He was going to be censorious. She knew it; he hadn't changed.

'I wanted to be here,' he said. 'When it happened. I'd have given anything.'

'I know.'

'I'm sorry you were left to cope.'

'That's all right.'

He was silent for a while. 'Thanks, anyway,' he said; and she knew he was sincere.

When they had had supper, which he helped her prepare in the bright steely kitchen, they both felt more relaxed and she knew he was going to talk about her future.

'What are you going to do now, Pip?'

'I don't really know. Work in London, I think.'

'Commute from here?'

'Christ, no! Share a flat with some girls, I meant.' She had made coffee and they took it into the living-room, she curling up on the sofa with hers.

'You don't have to, you know,' he reminded her. 'You'll be pretty well off. I don't know exactly how much but—'

'Yes, I know all about that.'

'You get this house and all its contents, the bus, the cottage, and three tenths of all the rest of the estate—which means the business shares. I get the remainder. We thought that was fair.' He was talking like the solicitor he was. Having just qualified in Law he had gone straight into the Canadian branch on the advisory staff.

She knew all about the arrangements. Her mother had expended her last strength explaining everything, making sure it was all clear. It had been painful. And clinical. And fair, of course.

'You might be better off staying here, doing whatever you want to do.'

'In this house? I hate it! Look at it!'

'Do you have to live in London?'

'Yes.'

'Doing what?'

'Photographic modelling. Fashion.'

'Oh Christ, Pip, grow up!' She could hear Uncle George in his voice, only thirty years younger. Nicholas was on the threshold of joining the establishment. He was going to lecture her. 'Do you realize what you're up against?'

'Yes, a lot of competition.' The only way to defend oneself against Nicholas's kind of superiority was to anticipate him.

'And a hell of a lot of graft and God knows what else. Do you imagine you've got what it takes?'

'I'm the right size and I've got the right sort of face. Reasonably intelligent and quite stubborn. What else does one need?'

He looked at her steadily. 'You're not stubborn; you're pliable, darling. Inside you're a kid still in the process of finding out about life. As vulnerable as a baby.'

'Don't be stupid.' She could feel her heart beating.

'Pip, you're so susceptible—you know you are. I'd rather you didn't. You'll only get hurt.'

'Oh God, here we go!' It was useless trying to argue with this kind of male sententiousness. 'Of course I could live with Mavis and George in Sheffield and look out for some Steel Board marketing executive with a minimum of five thousand a year. It's a different sort of prostitution but hundreds do it.'

'It's not what I meant at all. And it's not the only alternative. I think you ought to take those other "A" levels and go to university. There's still time.'

This silenced her for she knew it to be a point to him. She had wasted a lot of time three years ago scorching the town and countryside with Buzz Gregory on his motor-bike; she recognized that now. She had her English; she'd almost passed in French; she would certainly have got Art if she'd put in the time. It could be done; it was, as he had said, still possible.

'I'm not university material,' she said.

'Then at least go to art school.'

'Leave me alone. I know what I want to do. It's my life ... Tell me about yourself now—about Canada.'

He told her. Knowing her romanticism he tried to make it sound unadventurous, even humdrum, but she listened enviously. The names of places, dropped casually, mentioned in the course of business, were poetry. Elk Island. Buffalo Lake. Calgary ... Just to travel, to see places, mountains, forests, rivers, wide vistas, a different light, hear a different accent—the thought inflamed her discontent.

'Do you remember that film we saw years ago in Kingsbridge?' she said suddenly. 'What was it called? *Days of Our Eden*. A super western.'

Nicholas looked suddenly away from her, as he had done at the station when she'd first greeted him. 'It wasn't a western,' he frowned, 'strictly speaking. It was a screen epic about a pioneering homestead in Wyoming. An inflated lyric piece of corn.'

'It was my favourite picture, next to *Dr Zhivago*. I lived on it for the whole of the next year, back at school.'

'I remember you got very starry-eyed about it.'

'It must have affected you too. Didn't it help you to decide when the Alberta job came up?'

'Edmonton isn't exactly an old homestead where they make their own soap.'

'But it was a great film.'

'It was fair. You were thirteen. Your sense of discrimination had not then developed. If it ever has.'

She reached for another cigarette and he lit it for her. 'You're smoking too much, Pippy,' he told her again.

'Oh shut up! Don't be such a bloody prig!'

Nicholas watched her, spread comfortably on the sofa in a fashionable, very young-looking outfit. He had serious eyes that seemed to penetrate deep into the mind and character of his subject, the lawyer's stare. 'Don't go and try the London lark,' he begged her. 'You'll end up in the wrong set.'

'What set is that?' She was hostile.

'The Chelsea swingers, probably. Or whatever is current. I don't know. I've been away. But you'll get hurt, I tell you.'

'Well, I've got to find out, haven't I? I've got to find out for myself ... I could just as easily get hurt here. It's only thirty miles from the great metropolis. It isn't where you live, surely, that counts?'

'No. It's the ethic of your friends.' He shared the ashtray with her. 'Is that all you smoke?' he said, indicating her filter tip.

She narrowed her eyes at him in direct challenge. There was going to be a row. She could feel it coming. 'One goes to a few pot parties,' she said. 'Naturally.'

'That's what I mean.'

'Oh, bloody Christ! Don't tell me they're all spiritual virgins in Edmonton, Alberta!'

'No. But pot parties tend to develop into hash parties and from there to acid. After that you're usually on your own with a blunt needle.'

She rolled over on the settee, turning her back to him. 'Piss off!' she said.

Nicholas rose, collected the coffee cups and took them to the kitchen, putting them on the draining board. He stood there thoughtfully, she could see. Then he came back.

'Pip,' he said, 'don't let's quarrel ... I'm only over here for a week.' He watched the drawn-up bundle on the sofa, the neutral, silent back, unable to make out whether she was crying or just sullen.

'Give me time to have a shave and then I'll take you out somewhere. Think of a place.' He went out and collected his things dumped in the hall. 'Which room am I in—the old one?'

She came out to him, her fingertips brushing her eyes. 'No, I've put you in the small front, I hope you don't mind. I seem to have taken over your room. And I didn't think you'd want to go into Mummy's with all her things about.' Her eyes were shining. She found a tissue and blew her nose. 'If we're going out,' she said, 'I'd better make myself presentable too.' She looked round the traditional, middle-class hall and up the staircase, thinking: It was only two days ago that all those hawks were here. Sherry and sympathy, but not much trust.

Her brother had preceded her to his own room and, having washed, was preparing to shave, in open shirt and rolled sleeves, with the door open so that they could continue to talk. He plugged in an electric razor and set to work. Pippa came to the doorway and watched him. When it was complete he found a turtle neck sweater and dragged it on. She handed him a comb.

All at once she said: 'Nick, I'm sorry.'

'What about?'

'Just now. Downstairs.'

'Forget it, girl! ... Go and do something to yourself. You look a bit wan.' As he turned to face her, taller than she was, looking down at her with his mocking yet diffident smile, she suddenly took him by surprise and flung her arms round his neck. 'Oh Nicky, I love you!' she said, her head on his shoulder.

Embarrassed again, he made as if to disengage her as she buried her face in his sweater, and then relented, holding her lightly and gently instead.

'You didn't really want to take me out,' she was saying into the wool. 'You're the home bird. You wanted to stay in and talk about Mummy. You're the one who's going to miss her. You wanted to hear all the details, to go on and on talking. It's worse for you than it is for me. You were her favourite. And you're taking it all so stoically. I wish I could.'

He kissed the parting of her hair line, so gently that she didn't notice it. And then, lifting her face by cupping her cheek with one hand, he examined the beauty of it at close quarters for several seconds, then kissed her on the mouth, but still tenderly; compassionately but without sensual passion. It was very brief.

'You've got to grow up, Pippy,' he told her.

She closed her eyes.

'Now let's go out,' he said.

*   *   *

She was very drowsy still. This was partly because, although the long windows were open, she felt hot in the tight narrow bed hemmed in like a straitjacket, with her head flat on the severely laundered sheet, without any pillows. The ceiling was green and a long way up. It ought to have been the sky but it was the wrong colour. She turned her head slightly, or rather her eyes, because her head was too heavy and hot, and tried to puzzle out the meaning of the great mound of colour not far away. The focus growing stronger, it became more intelligible, until finally she recognized them to be flowers. They were roses, a pyramid of them, red and white and pink and yellow. Something about the sight of them made her happy but she couldn't define what it was, merely that it was a pleasurable unfinished thought, a half sentence left over from a previous chapter, before she went to sleep, which it was now nice to be able to continue and finish.

'Tom,' she heard someone say, softly, a woman's voice. It must have been herself.

There was a rustle nearby, a smell of soap.

'*Si sente meglio?*'

Pippa twisted her eyes again and this time, very slightly, her head. There was a dark young woman in brown and white, short sleeves, white head-kerchief, a nurse's uniform. She had spoken something, a question. Pippa tried to translate but it was too difficult; she was unable to concentrate in another language.

'Where am I?'

The nursing sister, showing white teeth, seemed delighted with the remark, smiled and came nearer, bending over her.

'You are-a well-a! Is nice!'

'Where am I? Please?'

'*L'ospedale di San Bernardino.* In Riva. You O.K. You notta worry.'

'Tom?'

The nurse shrugged and smiled reassuringly. She did not understand.

'Is Nicky here?'

The woman smoothed the bedclothes and tightened the straitjacket. 'Is nice you are-a well-a, you can talk! Now you must-a be quiet. You good!'

There was an accident, a smash, her motor-bike, a petrol tanker, a green Opel—the details of the event all came crowding back into her rapidly clearing mind. The light was beginning to make her head ache as she tried to think, and she pulled her hand out of the bedclothes and put it to her brow, frowning against the sunlight just catching her from the high window. The woman, perhaps seeing Pippa's discomfort, drew a cord which swished a cream curtain across and then bunched up the flowers proudly as though with vested pride.

'Is beautiful! Two three times he has sent you these beautiful flowers.' She was obviously so impressed she couldn't forbear to talk about it. 'Every day! You are a lucky one! Is so nice!'

Pippa found it difficult to concentrate. There was a dryness in her mouth, a stiff ache in her left arm, and she kept slipping away into a drowsiness whose Lethe she did not want to forego. She tried to come to the surface again, to give her mind to a complexity which was proving too much for her, she had to find the right thread which would unravel this tangle of confusion.

'Nicky,' she murmured, her eyes closed, 'has gone back to Canada.' She knew it couldn't be Tom. She turned her face to the flat pillowless sheet and sought the comfort of a patch of virgin coolness, unspoilt by the sun or her own sweat.

The nurse, warm, ebullient, and happy with the success of her patient's recovery, seemed to hesitate between her duty to keep her quiet and her natural inclination to gush. Finally she drew the roses nearer and picked out a greetings card with a scalloped gilt edge.

'Look, you will getta well quick when you read what he says, is so nice, ha? You are lucky to have this such a thing! Is worth being in accident, I think perhaps. He think of you so kind—nice thoughts. Two three times he send much a *biglietto*, and once he is calling in person!'

Pippa could not identify the card undulating in front of her; it was a white blur, twisted on its side.

'Who?' she said.

The nurse sat down on a bedside stool and examined the ornamented pasteboard for herself as though it were a holy relic. 'The Count Raffaele, of course! Who else? Is charming with you and full of sympathy.'

Pippa frowned again and put out her hand, searching for the card. The nurse gave it to her and she drew it nearer to her face. The salutation was in English, in a round meticulous, almost feminine hand; *Sincere wishes for your early recovery*, and was signed Raffaele d'Anza.

Pippa looked at it uncomprehendingly for a long time. 'I don't understand,' she said. 'How did he know? About me? About what happened and where I am?'

'But of course, he was in the car—the car which knockéd you down.'

'The big green one?' It was beginning to piece together.

'But of course!... Is so *romantica*!' The nurse's dark eyes were shining, enjoying it, swimming in sentimental dreams no doubt, living in some fantasy from her favourite pulp magazine. Here, week after week, it was always some pretty but lonely English girl, a governess perhaps or a lady's companion, who got knocked down by a rakish marquis on his way back from the gambling tables of Monte Carlo. Or else, sometimes, it was the other way round—the fresh Italian girl, modest and a good Catholic, of course, who was befriended by an incredibly rich if mentally simple English milord doing his nostalgic grand tour of the 1944 battlefields. It was always so very *romantica*.

'He was a pretty lousy driver,' Pippa reflected. 'Taking the corner wide like that, as though he owned the highway as well as all the rest.'

'No, no, he was notta driving. The chauffeur, he was-a driving. The Count, he was sat inside. He was seeing it all. He brings you to the hospital himself. The *carabiniere* wishes to question the chauffeur, to wait for the ambulance, but the Count d'Anza waves him away, is so grand, so proud. "*Presto all'ospedale!*" he says. He is furious. "The child is badly hurt. She must be transported at once!"'

Pippa, closing her eyes again, listened to the hot chattering of sparrows. There were a thousand things she wanted to know, but it was probably useless questioning the nurse, who would only give her fanciful answers.

'Is good, you go to sleep now.' The woman moved away. And in a few minutes Pippa lost consciousness again.

When she awoke later she was washed gently by two sisters with starched winged headdresses, who looked like nuns, and then she was given some soup. She asked for a mirror so that she could tidy herself but they only smiled and shook their heads benignly. During the washing she had examined herself to discover whether she was injured, and where, and how badly. Apart from a sore elbow and bandaged forearm she had been unable to discover anything seriously untoward. She could move all her limbs. There had been some grazing of her left leg but the suppuration had been treated and had now hardened, and in any case was no worse than things she'd suffered as a child coming off her push-bike. Now she wanted to see whether her face was disfigured. She put up her hand and felt it carefully, reading it blind with the tips of her fingers. The skin appeared to be intact except for a cheek scratch, but exploring her scalp she found that some of the hair seemed to have been cut and there was an adhesive plaster. She tried to ascertain the size of it by the width of her finger joints. It felt large but she judged it to be no more than four or five centimetres. If there was a patch, she thought, her hair, which was fine but luxuriant, would cover it. She pressed it cautiously. It tingled a little, otherwise there was no sensation of soreness. Why then did they deny her the mirror? She brooded on this fact for about half an hour, becoming more and more convinced that there was something, something she had not discovered which they did not want her to see. She felt her cheeks again and all her teeth, ran her fingers searchingly along her forehead, tried by squinting to see the end of her nose. Then at the end of this time a man in a white house-coat came in with the ward sister and stood for a moment looking down at Pippa thoughtfully. Then he smiled.

'I am Dr Rossano,' he said, in English. 'How are you feeling now?' A middle-aged man with a dark moustache.

'All right,' she considered. 'A bit weak.'

'But of course. That is only to be expected. You have been unconscious for several days, and have sustained only a minimal diet. You will soon be stronger now you are taking nourishment.'

'Unconscious? How long?'

'Several days.' He consulted a bed chart. 'Four days.'

'Four days!' It seemed impossible. 'What happened? Tell me.'

'Well, what do you remember?'

'I was knocked off my motor-bike. In Pianezze. A lot of traffic. Someone tried to lift me. I don't remember any more.'

'Yes, that was unfortunate. You had a dislocated shoulder. It was probably very painful and you fainted.'

'Dislocated?' She felt her left shoulder under the sheet. Someone had put her into a cotton nightdress, not her own.

'We set it immediately, of course. It was quite a simple job. Anyone can do it. But it leaves a certain weakness there, a propensity to dislocate again if you abuse it or don't give it time to knit ... Do you serve left handed at tennis?'

'No, right.'

'Good. And this summer if you swim it must be the breast stroke, not crawl. Not to go climbing ropes, mountaineering, that sort of thing, you understand?' He was smiling again. 'What is your occupation?'

'Anything at the moment. Anything I'm offered ... I've done office work, and been a model.'

'Fine. You stick to that.' He contemplated her gravely again.

'Dr Rossano,' she said, unnerved by his scrutiny, 'is there anything wrong with my face?' She could feel herself growing cold with apprehension.

'Your face, Signorina Rowantree?'

'They wouldn't let me have a mirror. There's something wrong with my face. Isn't there? What is it? What am I like?' She had a sudden nightmare vision of herself, as though she were standing at the bedside where Rossano was, looking down at herself. She was a witch. The skin of her face was tough and wrinkled, sprouting whiskers around the mouth and from the chin, and her lank sparse hair was grey, her teeth broken and discoloured.

'What are you like, signorina?' Dr Rossano smiled again. 'You are very charming. There is nothing wrong with your face.'

She felt an overwhelming, incredible relief, although her heart continued to pound with the shock of the strange, if momentary, hallucination.

'How old are you, Signorina Rowantree?'

'Twenty.'

'So.' He grimaced paternally. 'And I am fifty. So it is without offence that I can assure you that you have not lost your beauty. *Deo gratia!* It is just your anxiety.' He called a nurse and ordered a mirror to be brought. Given a small hand looking-glass, Pippa examined her familiar features. The face that stared back at her looked a bit pale, her eyes shadowy underneath; but otherwise, apart from the scratch, everything was as she remembered it—fair hair, straight nose, grey-blue eyes, long natural lashes, wide full mouth, firm and visible cheekbones. Why had she experienced that extraordinary delusion just now?

'What is this plaster?' she demanded, her hand to the back of her head.

Dr Rossano drew up a chair and sat down pleasantly. Short in the leg, like many Italians, he seemed more massive seated.

'When you hit the petrol tanker,' he explained, 'you suffered a grave—what is the term?—*una grava commozione cerebrale.*' He clicked his tongue and rubbed a finger and thumb together, cicada-like, seeking the English equivalent. 'A bad concussion,' he finally selected.

Pippa waited.

'The X-ray showed a minute hair crack of the skull—just here. The pressure of this concussion is undoubtedly what kept you unconscious for so long. There was danger of some bleeding and we had to relieve this to prevent a clot, you understand. I am being very frank with you. And I am happy to tell you everything is satisfactory. If you hadn't been wearing a crash helmet it would certainly have been fatal. You hit the suspension bar of the tanker.

You are very lucky. You are not disfigured, even temporarily. The hair will grow again where we made the small incision. And the fact that you can remember up to the moment of the impact, that is very good.'

'I'm glad.'

'However, we would like to keep you under observation a little longer.'

'Where?'

'Ah, this raises a problem, Signorina Rowantree. This hospital is small, is not well equipped, and like every other it is in constant demand for bed space. You could go to Verona, to the convalescent wing of the general hospital there, for a week or two. Or Padua.'

Pippa felt a little alarmed. 'Won't it be expensive? Who's going to pay for all this?' She was not sure how far her international insurance covered her for this sort of treatment, but Rossano reassured her. Standing up, he said: 'You are not to concern yourself. These things can always be arranged. When my daughter comes to London you can show her the sights ... Besides, you are a casualty. The state has to look after its road casualties.'

'I think I'd rather go home.' This reminded her of her Honda. 'What's happened to my motor-cycle, and all my things?'

He turned at the corner of the bed, looking down at her. 'Your machine I am afraid is completely smashed. It is in the hands of the civil guard. They will have all your possessions too, your passport and money. It will be all right. You will see. You are not to worry.'

'But I want to get home, to England. How am I to do that?'

'Have patience, my dear young lady. You are not fit to travel. We want to take another X-ray in three weeks' time, to see what that little cracked bone is doing.'

'They can do that in London.'

'True, but you should avoid the strain of a long journey just yet. You should avoid all excitement. Why not go to Verona? It is an interesting city. They will show you Juliet's tomb. Maybe you will get some ideas for your work, for your modelling. Leaning against it gracefully, advertising something in Italian silk—isn't that the idea? Or what about Padua? Do you know that it has a university which is older than Oxford?'

'I haven't any money to stay anywhere at the moment. Unless I work.'

Dr Rossano picked up his briefcase and fastened the clasp. 'Then the other alternative is the most obvious solution.'

'Which? Modelling silk in front of Juliet's tomb?'

'No, no! That I was joking with you ... I was referring to the offer of the Count Raffaele d'Anza, to stay there.'

'At the Villa Franceschini?'

'Yes, it would have its advantages. We could keep in touch. You would not have to travel far. And for you it would be a unique experience, certainly an interesting experience for anyone. The villa is a wonderful house, full of treasures. Rather quiet, of course, from your point of view; rather dull—no gay parties, no dancing till dawn—but from ours this would be an added recommendation. It is best for you not to get excited, until we are quite sure there is no danger of cerebral laceration. You would ideally convalesce there. It is large, restful, beautiful, plenty to read and look at—and all free. What more could you ask?'

Pippa, slightly taken aback, glanced sideways again at the roses, then at the sparse-haired man in glasses. He seemed honest and likeable.

'Is that what you think I should do?' she said.

'If it were me I should jump at the opportunity.'

'It's not quite the same though, is it? For you. You're not a woman.' She didn't know why she said this. It was not what she had meant to say at all; it sounded crudely melodramatic, as corny and prudish as one of those pulp magazines. A woman herself, as she had said, for longer than her two years of majority, she wasn't frightened of being invited into strange houses merely. She was quite capable of taking care of herself. It was something more than that.

Rossano, looking at her shrewdly, twisted his mouth into a little grimace, somewhere between a smile and a shrug, an odd foreign gesture of the lips. 'You are quite right, of course,' he said. 'But d'Anza is eminently respectable, a sober man. Cultured, a scholar, reserved. You need have no fear.'

She had no fear. This sort of male protectiveness only served to irritate her. Rossano, like Nicky and Tom and all the rest of the intelligent liberal humanists of this age, could not disguise his inbred conviction of superiority. Because she was a girl, and in their philosophy therefore the target for everybody's penis, she was in need of care, gallantry and advice on how to keep her virginity intact. It was not intact. She had willingly and joyously parted with it years ago, while she was still at school. And she was quick on her feet and good at running and knew all the trigger spots to jab her toe-cap or knee or elbow into in the art of self-defence. She hadn't come half way across Europe alone to be scared of an elderly quietist who sent her flowers.... It was something else.

'Perhaps I will go there then,' she considered. 'To the Villa Franceschini. For a while at any rate. Until my hair grows.'

She was feeling drowsy again.

* * *

A month after leaving her mother's house—hers now—she was ensconced in a flat in St John's Wood, shared with three other working girls. She'd found it the usual way, through a small ad. It wasn't Chelsea; it was a sedate neighbourhood with tallish, quiet houses set back in small gardens, the front doors above rounded stone steps mostly painted primrose or sage. Even Nicholas would have passed it for approval. It wasn't drab, but bordered on the dull. Better however than the awful sub-rural jungle where she lived, where everyone worked like mad in order to live genteelly when they stopped, and were prepared to travel long distances daily so that they might be within striking distance of countryside they never had time to walk in.

After a preliminary telephone inquiry she stood on the doorstep, rang the bell and waited. There was a short concrete drive blocked with two cars under plastic sheets. A good job she hadn't brought the Singer. The semicircular garden consisted of shrubs, bare now except for the holly and laurel.

The girl who opened the door was about her own age. She looked pleasant. 'Hello,' she said. 'You're Pippa?' It was a good start.

They went up the narrow stairs and she was shown all the rooms, the others as well as her own. It was all satisfactory. The communal kitchen was small but workable.

'All right?' inquired the girl. Her name was Jen. She was tall and clear eyed, businesslike, the organizer of the ménage.

'Super,' agreed Pippa. They stood looking at each other. It was going to work out all right.

'Tracy and Zillah work in the same office,' Jen explained. 'They usually leave at the same time and come in together. The Tube is just up the road. And of course there's the bus stop just down there.

Is that how you came? How are you going to get to work?'

Pippa explained that she hadn't actually got any yet but she was equipped with a number of addresses for inquiry. Jen didn't seem at all surprised.

'Cup of tea?' she invited. It was going to be that sort of relationship—no domination, no questions, freedom to come and go, to do as she liked. Pippa felt happy.

'There's just one thing,' Jen said. 'Before you join us. There's one thing I ought to tell you.' Now the snags, Pippa thought. Something to do with the bathroom—you can't get really hot water.

'Have you any racial prejudice?' Jen laughed as she said it, making it sound less absurd. 'I hope not, because Zillah is from Trinidad. You're not a militant Powellite or anything?'

'Of course not.'

'Good. Because she's a bit sensitive, like all blacks. And we want everyone to get on well together don't we? That's settled then.'

Jen helped her carry up her four suitcases and a hatbox. 'My word, you had a load on the bus!' she said cheerfully. Pippa hadn't the courage to admit that she had come by taxi. She had the impression that such a luxury, which she without thinking had regarded as a necessity, might be deemed ostentatious by Jen, who had an uncompromising northern accent and a room liberally lined with books on sagging homemade shelves—a sense of guilt which was confirmed a little later when Jen brought in two cups of tea and surprised her in the act of unpacking. There was very little hanging space in her room—only a curtained-off recess beside an old blocked-in fireplace—and Pippa had laid out all her dresses and tunics, catsuits, coats, skirts, blouses, neatly on the bed, wondering where to put them. Jen stared at them, round eyed.

'Wow!' she said. That was all. But it contained a wealth of expression—astonishment, envy, incredulous amusement. She was looking at one gorgeous thing in crushed velvet, all Pre-Raphaelite folds which caught and reflected the light. 'You've got some *lovely* clothes!' she said finally.

Pippa smiled sheepishly. 'I don't quite know what to do with them all,' she admitted. She was thinking of all those others she had been unable to bring, left behind in an agony of indecision and frustration. She had accumulated too many, she knew. The trouble was, when she saw something fabulous which suited her she couldn't rest until she'd acquired it—she just had a narcissistic lust for beautiful clothes.

Sitting on a painted chair and a soiled linen box they sipped their tea and chatted.

'What do you do?' Pippa asked. It occurred to her that Jen had peculiar hours of work—it was the middle of the afternoon.

'Me? Oh, I'm at Flyte and Coriander's, the publishers. But I have to do a certain amount at home. That's why I get time off for it. I'm really only a very small cog. They let me do indexes and collation, and sometimes I draft out a summary for the blurb writer—that sort of thing. Nothing special.'

Hence all the books in her room, Pippa decided, bearing the same imprint. They talked for a while and then, having finished the tea, Pippa turned to carry on with the unpacking but paused, aware of Jen's interest and curiosity, her hovering presence like a kestrel, quartering the area, missing nothing. For the first time in her life she felt shy. She closed the lid on the suitcase and helped carry the cups and saucers down to the kitchen.

The next morning, carrying her list of contacts, she began her search for employment. It was a dreary round, profitless at the end of the first day although she had visited four agencies before they closed. The first was typical of the rest—a brown-and-cream office in a side lane off Wardour Street, with a steep, thin-carpeted staircase, no lift, and a fried-oniony smell of hamburgers from a cheap restaurant next door on the ground floor. She waited a long time on a slippery plastic-weave chair with several other applicants, four girls and a man, before being called into an adjoining room with a faceted opaque glass door.

A young man, not much older than herself, in a trendy suit and sideburns, looked her over penetratingly for a few seconds, then took his glasses off and polished them with a paper tissue.

'Okay darling, what you do then?' He had a voice which, originating in Birmingham, was now somewhere in the mid-Atlantic.

'Well, anything.'

'Great! Lovely! I mean, what've you done up to now? Who have you worked for, chick? Can't seem to find you in the files.'

'No, I haven't had any experience in this sort of work before. I was recommended—'

'Oh! Yeh, I see! Well, honey, you look okay. What sorta line d'you want?'

She told him. Patiently. Fashion modelling. She was interested in clothes. She knew how to wear them. She wanted to design them too.

'Oh Jesus, darling! You're like all the rest. They all want to be little Twiggys. As soon as they leave school. There's thousands after that line—you'll grow old waitin'. I'm not kiddin'.'

She watched him coldly and a little desperately. He had finished polishing his glasses; now he lit a cigarette out of a packet, but didn't offer her one.

'Well, anything then,' she considered. 'Television ads?'

He glanced at her a second time but with hardly more enthusiasm.

'You an actress?' he said. 'You have to have training to do that crap. They're all pros, you know—even the dolly who eats the chocolates. You want RADA or something at least for that. You have to eat a choc bar like you was doin' something porno, you know what I mean?'

'I've done quite a lot of acting,' Pippa told him. 'I could try.'

'Yeh? What sort of like?'

'Well, I played Ismene in Anouilh's *Antigone*, which is only a bit part, I know, but important in a way. And Titania in *A Midsummer Night's Dream*.' She recognized, as she said it, that it sounded inadequate, even ridiculous. The man was looking at her seriously enough, at least with an expressionless face, but he was laughing at her inwardly. It was obvious. It made her furious with herself to sound so palpably naïve.

'Where you done that then? Amateur, was it?'

'The first was local rep. The *Dream* we did in my last year at school.'

'Yeh?' He was more interested in cleaning out his ear with the spent matchstick. 'Well, I don't know about that ... There's more doing right now in the girlie mags, but you're not exactly the right type. I mean you're pretty enough, don't get me wrong, but you're a bit thin, aren't you? Round the thirty-ninth parallel, I mean. That's what they really want ... Okay, leave your partic'lars with the girl at the desk on your way out and she'll put you in the files. Good luck, chick!'

At the end of the day, despite the fact that the four agencies were all roughly in the same area, all she seemed to have to show for her effort were cold, aching feet from the February slush of a London now beginning to lose its identity again in whirling wet snow which settled only on the pavements. And a deepening weariness of spirit.

After three more days of this sort of thing she gave up trying. Instead she went to the bank, drew another cheque and spent the afternoon at the cinema. When she got home she was told by Jen that there had been a phone message for her, to call at the first office the next day. A breakthrough at last, she thought, and slept fitfully with excitement that night. Presenting herself in high hopes at the address given by the agency she discovered it to be a large, cold, north-facing room in Kennington, the huge sloping attic window opaque with snow, and cluttered with all the paraphernalia of the studio photographer—drapes, floods, nests of tables, simulated fur rug, cables, Indian wicker chair, a palm, a long couch and a very inadequate electric fire. It soon became obvious what she was there for, but since the man's wife was continually present, helping around—indeed it was obviously a professional partnership—Pippa complied with everything she was asked. She undressed, lay on the rug, contorted herself to play with a feather boa as instructed, looked directly at the camera when told, and then put her clothes on again. She was invited to come again tomorrow to hear the result of the trial proofs. Well, it was a start—a bit sickening perhaps, and not what she'd dreamed of in those fantasies of herself standing on the Embankment swathed in Russian furs for Debenham and Freebody's, but it was a beginning.

The next morning, at ten o'clock, the light still murky, she listened to the photographer's unenthusiastic analysis.

'You don't come out too well, darling,' he said. 'You're a bit skinny, like we said.' He was a mild, thin-haired man in his late thirties; his wife, the same age, sported an elaborate coiffure even at that early hour, with rather dramatic make-up and long pendant glass earrings. They let it be known that they liked to be called by their first names, which were Malcolm and Wendy—except that in addressing each other they tended to abbreviate these to Malc and Wend. Looking at the big, matt, curling photograph proofs she was appalled at herself; she looked ten years older, excruciatingly arch, and as common as muck.

'You're trying too hard, darling,' Wendy told her. 'You'll have to learn to relax.' She had a deep, gravelly voice. Her eyes were screwed up against the smart of her own cigarette smoke as she examined the prints.

'I dunno, Wend, that sorta scared look in that one isn't bad,' Malcolm said. 'If we could keep that up. Maybe a line we could work on ... Look, kid, I'm on the look-out for a schoolgirl series I know a market for. Wend, would you get the gear—the gym-slip and stuff. You know where it is.'

Pippa, feeling depressed, took off her winter coat and hung it carefully on a hanger behind the door. She could hear electric trains rattling by somewhere outside, below her, unseen—in itself a wintry sound. She was even more depressed when she turned and saw the imaginative aids that had been brought for her to wear.

'Schoolgirls don't wear gym-slips any more,' she said incredulously. 'And certainly not all those other things.' They were probably Wend's, she thought, over twenty years ago. 'Whoever goes for those?'

'The market,' he told her '—this particular one—likes it that way.'

Pippa, saying nothing, went to the screened alcove where yesterday she had undressed, but the photographer, who had been eyeing her dress and boots with frank admiration, said: 'That's a nice outfit you're wearing there, darling. Pity to waste it. Hold on.'

She was persuaded to get out of it, slowly, in front of a bedroom set which was created simply but effectively by pulling over the divan, covering it with a sheet and quilt, and trundling across behind it a light wooden frame on castors giving the effect of a curtained window. This time the eerie pair used a ciné camera.

'I can tell you're new to this business,' Malcolm said pleasantly between buzzing short takes, crouched over the tripod. 'I mean, I'm right, aren't I—you haven't done this before.'

'Yes,' she admitted. She felt cold and suddenly hungry, regretful of the fact that she'd had no breakfast except a cup of instant coffee. He went on to give her some hints. On coming to work to wear nothing tight round her middle, no bra, since these left marks which made it impossible to take a close nude for perhaps an hour or more before they disappeared, which was a waste of professional time. Spots could be blocked out with make-up, but lines—no, definitely nothing you could do about it. Buzz. Come in a slip with your long coat over it. Or a mack in summer. Buzz. Can you look up a bit? Drop your shoulder—no, the other one. Nice. Bit more. Lick your lips. Great!

* * *

She met Tom two days later at a party given by the girls in honour of Tracy's twenty-second birthday.

They were surprised that Pippa, attractive and seemingly vivacious, had invited no one. Of course she hadn't been there long, although coming from so short a distance she would have had friends in town, or able to get there, one would have thought. But the truth was there was no one from her old life whom she wanted to invite. She was done with that episode in her history, and with them. This was a new phase and she was determined not to be reminded of an earlier. She would make the most of it. Even the Malc and Wend set-up was preferable to Bracknell. Getting rid of that sterilized atmosphere was like sloughing an old skin.

She picked him out of the small crowd immediately. He was long-legged, bearded, casual, not too clean, lazy-eyed and yet watchful, awkward and alert, squatting on the floor drinking beer. He was three-dimensional, an individual. Arguing with somebody, another man, his eyes closed as he sought some involved train of logic. He had bony wrists, she noticed. In his mid twenties. Talking not vehemently but with intensity in his corner, without raising his voice, so that she was unable to distinguish from where she stood sipping her cheap Cyprus sherry what was the subject of his argument; he merely gave her the impression of being an intellectual. She wasn't sure that she cared for intellectuals. More so than the crudely dominant, they made her feel inferior. Someone put the record player on and she gave herself up to dancing. The party continued. Dim lights. Talking. Sentimental clinches. Swaying together to slow music. Drinks and exotic oddments of food. Warm vital atmosphere. It was a nice party, a pleasant one—nobody sick in the loo, no stupid sex games, nobody talking shop. Or money. A hundred miles from Bracknell, a thousand from Sheffield.

She found herself dancing opposite the man whose name she didn't know. Two new things she discovered about him. Standing up now, he was tallish, burly across the shoulders, comparatively narrow in the hips; and his eyes were deep brown. In the subdued light of Jen's romantic gloom they looked almost impenetrably dark. She disliked their directness. An intellectual, permanently confident of his polemical superiority. Quiet but arrogant. She didn't want to know him.

'I haven't seen you before,' he said, taking her glass and refilling it for her. 'Are you one of Jen's?' He had a voice whose origin it was difficult to place, cultured but with overtones of what could have been deliberate roughness, perhaps a mask or the cabbala of some faction to which he belonged.

'I live here,' she told him.

'Then you're new.' He stared at her, drinking his canned beer at the same time, the directness of his interest over the top of the metal tankard disturbing her. A red-blooded intellectual then, not one confined to yoghurt and discussion. 'What is your name?' he said.

She had come down too late for introductions, and in any case it was the sort of party where everybody either knew one another or introduced themselves. She looked up at him. Oddly enough she didn't want to give anything away to him, not even her name. It was like parting with a bit of her personality. She didn't want to be dominated by him, or by anyone.

'Cathy Earnshaw,' she said. She often gave fictitious names like this; it was a habit she'd got into as a child.

He didn't flicker an eyelid. If it meant anything at all to him it didn't cause any reaction. Maybe, despite his argumentative appearance, he was not very well read. At least in literature. A scientist perhaps.

'Nice,' he said. That was all. An ambiguous remark.

'And yours?' she prompted, after a while. It was a spontaneous question, not of her willing, something thrown in merely to keep the conversation going. She couldn't think why she should want to know.

'Tom Pleydell.' He spread butter generously on a thick cut of French bread and folded it over a wedge of cheese and ate it hungrily. He seemed to have a virile appetite. 'All right, tell me about yourself, Catherine Earnshaw. Where do you come from? What do you do?' He picked the crusty crumbs out of his beard and washed them down with beer. 'Do you have a permanent place in this establishment, or do you just make a practice of flying in and out of the window haunting the unwary visitor?'

She had misjudged him.

'I model,' she said. 'When I'm in work. Can I get you some more to eat?'

'Thanks, I'll help myself. To tell the truth, I haven't had much today. Well, I knew I was coming here so there was no point. One has to economize.'

'And what do you do? Your work, I mean.' She watched him piling a small plate with ham, cheese, potato salad, shrimps, onions, and another round of bread.

'Work? You mean in order to make money, to live? Oh, anything.'

They took their food and sat on the stairs where there was more room. 'Anything' was rather vague and unsatisfactory, she thought.

She asked him to qualify it.

'Well, that's it. Any bloody thing. I haven't been a bog attendant yet, but I could be. I'm not proud.' They shifted apart, he to the wall, she to the banisters, to let two people pass, up to one of the bedrooms.

'And at present?'

'At present I'm eating my first meal of the day with this dolly peach called Tess Durbeyfield.'

She registered the name, made no attempt to correct it.

'You're out of work.'

'Christ, no, I've got enough to keep me busy for ten months. I ought to be at it now. I'm just taking a break. Having a day off because mentally I feel like a stopped-up drain.'

He was a writer. She might have guessed. He had that challenging and at the same time complacent truculence, with a crisp apt way of expressing himself as though he were a character in a book, always more pithy than life. Or he might have been a painter. She glanced sideways at his bulk across the shoulders, his spatulate fingers and flexible wrists. A sculptor perhaps.

'Creative work?' She licked her fingers clean.

'All bloody work is creative. Don't believe anybody who tells you otherwise. Did you see that paint scrawl on the building site down the road?—*Property is Theft*. I wrote that. That's creative.'

She didn't believe him—he was joking.

'Even routine work, office work? Filing cabinets and computers? Creative? Even machine minding in a factory?'

'Sure. Why not? It gets you money—and some leisure to spend it on. It's just tough luck if people are too ignorant to know what to do with either.'

She wasn't altogether impressed either by this argument which sounded too smooth to be convincing. 'Have you ever tried it?' she said.

'I told you. I've tried everything.'

'How do you earn your leisure—when you're working? When you were working last, I mean.'

'Hell, you ask a lot of questions. I should hate to be married to you. My last job? Casual labouring on a demolition site. I'm still on the books, only this week the weather's been too bad and the casuals have all been temporarily laid off. I could go on the dole but they'd find me another job and I want time off to catch up on things.'

'So you prefer to go hungry?'

'I never go hungry. I cultivate the acquaintance of good women, like Jen. And my landlady. When things get really bad I sleep with her in lieu of paying the rent.'

'You make it sound like a reluctant process.'

'Well, she's forty-eight. And has a complete set of dentures.'

Pippa looked at him cautiously. She couldn't be sure how serious he was. His face was composed, his brows knit; he was concentrating on mopping up the last of the Russian salad with the remains of the bread crust. With a glance at her, considerately, he had left the onions. They continued to talk. She told him something of her reason for coming to town, her discontent with suburban office life. It was all very general. She didn't mention her mother's death nor where she came from, and although he made occasional sympathetic grunts she felt he wasn't really interested.

He took her hand-warm glass. 'Like some more plonk?'

'Not really, thanks. Later perhaps. Shall we go down and dance?'

'I'm not much of a dancer.'

'So I noticed. But let's try.'

'Why not show me your room instead?'

She hugged her knees, flexing her ankles in their boots where her dress fringed over them. 'Why should I?'

'It will probably be full of your personality.'

'It's just a bedroom. And I have no intention of emulating your landlady.'

'We could go on talking. Comfortably. That's all.'

'No.'

'No?'

She stacked the plates and glasses together and stood up, shook back her hair and then carried the dishes carefully downstairs, endeavouring not to trip over her long dress. He followed her. 'Then we'd better try dancing,' he said.

'You don't have to hang around. There are plenty of others you can entertain.' She had put the plates and glasses on a little table. He waited for her to turn round, then took her elbow and propelled her into a comparatively unoccupied corner.

'Cheap,' he said.

'What is?'

'That was. A common little remark. Not in character with Tess Durbeyfield. She'd never have said that.'

'My name isn't Tess. I told you.'

'I know.' They began to dance. The music was slow and he held her. The feel of the firm but gentle male possessiveness of his hands on her waist, fingers touching at the back, those sensitive fingers unnaturally roughened with brick rubble, had the effect of making her breathe rather more quickly and deeply. She was all at once conscious of her heartbeats. She hoped that it wasn't communicable.

'What do you model?' he said. 'Fashion, presumably.'

She told him she hadn't really started; she was making contacts. She'd done some studio work. She avoided any mention of the Kennington pair. Then after a pause she added: 'Why "presumably"?'

'Well, you're not butch enough for an artist's.'

'Is that what you are—an artist?'

'No, I told you—I shovel rubble into lorries. Sometimes if the ganger is feeling in an expansive mood he lets me drive the bulldozer.' That was why his hands were calloused, the skin split.

'Why do you ask then?' she said. 'Do you know anyone in the business?' He might be considering putting her in touch with someone and though on the whole she disliked him she was not too proud to accept charity if it meant furthering her ambition.

'Not fashion. I know a couple of artists. But they're both skint. They have to sleep with their models.'

'Again?' The record stopped and they drifted away before the next started. 'Sex is such a useful commodity in a world of barter. No need for money in a truly co-operative society. Isn't that it? The commune?'

Tom grinned at her suddenly. 'You went to school somewhere,' he said. He seemed delighted with the deduction. 'You're not old enough to have finished university.'

'No?'

'Tell me about your school. It was a seminary for young ladies. Must be, with that little voice.'

'More or less. It was called St Helen's and St Catherine's, so everyone called it Hell-cats: It was aptly named. A sort of lesbian St Trinian's. But the teachers weren't bad, some of them. It was run by Anglican nuns.'

'Christ!'

She looked up at him. Offensive again after his momentary betrayal of humanity, he was back on form, coolly suspicious of her power to interest him.

'And where did you go?' she prompted. 'Approved school?'

Cheap again. You should know that every time you cheapen yourself by a glib remark, Philippa, the Sister Superior had said, you weaken your defences. The old cat. The most hellish of the Hellcats. Pippa bit her lip.

'Me? I went to a very common secondary modern.' Somehow this surprised her, she couldn't think why. Something to do with the tone of his voice, the pitch and quality of it, the easy phraseology. Under the rough edge, superficial she suspected like the abrased texture of his hands, the vowels were pure. She found her bag and extracted a cigarette, then offered him the open case. He took one, looking embarrassed, perhaps that he hadn't thought of it first, or had none to offer her. Instead he fished in his pocket for a box of matches and lit hers for her. Not looking at him, listening to the music and the blended laughter and conversation, she was yet conscious that he was watching her every movement. It made her nervous. She drew on her cigarette without savouring it and exhaled immediately.

'Where do you come from?' he asked. 'When you're at home I mean. With Mummy and Daddy.' He exaggerated the gentility of it, perhaps imitating her, she didn't know. She wasn't aware she spoke like that.

'Hassocks,' she said immediately, to annoy him. She had no idea why she lied so easily. Fabrications with her just came out, always had done. An indication of a fertile imagination, Sister Clare had once said, trying to defend her before the Superior Hell-cat.

'Christ!' he said again, this time sourly, more of a groan. 'The dolly deb from the stockbroker belt. Motion picture mock-Tudor with triple garage. Daddy is something in the City, where he commutes daily in the Jag, leaving Mummy to do a round or two of afternoon bridge before dressing for the After Eight Mints.'

'That's right.' She felt herself growing cold with suppressed anger. She disliked his inverted snobbery, his mocking superiority of manner.

'Meanwhile Daddy Earnshaw makes Catherine an allowance to live on in London while she looks for her Carnaby Street impresario.'

'For God's sake go away! Find somebody else to talk to!' She found she was smoking furiously and looked round for a diversion, someone to transfer to. Everyone was absorbed. Zillah, the nearest, pretty in white, was laughing with a fellow West Indian, a cat-like man with panné velvet trousers and a colourful shirt. The inside of her mouth when she laughed, Pippa noticed, was pink, like the palms of her hands. It made nonsense of the term 'black'.

The record changed and Pippa found herself another partner, a succession of partners. From time to time she could see Tom continuing to sit there on the corner of the table, drinking beer and watching her morosely. She drifted away, went into the kitchen to help wash up.

Jen, already there, said: 'You've found Tom Pleydell. Or did he discover you?'

'What is he? Apart from a casual labourer and a bore.'

'I don't know—it would be pleasant to think he's a genius but I doubt it. He's intelligent. But he's probably just a hanger-on.'

'Writer?'

'Writing something. Won't say what, which is unusual in itself. They can usually talk of nothing else. But I suspect that it's because of it that he cultivated me in the first place. As soon as he heard I was with Flyte. Might be a useful contact, I suppose he thought.'

Pippa, remembering that she had been motivated earlier by a similar impulse, felt slightly bitter with herself. It was all a rat-race, all this ambition to be noticed and to get somewhere. She re-joined the others to discover that an entertainment had started up. The West Indian was singing, breaking off to play a few bars on a harmonica, a few bursts of energetic gyratory tap, then a crescendo of singing again in his warm high-pitched gritty voice. Applause and laughter. Someone, evidently Greek, perhaps from the restaurant down the road, sang a plaintive love song full of nasal lyricism which bubbled up out of nothing, like a wild spring, and was followed by a rhythmic shoulder-to-shoulder, knee-swaying dance. Afterwards a couple of minutes of emptiness, only talk, no one offering to continue. Then someone began to croon a pop song, *sotto voce*, and it was taken up by others. There was a guitar hanging on the wall as an ornament. Tom took it down and tuned it. One string was missing but he was able to accompany himself in a folkish style in a rendering of a group of sung poems. Pippa thought she recognized the words of Brian Patten, Adrian Henri, Roger McGough, but there were others which were unfamiliar. He had a baritone voice, raw but pleasant. She watched him as he sat there strumming—singing largely to himself, she thought, for his own amusement, not theirs. He ignored everybody else, even when they applauded. Then he began a Hebridean lilt in a strange pentatonic mode about a grey selchie who swam ashore to become a girl by night and went back to the sea as the dawn rose over the mountains. During it, once, he glanced at her. It went on through rather a lot of verses and by the end not many people were listening. His voice had become correspondingly quieter as the conversation increased and he perched there bulkily with his head down, ear close to the strings, entertaining himself, completely withdrawn from the company. After a while he finished, sat there a little longer meditatively, then got up and replaced the instrument on the wall.

He seemed at a loss what to do next, morosely isolated, unsociable, hunched up, hands in pockets, looming largely over another girl, dissecting her narrowly for analysis but not talking; so Pippa went over to him voluntarily and offered him another cigarette. It wasn't so much a change of heart as an admission that she was bored with everyone else. The seal ballad had been weirdly beautiful.

His face lightened as she swung herself up to sit on the table beside him. He accepted the cigarette and this time she lit it for him, with her own small gold lighter. He cupped her hand in his own two, to steady and direct the flame, and the touch was somehow intimate and warming. Still holding it, lightly, he studied her face for a second over the red glowing tip of the cigarette in the dimmed room and then released her.

'What are you writing?' she asked. 'A novel?'

'Lord, no!' He didn't seem surprised at the question, only at her assumption of the medium. 'The novel as a form today is dead, worked out, finished—didn't you know that?'

'No. I was under the impression that a lot still go on being written. And read.'

'Of course they do! Because a lot of hacks continue to turn out the old derivative plot-situations while a corresponding set of morons go on lapping it up as though they'd never read it all before.'

'Does a plot-situation have to be original? Is that so important? I thought Shakespeare was supposed to have pinched all his.'

'True, but he could do new things with them. With him drama was just then setting out in full sail, exploring new worlds opened up by the Renaissance, the same as men were doing everywhere—freebooters, soldiers-of-fortune, navigators, merchant adventurers, exploiting the Americas. That was a dramatic surge. No nonsense about Art. The novel, born too late, had its dramatic surge in the nineteenth century. It came to an end with Virginia Woolf. There's nothing more you can do with it. Death by its own hand.'

'You could translate an old story like Oedipus or Cinderella or Aladdin into the modern idiom. Put it in a contemporary setting. Wouldn't that do?'

'Sure you could. But it wouldn't have any new ideas. It wouldn't have any surprises, any freshness. It would still be Cinderella or Aladdin, and we'd recognize it a quarter of the way through and it would flop out. We'd no longer be enthralled, like a kid reading "The Arabian Nights" for the first time, because we'd already know how it ends. And that's how an art form ought to be—completely dominating. The reader's got to have no resistance, no will of his own, he's got to be lifted up and carried off to some marvellous place he's never been to before.'

Pippa considered this. 'I don't know,' she said. 'I don't mind reading a story over again if it's a favourite. Sometimes it's an advantage.'

'The same story, yes. Exactly the same, the same words. But not a re-hash, something refurbished, Cinderella in terms of the football pools. There's no bloody magic in that.'

'I read somewhere once that every woman is a little girl who never tires of Cinderella, and every man a little boy who fancies himself as Aladdin.'

'Where'd you read that? It sounds like some old queen introducing a course in fiction-writing. You can do it all by formula, we guarantee success. That's not what I mean by creative exploration. If you think that, then we're not on the same wavelength, kid!'

'Oh, baloney! To hell with creative exploration!' Pippa disliked being called 'kid' by a man only a few years older than herself. 'What's wrong with the Aladdin formula? Treasure cave fraught with danger—a magic lamp and a faithful genie—death to wicked Abanazer—and reward for it all at the end in the beautiful form of a princess. Isn't that the plot of every adventure story?'

'And for our small girl readers—a poor little have-not has a ball, meets Prince Charming, nearly loses him, but wins through in the end with the aid of her pretty little feet and quick wits. Another wholesome fantasy next week ... Is that what you used to read under the bedclothes at Hell-cats? No wonder you look like that.'

'Like what?'

'Like any other starry-eyed doll from the typing pool. Listen, nobody reads novels any more—except the old dears who frequent public libraries and like a nice read. All about how poor Sandra loved a doctor all over the most picturesque bits of New Zealand. Culminating in the big set piece where the hurricane washes away the ferry, leaving them stranded all night in the bungalow; and her simple goodness, as she at last pours out her heart, convinces the great fairy that she is Miss Right after all.'

She continued to smoke coolly. She'd learnt to ignore his boorish manner now, regarding it as an accidental, and to concentrate instead on the development of the argument. To this purpose she waited for him to make the next remark, but her silence seemed to exasperate him for he snapped at her nervously like a goaded animal. 'If it's Perrault you want, kiddy, why not "Beauty and the Beast"? *There's* a nice erotic bedtime story for little girls when they're not playing with their genitals!'

Pippa slipped off the table and walked away without replying. She made her way into the kitchen but there was a couple there embracing against the pantry door, and Jen and another man holding hands watching the coffee percolate. A few moments later she heard Tom's voice behind her, more subdued in tone. 'I'm sorry,' he said. He seemed sincere. 'Look, I'm sorry! I shouldn't have said that to you.'

She accepted his apology gracefully by keeping quiet. She laid out saucers on a tray and he helped her, handing her coffee cups. Although she knew that her silence irritated him there was nothing she could do about it. He irritated her slightly too; and intrigued her too. She wished he wasn't standing so close. She was uncomfortably conscious of his breath on her neck.

Jen having disappeared with the tray of coffee, her man left there at a disadvantage smiled at Pippa and then at Tom whom he seemed to know. Tom introduced them. 'Haven't you met Pete yet? We went to school together. And got expelled together. But not for doing what you might suspect.... This is a little girl who doesn't really exist. Actually she's more intelligent than she looks. Her name's Becky Sharp.'

The other man nodded, seriously, interested, looking at her as men often did, she had discovered, when taken off guard—tenderly, as though enchanted by her prettiness more than anything, more than her sexuality. Pippa found herself laughing. Tom Pleydell no longer annoyed her, nor did she want to continue to fight him. She had lost the skirmish on that stupid deception of names. She conceded the point to him.

He too seemed relieved. 'Nice to see you laugh,' he said. 'It proves you have all your own teeth. Better than Nancy Miles ... My landlady,' he added when she looked puzzled.

Tactfully Pete left them and they took their coffee into a corner where they drank it in silence, not attempting to keep up an artificial conversation. They were aware of each other, sexually as well as personality to personality. They both knew it.

Later on, the coffee over, she continued: 'What is it you're writing then? If it isn't a novel. You still haven't told me.'

He was sitting on a window ledge on his knuckles, shoulders hunched up, head lost in his neck, brooding like some kind of predatory bird. 'I'm writing a play at the moment ... Trying to write a play. It's the only medium still expanding.'

'What's it about?'

'People.' He wasn't very communicative. She waited, but there was nothing more forthcoming so she did nothing to prompt him. She didn't see why she should. She swung her legs which were in the process of going to sleep from sitting on the sharp edge of the table and then, after another minute, she said: 'Had any success?'

'Anything accepted, you mean? Not a play, no ... Some poetry.'

'Where?'

'Oh, magazines.' He named two or three. 'The BBC took some. I've tried selling them in pubs. You know—broadsheets.'

'Any luck?'

'People listen. But they don't want to buy 'em. I occasionally get a free drink. But it's not exactly a source of income.'

'So you do casual labouring. But it doesn't have to be that, does it? Isn't that rather extreme. Couldn't you get a less exhausting job?'

'Like punching buttons on an adding machine in a bank, you mean? I could. God, you're all the same, you women—you're so bloody bourgeois! You're so timid! Supermarket orientated. It's the god-damn mother instinct. They want to emasculate all men by incubating them. You'd turn the whole race into a system of battery hens, safe in a tight little warm house without the birthright of dirt and danger. Despite the fact that you're being methodically exploited by society you'd barter the lot for three nice meals a day and a semi-detached with garage on some sodding new estate.'

Painfully she accepted the irony of the criticism; it was basically the same as she'd levelled at Nicky. She'd seen her brother as potentially authoritarian, giving protective advice which she didn't need, only his affection. Why don't we all mind our own business?

'The trouble with any desk job,' he was saying, 'is that it's too much *like* writing. I mean, you can't throw off one for the other.

In your spare time you can't think except in terms of office clichés and the jargon of commerce, a sort of sub-language for the semi-literate. I know, I've tried it. But if I shovel brick dust or drive a dumper truck I can think as I work. I can let my mind wander. It's not confused. It can go up over the filthy walls we're pulling down, over the top of that terrific crane, into the sky and expand like a gas and disperse over the whole bloody earth. Over the entire universe! God, I'm free, man, I say to myself—I'm flying! ... And after work, when I get home, my body may be tired but my mind is fresh. Because I haven't worn it down smooth balancing ledgers or teaching kids not to make blots. I don't want security; I want my birthright. I was born *Homo sapiens*. It took two million years to make me. I want the human right to think and reason. I don't want a perishing Ford Zodiac with cigar lighter or a Louis Quinze telephone extension on the bijou patio—I want the mental strength to write a poem, that's all.'

'In London? I should have thought you'd have found it easier to do that while growing cabbages in Wiltshire. That's not very mind-bending. Why don't you take a cottage? Or a caravan?'

'Oh, Jesus, you don't have to commune with nature in order to discover poetry. In fact you're not likely to find it there much at all in this non-rural age. What sort of a girl are you? You find it in people. People live in London. So that's where you find it. I should have thought that much was obvious.'

Though she pretended it was casual she found herself studying him with increasing interest. She looked for the most part beyond him, towards the dancing company drifting between the two rooms, but in the occasional glance she allowed herself at him she saw an intriguingly complex man, a paradox who drew his inspiration from company yet was shy of it (or contemptuous of it) and stood aloof on its periphery, withdrawn, observant perhaps but not exactly an integral and stimulating part of it. Nor was he conventionally good looking. The beard helped to disguise what she suspected was essentially a weak face, thin now because he had neglected himself but in more prosperous circumstances—with literary success, for example, later in life—it would probably become fleshy, even a little flaccid. Yet he was the most magnetic person she had met for a long time. She knew herself to be attracted towards him. It was immediate and positive, a sensation both exhilarating and disquieting.

A touch on her shoulder and she was invited back into the dance by the West Indian. His name was Grant. An insurance clerk by day, he supplemented his income by singing in a nightclub. This evening was his late turn. He therefore didn't have to dash off till after midnight. His energy seemed unbounded. Then, the piece over, she ran upstairs to her room; her boots had become uncomfortable and she wanted to change them. As she opened the door a pair of guests who had been reclining on the bed got up sheepishly and went out, passing her with an apologetic smile. After all it was her room.

She went in and was about to push the door to when she observed Tom on the landing outside. He had followed her up the stairs and was leaning back against the banister rail.

'You can't blame them,' he said. 'You weren't using it. In the commune no one has any possessions, not even privacy. If you have a pad you should share it.'

'What do you want?' she said.

'Like I said. I have a compulsive urge to see your room. If you'll let me. It promises to be full of your enigmatic little lady-like personality. I might even discover who you are.'

'You needn't think I'm going to let you sleep with me.'

'There you are—a euphemism from your convent days. What you mean is you won't let me screw you. I hadn't asked to. And I won't.'

She switched on the light. He looked around, taking everything in in one glance. Arrested by the portrait of Che Guevara he knit his brows and said in disgust: 'God, you're a bloody romantic Trotskyist!'

'Am I? So what if I am? I can please myself ... What are you? Don't tell me you're a Conservative.'

'Me? I'm nothing. I don't care two pins for any of them. Marx or Mao or President Nixon. I'm for myself.'

'You're a romantic anarchist. Hardly any difference.' Sitting, she began to unlace her boots.

'I'm nothing, I tell you. I'm for myself.' Fascinated, he watched her progress. Then he added: 'I could be for you too. Perhaps. I don't know.'

In her nylon feet she skirted him lightly where he stood inconveniently taking up space, and pulled open the big rocking wardrobe with care because the door tended to stick and the whole thing to sway forward. She was looking for shoes.

'It's nearly twelve o'clock,' he reminded her, toeing one of her collapsed white boots curiously with his foot. 'Are you going to leave that when the clock strikes and you trip wildly downstairs?'

For a moment, still searching in the cupboard, she didn't appreciate the allusion, then looking briefly over her shoulder, she grinned. 'It's not exactly a glass slipper,' she admitted.

He sat heavily on the bed, his face serious, even gloomy, as he contemplated her unenthusiastically as though he found her exasperating. 'It wasn't glass,' he said. It was her stupidity evidently then which irked him. 'It was ermine. Don't you know the difference between *verre* and *vair*?'

'Of course.' His tone, the male patronage, the airing of erudition for superiority's sake, point-scoring, nettled her. 'Everyone knows it. It's an old thing they teach you in the third form. Only I happen to think glass slipper is more romantic.' Then she added, spitefully: 'I also happen to know Perrault didn't write "Beauty and the Beast". It was Mme de Beaumont.' Advantage Miss Rowantree.

'Well informed with it too. They did you well at your convent.'

'Probably as good as your secondary mod.'

She passed him again on her way to her dressing-table stool and as she did so he caught her by the hand and held her. At the same time he stood up. 'I have news for you,' he told her. 'That was a lie.'

'I suspected it. Where was it?'

He was silent for a few moments. Then he drew her, still by the hand, towards him until her face was close, forearms crooked, shoulders almost touching. There was an odd tension between them, composed of suspicion, curiosity and, she thought, plain animal fascination. He twisted the corner of his mouth briefly. Apologetic, nervous, and genuinely amused. 'It was a large red-brick public lavatory on the A4 at Marlborough.' She found his grip uncomfortable but couldn't release her hand. Her wrist was imprisoned against his chest. 'Don't you want to know why Pete and I were sacked?'

'Not particularly.'

'Well, I'll tell you anyway. Otherwise you'll go away and die of curiosity ... It was for writing rude comments in the gallery of the Hall under the names of the old boys who had died in the last two wars. We wrote *"Fuck 'em all"* underneath and decorated everything with a pretty pattern of swastikas.'

'Is that all?'

'What did you expect?'

'Something more disreputable. Pushing hash at least.'

'There wasn't all that much about in those days. What we did was enough. It was a gesture.'

'Rather a stupid one. Typical of boys. You might have known what the outcome would be.'

'Of course you and your nun-ridden Hell-cats would have succeeded in thinking up something more subtle, such as anonymous letters containing contraceptives to the Sister Superior.'

'She was a tough old bird. She'd probably have filed them away in the cabinet under the appropriate reference.'

'Do you know why we did it?'

'No, I'm not in the least interested. However, it obviously means a lot to you.'

'It was a hysterical death-wish. Masochistic. A cry of despair. We wanted to be caught. A generation earlier and in other circumstances we would have been fanatical *Hitlerjugender* stamping through the streets of Munich. Or Marlborough. So would all the other clean-limbed, pie-frilled, masturbating products of the English public-school system singing *I vow to thee, my country* from the choir stalls over well-thumbed and camouflaged pages of *Men Only*. If Hitler had invaded, I tell you, seventy-five per cent of those illustrious heroes commemorated on the wall would have welcomed him with open arms. We wanted to repudiate our heritage. A sort of glorious abdication from a guilty kingship. We wanted to be found out and caught, so that we could purge ourselves of that conviction of guilt, by being rejected by that complacent, sanctimonious, officer-class cabal. Because it was only like this, by being rejected I mean, that we in turn could reject it. The old-boy caste system is like any totalitarian organization, like Communism, like the Catholic church—you can't resign from it, you can only be expelled. That was why I told you I was secondary mod. That was a wishful fantasy too, another death-wish. I want to lose my identity and regain the self-esteem which has been sucked out by generations of mental inbreeding.'

The fingers of his other hand while he was speaking had clenched on her upper arm and Pippa, with a wince and a slight indrawn gasp of discomfort, rose on the balls of her unshod feet with the pain of it. 'Well, I believe you,' she said. 'Only stop being a Nazi. You're hurting my arm.'

Immediately, as though he hadn't been aware of it, he released her and then, perhaps compensating for it or even out of genuine remorse, he took her again, re-capturing her more gently this time, and kissed her. His beard was soft; it surprised her. Somehow she'd imagined it would be coarse and whiskery, but it was almost as fine as her own hair. She made no attempt to resist; on the contrary she found it enjoyable. She didn't much like the man himself but his kisses, on a wholly sensual level, were stimulating. He released her mouth and then found it again, for the repeated pleasure of its contact, and she in turn responded by returning the exploration. A feeling of sweet drowsiness began first to trickle, then to flow, through her veins. She felt weak on her feet.

Sitting with her on the edge of the bed he said: 'You haven't disappeared yet.' It was a growled whisper in the region of her ear.

'Why should I? I live here, remember.' He puzzled her. Deliberately fanciful, but under that tough writer's mask of obligatory cynicism was an enigmatic earnestness; and beneath that again, further recessed, a vein of poetry—or perhaps merely sentimentalism, either way an introspectiveness which perhaps accounted for the soft element she'd recognized in his face. She was beginning to understand him. It was all play-acting, he was creating for himself a part he felt he had to live up to.

'Why should you?' He repeated her answer. 'I'm not sure of anything.' He found her ear by parting the hair from it, contemplated it for a moment and then kissed the lobe. 'All I know, *inconnue*, is that I was at this party and I was feeling like bloody piss and wondering whether to go round to somebody else's and suddenly there was this gorgeous little bird who floated down the stairs and said she was La Belle Dame Sans Merci, a faery's child, and took me to her elfin grot.'

She laughed. 'It's Pippa Rowantree,' she confessed. She no longer felt tense and the information was given painlessly. From down below they could hear a burst of laughter and ironic cheers, then more animated talking and another record.

'It's damn cold up here, Pippa,' he said. 'Don't you have any heating?' Her body was shivering under his hands.

'There's a gas fire. I didn't intend to stay. We'd better go down.'

He held her. 'We could always get into bed.'

'No.'

'No? Why not?'

'Because I'm not promiscuous. Amoral but not promiscuous.'

'Making love isn't promiscuity. It's common sense. Almost an act of courtesy.' Her head being turned away from him, listening nervously to footsteps on the stairs, he kissed the side of her neck where the tendon strained. 'Your heart's beating like a drum,' he told her. She was aware of it. 'And what's this nipple standing up for if it isn't interested?'

She disengaged herself and stood up, arranging her dress.

'I'm going down,' she decided.

* * *

The green Ascona, comfortable rather than stylish, with the chauffeur leaning against it, a short raven-haired man trimming his nails, was waiting for her in the courtyard outside the hospital. Shadows from the arched arcades looped across the granite cobbles, the sun reflected from the sage-coloured cement walls, an old man in black sat motionless on a seat, his thin wrinkled hands like brown leather folded on his stomach. The chiaroscuro of bright sunlight and deep shadow after the cool white flagstoned corridors of the interior made Pippa narrow her eyes and filter everything for a moment through her lashes. In her hand she carried one of the panniers of her motor-cycle. The porter at her side had the other under his arm and a tall multi-coloured paper carrier bag with the name 'Casa Verdi, 27 Via Pescolati, RIVA', on it, containing the rest of her belongings. The whole complement was not much.

There was a smell of soapsuds. A watery gush down a pipe on the wall and an ejection of milky-blue foaming liquid issued from a waste pipe to find its way into a gully by the side of the paved walk. She stepped out of the cloister into sunlight which immediately penetrated her skin, enfolding her like a golden anemone. As she walked across the yard towards the shining car the chauffeur came to life, put his manicure set away and moved round to the other side to open the door for her. The old man on the bench paid no attention as she passed. But for the fact that his faded ochre eyes were wide open one might have thought he was asleep, or dead, he was so still. Perhaps he was blind. But he didn't even turn his head to the sound of her feet. His chin was white with stubble, the raised veins on the back of his hands a black embroidered network of old leather. He was content to sit there, to be alive, grateful, knowing it was a bonus on his rightful expectancy of days. He was very old and very frail. If she'd said *'Buon giorno'* it would have broken the calm surface of his euphoria. He would have had to start thinking, focusing the meaning of her voice, then having to reply. As it was he was experiencing the simplest of pleasures, as unintellectual as an amoeba. She got into the car.

The chauffeur, handing in the rest of her frugal luggage, glanced at her for a fraction of a second as a man, then became a servant again, impersonal and incurious, adjusted his white-crowned cap and swung heavily into the driver's seat. They slid quietly out of the courtyard, under an arch, and Pippa, sitting at the back, feeling small in the alien limousine, turned to acknowledge the farewell wave of the nurse on the steps, but it was almost too late. The car had passed into the main road joining the sunlit traffic. All at once she felt apprehensive, made edgy by the stream of vehicles and the traffic noises, and she realized with surprise that she was still not over the shock of her accident. To this extent at any rate she was indeed still convalescent. Otherwise she felt relaxed and normal.

Out of the town she became calmer. The road followed the lakeside, rising and falling occasionally, twisting with the indentations of the lake's contours or cutting through a knoll of pines, with the sun flashing past the columns of sycamore, cherry and sweet chestnut, always heliographing a morse code across her absorbed eyes. There were long, thin plantations of conifers and apples. She thought she saw the dark green of orange trees. Then came terraced vineyards, the young plants growing out of light stony soil beginning to haul themselves up the rows of wires running north and south to catch the sun.

The road had climbed higher now and coming out on to an open curve she saw a great arm of the lake shining in mackerel ripples and caught a glimpse, for a moment only, of Isola Malcontenta—a green-and-pink hummock with a doll's-house villa and one flashing window, a diamond laser of pinpoint reflection, and then it was gone. They were dropping down into Pianezze. In the centre of the town, recognizing the spot where she'd had her crash, Pippa felt once again the cold spasm of panic which had overtaken her earlier. An internal brief shiver like a chill, icy and burning at the same time, it ran up through her from belly to shoulder-blades and then it was over. The place was quiet now at any rate. Midweek, late in the afternoon, it was almost deserted.

The car turned into the private approach, crossed the short causeway with the two or three boats moored there from iron rings, and passed through the lodge-house gates, which were already open. In a moment, having encircled the villa, they pulled up on the other side in front of the main entrance. A double flight of stone steps, lozenge shaped, curved upwards from the urns of orange azaleas and at the top stood a tall elderly man, watching them from the balustrade. It was the same one she had met before. Accompanied by a spaniel, well to heel, he came down slowly to greet her as the chauffeur handed out the ridiculous bits of impedimenta.

Count Raffaele d'Anza held out his hand. It was thin and bony, smooth, the colour of old ivory, but the grip as he shook hers was both gentle and firm, dry and warm. It was the sort of handshake that gave her confidence.

'Miss Rowantree.' His acknowledgement was accompanied by a formal continental bow, slight and unostentatious, somehow rather old-fashioned and, she thought again, military. 'I am sorry that our short acquaintance was destined to end in such an unhappy accident. Believe me I was shocked, devastated. Now it is my duty to welcome you to my house for as long as you care to stay, in an effort to make amends, and indeed I am delighted to do so.' His English, though rather pedantic, was charming, as was his whole bearing. Thin, even slightly emaciated, though he had once been big, she considered, his grey linen jacket hanging loosely upon him, his straw hat in his hand, he smiled down at her. She smiled back, and said simply: 'Thank you.'

D'Anza then spoke to the chauffeur in Italian and the man picked up her belongings and carried them up the steps.

'At this time of day,' the Count said, 'I usually take a little refreshment—some wine and a biscuit—on the terrace up there. It is cool and pleasant. Would you care to join me, before you are shown your room?' He held out his arm by way of invitation, another old-fashioned gesture, and she took it, feeling by the action somehow less diffident as they mounted the splendid steps, less conscious of her inadequacy in this setting, of the absurdity of her mended shirt and frayed trousers, tissue thin at the knee and still bearing stains of oil and road grit. At the top, in a corner of the flagged terrace, under the shade of a fig tree, was a small table set out with a white cloth on it and two wicker chairs. 'Of course, if you prefer it, you can have tea. Or coffee? Whisky. Coca-Cola.' He smiled. 'Anything you like. You must speak up. I don't as yet know your preferences or habits.'

'Thank you, Count d'Anza. Wine will be splendid.'

He arranged her chair, made a vague waving gesture towards the house and then he too sat. 'I find I do not eat too much these days,' he apologized. 'A sign of approaching senility, do you imagine? It is a sobering thought, to reflect that after middle age one's stomach begins to atrophy and the cells of one's brain die off one by one, irremediably, like so many burnt-out Christmas lights. There was a time, not so long ago, when I had a tremendous appetite—great dishes of *jugànega* and *lasagne al forno*—but now I am content with wine and biscuits. However, let me not dishearten you, Miss Rowantree. You are young and I am sure are able to enjoy good food. Tonight I have ordered something special in honour of your presence, for it is not often that we entertain a beautiful woman at the villa nowadays; so you will not retire hungry I assure you.'

She smiled and sat there demurely, reminding herself to try and be as graceful as his compliments. Upright and aristocratic in his woven chair, he was as remote as the two generations separating them. Again she thought that, but for the rather florid wet lips, he would, in his day, have been handsome. Even now he was commanding. The dog had meanwhile flopped down on the slabs, near by, panting.

The wine arrived.

A short, middle-aged woman, dark-eyed, black-haired and sour looking, in some sort of a black uniform with a lace edged apron, shuffled out on low-heeled court shoes with a tray containing a carafe and glasses which she dumped without ceremony on the table between them. D'Anza, acknowledging the woman's service with a raised hand and an inclination of the head, an absent-minded rather than an imperious gesture, though it tended to look like the latter, poured the wine carefully. His hand was steady, the grip on the jug firm and calculated. The glasses were old, conical and finely chased, and the light made a twisted rope inside their stems.

'You will find this is quite a good wine,' he said. 'It is our own.' He said it proudly yet without any kind of arrogance, still meek as became his nobility, valuing the achievement rather than the prestige. 'The vineyards to the north of Pianezze, around Brecchio, belong to the villa; and we have others in the Valpolicella, near Negrar, just above Verona. In fact they are our livelihood. They just about pay for the upkeep of the state and the house. Without them I should be penniless. We produce a *spumante* which is quite well known and fairly popular—many people enjoy it at this time of the afternoon—and also this, which I personally prefer. Not as rich as a Frascati perhaps, but I think you will like it. Tell me your opinion. You can be honest.'

The wine, crystal clear in the glass, was pale olive in colour and smelt fragrant. She raised the glass. It tasted moderately sweet and benign, with a good pleasant body. She was no connoisseur, even though d'Anza paid her the compliment of assuming that she was; nevertheless she liked this one. It was a wine she could have gone on drinking happily, she felt, until she was conscious that she'd had too much.

'Lovely,' she assured him. It seemed an inadequate report but he accepted it gracefully.

He took up one of the long brown biscuits and dipped it in his glass. 'These we call "*ossi da morto*",' he told her. 'Rather a macabre title perhaps—"dead man's bones". But they go well with a robust wine. The others, the little round ones, you will find more delicate, more feminine. They are called *bianchetti*.'

She found them delicious and said so.

He inclined his head again appreciatively. 'Giulia is a good cook,' he conceded. 'The woman who served us just now. A taciturn creature possibly, but invaluable notwithstanding. I have very few servants now. After all, my wants are few. There is only Giulia and Carla and another woman who comes in daily; Marco my chauffeur and general man; my personal valet Enrico, an old faithful from before Sidi Omar; and of course the gardeners—we have to keep them on. Not a staff in the sense of the old days, before the 1915 war. Then you would have experienced the real *villeggiatura* in the true sense of the word. Since my wife died there has been little gaiety here, I am afraid. However, Giulia insisted on staying. That is why I am grateful to her. She is a link with the past, the only one left....' Then perhaps thinking that his conversation was in danger of becoming morbidly retrospective, he smiled and refilled her glass. 'When you are sufficiently rested,' he said, 'I will show you around. I hope you will not find it too Spartan an existence.'

He raised his glass and contemplated her silently over the top of it. Pippa, smiling in return, drank—and looked out across a corner of the lake to the bumpy haze which might have been mountains or simply clouds. The effect of the rich wine on this warm afternoon with the breeze stirring her hair and breathing cool through her shirt was to make her feel relaxed and suddenly incredibly happy. She had the pleasant illusion that she had been drinking white wine on this terrace with this civilized man—her father, was it?—her grandfather?—all her life. All this, the house behind her and the lake and the village and the vineyards out at Brecchio and elsewhere, all these were hers by birthright and she was enjoying it. At least she was going to enjoy it while it lasted. She could hear the scream of peacocks—a sound which she fancied she would always associate with this place.

'Rossano tells me that you must rest,' d'Anza was saying. 'You are to have peace and quiet for a while. I think we can offer you that. As I told him, we cannot introduce you to a gay life; you will not find that at the Villa Franceschini. But I think you will not find it boring.' His eyes were very steady, brown and penetrating.

She looked at him warmly. 'You are very kind,' she said. 'And I am truly very grateful, Count d'Anza.'

He seemed pleased. He watched her nibble the last of the frosted *bianchetti* and then said, in his old-world phraseology which was like a translation of Henry James: 'When you are agreeable, Miss Philippa, you will allow me to conduct you inside. You would doubtless like to see something of the villa and your own quarters before dining.'

She rose, a shade unsteadily. 'My friends call me Pippa,' she assured him. The wine was heady. She had the odd sensation that she was going to topple over the terrace wall and plunge into the rhododendrons below.

D'Anza, also standing, glanced at her with a certain wry amusement, his strange mouth flickering for a moment before composing itself once more into its customary gravity. 'Indeed?' he said. 'That is singularly appropriate.' But whatever the inward joke was he evidently chose not to enlighten her. It was something private, no doubt. 'When I feel that I have earned the right to such an honour I shall certainly refer to you by that charming diminutive.' The dog had scrambled to its feet as soon as the Count stood up.

Together they walked across the flagstones, up a step to another level, and thence across grass to a paved circumambulatory. From here they were able to enter the house through a long, open french window directly into a large room full of pictures and, it seemed, clocks. Gold clocks under glass domes, ormolu clocks on black plinths, clocks on walls, in one corner a grandfather clock with figured blue tiles. Escapements swinging, rotating horizontally, pendulums clicking softly, plunger movements rising and falling like weightless pistons in some scientific model on exhibit in a museum, all catching the light and reflecting it in little silent flashes of yellow and silver. She could have stayed to see more of the marvels but he escorted her through a double door while she was still wondering what the room would be like, what Hoffmanesque music there would be, when they all struck the hour together.

They were in the entrance hall. A great assembly area with a floor of alternate brown and black marble slabs, a curved staircase itself as wide as a room, with shallow risers and broad treads carpeted in turkey-red, with wrought-iron dolphins and cherubs besporting themselves under a grey-brown walnut handrail, smooth as glass but softer to the touch. Pictures mounted the stairs at discreet intervals. One, an enormous classical group in browns and crimson on the first landing, framed in gilt, looked a showpiece for it sparkled under an electric pencil light all to itself. Some alabaster figures, a putty-coloured, grim-looking nineteenth-century bust of a bewhiskered gentleman, a few potted plants, a white rug on the floor in the centre—these were about all the remainder of interest in the room. The design and lofty sweep of the architecture were the impressive features.

The house had been built in 1775 by Giovanni Muttoni, she heard d'Anza saying by her side. She was gazing up the perspective of the staircase, her eyes drawn to the elaborate cornice above, and the chandelier suspended over the well. How did they ever get to clean it, or to repair the electric lamps when they went wrong? Or was the whole thing lowered perhaps by means of a pulley? 'At least it was begun by Muttoni. This part is his. The house was continually developed and altered throughout the last century—pulling bits down and re-designing others. We Italians have a great propensity towards that sort of thing. The conservatory is quite late Victor Emmanuel II. Victorian I suppose you would call it in England. You may have heard of my great-uncle, Dr Maurizio d'Anza—he had a lot to do with it. He was a naturalist-explorer who helped survey part of Eritrea and the White Nile. There is an African lily named after him, *Agapanthus rubens danzae*, which is hence wrongly, but popularly, known as the Dancing Lily.' He was guiding her up the staircase and through another room, leading off from the first mezzanine. 'The guide books tell you that it is in the Palladian style,' he said, looking back the way they had come, at the view of cream walls through open mahogany doors, 'by which they mean that it is reminiscent of Andrea Palladio. It is a fairly meaningless observation since the genius of that remarkable stonemason of the *cinquecento* has in fact influenced most Italian architecture right down to the present day, when Palladian cinemas and offices abound in every city.... Have you been to Treviso yet?'

Pippa shook her head. She was gazing up at a painted ceiling—a flaky gamboge version of (apparently) the four winds arriving to pay homage to the birth of Venus at that moment curled up coyly asleep in a scallop shell. Only the placing of the hands was Botticelli.

'You must go to Treviso if you wish to examine the best original work of Palladio.' He recited a list of which villas and castles to see, a full and exhaustive itinerary. She found his grave assumption that she was a woman of wealth and infinite leisure, with all the means in the world for the grand tour, both amusing and, as she looked down at her threadbare appearance, undeniably bizarre. He was of course an eccentric. She had already decided that. The whole house, she considered, was probably just a little eccentric. She was thinking of the room full of clocks all ticking away in pointless rivalry.

As though sensing something in the trend of her thoughts he went on: 'This place is like a museum. It is too empty. It grieves me sometimes. This exquisite Mary Magdalene, for example—' he had paused in front of a small painting, unlit but under a window, with a table and boat-shaped display of flowers in front of it, 'is a Correggio, but who is there to see it? It might as well be in Rome. I normally keep it in my private gallery, under lock and key.' He stood and contemplated it, forgetful of her. There were still more paintings, dark and mysterious, leading away to left and right.

'You could open the house to the public,' she suggested. 'That would be one way.'

He took her arm and led her on. 'I don't know that I find that idea altogether agreeable,' he said. 'The public is such an anonymous body. Holidaymakers who come in coaches or park their cars on the lawns and tramp their way up and down my carpets and are gone for ever after tea. I should much prefer a few friends. But perhaps it may have to come to it yet.'

'A good many owners of English mansions have discovered that their estates have been improved by the social revolution,' she said stubbornly. He was just an old reactionary. 'It may have swept away the hunt dinners but it's filled the rooms with life for the rest of the year.'

'You are too young to be sententious, my dear,' he reprimanded her gently, 'although you may well be right. And I am not the Duke of Bedford or the Marquess of Hertford. I am a recluse. No longer sociable.'

'I cannot believe that,' she said gallantly. Although he walked slowly she found it impossible to keep in step with him; he had a long, dignified and virile stride.

'I like to choose my acquaintances ... However, we recently had life enough here.' They had come to a lengthy dining-room, all crimson and brown, with an oval draw-leaf table fully extended but bare except for two silver candelabra. 'Last autumn we endured the presence of a film unit. They used the villa and the gardens as— what is the term?' He visibly searched his English vocabulary and then found it. 'On location. The technicians descended upon us and for ten days it was like a state of siege. Then the shooting started— is that the correct phrase? Only two days of that. Then it was all over. Peace again. It was my fault. I knew the director years ago, when we were in the war together. I offered him the facilities. I have only myself to blame.'

Pippa, immediately interested, asked him who it was.

'Gian-Mario Agosti. You have heard of him?'

She had to confess that she hadn't. She was not very familiar with the film world, she tried to excuse herself, nor with Italian directors in particular. She'd heard of Fellini, of course, and Antonioni, Visconti, and Zeffirelli. She tried to think of some others. 'What is the picture called?' she asked. They had entered the conservatory and were moving among humid ferns, beaked cacti with red mouths, soaring rubber plants, exotic but drooping flowers in pots, all rather papery and neglected, the labels indecipherable.

He ducked his tall frame under an overhanging creeper. 'I believe the title is to be O *Paolo, O Francesca*! A reference to Dante, I imagine.' He looked at her sideways, shyly; a glance that she felt had some intention, a quick search of her face for a reaction perhaps but the phrase held no significance for her. 'A satirical fantasy, I think Gian-Mario called it, in the modern idiom. I don't know. I am ignorant of these things ... Have you seen it?'

'No, it certainly hasn't reached London yet. Perhaps it's still to be released, if it was only last autumn they were here. Studio work probably came after that.'

'Very possibly.' They had passed under a seedy-looking banana palm and now stood at the end, in a doorway arched like a fan, looking out at the deserted formal gardens dropping away in steps, and beyond them the lake. 'The park was laid out by Negrin who was responsible for the gardens at the Villa Revedin-Bolasco at Castelfranco Veneto. The statues, too—some fifty of them—are similar. They are by Marinali ... I think we will leave the rest for another day. You are no doubt fatigued.' He looked down at her half hidden among the bamboo ferns. 'You would like to see your room. You can rest there if you wish until you hear the bell for dinner. There is a small campanile which you can see from your window. We use its bell for such occasions.'

'Really, I'm not tired, Count d'Anza,' she assured him. She wanted to go on seeing everything in this fabulous and enchanting place.

'Nevertheless I regret I must leave you for a while, Miss Rowantree. I have some work to do; some writing to finish.' It was the first time she had been conscious of a real note of censure in his voice. It was gentle, it was dignified, but it was firm. She recognized it as a command. He was still in authority, and he was dismissing her.

'Very well,' she agreed, and followed him dutifully back into the house and up the staircase whose dimensions made her feel small. She could remember as a child being suddenly conscious of this form of agoraphobia on a visit one wet day to Wilton House when she and Nicholas and her mother had been the only visitors in the echoing hall.

'Actually you have seen most of the house now,' the Count told her. 'My study is along there.' He waved a delicate and parchment-yellow hand down a corridor. 'There is a basement, of course. That is quite a labyrinth and extends under the whole villa. Some of it we keep for essential equipment and storage; the rest is a sort of museum of eccentricities instigated by my grandfather. You will have already observed that eccentricities abound in my family.' The shot went home. He smiled at her again, the same shy sideways glance of apology and amusement and a hint of self-satisfaction.

At the top of the staircase she looked down vertiginously over the balustrade. 'Who was in the film?' she said. 'Who were the stars?' Her imagination kept coming back to the picture which had been made here. It was certainly an ideal setting, a wonderful location for a romantic drama. Already in her mind she had begun to cast and direct it.

'Oh, there was that young actress—what does she call herself?' D'Anza was staring at a cobweb which had escaped somebody's long feather duster. He tried to hook it down with his stick from its anchorage above the plaster cornice. 'She chooses to go by a single name. A conceit of her profession, I suppose ... Vanessa, is it? Valentina? ...'

'Valencia?'

'Ah yes, to be sure—you are correct! Valencia. That was the name. A young woman with long auburn hair.'

Pippa was as thrilled as if she had still been at school. 'Valencia was in it? Here? But she is *beautiful*!'

D'Anza chuckled. 'Yes, I suppose so. Yes indeed—one must allow her that. Though that is about all she is ... Not a great actress. She couldn't even walk down this staircase like a lady. As if she'd been born to it, I mean. She was very hard to direct.' And then, significantly, as if it explained everything he added: 'I understand she is a Neapolitan.' He had succeeded at last in poking at the cobweb which came away in a festoon of gossamer and dust. 'The other— her leading man—was Angelino Franconi. You know him? But yes, I see you do ... They didn't have much to do, I thought. It consisted mainly in walking about from one room to another holding hands and carrying oil lamps. Or else playing hide-and-seek and other children's games in the arboretum. Or holding each other very wetly under one of the fountains. No doubt it will be extremely pretty. Photogenic—is that the word? Of course there was also some going to bed. There seems to be a lot of going to bed in motion pictures nowadays. In my young days Rudolf Valentino managed to do it all fully dressed.'

The remark, opportunely or not, had brought him to a door at which he paused. It had a china handle and in the lock a huge brass key which he turned, pushing the door open and standing aside for her to enter. 'Your room,' he explained.

It was large and airy. High sash windows. Shutters. Sage green and old gold tapestries on the walls. A huge Italian brass bed that reminded her of an illustration to 'The Princess and the Pea' in one of her pre-school story books. Piled high with softness, it had a red brocade cover and lace-edged eiderdown pillows. The period was 1910, like the ornate tiled washstand and commode set. Everything in the room was of that period, except for the tapestries and a rococo wall mirror, all wildly florid gilt plaster curves and pink Versailles rosebuds. She thought it was all delightful.

'Satisfactory?' Standing there, leaning both hands aristocratically on his stick. He was watching her reaction eagerly, closely, almost sentimentally she thought, like a father indulging his youngest daughter.

'It's charming, Count d'Anza. Wonderful!' She went to the window, which was open, and pushed out the shutters, closed against the afternoon sun. It revealed a view of the terraced gardens and the lake. 'It's beautiful,' she repeated. 'Beautiful!' She looked all round. A glazed door led out on to a balcony from which a stone staircase wound down in stages to the terrace. 'Beautiful!' She could think of nothing else to say, suddenly bereft of vocabulary. At home—it seemed like a former life—she would have said 'Wow!' or 'Super!' Here not only would they have been inappropriate, they didn't even occur to her. She came back and touched the dressing-table, smoothed the figured brocade on the tall square bed. 'I shan't want to leave. I shall want to stay here for ever!'

On the table against the wall were the two motor-cycle panniers and the paper bag, reminding her of reality and something that had been worrying her ever since she had arrived. She turned to the silent man behind her.

'Count d'Anza, is it possible for me to buy some clothes, do you think?'

He smiled gravely. 'You won't find anything much in Pianezze, I imagine. However I have no doubt, when you feel up to it, that Marco can be persuaded to take you into Garda, or even Verona perhaps. When Dr Rossano agrees that you are well enough.'

'Not until then?'

'Is it so important?'

She looked down at herself and grimaced. 'I'm afraid I shall disgrace you.'

'I assure you, you look very acceptable.'

'But not to myself.' She went over to the table, unzipped one of the panniers and pulled out a crumpled short dress more appropriate to the discotheque than to that formal, ambassadorial dining-room downstairs. To Pippa, adoring clothes as she did, it was something important enough to make her miserable, spoiling the pleasure of the day and all that had built up to this point. 'This evening,' she told him bitterly, 'it will have to be either this or jeans. I don't carry anything else much.' Her voice faltered away with disappointment and she could feel the tears pricking the back of her eyes. It was so stupid. She had no intention of letting herself cry. She rarely wept, the last time was when Nicky had come home. She hadn't even done so when she had walked out of the Notting Hill flat and left Tom leaning against the draining board. That had been something too deep for tears. But the thought of being a guest in this noble house, with all the graceful past life that it reflected, with only this crushed dress and a couple of pairs of grubby slacks and superficial shorts was important enough to make her feel emotional. It was true what she had told him. Her mortification lay in the fact that she was afraid of disgracing him, the elderly aristocrat, paternally forbearing yet brought up in a remote pre-war world of forgotten manners and a required code of etiquette. Clothes were important. It was difficult to explain this to him. Probably only another woman would have understood.

He stood there, Prospero-like, watching her; tall and distant, autocratic, courteous, enigmatically complacent.

'You have not as yet examined your wardrobe,' he observed.

Into her mind instantly a strange telepathic illumination. Not so much a thought, an intuitive feeling rather than reasoning or comprehension. It was like what is glimpsed in the snap of electric light, that moment switched on, before the bulb fuses. A momentary revelation of more things than can be taken in. She had to examine the wardrobe.

It was a great auburn mahogany cabinet like a baroque cathedral, as solid as the post-Garibaldi régime in which it was created. She opened the left-hand door. Inside were the glimpsed edges of girls' clothes, suspended from hangers. For a moment she assumed that they were all period 1910, having been left in the cupboard by some past occupant. Astonished, she put in both hands, spread them apart, examined them. They were as modern as this week. Three day dresses, an evening gown, a couple of cocktail tunics and trousers, a pair of white slacks. Below, on a metal rack, were shoes. It was incredible. She didn't understand any of it. She glanced at d'Anza for enlightenment but he was standing there inscrutably, watching her like Prospero, unsmiling but reasonably pleased with the success of his magic. She opened the other door. Two more dresses. Shirts. A printed silk scarf. A short skirt, a long one. A kimono bath wrap. Below, standing up tall, a pair of boots.

It was all incredible. She supposed, she had some idea, that d'Anza must have acquired all this specially for her, but the notion was hardly formulated; her mind was in a whirl. And for what purpose she hadn't even got as far as guessing. She slid open a drawer. It contained underwear; soft, pretty and sweet smelling, freshly laundered.

Pushing it shut she turned and leaned her back against it, looking at him directly. She was unable to say anything. Surmise and accusation and disappointment and hope, all mixed up in the whirl. Perhaps seeing something of this expressed in her wide grey-blue eyes, the man, leaning on his stick with one hand, spread the other in a deprecatory gesture of explanation.

'It is very simple,' he said gravely. 'These are some of the things left behind after the filming. Those people made such nuisances of themselves I became angry and pushed them out. Well, I mean to tell you! Giulia was very upset—her routine disorganized. She is a peasant. Independent but indispensable. She was in a mood to leave. I could not have that. I need her. I could not afford to have her go; she understands my way of life. So I told Gian-Mario they must all clear out. They finished the rest of the takes quickly and moved out, vans, trailers, equipment—like a circus caravan. Only the litter and breakages left, trampled gardens, bits of wire. They had to come back to replace the electric light fittings they had taken down. It was a period picture, you understand ... Or rather, a fantasy, a mixture of periods. It opened in the present, I believe, with flashbacks. Something like that. I am not wholly conversant with these matters. Anyway these few things were left in a cupboard downstairs in the basement which they used as changing rooms. I saw no reason why they should be returned. We had been put to enough inconvenience. As it happens they may prove useful. Will you accept them?'

She was still cautious. Amazed but sceptical. Delighted but still not wholly comprehending. Drawing out one of the shoes, she slipped it on. Sveltely Italian, it was her fit. She re-examined all the things, looking at concealed labels. It was wonderful. Suddenly another wild surmise. 'Are these—? Were all these things for Valencia? Did she use them?'

D'Anza laughed at her tone of awe. 'I very much doubt it,' he said. 'Not quite sumptuous enough for her, I imagine. Furs and pure silk crepe for that one. No, I don't know whom these were for. Extras. Guests at the birthday party scene. I don't know ... Will they do, do you think?'

She felt ecstatic with gratitude, to him or to circumstances. 'Of course they will do! They're marvellous! Count d'Anza, thank you.' There was nothing else she could properly say with any dignity. He inclined his head again, that little obsolescent continental bow of acknowledgement, his appreciation of her pleasure. 'Then I will take my leave of you,' he said, and put his hand to the door.

But she restrained him a moment longer. With both compartments of the wardrobe open she said: 'You must tell me which one I am to wear. It's your occasion. You choose.'

He contemplated the display for a little while soberly from a distance, his head back and eyes narrowed slightly as though he were long-sighted and he could see better that way. Then he raised his stick and pointed with it to the classical evening gown, a fall of vanilla rayon so simple as to be almost austere. 'As it will be our first evening,' he said, 'and therefore something of a formal occasion —that one will do very well. You need nothing more. Except some ear rings. You will find a selection in the fourth drawer.'

*   *   *

Tom Pleydell lived in one room, a converted bed-sitter at the back of a terrace block of featureless shops and offices somewhere behind Westbourne Grove all carved out of what had once been elegant houses with servants' attics and basement areas. Now it was a warren of what the estate agents called high density living—a near slum of mixed races all unaware of anyone living farther than the next apartment. To reach his cell of the honeycomb one had to climb an iron fire-escape and cross the concrete roof of a garage, then step over a low parapet wall some four bricks high and select one of four unpainted doors. His was the one with the sour milk bottles.

It was here, three weeks after their first encounter, that Pippa moved in with him. It had been both a capitulation and an inevitability. They had met frequently during the lengthening days of February, as often as possible, every evening, half day together on Saturdays, all day Sunday except when he was on overtime. They had more in common than separated them; both romantic anarchists, dissatisfied with the circumstances of their origin and what the normal development of those circumstances had to offer, namely an established middle-class routine. They were two young members of the society which had produced them, intelligent, modern, passionate, and dissatisfied. It was inevitable that they should be mutually attracted, not unnatural that they should finish up living together. The capitulation lay not in this but in the fact that Pippa finally gave up trying to make it in the world of modelling. If she'd had patience, more tenacity, no private means, it might have been a different outcome. The prospect of a little starvation could have stiffened her determination to persevere, but as things were it was always too easy for her, when the rent money ran out, to go to the bank and draw another cheque on her account. Not being forced by privation to continue the glamour-pose sessions with Malc and Wend, which though disheartening might in the long run have been good for her, she left. In actual fact it came to a head the day before she moved out of St John's Wood and farther down, across the railway tracks, into Notting Hill.

Malcolm had been pleased with her intelligent progress; she had learnt the techniques quickly, he told her, and suggested she might soon be ready to go on to more advanced work. She was not curious about this. The only advanced work she was interested in was fashion, which she knew he didn't do. After the first disappointment she hadn't been too depressed by the realization of the dead-end nature of this job. It was pretty squalid but not actually degrading; one could get used to it probably. It could lead to other channels, she was confident. Nor was she even particularly deterred when she chanced upon an awful picture of herself peeping mischievously through her fingers from an open page of a magazine blowing in the breeze on a Soho bookstall. If Tom had seen it, of course, there would probably have been a row; his communal philosophy stopped short of sharing her with voyeurs. But he wasn't with her and didn't appear to frequent that sort of bookshop anyway, and in any case would most likely not have recognized her behind those Japanese fan-shaped hands and in that dark wig—she had no other distinguishing features. It wasn't even the idiocy of dressing like a schoolgirl, with false plaits, in order to undress again and hang on a rope in a deserted drill hall gym, that decided her. It was Malcolm's enthusiasm for her ability to learn new techniques.

'You're doing okay, darling,' he said. 'That last set sold straight away. You interested in working with a partner?'

'I don't know. Possibly. What is it?'

'Oh well, the usual; you know, doll.' He attended to a kettle which was whistling on a gas-ring. When he came back he went on: 'You can take a butcher's at him in a minute, if you want. He's coming round for a short session.'

'An actor?'

'Well of course!'

She had almost forgotten about him when he walked in later, a six-foot-three guardsman—except that from his hair he couldn't have been a guardsman, she judged, unless he was still wearing his busby. He ducked under the wet prints hanging from bulldog clips on a line as he entered the studio and she grabbed a towel. It was odd that although she'd got used to Malc and Wendy (they were such a sexless, if creepy, pair) her reaction to this stranger was to shoot back quickly into the alcove. It didn't augur well for the success of their partnership. And when she discovered what the proposed series involved she was even less enthusiastic. Still, he was an actor. And photography was all an illusion.

But after the preliminary poses she wasn't so sure of his acting ability, nor of Malcolm's intentions. Her nerve failed her. She dressed and walked out, bought herself a coffee and Cointreau at a pub on the corner and went home. She never returned. She'd had enough. And she knew that if anyone was to handle her she wanted it to be Tom, not this handsome giant with the cleft chin.

She paid Jenny, who asked no questions, up to the end of the week and moved her suitcases out. She had already got rid of the Che Guevara poster. In the honeymoon days that followed, life in Tom's hovel was joyous if squalid. She tried to clean the place up, or at least to tidy it, and succeeded to a certain extent; but she was not by nature a devotee of the kitchen, and besides, as Tom said, it really needed tearing apart and re-building, re-plumbing and re-decorating by a team of contractors. Grease lay congealed and encrusted in the shrunken wood cracks, and the draught poured in through the ancient mouseholes and under the sagging door, despite the bit of carpet tacked along the bottom. She stuffed the holes with old tights and went out and got herself a job as a waitress at an orange-fronted restaurant down the road, in Bayswater, called La Tarantella. Strangely enough she loved the cosmopolitanism of Bayswater. The Indian saris, the animated conversations in Polish or Greek on street corners, the delicatessen shops and rows of intriguing foreign papers hanging up outside tiny newsagents, all gave it an exotic appearance and helped her forget the dreariness of the rest and the biting winds and sleety rain.

Life with Tom was never dull. When they were not arguing about the world or having rows they made love, frequently all night, each time as she became more aroused getting better and almost more unbearable until, exhausted, she fell asleep, only to be awakened an hour later, dragged deliciously out of her floating unconsciousness by the feel of his hands gently but importunately at work on her body, his lips on hers, one finger slowly, insistently caressing an oval round her vagina. Then with only a smiling moan of protest, 'Tom' becoming a murmur, his name a sigh, she would accept the last coitus, still more than half asleep, sweet and unworldly, as though it were all happening to her in a dream, too limp almost to arch her back. They even set the alarm clock, a tin affair from the British Home Stores, half an hour early so that they could wake up and make love before he went to work. It helped him, he said, through the worst part of the morning, making his way to the site before it got really light. The sensation which he called the afterbliss stayed with him, he assured her, until the first tea-break.

But they had rows.

They argued about practically everything, from the price of tea to the poems of Donne. At first she had taken the arguments seriously and got heated. Then, as she came to know him better, she made due allowance for his provocative nature. It was all a tease, play-acting. He contradicted for the sake of contradicting, argued because he liked it, and there was always a slight sadistic streak in his intellectual one-upmanship. Thank God he'd never had a sister, she told him. As a boy he must have been insufferable. Then she would think of Nicholas—their old partnership in childhood, a teasing love-hate relationship, an affinity which drew them to each other even when they fought each other, which had sustained them to lie for hours on the sharp rocks by Lannacombe gazing into still pools for marine life, and to climb out on to the roof of the old house in Putney, through a trap door, because he had dared her, and to dance there together to the strain of a transistor radio. She could remember that very well. Hanging on to his tie with her eyes closed and only a bit of a wire frame, to keep the snow from falling off the roof, between them and the railings below. The traffic noises coming up clear on the night air. Cars, a lorry, an electric train flashing blue somewhere. The rattle of the wind in the television aerial ... There were times when she found it difficult to distinguish between Tom and Nicky.

She had discovered what his play was about.

'Well, it's about this boy who hates his schoolmaster,' he said. 'And pursues him into retirement, years afterwards, blackmailing the old bastard about an incident that never happened but he thinks it might possibly have. The old man, I mean. And then things get twisted, and the blackmailer feels sorry for his victim because he meets this girl, the old man's niece. Only she isn't his niece. The old schoolmaster's just living with her, the dirty old sod—she's very young. And he turns the tables and cooks them both by telling everybody they're brother and sister. So they have to murder him. Are you with me?'

'I think so.'

'Then they find out they really are.'
'Are what?'
'Brother and sister. Last laugh on the old man. Curtain ... Now say it's bloody.'

This was before Pippa had joined him, while she was still at her own flat.

'Well, put like that it sounds a bit melodramatic. Not at all the sort of thing I thought you were on about. Depends on how you treat it. In the writing up, I mean.'
'I thought it would sell. I'm doing another which won't.'
'As a plot I still think it might make a better novel.'
'Oh, Christ!'
'What's that supposed to mean?'
'I told you. The novel's dead. It's all bloody twat. Nothing happens any more. It's about how poor Auntie Jane didn't have it off with the lodger. Or 180 pages of chat disguised as social comment. Or else it's poetry. With lots of spaces in between the pages.'
'And the drama goes on living?'
'Of course it does! It's still got space to develop in. It can spill over the stage and involve the audience. Or it can pick up visual hints from the cinema. Or it can burst into TV—two people battling their wits out in one room, that's drama. Not in the theatre, on telly. It's alive? Of course it is. It's not fettered by a limited number of words between covers. It can go in any direction.'

Pippa was still thinking about the battle of wits in a television set.

'Anything as intimate as that would need good dialogue,' she reflected.

'You're too right. And have you noticed how often it sounds like somebody's been trying to mould it out of very wet clay? With boxing gloves on?... That's where the drama can develop. You need to go around with a tape recorder. Or just an ear for the way people talk.'
'And you think you have that?'
'Better than some.'

He was given to illustrating his more muted arguments with strange fairy tales, sometimes softly spoken over a guitar accompaniment.

'Are you sitting comfortably? You are? Then I shall begin... Once upon a time there was this great film director named Henrik Ibsen. He made some fantastic movies about Roman orgies, and

Raquel Welch playing Santa Claus in a remand home for boys where she gets stuck in this chimney and it's so hot up there she has to wriggle out of all her clothes. Well, one day he got fed up with all this because he had no more room on his shelf for the Oscars, he was fed up with the whole stinking stupid roundabout, so he packed all his gear into a small boat with twelve chosen disciples and sailed off to Fetlar, which is a remote island in the Hebrides, my child, and there he made a picture about the life of the Snowy Owl. The only people in it were a man and a girl who loved each other. Very much. No visible sex, just eyes full of mutual tenderness. They were trying to protect the miraculous bird from exploitation—such as the film unit. So art and reality became blended. No dialogue—just the poetry of seascapes and skyscapes and the sound of the wind. It was very beautiful. No orgasms. Ibsen even cut out a lovely shot of the lighthouse in case some Fleet Street hack with a tripos, writing for the *Custodian*, should see in it a phallus. The censor reluctantly gave it a U certificate, the critics didn't know what to make of it, and the public were bored. It was box office poison. The distributors took fright. The old man was clearly past it, everybody said. So he went back to his native village and got a job as a caretaker at the little wooden school. He had to empty the earth closets because it was a very primitive school, but somebody had to do it for the kids and he was happy. Happy! And one day...'

Once started on one of his allegories he tended to go on. She supposed it was the author in him.

There were rows. After they came to live together these tended to be shorter but often more violent. He frequently picked things up, whatever was nearest at hand, and threw them at her. Once in a rage he slammed the back door and all the glass fell out; and they had to patch it up with cardboard until he could get out next day to buy a new pane and re-glaze it with putty, which he was not very good at doing. Then there would be remorse and a gift of a dozen daffodils and more lovemaking.

Mrs Miles, his landlady, who leased the room along with the rest of the tenement from some remote syndicate, was a sad-dispositioned woman who clutched herself in various cardigans and kept the sweetshop and newsagent's on the ground floor. She made no objection to Pippa's arrival and took the opportunity to put up the rent.

Once after one of their rows (usually over money but this time because he had called her a sham) she had said: 'What about you? You're not really a hippy. You could never be. You're just a renegade, like me. But you make too many demands on life.'

'Listen, all I want of life is to go on living, to have you to make love to, and to write. That's not too much to ask whoever put me on this planet, is it?'

'I don't know. Those are three tremendously big requests, if you think about it.'

He kissed her hair, standing behind her as she worked in the kitchen.

'Once upon a time,' he said, 'there was a young woodcutter and he went into this gingerbread house and on the stairs he met a faery's child who made sweet moan and granted him three wishes, because he was very handsome and talented and her heart went tick-tock every time she looked at him.' She went on cooking her risotto over an old black gas-stove which never seemed to have any heat in it. She turned the rice with a fork while he parted her hair at the back of her neck and softly kissed the nape.

'Do you make up stories even in your sleep?'

'Yes. Mostly about you.' He stood behind her with his arms round her middle. 'Once upon a time there was a little boy named Hans Christian Andersen and he was very lonely and sad because he had no brothers or sisters to play with. And he used to lie on his midnight pallet at Marlborough trying not to weep. But he kept his head while all the others round about him were having a good wank and comforted himself with stories in which he sailed up the Amazon and found lost cities and rescued Professor Challenger's daughter, a beautiful princess who was female only insofar as she wore a dress and didn't use rude words like the other boys. He hardly knew what one looked like. Not having had a little sister to share the bath with, you see.'

At least she was able to do his typing for him, making a better job of it than his own two-fingered efforts. The first draft of the play displeased him when he re-read it, and he began again. She had to cadge the paper from Jen because he said it was expensive and they couldn't afford to buy it when they had friends who worked in publishers' offices. Pippa, in order to prevent another row, had to pretend she had no money of her own and this in turn led to a deception which culminated in the final and irrevocable row two months later when she had walked out on him. His total literary success during this time was a short story accepted for radio. They celebrated the cheque by going out to eat. Not to La Tarantella. That would have been too much like a busman's holiday. They chose a place a little nearer Greek Street.

Pippa didn't mind working at La Tarantella. She liked the warmth and the company. It was conveniently within walking distance, no transport fares. This left Tom free for the most part to use her Honda for work. She had sold the Singer—one more item in the bank she had kept quiet about. The house in Bracknell was let furnished, the rent piling up somewhere with the dividends, and the cottage at South Pool empty at this time of the year—she didn't want to know about either. She was in love with Tom. She wanted to keep him, to hold on to him. To do this she had to meet him on his own terms, to share his philosophy and his way of life, to alter such circumstances would be to kill their relationship. After all, they had deceived each other before, about their origins; it was easy to go on with further deceptions.

La Tarantella was owned by Luigi Marciano, inevitably known as Rocky, a stout happy man who liked to keep himself and his customers warm in the steamy atmosphere of the Italian restaurant decorated with blown-up colour prints of Capri and San Remo; which was just as well in view of the fact that he had a sentimental predilection for the mini-skirt, whose passing he regretted, and in an effort to arrest the process had designed the costume of his young waitresses himself—a mauve concoction with a halter neck and what at that time were known as 'hot pants'. Despite a tendency to pinch her bottom as she was engaged with the till, or to count her vertebrae with his fingertips, he was harmless—a genial man who led his large family to Mass every Sunday and loved to see everyone around him happy. She had more reason to fear the customers.

It was he who directed her thoughts towards Italy when she finally ran away.

'She is so beautiful,' he used to say frequently, kissing his own fingers. He came from Genoa. 'You go there, Pippina mia; you never come back no more.' In order to improve his English he had remained in this country for a while after demobilization—he had been a prisoner of war—and business success, together with family ties, had kept him there. (He now had a chain of small restaurants; his wife was a Londoner.) 'Good food, good wine. Every day you have breakfast in the sun. Everyone your friend, everyone know you. Is all so happy and so nice.' She looked at the impossibly cloudless, blue-vaulted pictures of Venice and Rimini and then, beyond the bamboo partition, at the big street windows running with condensation from the dull cold outside and the hot-house atmosphere within.

Another advantage of the Tarantella was that she was able to bring home certain perks—rounds of unwanted salami or a tinful of instant coffee which had got damp in Rocky's steam bath. She and Tom were also able to eat there at reduced rates. Quite often Luigi forgot (deliberately?) to charge them anything at all. The intellectual arguments went on even here, over the glass table top.

'What are these cinematic methods then you say the drama can borrow?'

'Plenty! You can mix the media, for a start. You can have back projection. Cartoon techniques. Slow motion. You can freeze the action while Hamlet soliloquizes. A synchronization of sound with vision—overlap by playing one scene while speaking the lines of another. Double image. Tons of things to experiment with. Or you could reverse the clichés—take everything apart and send it up with love. Parody.'

A sizzle of chips from behind the stainless-steel operating theatre. A call from behind the hatchway. 'Number sixteen!' Their omelette is ready.

'Think of a typical situation. The latest screen epic from Sweden or whatever. Elektra is seated at her Louis Quinze dressing-table in a deeply cleft Empire nightdress, flanked on either side by candlesticks. She is brushing her long hair. The candles gutter gently in the faint breeze from the wind-machine. Suddenly in the dressing-table mirror we see the door pushed open. Orestes is standing there looking wildly Byronic in an open-necked bishop-sleeved shirt and holding aloft an oil lamp. Much photographic play is made of the oil lamp (a) because it looks pretty on the screen, and (b) because it's a phallic symbol. We see his feet cross the carpet. Elektra, turning, recognizes him and makes sweet moan. They are in each other's arms. The lamp is on the dressing-table. Reflected in the mirror again we see fumblings. Camera at floor level, the nightdress drops; she steps away from it out of focus. The bed rushes towards us. The candle flares up in a sputtering orgasm and goes out, to the strains of surging Tchaikovsky. Romeo and Juliet ... Francesca da Rimini ... Hamlet ... The B Flat Concerto ... Who cares?'

'Sounds quite good.' She investigated the contents of her omelette. 'You ought to be writing film scenarios.'

'No, I ought to be writing for television. Why doesn't somebody give me a job?'

'You haven't had a success yet.'

This reminder always silenced him. And hurt him, she recognized. She was invariably sorry afterwards to see the effect of her jibe; but he did talk so much. And anyway it was never long before he came back. Resilience was the key to his survival.

'The next contribution I shall offer the BBC is a fairy tale for *Watch with Mother*. "The Tortures of Genghis Khan, and how to make your own kit." Or possibly "The True Story of Susannah and the Elders". Or what about "The Beauty-and-the-Beast Syndrome in Western Psychosomatic Culture"?'

'That again?'

'It fascinates me. Listen—I saw an old film once at an arts cinema. Made by Cocteau, ages ago. It was beautiful. Fantastic disembodied hands beckoning this girl through an enchanted garden. It was Josette Day. Lighted candelabra floating in the air. She seems to be floating too, just off the surface of the ground. Pink roses flow open from buds. Briars uncurl and pluck at her draperies as she goes, wide-eyed, to meet the Creature. Clichés today, but a breakthrough then, all that time ago. It must have been '47. Sheer Existentialist poetry. Only he was writing it directly with the camera. That's creative borrowing.'

He talked like this when he was happy, when he felt her love to be secure. At other times, when a row had temporarily separated them, he was morose and dispirited.

'I don't see how you could develop that idea much,' Pippa considered.

'No? Think of the universality of his theme. It's the basis of every erotic horror story—from Andromeda through Nebuchadnezzar to King Kong. Girls for the Minotaur. Shakespeare did it. He had Caliban close-neighboured with Miranda. In the *Dream* he sent it up as a sardonic joke. His audience laughed but I bet it gave them the shivers. It all derives from the ancient fear-fascination, universal in folklore, of the idea of copulation with an animal.'

'It didn't strike me like that when I played Titania. We did it at school.'

'God, I bet you did! I can just imagine it as done by the girls of St Helen's. Just because it has fairies in the cast doesn't mean it is a play suitable for kids. It is saturated with sex, I tell you, both straight and deviant. Witchcraft and animalism. A weird sort of epithalamium for a wedding-night! It convinces me more than ever that Shakespeare was a queer.'

'Oh, bosh!'

And there were always arguments about money.

Pippa, in order to buy a few extras (new clothes for herself, a decent shirt for Tom), dipped into her own account and lied about the rise she had just got from Rocky. Tom's jealousy flared up, suspecting the worst. He went round to have it out with Marciano and discovered the falsehood. So where had she got the money from? A gift? Favours? She tried to keep her temper against his outright and childish accusations. She had saved it—when she was in the photographic business.

Then why the hell had they gone without weeds for a month?

An itinerant Pakistani named Murad, whose legitimate trade was household goods out of an attaché case, called from time to time and supplied Tom, when he had the money to spare, with a few sticks. Buying the resin and making your own was of course cheaper, but it was better than hanging around the Portobello Road for a contact. Handed over in an old flattened Embassy packet, at the current price of seven for a pound, these were a luxury which Pippa had thought they could perhaps cut back on. She had no moral objection to cannabis smoking which, as she'd told Nicholas, she'd indulged in herself as part of her adolescent experience. But it remained a luxury. Other things came first, she maintained. In this category she put clothes. She could, of course, have subsidized Tom's habits out of her own resources, but he was shrewd, he would have suspected something if they suddenly didn't live in the penury he was accustomed to. He recognized the simple arithmetic of two at work being able to live better than one, but the improvement in their standard of living had to be gradual. This was complicated by the spasmodic nature of Tom's employment; he never seemed to keep any job for long.

For entertainment they usually went to the cinema, in the outer ring area where it was cheaper. The Notting Hill Library supplied them with books. They went out and met friends occasionally, in pubs and rooms. At one of these, not at Jen's, the West Indian friend of Zillah's, the cabaret artist named Grant, was able to supply them with something different.

'This here's a twin jet, man!' he told Tom. 'You can have twice the trip on that.'

So they carefully cut the two pounds' worth of oblong blue tablet in half with a penknife and Pippa took her first experience of Instant Zen or lysergic acid diethylamide. It was not a particularly successful trip. She was 'brought down'—that is, first elevated and then suddenly and unexpectedly frightened and depressed.

Pippa and Tom were sitting together, she in his lap, in a large dust-smelling upholstered armchair with the stuffing coming out, at somebody's pad in Fulham.

'It's not working,' she said. 'Nothing's happening.'

'Well, give it time, darling. It takes half an hour. Look at something nice. Don't look at me. Something nice. The last thing you look at may be important.'

'It's just a lump in my stomach. Like indigestion.'

'Give it time. I'll tell you a story while we wait. Look at something nice.'

So she stared at a bowl of plastic tulips.

'One day while he was cleaning out the earth closets Henrik Ibsen had a thought. He found he couldn't live without his art. Life without film-making was like life without God, for I forgot to tell you that he was essentially a religious man. So he made one more, all on his own, just for himself. It was about his childhood. No sex, no violence. Just an aching nostalgia. Simple people, with beliefs, a quieter pace. The walk to church on Sunday morning. Melting snow. Fishing in the lake. Teaching a little girl in a patterned jumper to ride a bicycle. The first sloe blossom. Spring and sincerity. Innocence ... And he sat alone in his cottage and watched it on his home-movie set like mad King Ludwig in his empty Bavarian opera house. And he saw that it was good.'

'And it was a box office success.' Pippa had to take part in these fairy tales. Indeed she quite enjoyed doing so. They were part of his individuality. It is the individuality of a person that one loves; the rest is decoration, icing-sugar.

'Not yet. Wait a minute. You're way ahead of me ... The old man died. Really it was because he was disappointed. The film needed a proper sound track, music, a cinema, an audience—things he couldn't provide. So one day, just as the cranes were flying south, old Ibsen snuffed it. But there was this Wardour Street mogul named Aristotle Croesus who'd heard about the great man's last opus, so he went to Skein and bought up the entire village. School house, earth closets and everything. And he and a few dozen others fitted out the picture as a musical. Did a studio mock-up of romantic old pre-war Elsinore where they'd moved the setting slightly, with lots of artificial snow and zoo reindeer, and had the Black and White Minstrels do the song-and-dance routines. Music based on an idea by Grieg. And of course wrote in some comic bits because let's face it the old boy hadn't much humour, and this is a humorous age. Two million

Jews went laughing like hell into the gas chambers ... Still there, Pippy? ... And it was a great success and ran for twenty-five years to coach parties piled up around Leicester Square. A nice family show. They called it "Son of the Master Builder".'

She continued to stare up at the tulips.

*   *   *

Left to her own devices after d'Anza had gone, Pippa first explored all the other drawers in the wardrobe, discovering an assortment of useful accessories from hair grips to a gold clasp. Then she examined the rest of the room. A delicate little Swiss night clock, with a button which when pressed, she discovered, closed it up like a silent oyster for sleeping, stood on a bedside table with a cut glass ashtray. Underneath on a half shelf was a small mahogany box inlaid with a pattern of mother-of-pearl. It contained tipped cigarettes in one cedar-lined compartment, a lighter in a chamois hood in another. A glass paperweight with a vignette of pressed flowers inside. On the wall another glazed conceit of pressed flowers surrounded by arabesques of gold and silver wire as fine as hair. Around the edge a legend: *Difendiamo i fiori dei nostri monti.*

There were a few books on a shelf between asymmetrical bookends—a goat-footed Pan seated on his haunches at one end playing to an enchanted, and enchanting, fawn at the other, as though time and music and the delicately chiselled cascade and the animal's movement had all been transfixed. She ran her finger along the book titles. The poems of Keats, Browning, Shelley, Byron. Four uniform volumes in green ... E. M. Forster, *Where Angels Fear to Tread* ... D. H. Lawrence, *Travels in Italy* ... D. H. Lawrence, *Collected Poems* ... Shakespeare, *Complete Works* ... Orlandi's *Dizionario* ... Giovanni Verga, *I Malavoglia* ... Michele Prisco, *I Cieli della Sera* ... Dante Alighieri, *Inferno* ... *Purgatorio* ... *Paradiso* ... Three uniform volumes in blue ... Alessandro Manzoni, *I Promessi Sposi* ... Giuseppe di Lampedusa, *Il Gattopardo* ... She wondered if they had been specially chosen for her from the library downstairs or whether they just happened to be there.

A wide dressing-table, matching wardrobe, supported china-backed hairbrushes, a silver comb, two hand mirrors, a spray deodorant, manicure set, and a mysterious little elongated cabinet which, when opened, revealed a set of stoppered tiny amphorae, each containing a few millilitres of liquid. She unplugged one and sniffed it. It was scent. She tried the others. They were all different; each with its subtly individual fragrance.

When she had sufficiently amused herself with the interior of the room she opened the door on to the balcony and walked out. It was a paved rectangle about eight metres by four with a rather desiccated hydrangea in a tub in one corner, and a flat stone bench near the wall facing the lake. On the parapet, where it made an angle, stood one of the marble figures she had seen from below—a Junoesque lady clutching with one arm a sheet which was just slipping from her shoulders, the other hand raised in the act of releasing a dove. Pippa sat on the bench for a while looking out. There on the water was the same arrowhead ripple she had seen before, arcing slowly; it was the launch crossing the lake to the next village. There were also three or four sturdy-looking little craft with red sails—she thought they were probably fishing boats. She was in full sun, yet it was airy here exposed to the warm breeze. The air smelt piquantly of cinnamon. Were those seagulls on the lake? Little pinpoints of white. On her left could be seen the top of the miniature campanile.

Her mind was still slightly dazed. Not only with the beauty of the house and its setting, but also with the puzzle of d'Anza and his solicitude for her, which she felt was still not quite resolved. She wasn't really sure about that wardrobe of delights; not wholly convinced of the truth of his story about their origin, that these things had all been left over from the filming. It was a coincidence, to say the least, that the clothes should be all her size and style. It was the sort of thing one experiences in dreams, wishful fantasy usurping logic—except that this was no dream; the hard bench under her thin trousers precluded that; it was uncomfortable and real, pinching her bones ... And, she continued, no matter how precipitately the unit had departed, d'Anza waving his stick at them in wrathful exasperation, was it altogether likely that someone had left a gold clasp behind, and a gown that must have cost almost as much? The more she considered it the more she felt that d'Anza must have bought them, or acquired them from somewhere, specially for her.

Yet she was not particularly dismayed. The Count did not frighten her. He was strange, certainly, but no more so than many a wealthy eccentric and scholar—she felt sure he *was* a scholar—living in similar circumstances, head of a noble house, used to giving orders, the last of an old régime, with a dwindling staff and few relatives, an essentially shy man who probably enjoyed doing anonymous philanthropic acts and watching the result from a safe distance. The obvious inference, which she was not blind to, was that he was an old Casanova setting his premeditated trap for her seduction—yet this she found difficult to believe. His whole manner was against it. He hadn't looked at her like that. How had he looked at her then? Gravely thoughtful, sometimes absent-minded, occasionally delighted with her response. Her response to what? The house, the villa, the island setting. Her appreciation of its beauty. His normal manner when she had walked about with him, talking of London, her journey across France, Munich, a blocked carburettor on the Brenner Pass, had been almost off-hand—he had merely raked gnats and clicked his fingers at Giulia to take the tray away. But the moment she had indrawn her breath at the sight of the great ceiling of the hall, or stood and gazed at the little Correggio, suddenly reduced to silence —then he had looked at her with real interest. With tenderness? Yes, a suggestion of that too, she thought. That was where the mystery lay. Well, no doubt if she stayed long enough it would be revealed in time. But she was not afraid of him. She was quite able to take care of herself. He didn't strike her as being violent, and in any case she had successfully defended herself against violence before now. The German truck-driver on the Brenner. Intelligence was a good weapon.

She wished the bench had a back to it. Flat and hard, it was obviously designed for its classic beauty rather than its comfort. If she was going to spend much time out here, she reflected, she would make a request for a deck-chair. She had no doubt that d'Anza would be able to click his fingers and conjure one up from somewhere. Getting up, she explored the rest of her little patio. Built on a corner of the house, it was separated from the rest by a high wall and was quite private. The wall had a projecting flat top with a frieze of circular spikes. No one was likely to be able to climb over it. The stone staircase which led down to the terrace was also under her control, she discovered, because a few steps down there was an arch with an iron gate set in it, and on going down to examine this further she found that it had an antique but well-greased mortise lock with a key in it on her side. First making sure that it was secure she withdrew the key and carried it back with her to her own room where she placed it in the cigarette box.

Everything was so still and quiet; it was like being alone on a desert island, yet strangely she didn't seem isolated. This was the experience she'd had when first setting foot here; and it was odd, it was new for her. She, like everyone else of her age, she supposed, had always thrived on company, eschewed solitude, did everything she could to break it by playing records or phoning somebody, because nothing bored her so much as silence and her own company. She was not afraid of going it alone. But she disliked silence. Yet here, today at any rate, she felt content in this silent house. Perhaps it was because there was so much magic in the air.

She opened the door and went for a walk down the short corridor. At the end of it she discovered a bathroom. An old-fashioned bath with brass taps and claw feet, almost an heirloom, but spotless. Also, in one corner, a more recently fitted feature—a modern shower over a black marble, square, recessed basin. She tried the taps. After a long wait the water eventually ran hot. Deciding to freshen up before dinner she returned to her room, undressed, put on the kimono, selected two of the Turkish towels laid out on the wash-stand evidently for her use, and made her way back. There was something very strange about the extraordinary quiet of the great house, something not quite real. She had the sensation of watching herself performing all this in some other medium, from a point outside herself, as though she were asleep or seeing a film, herself the actress in it. She was looking down on a set, with the roof off, a doll's house; she was swinging down the corridor, viewed from above, her hair bouncing. She had never seen that angle of herself before; and the sound had gone.

This was the first of many peculiar impressions she was to receive at the Villa Franceschini.

Presently, feeling cool and refreshed, she stood looking at the contents of her wardrobe. She took out the creamy gown and put it on. Then, because the rococo wall mirror did not show her full length—most of its area being taken up with whorls and extravagance—she turned herself around in front of the long wardrobe mirrors inside the doors, arranging them so that she could see herself from all angles. She was thrilled with it; it was so beautiful. Not what she would have immediately chosen for herself perhaps but, viewing it on, undoubtedly effective. It draped simply and gave importance to her smallish bust, her least satisfactory feature. From the drawer she chose a pair of gold wire earrings. She wondered for a moment whether she should also wear a velvet throat band she found there, but then decided against it. D'Anza had said she needed nothing else. And it was his dinner party. To please him she would do as he requested. After all he deserved it. Then she went to the little cabinet of perfumes and after playing with them found one she liked. When she had brushed her hair and arranged it and touched up her eyes she felt quite pleased with herself.

A silly expression from somewhere in the past came into her mind to amuse her, and then sadden her. And Cinderella *shall* go to the ball! She grinned at her own reflection, holding the little eye-brush. Tom would have found that funny and capped it with something better. And at the thought of him the grin disappeared. A cold jab to the heart. She had taken off the dress and earrings to do her hair and she now lay on the bed and read. She decided she might as well try the Forster since she had not read this one and it promised, on inspection, to be the only book on this shelf she was likely to be interested in. She was some thirty pages into the story, and quite absorbed, when she heard the bell. It was a sweet golden sound, quite unlike any English church bell, which she always associated with verdigris bronze dreariness, Easter offerings, mothballs; or with mourning, the death of her mother. This was somehow both more melodious and more dramatic, like a temple bell, a call from Bali. It had a connection in her mind, this sound, this operatic summons, with the other half of something she had already experienced here, but she couldn't think what at the moment, and there was no time to puzzle over it. She slid off the high bed and dressed quickly.

She walked down the corridor and thence the staircase, holding her dress off her shins, glad that her host wasn't about to see her descent. If he had been dissatisfied with Valencia then he must be a hard taskmaster. Making her way to where she remembered the large dining-room to be situated she discovered it, on opening the door, to be empty, the table still bare, the room unlit except for the last of the greenish twilight coming in through the lofty windows. She was a little taken aback. What was she supposed to do now? Wait? Go and sit down? Amuse herself at the pianoforte in the music-room opposite?

She heard d'Anza's voice behind her. 'A thousand pardons, Miss Rowantree. I did not hear you come down.'

She turned. And as she did so, facing him, full length, front view, she saw his expression momentarily unguarded. It was a revealing look. A flicker of astonishment, a little raising of the thin dark eyebrows, a freezing of the eyes, widened as though he had confronted a ghost. Then it was gone. He was upright and polite and impersonal again, tall, suave. 'Very good,' he murmured, perhaps at her overall effect. 'Very good indeed!' A swift glance from her face to her ankles and up again, once; a nod, as though he approved; then he offered her his arm. 'I thought as there were only the two of us we would dine in the smaller room. It seemed so pointless to sit in this lonely place—it's like a banqueting hall. Although Gian-Mario had them do it, I seem to remember, in the picture—one at each end of the table. I must say it seemed a little contrived to me, over theatrical, you know. It would be difficult enough to hold a conversation in those circumstances, let alone pass the salt. Would you care for a short stroll before dining?... Or perhaps no, on second thoughts; we had better not. Giulia has doubtless prepared an excellent soup and she will be displeased if we let it get cold.'

He led her down the passage to an adjacent, smaller room, square in shape, with a round rosewood table laid out for a meal. Three of the walls housed glass-fronted china cabinets.

'This is known as the Worcester Room,' he said. 'I am something of a collector of fine china and this is where most of it is assembled. There is some very precious Sèvres here, and some Dresden of which I am proud; but also a representative sprinkling of fine ware from your own country, the best examples of which I rate highly. Hence, you understand, the name. It has the advantage that it renders this room exclusive to my friends. It's title is a means by which I can select them. Nobody but a cultivated person can pronounce it.' He chuckled. 'You think I am an intellectual snob?'

She shook her head and smiled. She merely thought his command of English was remarkable.

Marco, the general man, in a dark suit with a black cummerbund, who seemed to be in attendance, arranged her chair for her as she sat.

'You are not cold, Miss Rowantree?' d'Anza continued. 'It frequently sets in cool here with us in the evenings. Mist rises from the lake. Visitors often tell me that the house strikes them as damp, although I must say I do not notice it myself. But we Italians are incurably optimistic about the weather. We have always built houses with inadequate heating, believing I suppose that the climate is a sufficiently benign one. The fact that south of the Alps spring comes early and autumn tends to go on until Christmas does not mean that we have no winter. As some of your soldiers discovered, I believe, in the last war.' He was looking at her over folded hands.

She assured him that she was quite warm. It was inclined to be close, she thought.

'Yes, indeed. Thundery. It may be building up for a storm. This happens in this area. The mountains and the lakes conspire to produce it, something to do with the differential of latent heats.'

If she had been suffering from the cold the soup would have dispelled it. It was scalding. D'Anza was not too pleased, however.

'*Pasta e fagioli.*' He frowned at it, holding his spoon over it dubiously. 'A peasant broth, although nourishing enough. This is the trouble with Giulia—she is a good cook but she has little finesse.'

Pippa enjoyed it.

'The wine,' d'Anza said, pouring it himself, 'is a *prosecco* from the Valdobbiàdene—not one of ours, which are all rather too sweet for this part of the meal. For the main course is another of the *amabili* that you seemed to care for this afternoon. It is called "Il Giovanotto". I am anxious to see what you think of it.' He filled his own glass. 'Later we will try the *spumante*.'

The fish was salmon trout ('*Carpione*,' he told her, 'from the lake') done in a yellowish parmesan sauce tasting faintly of cider. 'Better,' he pronounced. There followed a chicken which fell apart with tenderness. Adorned with vermicelli, tomatoes, peppers and strips of veal, it was simple but delicious. Marco, serving from a trolley, hovered in the background and said nothing.

When he had gone, back to the kitchen presumably to replenish the sideboard, d'Anza said: 'Tell me more about yourself.'

'What do you want to know, Count d'Anza?'

'Your origin will do, for a start.'

It was difficult to do justice to the meal and talk gracefully at the same time—she was very conscious of his out-dated idealism in the code of behaviour—but she gave him an account, albeit very brief and factual, of her early life, her mother, holidays in Devon, Nicholas, her school. He replenished her glass.

The pudding was a strudel, peaked with yellow cream and scattered with almonds.

'And then, after your mother died?'

'I went to London.' She said no more. Nothing about her modelling, nothing about Tom. He seemed to respect her reticence for he did not press her further. Her plate was confiscated by Marco in an off-hand manner. She'd half expected the dishes to be silver—the slightly unworldly atmosphere of the place up to now seemed to warrant it—but in fact they were plain Italian earthenware, large and biscuit-coloured, not even Worcester. The cutlery too was huge, as though the knives and forks and spoons had all been specially made for a family of giants, but these in fact were of silver, and crested with a monogram. There was the spread eagle again. She had noticed it elsewhere, over fireplaces, leaded into a window.

A great dish of fruit was placed between them, but Pippa declined. 'No more!' she smiled happily. It had been a wonderful meal. 'I shall get fat.'

D'Anza smiled too, gently. 'Not very fat, I think. Finish your wine.' He had topped it up while she hadn't been looking.

'Tell me something now, Count d'Anza.'

'Certainly.' He waited.

'Why did you say it was appropriate this afternoon that my name should be Pippa?'

He laughed outright, cutting himself a pear. 'Oh, that is very simply explained, my dear. I am at the moment engaged in writing a small work. You would class it as a commentary. Its subject is concerned with English poets who have found some inspiration in Italy. I am just now dealing with Browning.'

Pippa laughed too. She understood. 'And I happened to be passing.' She watched him scooping round the core of the pear with a kind of marrow spoon. 'Except that when I came off my motor-cycle all was *not* right with the world. I've always thought that was rather a silly poem. Now I know.'

'Really?' He abandoned the empty skin and wiped his fingers. 'Have you read the play?'

She shook her head.

'Then you must be forgiven for not knowing the context ... Would you care to join me now in a *grappa*?'

'I think I'd better not. Thank you.'

'As you prefer. You are of course just out of hospital. You must not tax your power of recovery ... Shall we sit somewhere more comfortable?'

She accompanied him into a pleasant room with windows which in daytime doubtless overlooked the lake but were now curtained.

'You will have a cigarette?' He opened an engraved metal box for her; it looked like black antique silver. 'Forgive me if I prefer a cigar.' He settled himself down in a winged armchair with his *grappa* which Marco had brought in, having signalled the man with a frown to light hers first. For one who professed to live only on biscuits and wine the Count was, she thought, not doing badly. He seemed to be considering something as he watched the smoke rising from his cigar. It was evidently the matter they had just been discussing, for he continued: 'It is a song which is heard offstage at the end of the first act, a sort of chorus to the previous action which has included the utmost violence—murder, lust, adultery, jealous revenge. In its context then you will see that it has something of the satirical equivocation of Hamlet's "What a piece of work is man!" They put that in my school anthology. But it depends on the way you say it. "How noble in reason! how infinite in faculties! in form and moving, how express and admirable! in action, how like an angel! in apprehension, how like a god! the beauty of the world! the paragon of animals!" And it also depends on what follows. "And yet, to me, what is this quintessence of dust? Man delights not me; no, nor woman neither." They left that out of my anthology. "Morning's at seven" is not the whole of *Pippa Passes*.'

Pippa, who had already been impressed by his knowledge of English, looked at him with further interest. 'I must read it sometime,' she decided, 'and find out what else I do.'

'She is merely a simple village girl who links the disseminated episodes together. It is hardly an actable play; not surprising that it has rarely been performed.' He tapped the ash from his cigar with a flick of his index finger. 'You must go to Asolo.'

She wondered why she must go to Asolo, but said nothing to betray her ignorance.

'The Brownings lived there,' he explained. 'So did Eleanora Duse, Stravinsky, Malipiero, Giorgione, Lorenzo Lotto. It is still a beautiful and absorbing little town. Old shadowy arcades and porticoes. A cathedral. Fountains. Did you know the one in the Piazza Maggiore is still supplied with water from a Roman aqueduct? This is what time means in Italy. Nowhere will you feel a greater sense of continuity than here.'

'I can believe it.' Already she had caught something of this agelessness of her surroundings here on the Isola Malcontenta.

'We, too, have a Via Roberto Browning in Pianezze,' he told her. 'Had you discovered that? It has no fountain, alas, like that in Asolo, but it has a little *trattoria* where they sell "English toasted bread" for tourists. We have a long tradition, our two countries, of mutual admiration.'

'Is that bad?'

'On the contrary. It is a pity we do not live closer. As things are, our people—especially the young, your generation—are more likely to be increasingly influenced by America.'

'Surely that's inevitable.'

'Yes, Miss Rowantree; it is inevitable. So much in life is inevitable.' He seemed very remote and old all of a sudden, sitting there with a cigar in one hand, glass in the other, both arms stretched forward like his feet. 'Its predictability is what makes life comprehensible. A universe without cosmic design would not be bearable to a thinking being.'

The curtains stirred a little. She thought she could hear a dog barking somewhere. Perhaps it was the spaniel.

'You love Italy, Count d'Anza.'

He came out of his distant reverie and smiled. 'I am old fashioned and a patriot,' he said. 'I also love Italy, yes. I know it most acutely when I am absent from it.'

'Haven't you lived here all your life?' Somehow she couldn't imagine him anywhere else but in this elegant house, growing old with it. Even his appearance fitted the place. He wore a satin-faced dinner jacket with a stiff, outmoded formal shirt but the tie was velvet. She didn't know whether this was as a concession to the present day or harked back to some earlier fashion she knew nothing of.

'I have to travel occasionally. During the war I was in Africa. Then a prisoner of war.'

'In England?'

'In Scotland. Near Edinburgh. It was not as unpleasant as you might think, apart from the cold and the boredom. A bitterness arising from a sense of failure, a conviction of inadequacy which is the experience of every prisoner, I suppose. Then I was put in charge of the library—we were allowed a few books—and things got better. I was happy when I could read. And I began to write. That was better still, for I was able to escape, if not in reality, at least in effect. I was able to live elsewhere, in a world of the mind. I suppose it is a universal truth that man in his spiritual loneliness must create himself an illusion in order to survive. If, after all, there is no cosmic design. Have you not discovered that, young as you are?'

Pippa's fingers smoothed out the cream material folding over her lap. 'I think we're all too busy enjoying life to worry about it overmuch,' she said.

'Indeed? I wish I could see it that way.' He looked at his pocket watch. 'Why do you imagine that drug addiction is most prevalent in your age group, not mine, if not in order to escape from life, if only temporarily? In this flaunted age of Aquarius this is not the behaviour, I should have thought, of a civilization which is enjoying itself or even knows how to do so. All those sad or excruciated faces in some back room, together in order to be withdrawn, a community of isolation! I think I would rather be a monk. Equally pointless but at least my happiness would be visible.'

It was so accurate a shaft, with so personal a target, she was unable to counter it.

'Come!' he said suddenly, standing up. 'As you have finished your cigarette, let me show you one or two other things.' He raised her by the hand, another unexpected and archaic gesture. 'You haven't yet seen the Little Gallery.'

They passed down the corridor and up the staircase to the mezzanine. Opposite, leading off from an alcove, was an unexceptional door she had not noticed before. This he now unlocked from a key on his watch-chain and she found herself in a small room, almost like a corridor in itself, lined with pictures and containing, down the centre, a row of tables and cabinets.

'Most picture galleries in country houses,' he said, 'are vast showplaces of mediocre portraits, the commissioned likenesses of family ancestors. This is not quite so dreary. As you see there are but few, and for the most part they are small.' They went round together. Bright Madonnas, triangular Calvaries, venerable Peters, rock-strewn Resurrections, extended down one side; up the other were subjects from classical mythology—Daphnis serenading Chloe, Narcissus mourning Echo, Jupiter in the form of a fearsome bull carrying off a swooning Europa. On the tables were a few ceramics, plaster casts and silverware.

'Few of these things are of great intrinsic value,' d'Anza said. 'The Correggio you saw this afternoon was the most rare. But they are all noble—crude in actual workmanship though some of them are. Others are mere modern copies. For they represent the inspiration of Italy, and therefore civilization, upon the rest of the world. We must not allow the latter to forget that it was here that the Renaissance originated nor that it remains the most important development in world history since Christ, despite any claim of the modern world's scientific endeavour. That is why the Correggio has pride of place in this room. It is normally kept over there.' He indicated a blank space on the end wall. 'But I cannot bear to keep it unseen, locked away. I have it moved out to a more conspicuous position for special occasions.'

'Has there been a special occasion then?'

'Why, yes.' He slid back one of the drawers containing examples of native silk. The one below had been full of folded lace. 'Your arrival. I thought it would be nice to put it out for you.'

She was rendered silent.

When she had seen and admired everything they went back to the small drawing-room where they went on talking for another hour or so. When he reached forward to switch on a standard lamp she noticed that his left wrist was disfigured with a scar which curled round almost the whole of it. It had been covered by his sleeve before and she hadn't spotted it. An old war wound, she supposed. He had been in the Ariete Division, she learned; taken in a surprise attack on Sidi Omar in 1941. The names meant nothing to her.

He insisted on her trying the *spumante* with a little slice of rich cake. The bubbles sang gaily at the back of her nose.

'Not my favourite,' he said, 'but I should be grateful it sells so well. This is the one you see advertised everywhere.' He looked at her with his customary gravity over the top of his glass, eyes slightly narrowed, head thrown back as though with presbyopia, examining her progress with the refreshment.

'You are very beautiful,' he said quietly.

'Thank you.' She had never been embarrassed by compliments before. She had always known what to say, to make a pert reply, to Tom or any of the others. Only it was the difference in style and vocabulary of this man that silenced her. Tom would have said: 'Jesus, darling, you look sensational! Groovy! Like a million!' and swung her to her feet and danced with her. She could react to that kind of treatment. All she could do in the face of this courtesy of d'Anza's was to try to be still, to look tranquil, to behave like the rest of the furnishings, pre-1915 *Imperio d'Italia*.

Presently, feeling a little unworldly in the head with all the wine she had got through today, and rather warm in the close atmosphere of the late May evening with its threat of storm, she excused herself as being tired and said she thought she would go to bed.

He rose immediately.

'But of course, Miss Rowantree, you must do whatever you wish. You are still convalescent. I have orders to see that you rest.'

'Something I do wish is—that you would call me Pippa. I hate the other name.'

He bowed. 'You are too kind. Very well, it shall be so, Pippa.'

He insisted on escorting her up the staircase to the end of her corridor and there wished her goodnight. He would continue for a while to write, he thought, and made his way back to his study.

On her bed someone had laid out a nightdress, a thin white fluted affair like a Greek chiton, with a tie below the bosom and a short mantle looping over it from fastenings on the shoulders. It had been splayed out artistically like a display model in a shop window and was, like the other things, quite lovely. On the floor was a pair of bedroom sandals which might have been designed to match. She removed the nightdress to the brass bed-rail and lay for a time, fully dressed, on the bed, thinking, smoking another cigarette. She tried to read but found she couldn't concentrate. She didn't know exactly what was happening but she was going to be pampered, that much was clear. Well, she could take that. She liked being pampered. She closed her eyes.

Why was the gate electrified?

Why was the house so silent?

What was Nicky doing at this moment? Still at the office; presumably; in Edmonton it was afternoon. She didn't allow herself to think about Tom.

After a while she got up and opened the windows wide. The shutters were fastened and only a faint breath of air came through the louvres. Then she locked the corridor door, leaving the heavy key in it on the inside, found two bolts at the top and bottom of the door on to the balcony, shot them across, put on her Hellenistic nightdress and got into bed.

But she could not sleep. Her brain was too active; she was too excited. She lay there listening to the sounds of the night in a strange place—an owl moaning, a distant lorry, very faint, climbing the incline this side of Pianezze. She twisted and found she was hot. The underlay was soft and apparently full of feathers. She sat up to remove the top cover.

And as she did so she heard the most beautiful yet unearthly sound, like a liquid bubbling flute. This was repeated several times; then a pause. Then came a different sound—the same instrument but more of a chug-chug-chug. It had almost an oriental timbre, something out of ancient Persia, from the Arabian Nights, gorgeous and at the same time plaintive. She slipped out of bed and went to the window, trying to peer through the slanting louvres, but she could see nothing but a general impression of bright moonlight.

Then the sound came again.

And this time she knew what it was. It was a nightingale. She had never heard one before, except on a record, but she recognized it now with a little thrill of delight. It was the same sound as on that old school record of birdsong. A nightingale was singing down below in one of the bushes. The sound was positively loud, ringing, insistent in the stillness of the May night, seeming to fill the room. She unfastened the shutters and looked out, but there was nothing to be seen—only the staring moon and the tops of cypresses. The thing was too far away. There had been nightingales in Devon, they had been told, but in the summer they had always finished singing, or migrated. This was the first she had ever heard.

She stood listening to it for a while longer and then closed and bolted the shutters again. Discarding the nightdress, whose nylon fabric was airless and sticky, she returned to bed and lay naked under a single sheet. With the sound of the legendary bird pulsating in her ears she turned her face to the pillow and this time truly wept; she didn't know why, unless from sheer happiness.

And in ten minutes she was asleep.

* * *

Pippa had continued to stare at the Woolworth's tulips.

After a while they, or rather their colours, seemed to come towards her and she had the impression she was standing inside one of them. The petals were waving around her and over her head like a huge soft sea anemone, the stamens were fronds of upstanding floating hair, and there was a rushing Aeolian sound of twangling wind, or water, or pleasure. This was the intriguing thing—there was no distinction between the five senses. The changing luminous colours of the petals revolving outwards were notes of electronic music; the voices of people talking in the background, all around her, were changing scents; she was aware of the individual physical textures of the words that each person was using as though they were composed of silk, or needle points, or dry sand, or water. The five senses, set free, united to make a sixth, greater than the sum of its parts. She was observing all this from a vast distance away, out in space, where she was floating in a kind of free-fall weightlessness, her head and limbs a five-pointed starfish in a limitless swimming pool of clear warm water. Looking down, or rather perceiving with the mind for there was no sensation of looking, she could see herself in the chair of a house in Fulham which was a sort of doll's house, itself containing a smaller room with a Pippa-doll in a chair inside another doll's house—and so on, *ad infinitum*. This was all very delightful, amusing and expansive, a feeling of intellectual exhilaration as if the mind had been allowed to breathe pure oxygen. Then after a while came a change. She became concerned about the growth of the tulip in which she was imprisoned. Everything was expanding outwards like the universe, the speed relative to its distance, the farther away the faster. Pinpoints of light evolving and moving outwards with mathematically increasing acceleration to the farthest corners of her ability to comprehend. In the centre was the tulip's pistil which was also expanding. It was growing upwards and waving about slightly, antenna-like, between her legs in a way which somehow repelled and terrified her. She heard herself, or rather knew herself to be, calling out for her mother. But her mother was walking away rapidly down a sloping corridor which was like a pink alimentary canal, with doors of plastic tulip petals which closed after her, one upon the other, enfolding and digesting her. She tried to scream. It came out as a bubble. The passage was leading to a beautiful sun and Pippa understood that if she could only launch herself into this she would reach her mother and escape the pistil which was weaving lengthily down the corridor after her like a Jules Verne serpent with eyes like gig-lamps. She could not balance this simple conviction therefore with the voices of people near her who were trying to 'talk her down' from her bad trip.

At these sessions it is always advisable to have at least one member not under the drug in order to restrain a girl with an ecstatic urge to throw herself into the gasfire from actually doing so.

* * *

The sun was shining through the vents of the shutters when Pippa awoke next morning to the repeated tap on her bedroom door. She stretched lazily and murmured, 'Come in!' Then when the tap was reiterated and the handle turned several times she remembered that she had locked the door and slid herself out of bed. Discovering herself to be naked she put on her kimono and then went to the door and unfastened it. A woman—not Giulia but someone younger, though gaunt and dark, with black hair pulled back in a knot—stood outside with a tray. She bobbed a pleasant half-curtsy, smiled and said: 'Buon giorno, signora! Ha dormito bene?' So much was clear. Then followed a sentence in harsh local Italian which Pippa was unable to follow. She guessed however that it conveyed an explanation that the woman had brought up her *colazioncina* and she hoped it would be found suitable. Pippa thanked her and the tray was placed on her bedside table. Then the servant busied herself unfastening the shutters, closing the windows up tight, laying out a fresh towel and finally picking up the abandoned nightdress from the floor. She laid it across the foot of the bed carefully and turned and went out without a word or expression on her face.

When she'd gone Pippa opened the windows again and looked out upon a sunlit world already warm. It must be quite late, she thought, and confirmed the fact from her watch and the oyster clock. She had slept well. She decided to take the breakfast tray, which consisted of coffee in a jug with a cloth over it and twisted rolls, butter and cherry jam, out on to the patio, and she sat there on the hard sun-heated bench with the tray beside her looking down at the rippled lake. The coffee was hot; the butter cool, with drops of water winking on it. Enjoying the breakfast she wondered what she would do with herself today. There was so much to explore; so much to discover.

She felt well and fully rested. The stress of the motor-cycle accident and the subsequent memory of it was fading rapidly. She put her hand to the back of her head. The little plaster had long been removed and with her fingers she gingerly felt her scalp at that point. It felt quite small, a little groove, that was all. She even persuaded herself that the hair was beginning to grow over it again. At any rate Dr Rossano had assured her it would eventually, and until then, by the way she brushed her hair, it would be quite simple to camouflage it.

When, her breakfast finished, she went to the bathroom she found the bath already filled with hot water growing cool. The dark woman had evidently run it for her. Perhaps this was what she'd been explaining in her incomprehensible sentence. After Pippa had soaked for a while and then dressed she went downstairs, taking her Forster novel with her. There was no sign of d'Anza anywhere so she went out through the conservatory and wandered through the gardens. She soon discovered that these were not the same as those she had seen on that first day, when she had come here in flight from the village gallants, the day of the crash. These were less ornate, more neglected, yet fascinating enough in themselves and full of interesting things. She recollected then that the guide book had said that the house and its environs were not open to the general public, and she guessed that the showpiece gardens were those reserved for display on the other side of that electrified gate. With his depleted staff of gardeners the Count had probably decided to concentrate those forces on maintaining only those enjoyed by the tourists. It didn't matter so much if the others were wild and overgrown; he was the only one who had to put up with the fact. Well, that showed a certain sense of public spiritedness. She didn't think any the less of him for that. And she quite liked wild gardens. This was where her nightingale must have sung for her.

She found some steps which led down through fairly lank grass to what had once been a promenade by the lake's edge but which was now no more than a stage of broken uneven flagstones with weeds growing up between them. Yellow stonecrops and pink sedums. Growing out of the rocks plantains and giant mulleins. Darting lizards everywhere. Chocolate-coloured butterflies. She wandered about discovering things.

There were some weedy steps going down from the promenade into the water, an iron ring suggesting that, at one time at least, a boat had been moored there. She looked around and noticed a boathouse half hidden under the root-swamped alders. It must have been the one she had seen from the launch; she remembered the trailing vines of creeper. She walked out to it along the half rotted staging, only to discover it was empty. The water inside sucked and gurgled blackly with the swell of some steamer long since passed, now reaching the shore, and there was a creek-like smell similar to that of an English river. Coming back, cautiously over the unfirm staging, to sunlight, she stood on the little quay and wondered if it would be possible to swim from here. She would ask d'Anza. She had no costume but perhaps Prospero could click his fingers again and procure one from that mysterious bargain basement. In any case it was so deserted here on the lakeward side, screened from the village by a promontory, that she doubted if she needed one. Just something to tie up her hair, that was all. She knelt down and tested the water with her fingers. It was like silk, cool but inviting, eloquent with flattery.

Not this morning though, she decided. Better ask first. And to make sure that she wasn't interrupted she would confine her swimming to those times when d'Anza was busy, doing his writing perhaps. It would certainly be nice. She even thought she could make out, in the angle made by the jutting out promontory, a corner of gravelly beach, but when she tried to reach it she found herself prevented by a rocky stream in a declivity over which there seemed no easy way to cross. Perhaps there was one farther up. She decided to leave this for another day and instead discovered a shady arbour for herself where she curled up and read her book amid blue chicory flowers. At half past twelve she thought she had better go back and present herself, and she was actually in the upper gardens, near the terrace on to which her staircase led, when she heard the *campanello* summoning her to luncheon. And at almost the same time there was the young gardener's voice again, singing as he worked in the shrubbery. This time it was *Nessun dormir*. He evidently specialized in Puccini. And the combination of the two sounds solved one little puzzle which had been there since yesterday unresolved at the back of her mind. She knew now what the *campanello* sounded like—it was a tubular bell used on the stage. That last act of *Tosca* illuminated by *E lucevan le stelle* was introduced by a prelude, she seemed to remember, which made use of a whole panorama of them. Nicky had a lot of Puccini records, his weakness. There was a certain sense of the theatre about this whole place. But perhaps Italy was like that.

She found d'Anza waiting for her by the door into the room full of clocks, where they had first entered the house. He wished her good morning and apologized for his not seeing her before. It was an unintended discourtesy, he assured her; she had disappeared no one knew where. He was more than a little anxious for her. She explained her morning's activities and apologized too for not having asked if she could wander down there.

'But of course,' he said. 'I am only concerned that you will not overtax your strength or come to any harm. And also that you will not be bored. You are going to find life very dull here, I fear.'

'Not in the least,' she told him. 'I'm quite happy so far.'

He had conducted her into the small dining-room again. 'This time,' he said, indicating the table, 'I have given instructions to Marco to use the proper ware. He is from Milan; they are all so prosaic, these Milanese.'

She observed that rather more refined cutlery had been set out, together with the Worcester plates. 'For an English rose,' d'Anza said quaintly.

They ate their *colazione*.

She told him about the cove she had seen. 'Is it possible to get down there to swim?' she asked.

'Why, yes.' He gave her instructions how to take a path. There was a rustic bridge. 'But you must be careful how you swim.' He was gravely concerned for her. 'You must not tire yourself, Pippa. Rossano told me about your shoulder. You must be patient.'

'Just a little swim. Please. Or even a bathe. I shan't do anything silly. And you said you didn't want me to get bored.' She thought she could get round him if she made herself sufficiently appealing.

'Very well. You had better take Carla with you.' She gathered that Carla was the young woman who had attended her that morning. 'She speaks no English but she is intelligent enough to make signs, and you speak some Italian I perceive. You should have someone with you—always.'

'So that I can't swim away?' Pippa said it as a joke, intending to be facetious, but the effect upon d'Anza was unexpected. He glanced at her quickly with a look of cold suspicion. It sobered her.

'I promised Rossano that I would see that you would come to no mischief,' he said. 'You must do as you are told.' There was silence between them, definitely a chilling of the previously cordial atmosphere. Then, perhaps in an effort to retrieve it, he smiled and said: 'No doubt we can find you a swimsuit.'

Pippa thought about this for a moment. 'Perhaps I could get one in Pianezze,' she considered. 'I have some money. Could Marco take me in, do you think?'

The general man, clearing the table and hearing his name, looked at her. He had a dark blue chin, shiny from close shaving. The rest of his face was pale.

'Later. All in good time,' d'Anza said. 'You must not be in such a hurry to rush about. You must rest. There is nothing much in that line in the village. Don't worry, we shall find you something agreeable. I will send Carla into Verona.'

'I really wanted to get a couple of airmail forms.' She ought to write to Nicky and tell him her whereabouts. She might even send one to Tom if she felt in a charitable mood.

'You can write from here,' d'Anza assured her. 'There are plenty of materials in the guests' writing-room. You do not need to go out for special forms.'

'I like writing long letters,' she persisted. 'Airmails have to be on thin paper.'

'Very well. Marco shall bring some back.' He gave the man an order.

'But—' Why did she suddenly feel stubborn? Was it because for the first time since her arrival she felt she wasn't being allowed to have her own way? 'I need to go in myself, Count d'Anza. There are certain things I must have. Marco cannot get them. Personal things.'

'Such as what?'

'I have to go to the chemist's,' she told him. 'It's to do with the calendar.' She thought his knowledge of idiomatic English might not run to 'the curse'.

D'Anza understood. He inclined his head in an old-fashioned way, a courteous recognition of her femininity and his respect for it. 'Carla will get whatever you want. Tell her what it is you need.'

'I don't think my command of Italian is sufficient. And I'm fussy about what I use.'

It seemed an impasse, but after a moment's reflection d'Anza said: 'There are a lot of magazines in the writing-room. Find an advertisement in one and show it to Carla. She is quite intelligent.'

Pippa had to leave it at that.

After lunch he took her out on the terrace, found her a shady corner where there were two chairs, one a chaise-longue type into which he saw her comfortably stretched, the other a wicker for himself, and proceeded to give her all his customary attention. He lit a cigar and talked to her, politely and affably, about all manner of things.

'If you should doze,' he said, 'do not worry. It is very good for you to have a siesta in the afternoon.'

She thought she would rather be doing something, playing tennis or rock climbing or whatever—why did he have to keep treating her like an invalid?—but since she couldn't do much of either here, being lazy was the next best thing. Lying in a swinging lounger and being pampered was quite nice.

'You are enjoying your book?' he asked. She still had it with her, tucked under her feet in a corner of the chair's extension. 'When you have finished it you must try something in Italian.' She didn't think she would be there long enough for that, and said so. To this he made no reply, but went on to talk about Verga and the more modern school of writers, those of today. She closed her eyes. It was very pleasant swaying there with the sound of doves cooing and the warm air kissing her, but she wished her host had been younger and less of a scholar. Then he wouldn't have been content to sit there with his hands folded on his stick and go on talking about Luigi Capuana and Aldo Palazzeschi. For the first time she felt physically lonely.

She must have dozed as he had suggested for when she opened

her eyes again, conscious of the cessation of his voice, he was gone. Leaving the book where it was, she got up and wandered off again. She thought perhaps she would see if she could go through into the gardens she had walked in the first day she had come over here, the terraces with the arboretum and the peacocks, mingle perhaps with the visitors. She could see that if she was going to remain here for many days there was a danger, as the Count had feared, of her becoming bored. Perhaps if things got too bad she would seek out that singing gardener and discover what he looked like.

'Once upon a time,' she heard a voice in her memory say, 'there was this princess and, walking in the palace yard one afternoon, she was accosted by a common swineherd—or so she thought.' A voice so familiar. She didn't want to be reminded of Tom. It was still too painful. Her heart felt as bruised as her shoulder had been.

Passing round to the other side of the house and guided by the cries of the peacocks she at length found a gate similar to the one she had stared through when she'd first encountered d'Anza. There on the other side of it was the empty garden she had seen and beyond that the gate which was electrified, or so it said. There was no such notice on this one anyhow. She didn't know how alarming the effect would be but she put out her hand very gingerly to touch the metal handle, ready to jump back if she felt the slightest tingle. There had been encounters with electric cattle-fences in Devon. They didn't give you much of a shock. Her fingers stretched nearer and nearer. She gritted her teeth. Almost there. She touched the handle quickly and shot her hand back again. It was only a psychological reflex—the metal was not live. Emboldened, she grasped the handle and turned it. The gate was locked.

She shook it but there was no doubt about its being secure. Suddenly she heard a shout behind her and she turned to see Marco approaching. He was shaking his hand and wagging his head from side to side to indicate, obviously, that it was no use her trying to get through. He was repeating the warning on the public side of the further gate: *'Divieto d'ingresso!'* Coming up close to her, he went on in strong Italian to tell her that no one was allowed in this garden; it was forbidden; it was the order of the Count. And then, in English of sorts, he added: 'Out of bounds! Is forbidden! Not for you!' And in similarly mangled German, in case she still hadn't got it: *'Verboten ist zu hineingangen!'*

He had a pallid unhealthy face which reminded her of one of the men who worked in Rocky's Tarantella, in the kitchen, and never came out during the day. She disliked the way he looked at her in close proximity. His eyes examined her too intimately. It was only the fact that she was his master's protégée, she felt, that prevented him from grinning and becoming familiar. He was near enough for her to smell his violent after-shave and touch of garlic.

She nodded her understanding and her acceptance of the position, and walked away (with dignity, she hoped) along the gravel path which ran parallel with the iron railings until it lost itself in the maze of shrubs and stone walls further down towards the lake. She could hear the peacocks and from time to time she caught glimpses of the visitors, little moving patterns of colour, through the trees on the other side of the garden which was like a barrier between them, or a no-man's land. Once again she had the sensation that she was deliberately being discouraged from mixing with people. Otherwise why shouldn't she go into Pianezze and buy things? Being kept isolated. A prisoner? Was that too fanciful? Of course it was. D'Anza was kindness itself. He was an old sentimentalist. Indulgent in a schmaltzy sort of way. She wasn't afraid of him. She didn't care for Marco, who gave her the creeps. But the Count was quite different. He might want to dress her up in opera cloaks and pour the wine for her, but his was strictly a romantic world. She knew his elderly type. He was like a more aristocratic version of Terry Macdonald, who had always looked at her sadly and honourably as if he couldn't forget the fact that he was forty-five and married. D'Anza was rather sweet. And if he was rather sweet on her (in 1930-ish language) then that could be made amusing too. She could list him in her personal inventory of conquests. 'Item, one slightly stiff Casanova aged sixty. He didn't really stand a chance. I could run a lot faster.'

Somewhere at the back of her mind too she could hear another familiar voice. It was Nicholas with his solicitor manner and sober concern. 'Pippy, what in God's name do you think you are doing?'

And her flippant reply: 'Don't know, darling. Waiting to see what's going to happen, I think. In the meantime I'm enjoying *la dolce vita*.'

And finally, as always: 'Pippy, you've got to grow up!'

She went back to the terrace and picked up her book where it was still lying, but she did not go on reading. Instead she made her way to the writing-room, found some headed paper and wrote a fairly straightforward letter to Nicholas in which she gave a detailed account of the accident and the hospital treatment and a somewhat less descriptive one of what had happened since. She spoke of her convalescence at the Villa Franceschini in generous but restrained terms which could not give offence to the Count if it should fall into his hands. She didn't think he would be likely to open it—he seemed almost pedantically a man of honour—but she was of a shrewder generation than his, one that trusted nobody. When she had addressed and sealed the envelope she propped it up on the escritoire. Then she looked through the magazines which, true to d'Anza's promise, were to be found on a near-by table. At last in a copy of *Oggi* she found what she wanted. She had lied to the Count about her personal calendar, as she had always lied about so many things, in order to score a point; but having done so she thought she had better go through with the deception. She intended to be one step ahead of everybody.

She tore it out for Carla.

She wore her cream gown again that evening but on this occasion, with more time on her hands and with Carla to help her, she took some trouble with her hair. She found she had everything she needed to persuade it into ringlets. The day was fading again into an amethyst twilight, still sultry like last night but with the pending storm no nearer. She had the windows wide open despite the threat of gnats. Carla smiled, stood behind her with deft hands and spoke encouragingly in her local Italian. Then she left. Pippa gathered she would do.

D'Anza had taken charge of her letter. Soon after it was finished he had come into the writing-room to see if there was anything she needed and he'd taken it from her, to go with his personal mail. It would go out that evening, he assured her. He would see that it was marked *Espresso*. He was very attentive and kind, but aloof. He didn't hover over her or threaten her with his presence, or indeed pay much attention to her beyond what politeness required. He stood on the other side of the table and gazed round the room at the *objets d'art*. Now, to repay his kindness, she was making herself look presentable. She thought that the probability was he liked having *objets d'art* around him, not to handle, just to contemplate.

Sitting at her dressing-table now, alone, listening to the dry stirring of leaves outside (the hydrangea, the cypresses) she heard another sound. Intermittently and from no particular direction. Not nightingales this time but something more familiar. It was a guitar.

Not so much a tune as mere lazy arpeggios and single plucked chords, the lower register notes throbbing metallically until they died away. The sound clutched at her heart, disturbed her deeply. And immediately she knew why. There should have been a voice to go with it. It reminded her again of Tom. He was a whole part of her life that she wanted to forget.

Unbolting her balcony door she went out on to the patio to see if she could discover where it was coming from. Perhaps it was the musical gardener. She listened ... Only the squabbling of sparrows late to bed. Then it came again, briefly. No particular direction. It was in the air. It was below her, somewhere near the foot of her staircase. Preliminaries to a serenade. She looked over the balustrade but could see nothing. Going back to her room quickly she extracted the key from the cigarette box where she'd hidden it, unlocked the arched gate and descended the steps. But the sounds had stopped now, and though she waited in the shadow of the wall and the hibiscus flowering red at the bottom, and then walked up and down the length of the terrace, she heard no more. She was still there, waiting uncertainly and a little foolishly, when the *campanello* went, so she made her way in to the house through the room of clocks which all seemed to be speaking to her, if they could have made themselves understood, and watching her with their faces. Scanning eyes, remote controlled, instruments from science fiction.

When she was seated at dinner she asked the Count, not too eagerly but during the course of conversation, if anyone in the household played a guitar.

'A guitar?' He looked at her sharply, but he was also puzzled. 'No, I don't think so. I know of none.'

'I heard a gardener singing this morning. Do you think it could be him?'

'You mean Bertoldi? I believe he does fancy himself to be something of a natural Caruso; he sings, yes. But I don't think he plays an instrument. Why?'

She told him about the tantalizing chords she had heard.

'From the terrace?'

'Well I had that impression. But it also seemed to be everywhere, or sort of nowhere. In the air. In my head.' She knew it sounded ridiculous.

D'Anza crumbled his bread. He promised to make inquiries. 'Don't worry, I will see to it that you are not disturbed,' he said.

'It's not that,' she assured him. Why did he have to be so

solicitous? She wasn't an invalid. She didn't have to have the fountains turned off just because they splashed at night. 'It's simply that I'd like to know where it came from.' But it *had* disturbed her, she reflected. It was odd how much this incident had disturbed her, just as she was feeling happy.

The Count must have sensed her mood, or perhaps it was her unaccustomed quietness that told him, for he did his best to be gay in a stiff Colonel-of-the-Regiment manner (always attentive at the Parade Ball to a pretty face), plying her with wine, flattering her with small courtesies, compliments (her ringlets were charming) until, under the influence of the *Giovonotto*, she brightened up and smiled.

'Is it.possible to get through into the public gardens?' she asked him. 'You know, where the peacocks and things are?'

He nodded. 'It is best to do so in the evening, or very early morning. Before the public arrive and the dividing gates are closed.'

'Not in the daytime?'

'You would not like the crowds. Why be jostled by them when you can have everything to yourself? However, take Carla with you. She will show you.'

She did not answer. She didn't want Carla with her, tailing her; she wanted the pleasure of discovering things for herself. There was a banyan tree to be found somewhere. She had vague ideas of what one looked like from *Coral Island*. It would be fun to track it down.

It was another splendid meal. Afterwards, conducting her into the library following his customary *grappa*, he went on to improve her education. She had the impression that this obligatory evening lecture was going to become a custom. He was talking about Gabriele d'Annunzio.

'Are you familiar with that name?' He turned to her.

'Wasn't he a Fascist?'

D'Anza replaced a volume with his large but delicate hands. 'He lived through an unfortunate period of our history,' he said euphemistically. 'Nevertheless he was a remarkable person—poet, mystic, soldier-of-fortune, novelist, philosopher, politician, libertine and satanist. Did you know he lived near here? At Vittoriale, a villa on the other side of the lake. It is something of a showplace now. I met him once when I was very young. There were great dinner parties, good company ... It was all a long time ago.' He looked wistfully reflective.

They passed on through double doors into a room adjoining.

'This is my study,' he told her. It was dominated by a huge leather-topped desk littered with bric-à-brac, a pile of odd-sized books, loose papers, pencils, a manuscript rack, enormous ashtray, an old sit-up-and-beg typewriter with a paragraph about Browning still curled in it, but one in such involved Italian that she couldn't follow it entirely. She felt honoured to be allowed in this place. It was a delightful room, cluttered and untidy and full of life and personality. His personality. Even in his absence the room would seem to contain him still. Things put down as they were discarded and not immediately tidied up. An empty glass. Slippers as though they'd been kicked off, not placed in a symmetrical pair. It suddenly humanized him. And evidently no servants were allowed to disorganize his chaotic intention by daily fuss—once a week was sufficient. She immediately took to this study. It reminded her of the old rectory where she used to go to meet her spiritual pastor at school. It was a routine. Flowers and confirmation chat. Afterwards scones with jam. The old man had been nice. Uncensorious when she didn't know the answers, and patient. He was a gardener. The jam came from his own strawberries, which he showed her, and he knew about the Rolling Stones. Didn't approve of them but didn't have to ask who they were. He had come near to giving her faith. This room was like that study, warm with comfort.

'Who is this?' she asked. She had found a photograph of a handsome young man in military uniform. And then having said it idly, without thinking, she knew immediately that it was the Count himself, taken thirty-five years ago. There was the same mouth, the same broad forehead, the same proud and yet sensitive carriage of the head. The expression of the eyes was slightly different; they were wider, less hooded and sardonic then, more idealistic.

'The 3rd Veronese Light Infantry,' he said. 'I was only a second lieutenant then.'

'My father was in the Royal Engineers,' she volunteered. She didn't know why she'd mentioned that; he didn't seem to want to know about it. He passed on, showing her other treasures—a letter from the composer Menotti, a scribbled note of invitation from d'Annunzio, a Christmas card from Prince Giuseppe di Lampedusa wishing him *'un buon Natale sereno'*. He was in a proud and sentimental mood. He wanted to share his great days, even with a child and a foreigner. She found it rather touching.

For here they went through into the Little Gallery where Pippa admired all the exhibits again, finishing up, automatically it seemed, at the plaster cast of Michelangelo's David which had drawn her equally the first time.

'You admire him,' d'Anza said gently, behind her.

She turned to say something and to her annoyance found there were tears in her eyes. She was infuriated with herself. The Count pretended not to notice. 'Imagine the impact of that, full size, in the Florence Accademia. (You have not seen it?) Something in the region of five metres high. A giant, Promethean, yet so beautiful, so perfect. The swelling flesh here—and here—' He demonstrated with sensitive but firm hands. 'These tensed muscles, the veins here... The expanding chest, as though he is breathing. The rich shock of hair falling proudly over a threatening brow ... Scorn, defiance ... And yet watchful. See how the weight on one leg causes the body to balance, almost to sway, as though the sculptor has arrested rhythm itself. You are right to be moved, for this perpetuates the glory of young manhood. Of life. Sometimes when I am in danger of losing my faith I come here and look at it. The man who carved this, it tells me, was not just a haphazard collection of dust thrown together for no other purpose but to procreate. Michelangelo, the Beethoven of the last quartets, the Shakespeare of the sonnets, these were something more than that surely? Is it so difficult to believe that they were the product of some intelligent design? Not just a felicitous chance pattern, but an *intelligent* design? And when I consider that whatever God created them must also have made me— then I am comforted. The beleaguered world may be disintegrating. The Goths are here. But this is my comfort.'

He went on to speak of other things. He showed her the Donatello David and that of Bernini, comparing the three. 'The Bernini is charming,' he allowed. 'After all he was the greatest Italian sculptor since Michelangelo. But he is a sensualist. He is too concerned with the joy of the form. The flesh. In this respect he is more at home here in the Daphne and Apollo.' He took her over to another corner. 'This is in Rome, the Galleria Borghese. It is indeed a masterpiece.' She found herself looking at a nude pair frozen in a sort of dance of yearning. 'Look at that upward surge!' he said. 'Her lips parted in a cry of anguish, her hair tossed in the wind! The slender lines! Her fingers already beginning to sprout into leaves at the very moment he catches and touches her! Is not that magnificent?'

She had to agree that it had an erotic impact that was sensationally beautiful.

D'Anza looked at her for a moment, and then suddenly changed the subject, his mood with it.

'Now if you will excuse me I will leave you. You have seen everything in the house there is to see.'

She was taken by surprise and thought she ought to show reluctance at his departure, to be polite. 'What about the basement?' she said.

It arrested him in the act of turning away. 'The basement?'

'The museum of eccentricities. Your grandfather.'

He shook his head. 'That is precisely what it is—a museum of bad taste. Such trivia are best thrown away, or else relegated to the cellar or the attics. You would be happier here. He was a joker, my grandfather Alessandro. In some respects an unpleasant man. There is nothing down there, only rubbish. The boilers that heat the water, that sort of thing. I use it as a dark room.'

'A dark room?' She looked puzzled.

'For developing photographs. Among other things I am interested in microphotography. The teeming world seen through a microscope. I picked it up from Gian-Mario. The subject from him, I mean. The techniques I learnt elsewhere.'

He was a man of many parts, she could see that.

As soon as he departed to his study she went out, waited for a moment in the hall to make sure that he was busy and wasn't going to return, and then opened the door and went outside. She made her way to the gate which that morning had been locked. She wanted to find those gardens again. And without Carla. Although the moon was not yet up it was not completely dark. The twilight seemed to linger still in the sky, a luminous streak of it beyond the foothills. There were also spasmodic flashes of distant sheet lightning, so far away to the north, somewhere up in the high Alps, that nothing could be heard of the thunder. Only the rasping of palms, a creak of an old cypress, the continual splash of fountains. It was warm still and she wore nothing extra over her dress. She was listening for guitars, for nightingales. But both seemed to be absent tonight. Everything was so still. The storm was no nearer except in threat.

The first gate was unlocked, she discovered. This at least was encouraging. It was true what d'Anza had said then. They were separated from the public only during the day, when the visitors crowded the place. It was probably Marco's job to see that everything was secure, and to turn the electricity on and off. She hoped he had remembered to throw the master switch, or whatever it was, that evening. There was nothing remarkable about the intermediate garden, the one before the electrified gate and the no-man's-land beyond. It had a few winding paths and varied levels, misleading to anyone in a hurry perhaps, but she kept her eye on the silhouette of the big filigree farther gate, black and greenish in the half light as she came up to it, zig-zagging her course towards it. She was conscious of some flowering bushes and shrubs—myrtle, could they be?—or veronica?—bougainvillaea? It was really too dark to identify them. When she reached the gate she was relieved to see that it was actually ajar. She had been steeling herself, all this while, for a repetition of that grasping of the nettle that she had undergone that morning, but there was no need. Not only was the current turned off but someone had actually gone through the gate recently. It was half open.

Now, for the first time since the day of her accident, she was standing on the other side of it. She hadn't thought then, she reflected gaily, that within a fortnight she would be walking here in the evening in a super dress, with her hair done like a Grecian princess, sandals to match, a whimsical old man's protégée and monarch of all she surveyed.

She passed through the sunken garden, up the further steps, and then made her way down through the steeply layered walks by the familiar wide paths overhung with oleanders and tamarisk and all those great spraying bushes she couldn't remember the names of, colourless now in the pale light, with dark rustling interiors like whispering caves; then on down the curved steps flanked with the marbled figures (by Marinali) which had been proudly naked by day and now by starlight were gently and poetically nude, ranged in tiers down the steep descent, their backs to her, designed to beckon the oncoming visitor upwards. The clouds were clearing from the sky and the green twilight patch was larger, or perhaps it was the moon beginning to come up that made things more visible for she could pick out the details of bamboo fern, laurel flowers, fountain and petunia-filled urn more easily. Yet she could have found her way down here again, she thought, by the perfumes— the verbena, the night-scented stocks, the eucalyptus, the wafts of nicotiana, the vigorous entangling Italian woodbine over the pergolas.

At last she reached the level of the water and stood on the landing stage where the boats came in. She could see the lights of

Pianezze, those on the promenade being looped and festooned like a distant fair, all reflected and broken in the lake. She ventured out on to the floating pontoon and felt it rock slightly beneath her, a gentle swaying motion. Leaning herself against the Venetian pole, her arm round it, she listened to the sounds across the water. Traffic, a few shouts, the thump of a dance band with an accordion. They all emphasized the silence. She would have liked to dance too. Only there was no one to dance with. A pity. It was all so beautiful she needed someone with whom to share it. Not even Bertoldi, the rustic Caruso. She needed someone to talk to. Well, there was d'Anza of course. But she meant someone of her own age. Well, not *talk* to.

It was that Daphne and Apollo. That's what had started it.

She decided to work it off by throwing stones in the lake. There were several flat broken bits on the terrace level and she wandered about, picking them up and pitching them into the water, first idly then trying to make them skim in ducks-and-drakes as she and Nicky used to do at Lannacombe. Whizz! Skim, skim, skim, plop.

Her searching for suitable ammunition led her farther from the pontoon, along the walk towards the basement gate which was like a portcullis. Suddenly as she approached it she saw that there was a man standing there. It was Marco. He had just come through and was in the act of locking up behind him.

It was stupid to be afraid of him, but she had more than once noticed in him a lecherous look, barely suppressed, which she could have done without. She began to return the way she had come, climbing the ramps and the stone steps awkwardly in her long dress. Marco was left below, scraping keys in metal.

There were two kinds of men, she thought (well, three if you counted the queers)—those who looked at her like Tom, and the others who were like Marco. A sort of knowing but furtive leer, as if he wasn't quite sure whether he was familiar enough yet to tell her that dirty joke. He was the would-be Don Juan of the office party, who took a delight in trying to get the youngest girls going with a succession of drinks they weren't used to. He was always over thirty; short well-oiled hair, white collar, prim dark suit, a briefcase-and-*Daily Express* man, a boss's man. Everything she hated. There had been one at her work. His name was Ron Hunter; he was head of her department. He used to collect the returns from her table in such a way that his hand invariably touched her breast as though by accident. Or brushing past her in the corridor he would pretend it was much narrower than it was, putting his hands on her waist and squeezing past with a bright little apology while she had her arms full of files; and then trailing his hand by chance again across her bottom, a touch just firm enough to discover what she had on underneath. He would never dream of pinching it honestly. Always the ambiguous touch, in case she should complain to the boss and he might lose his promotion. No evidence, he could always deny it. And the infuriating thing was (she knew) he considered he was giving her a thrill. God's gift to the sex-starved girl. The sheer masculine self-opinionated boorishness of it! It was enough to make one want to join the Women's Lib. Marco was that kind of person. Not openly villainous, like the German truck driver. Just smoothly repellent—a boss's man with hands.

At the second terrace, where the way turned back on itself, she paused and looked over the retaining wall. There were crunching footsteps below, a man climbing the path heavily. He was following her.

Her reason told her that he was probably only doing his rounds; but then reason suddenly left her. She wanted to get back to the villa quickly, to the nobility of it, the Little Gallery, the statuette of Michelangelo's David and the Pietà, even to d'Anza. She picked up her skirt and ran. Up the long flight of steps with the beckoning figures, along the avenue of lofty, arched bushes, down and up through the sunken garden, and so to the iron gate. She was running away from her past. From Mr Ron Hunter, B.Sc. (Econ.), the well-shaven Bracknell ladder-climber and woman-fancier.

She had paused, out of breath with her uphill flight. Her heart was pounding and her lungs stabbed with the exertion. She leaned against the arch for a moment and gulped air, her angry panic subsiding gradually. Then she heard Marco's footsteps again and the metallic screech of the other gate, and immediately it returned.

During the time she had been skimming stones the moon had come out and it was quite easy now to see her way in and out of the zigzags. She took a short cut across one set. And then almost straight away she realized that in doing so she had made a mistake. The gate into the villa was not where she had expected it; in its place there was a brick wall with an apricot trained over it, the little green fruits all silvery. She dashed back down the path, catching her dress on an unpruned briar. She heard it tear. Now she couldn't find the other fork. She was lost. Hysterical fear again, increased by the unearthliness of the moonlight. It was as though she was in a dream, walled in in a strange garden. Walled in. There was no sign of

Marco but this only increased her fear. If she'd known where he was it would have been better. He could step out suddenly from any of those neglected bushes. Veronica, bougainvillaea, laurel. Wildly she picked up her skirt again and ran headlong. She could hear her heart pounding and her breath gasping. All the paths looked alike, none was familiar. The gate had disappeared. Laurel. Her name should be Daphne. The slender lines. That upward surge. Her lips parted ...

She was at the wrong end of the garden, boxed in. There were three ways. This was not the way. She stopped and turned around.

And screamed.

For there, screened from the direction in which she had come by a great flanking hedge of laurel, was the most hideous creature she had ever seen in her life. Grey in colour but light in contrast with the heavy bushes behind it. It was a monster. A man, naked, squat and thick set, hairy. With horns. He was crouched with his gross legs apart showing a bull's pizzle rampant. The face was brutish, grotesque, the chops sagging, the mouth open in a bellowing laugh. And he was staring at her, not three yards away, ready to spring upon her from those powerful bent haunches.

She screamed again.

There were running footsteps and she realized several things simultaneously. The creature had not moved; it was another statue; it was the Minotaur; this was the celebrated Minotaur Garden; and the footsteps belonged to Marco.

He thundered heavily round the corner on his short legs.

'Is all right, il *Minotauro*,' he reassured her. 'Not do nothing to you, that one!' He laughed all over his square face, showing a good well-cared-for set of teeth. One of them was gold. He seemed to be very amused. He threw back his head and laughed again and again. 'He frighten you, eh?' Her fear had given him pleasure. He looked at her more closely now. 'You have tear your dress. Come, signora, I take you back.' He proffered his hand. He was close. She could smell after-shave and garlic. 'I take you back now. Show you the way. Take my hand.'

Another paroxysm of laughter overtook him, and taking advantage of this Pippa suddenly unparalysed herself, galvanized her feet and doubled back the way she had come, was successful this time in finding the gate and ran pell-mell for the villa with her dress clutched round her waist.

She went straight to her room and locked the door. She flung herself on the bed. There was a great triangular tear in her gown at the thigh and her leg was scratched.

The nightingale was singing again.

*   *   *

It was jealousy and sheer bloody-mindedness that caused her to leave Tom.

It was nothing to do with the argument which had followed the discovery of her photographic modelling. That had been comparatively mild. Not even a row really. She'd been quite surprised. Nancy Miles had come up from the shop one evening all delighted with herself, a copy of that month's latest glossy in her hand. It was a specialist magazine called *Master*. On the front cover, as though ducking her head under the title, was a half-length of Pippa. Full face, look at the camera, no disguises.

'I say—is this you, love?' Mrs Miles wanted to know. 'It's ever so nice, I must say.'

Pippa reclining on pale green satin, lightly sprinkled with real snowdrops and with one carefully placed dewpearl of glycerine on her hip. It was in fact one of Malcolm's better efforts, the composition aspiring to be quite artistic.

She had to admit her identity. She had to tell Tom everything, including the reason she left. It helped to soften the row. That was why it was only an argument.

'So that's where the money came from,' he said. He was thinking of the Rocky incident, of course. 'You should have told me.'

In the end he came to live with the picture, literally; he cut it out and pasted it on the wall near the bed.

When Pippa had first arrived at the flat Mrs Miles had taken little notice of her. Her lodgers' visitors were none of her affair. It was Friday. On Saturday when she had gone upstairs to collect the next week's rent she had found them both in bed. When Pippa was still there on the Monday she said: 'You staying here long, love?' Tom had gone to work. Pippa was not yet fixed up at La Tarantella. 'Because if it's to be permanent like I shall have to charge.' And she put the rent up five pounds. Tom, when he returned, called her a skinflint, an enemy of the alternative society and a miserable old bag. She understood the last part.

'Well, if you don't like it you can go, both of you. There's plenty after this pad. I could let this room half a dozen times over any week. It's nice and central.'

So Pippa found herself a job.

Out of her first week's wages she put down a deposit on a transistor tape recorder. It was for Tom.

'What's this?' he said.

'It's for you to dictate into. I thought it might help with your play. You know—dialogue like wet clay and all that.'

She never knew whether it helped. He was shy about using it in front of her.

One day Tom was sitting cross-legged on the bed playing a tune which happened to be popular at that time, 'Listen to the Pouring Rain'. It was evening. Frowning over the strings of the guitar he concentrated on the chords and sang to her. She began to prepare a meal.

Pippa spread the newspaper in which the fish fingers had been wrapped and, leaning on her wrists, was studying one item. 'There's an idea for you,' she told him. 'For a book. "Father's Death Search for Julie, Half Mile Away".'

He did not get up.

'I told you. The novel's dead. It expired when Henry James turned the screw a shade too far. Death by exquisite torture.'

'You said it was Virginia Woolf.'

'They were brother and sister. Or possibly even the same person ... What's it about—the news bit?'

'A man, a widower, travelled all over the States, spent all his life savings—looking for his daughter. Evacuated from London during the war, as a baby—with her mother. He came home and found she was alive and well and living in Surbiton. Become what the *Mirror* primly describes as a "dance hostess". She knew he was looking for her. Didn't want a re-union. He left a note and jumped in the Thames. Verdict: Unsound mind.' She threw the paper across to him. 'There must be novels all around us. There's probably one going on downstairs. Nancy Miles. What do we know of her?'

'Or anyone. The trouble is, we don't read one another ... God, man's non-communication is incredible! He's so *lonely*!'

They were probably nearer to each other at that moment than at any time.

He picked chords from the guitar again. 'Do you know a short story called "The Prodigal Son"?' He began to do one of his parodies but she knew he was talking about himself. It went on, whimsically.

'Then the old man said: "I've given you a first-class education, boy, which for some reason you choose to despise. You could have gone on and made a lot of yourself. Well, that's your affair."'

'"Yes, Dad," said the boy.'

'"All you seem to be able to do is play that damn guitar. And write poetry."'

'"You think so, Dad?"'

'"Why don't you marry and settle down with some nice girl?"'

'"Because I haven't met one. I prefer riotous living in one room."'

'"Well, all I can say is—don't come to me when you've had enough. Your mother and I will show you the door."'

'"Thanks, Dad."'

She thought under the bitterness he sounded wistful.

'So you're doing a labourer's job to prove you're a man. Or rather to prove it to your father.'

'He would prefer me to be a eunuch at the head office.'

'There are other alternatives.'

'I suppose ... What would you like me to be, Pipit?'

'You. Write poetry. And a good play. Not that one about the schoolmaster, a proper one. I'll help ... Don't I help?'

'Yes, I send you out to earn the bread when I have a row with the ganger and get the sack because he's a stupid Scotch git who calls me "College Boy".'

'Apart from that ... Don't I help?'

He got off the bed, put the guitar on it, and came over to her. He found some knives and forks from a drawer, a can of beer. 'I don't know what you see in me,' he said. 'God knows, I don't deserve you.' It was his oblique way of saying that he loved her; he rarely did so directly.

'Write poetry,' she said. 'Never mind the other job. Go on writing. That's the way to show your father you're a man.'

He'd finished laying the table; now he untagged the beer can and poured two glasses. He drank one standing up. 'Before I started writing properly,' he said, 'just stories and things at school, I used to dream about best-sellers, all the money I was going to make. I'd go and live in the Bahamas with lots of adoring women and never get married. Then, when I began, that didn't seem so important. I wanted to see my stuff printed, this play performed. And all the critics would rave and I'd be bracketed with Harold Pinter and Samuel Beckett. Then that didn't seem to matter much either. I just wanted someone, some person I loved, some *one* person, like you maybe, to read it and say, sincerely, "That's nice." One day I'll be able to do without even that. Without you even. I'll write for myself. I'll sit in my opera house alone, mad King Ludwig, and watch it all perform on the empty stage of the wall in my little upstairs room.'

'Now you're being sorry for yourself. That won't get you anywhere.' She began to dish up. She could be resentful too. 'Do you know you haven't written me a poem yet?' She couldn't understand this. Her remark had hurt him again, and she was glad. She also was hurt.

Screwing up the newspaper, he threw it away and arranged the daffodils he had bought her. They were now past their best and going brown and papery.

The end of the affair, exactly three months after their first meeting, was explosive and miserable.

One day Tom had come home early, the job having been temporarily suspended because of a collapse of scaffolding, and found her cheque book on the kitchen table. With it, opened and folded on top of its envelope, was her bank statement. It might have been worse, she told him, afraid suddenly after the row which followed and trying to laugh it off. She might have been in bed with the milkman. Oddly enough she thought he would more readily have forgiven her that. The cheque book was an insult to him; the healthy bank statement inflamed his anarchy. There was a tempestuous row, the worst they'd ever had. He had forced out of her the story of her mother's death and the arrangement of the will.

'Why the hell are we living like this then? In bloody penury?'

She tried to explain. 'Because you'd only rocket off about the capitalist society. Anyone with a bank account according to you is a Fascist.'

'Too bloody right! But I don't mind living on little Fascists. That's the sort of parasite I've always longed to be. Sucking one of the stupid buggers dry! Why didn't you offer to keep me while I got on with the play?'

He was being quite impossible. Because he was angry. Because he hated recognizing her superiority in anything, even possessions. And because of her deception. Her lies, and her silence (which was a form of lie), questioned the validity of her love. She knew all that, could read it in the direction of his anger, all that silly play-acting. Being a Jimmy Porter looking back in anger. It was just an out-of-date pose. Sponging on her would have been the last thing he would have accepted; he was just trying to goad her into retaliation. 'You know very well what would have happened if I'd suggested it,' she told him. She was trying to keep her voice flat. 'You'd have thrown a fit of temperament and screamed the place down. A lot of big talk about being an intellectual pimp.'

'You're dead right, skinny! I would. I'd have rubbed it in hard! I'd have let you know every minute of the day that you're a little Fascist whore. Living on unearned income. But I'd have taken the bread. I want freedom. And I want to write too. So I'd have accepted your kind offer and said bollocks to the foreman and gone to bed with a notebook and ball-point. Instead of pissing around on building sites trying to earn twopence to live on, the pair of us.'

It was because she wanted to be sure of the permanence of his love, the security of it—that's why she hadn't told him about the money. He had to be independent. To *feel* that he was independent. He had to learn to stand on his own two feet. Then, later, she would have told him, when their love was cemented. A child coming perhaps. And all this she wasn't able to tell him. Instead she said: 'What about all that Geordie Mac spiel about flying, man, above the crane? You enjoy scraping twopence together that way.' It was a spiteful remark, stupid. She too was angry, at his ingratitude.

'Oh, Christ, get stuffed, will you! You don't know anything. Go back to Daddy Nicholas! Go and shack up with Terry Macdonald! Somebody else!'

He had gone out and slammed the door again, but this time the putty was soft and generous, and the glass hadn't fallen out.

He did not come back that night.

She had at first thought he had gone off to the pub in a fit of pique. When he didn't return at closing time she realized it was more serious than that; perhaps he'd put up there for the night (they took in commercial travellers), or he'd found a lodging house. Just to show her. She sat up till one and then went to bed. The next day with still no sign of him she began to worry. His typewriter with the sheet still curled in it was on the table where he'd left it. It was out of character for him to go off and leave that. He must be coming back. He must. Eventually she went out, checked with the pub that he hadn't been there, and then came back. She was worried that he might have had an accident, maybe not looking where he was going in his temper, crossing the road somewhere. She went out again to the phone box, told Rocky that she wasn't feeling very well today—her shift wasn't due until lunchtime—and then rang the police and the London hospitals. Every one with casualties; none answering to Tom's description. No satisfaction. She returned to the flat. Alone in the one room she sat for hours staring at the unwashed dishes. Sick within. She had to do something. She was just about to get the motor-cycle out and go round to Jen's when she heard him on the iron staircase outside, their private entrance. The door opened and he stood there, his hand still grasping the Yale key. He seemed surprised to see her. Behind him was Zillah. She had a suitcase.

'Haven't you gone?' he said.

Of the three Zillah was the most embarrassed.

'I'm sorry, Pippa,' she said. 'He said you'd broken up and left. Honestly. Honestly I didn't know you were here.' She turned to go.

'It's all right, I'm just on my way.' Pippa rose, white with anger and sickness and suppressed tears. The end of an affair. She had known it.

'Look, Pippa, if I'd thought—'

'Don't worry. It's all right, Zillah.' She busied herself throwing a few essentials into her bag—cheque book, purse, a clean pair of pants. She didn't really know what she was doing.

'Look, he told me you were through. If I'd known—I'll go, shall I?'

'He's a bastard. He'll tell you anything. He makes up fairy tales.'

And all the time Tom had stood there half perched on the corner of the draining board, watching them both, looking sardonically amused. She didn't know whether he really intended to live there with Zillah or if it was just a mockery, a gesture at her expense. Either way it was heartless; and she didn't wait to find out.

'I'll leave you to do the washing up,' she said. 'The bed's aired.'

When it came to it, despite his play-acting, she had the best exit line. But she wasn't conscious of point-scoring, this time. She felt too miserable.

* * *

'Marco should not have frightened you like that,' d'Anza said severely. He was very concerned for her the next day when she told him about the incident. He had been sitting at his desk writing, wearing heavy dark-rimmed spectacles which he took off when she entered. Now he picked up his pen again. 'I will see that he is dismissed.'

'Oh no, please!' She was horrified. This was not what she had intended. She had only mentioned it in order to explain the torn dress which Carla had taken away that morning. 'I'm sure he was only doing his duty, patrolling the grounds. And I think he was trying to protect me. That's why he followed. And ran when I screamed. He came to help.' Sacking Marco would be a mistake, something told her. It would be better to keep him as a friend than to make an enemy of him.

'Nevertheless he had no right to speak to you as he did. He must show you more respect. He need not wait at table in future. I'll get Enrico to do it. He is my valet, a much better type of man. An old servant.'

'No, really, I don't want him punished.' A vindictive Marco, he really could be dangerous. That could be frightening truly. But the Count was adamant.

'You must let me do as I think best,' he declared. When he was in this sort of schoolmasterly mood she dared not gainsay him.

'I'm sorry about the dress,' she said penitently.

'It is of no consequence. It shall be replaced. It is time you had something else. Find yourself something nice in one of those magazines and I will have it copied in Milan.

Startled, she thought of all those lovely romantic Italian swirls she'd been admiring on some young fashionable marchioness yesterday. A tall pedigree girl leaning against a high marble mantelpiece. 'I shall be quite happy to make do with all the other things you provided,' she said. She'd been about to say 'so kindly provided' but didn't want to sound obsequious. 'And the gown can be mended. I expect Carla's good at sewing. I'm only afraid if I carry on like this they may not be in a fit state to go back.' She laughed.

But d'Anza raised his thin eyebrows. 'I thought I made it clear. All those things are yours. To keep. There is no question of their being returned.'

For the second time she stared at him warily.

'I'm afraid I couldn't take them as a gift,' she told him. 'You must understand that.' She couldn't make him out. He seemed so casual, documenting his papers.

Suddenly he threw down the pen, where it rolled across the blotting pad; then he stood up, whipping off his glasses again. 'Now you are being stupid!' he said angrily. 'You are talking like a shop girl. Yours is the behaviour of an *ingénue* who has been told by her mother never to accept gifts from a man before marriage. I tell you, I have given you these things because I enjoy the cordial pleasure of giving people presents. I have no intention of putting myself in the ridiculous position of offering you marriage, or anything else for that matter, child! Let that be understood. You are my guest and I wish you to be courteously provided for.'

She felt slightly abashed. 'I'm sorry,' she said. And then she added, because she knew that, despite feeling nettled by his outburst, she ought to remain polite, '—Count d'Anza.'

He opened the door for her. Something in her manner must have touched him for his features had softened, his eyes were a little less hooded. 'My friends,' he said, 'call me Raffaele. Those who are very close abbreviate even that, to Raf. I prefer either to my surname which, like you, I do not care for.'

Even that invitation he made grave, diffident and graceful. She said nothing, so he went on. 'Do not worry about Marco.' He looked down at her seriously. 'I promise you, Pippa, that no harm shall come to you here as long as I live ... Nevertheless I suggest that if you want to go down to the lake again at night it might be better if you were to confine yourself to this side, to the part by the old boathouse and the cove you wanted to swim from. However, daytime is best ... Tomorrow you should have a costume. I have given the order. You can amuse yourself ... But don't stay in too long.'

She was dismissed, like a child; but kindly, she felt.

Leaving him to his work she wandered back through the Little Gallery which he had left open for her and, of all the rooms, had become her favourite. She had finished her Forster and didn't know quite what to do next. Try the biography of Gabriele d'Annunzio perhaps. The Count had found her one in English. She felt too lazy to tackle any of the Italian novels in her room, and she wasn't in the mood for Browning or Shelley. Poetry held too many memories.

Her steps had taken her back again (automatically?) to the three Davids. She gazed at them. It was true: the Michelangelo was perfect. The others, by comparison, were conscious posing and rhetoric. With a smile she put out her hand and touched the shoulders, the cold little phallus. Why should this make her feel both so tender and so humble? Then she looked up—and at the end of the Gallery, where the Correggio Magdalene normally was, she saw a picture which had not been there yesterday. It was of a young woman kneeling on all fours, naked, her drooping breasts like upturned bells, her head turned upwards and over her shoulder, towards something out of the painting, on her face an expression of anticipatory ecstasy, lips parted, eyes widened glassily in sensual supplication. Pippa went towards it slowly. It was horrible. Absolutely horrible. She had no idea what it was supposed to represent but it made her shudder. It was disgusting. Not the fact that a woman was naked on all fours—there wasn't anything particularly revolting about that. Gauguin would have made a magnificent job of it. It was something it stood for. It was the expression on the face that made it so repellent ... What a substitute for the compassionate little Correggio! And why on earth was it there? In the place of honour. She would have to ask Raffaele. But not now. He was busy and it was more than she dare do to go back and disturb him.

She moved to go down the staircase.

And immediately she heard the guitar again.

It was inside the house this time. Quite definitely. An arpeggio, then a chord in G, then silence. Then two notes repeated, a minor fifth apart, continuously, as though a singer was about to croon a quiet ballad. But there was no song, no voice ... Then it stopped.

She looked all round. It had been inside the house, of that she was certain; but where? She had no real impression of its coming from anywhere, above her or below. It had no direction. Like the last time, it was just there. Not even in the air. Just in her ears. She ran up the stairs to the top and listened; but there was only silence. Then after some time with nothing happening, she went slowly down the staircase to the bottom and waited there for quite ten minutes. Nothing.

Perplexed and feeling a little strange, she went out into the sunshine, dazzled by it for a moment, so that she had to narrow her eyes and look through her lashes. The only person to be seen was Giulia, in black, clumping in stiff shoes across the flagstones which formed the yard of her quarters. She didn't look as if she could play a guitar. And in any case it hadn't been out here; it came from somewhere within.

She shivered a little, despite the sun, and made her way down to the boathouse.

* * *

That day.

She had dragged the Honda out from under the angle of the iron staircase where they kept it and set off, into the rain. No helmet, no proper gear, riding blind with tears and rain. No one could see her anyway, or she was past them too soon. She could ride and cry without restraint. That at least was a relief, comforting somehow. Traffic lights. She stopped automatically at those. Otherwise she didn't care. Roads. Signposts. She didn't really see any of them. She found herself in Clapham. So she must have crossed the Thames somewhere. Battersea Bridge? She didn't remember it. After another hour she knew she must be somewhere in Kent and that she was wet through, her hair sticking to her face, getting in her eyes. And by this time her passion had subsided; she could think coldly again. She was no longer shattered. She could think about it and make plans. Well, for one thing she wasn't going back. She couldn't trust herself. Not a face to face meeting. Better to make the break clean.

She found a ladies' lavatory and went in and tidied herself up, then bought some essential clothes, a crash helmet, and came back and changed. The rain had stopped. That night she stayed in Folkestone. Not much sleep. But she had her passport. The next she was in Rheims.

She had survived.

* * *

'Have you finished your book?' d'Anza inquired that evening at dinner.

'Yes, I'm just beginning the other. The life of Gabriele d'Annunzio. You're perfectly right—he was quite a character.' She had noticed that Marco was no longer present. Instead an upright man with grizzled curly hair like wire was serving them. 'But from what I've read so far I don't think I like him,' she added. 'As enigmatic a person as Lawrence of Arabia.'

'Oh, a lot more flamboyant. He called himself *"Duca Minimo"*— the least of the dukes. That was just his arrogance. But he was colourful. In the 1915 war he served successively in the Cavalry, the Infantry, the Navy. He invaded Austria in a small motor boat— and escaped unharmed. As an aviator he flew over Vienna dropping leaflets calling on them to surrender. He got a bullet through the wrist. Another ended the sight of one eye. In 1919 under the Treaty of Versailles, Dalmatia—formerly Austrian—was made a ward of the League of Nations. D'Annunzio declared that it should belong to Italy. At the head of twelve thousand Arditi, his personal bodyguard, he made what he called a "holy entrance" into the city of Fiume, and ruled it as dictator for two years. When the Treaty of Rapallo gave Dalmatia independence he actually declared war on Italy. "Even if the people of Fiume do not desire annexation, I desire it," he said. "The fact that it is against their wishes is immaterial."'

'A megalomaniac. Another Hitler.'

'Possibly. His Arditi certainly grew into Mussolini's Blackshirts. But his private life was less secret than either of those two's. His liaison with Eleanora Duse, in his youth, caused something of a scandal. Later, at Vittoriale on the lake here, there were stories of wild parties, orgies. Exaggerated probably. I do not remember any. But he was a voluptuary. And evidently fascinating. The concert pianist, Luisa Baccera, gave up her career to live with him, though he was married.'

'And he had a strange "Room of the Leper" according to one chapter heading. What was that?'

D'Anza shrugged. He looked uncomfortable. 'Something to do with witchcraft, black magic. He was interested in that sort of thing. He planned to die there. But it didn't work out like that. He had a stroke and collapsed at his desk.'

He said no more on the subject. Pippa waited until Enrico had gone, then spoke. 'Raffaele, I've heard the guitar again.' She played nervously with her glass.

'Bertoldi, the gardener? Was it he?'

'No, it couldn't have been. I mean, it was inside the house. Somewhere on the stairs.' She gave him the details.

D'Anza frowned, was silent for a while, then looked at her thoughtfully. 'It was your imagination, Pippa.'

'No, I don't think so.'

'There is no other explanation. It was in your head. It derives from something you have been thinking about—some place or some person, some incident ... Tell me more about your brother.'

The last took her so much by surprise, coming straight after the previous remark, that she looked up from her plate astonished.

'Nicky?' She hadn't been thinking about him. 'Oh, he's all right.' It was a silly observation but all she could think of.

'He is an interesting young man. Sensible, from what you have told me. You owe him much. But there were amusing times too, no doubt. These holiday escapades.'

She told him about the adventure on the roof slates, a slope of forty degrees and some of the tiles loose, crackly underfoot. Not so sensible, she thought now, and changed the subject. 'Tell me, what is that picture in the gallery? The one where you usually have the Magdalene? It wasn't there yesterday.'

'What picture is that, Pippa?'

'A nude woman on all fours.' It was as brief a description as she could make it. She had no wish to dwell on it. It was loathsome.

'Ah, that one.' He seemed to recognize it anyhow. He laid down his knife and fork. 'That must be Pasiphäe. Are you not familiar with your classical myths?'

'Not that particular one.'

'She was the wife of Minos and reputed mother of the Minotaur ... But it should not have been hung there. That was unpardonable. It was removed for cleaning. Someone must have put it back in the wrong place. That space is reserved for the Correggio. I will look into it.'

'It's horrid, Raffaele.'

'Well, perhaps not that. But a crude painting. It is a Castelrotto, an artist much influenced by the German school, and rather indifferent.' He refilled her glass, discovered that it was warm from her clutching it, and had it replaced.

'It's beastly,' she insisted. That was precisely what it was—like a beast. She remembered now seeing something like it in one of the girlie mags cluttering Malcolm's studio. That was probably why she found it repellent.

* * *

'*Ecco!*' said Carla, producing the swimsuit out of a coloured paper bag and holding it up with the air of an old-fashioned conjurer. She had brought it in with the breakfast tray.

Pippa sat up in bed and hugged her knees. It was going to be a beautiful day, she could see when Carla opened the shutters, and she confirmed it on going out on to the patio and looking over the little wall. The mist lay over the lake to tree top level, making even the fishing boats invisible. Raffaele had told her they were sardine trawlers. She had never thought of sardines in a lake; she'd always associated them with the Mediterranean. Too cool for breakfast outside this morning, it promised to be scorching later. She returned to her room. Carla had turned down the bed, tidied things. Now she stood there smiling. When Pippa came in she opened the wardrobe for her and ran her hands cheerfully among the dresses, dividing them.

'*E stamane, signora, quale vestito preferisce?*'

Pippa chose one and the woman laid it out. Making her understand that Pippa wanted to go swimming that morning wasn't as difficult as she had anticipated. She chose her words carefully (shades of Sister Theresa who had tried to drum some Italian into her as a third language at Hell-Cats) and pointed to the bathing costume, but Carla nodded immediately. She had evidently been instructed as to her duties. And responsibilities, no doubt.

At ten o'clock they were making their way down to the cove by way of the rustic bridge. From here the track led down steeply through a spinney of grey olive trees. The little beach was stony, consisting of grey, green and russet pebbles, and shelved rapidly into incredibly clear blue water littered with rocks. The day was now hot. The 'laughing lake' of Catullus, Raffaele had called it. She could see why. And the bay, cut off from view on two of its sides, was ideal. Pippa undressed, threw her clothes over a laurel, and put on her costume. The water, though cold after the air temperature, was not as bad as she'd feared it might be here in this mountainous part so early in the summer, and after the first gasps on entry she plunged forward and struck out. She swam gently, remembering her shoulder. It no longer gave her any trouble but she thought she'd better do as Rossano had said. Farther out she found a sloping rock, sheer on one side, tiered on the other, from whose point she could dive. Carla sat in the shade under the trees where she could keep an eye on her, obeying her orders, no doubt, to see that Pippa didn't overdo things. In grey, with her severe hair style, she looked perhaps a little like a prison wardress but she also smiled pleasantly from time to time. Pippa had brought an armful of magazines for them both to look at, but they were not used. Perhaps she wasn't able to read. Instead she produced from a bag a set of tiny bobbins and cottons and was soon absorbed in making lace, her fingers flying about nimbly while she continued to look up from time to time, watching Pippa, and smiling, and occasionally giving her a nod of encouragement.

When she had swum sufficiently to tire herself Pippa climbed up on the stratified rock and found herself a comfortable place to stretch herself and sunbathe. The beneficent sun. She could worship him as a god. He was aware of her too. He caressed her.

She was almost asleep in her hard, smooth marble-veined hammock when she heard the children singing.

It sounded rather faint, yet immediate—an odd description but accurate; as though it were not far away, yet too indistinct to be presumed close. In her head? She sat up. The tune was familiar—it was the same as the traditional 'It's raining, it's pouring', which she could remember from her infant playground days—but the words were vaguely Italian and she couldn't make them out. It sounded like two people singing. A boy and a girl? She looked all round. There was no sign of anyone, except Carla, fiddling away with her bobbins, quite unconcerned.

'It's raining, it's pouring;
The old man is snoring ...'

Only those weren't the words. The voices were elfin, plaintive, yet rather sweet, the sound coming and going in drifts as though blown by the wind, except that there was none to be borne on. Ethereal. And not strident like continental voices. The English liturgical gentility.

'Carla,' she called out, choosing her words very carefully in Hell-Cat Italian. 'Can you hear anything? Can you hear children somewhere? Singing?'

But Carla did not understand.

'*Ragazzi?*' She smiled and nodded, then went on with her bobbins. Clearly she had neither heard them nor understood the question. So Pippa slid off the rock and swam over to her. When she emerged from the water the voices were no longer discernible. There was only the sigh of the larches and the slight rattle of the olive leaves, the splash of her own ankles as she moved through the shallow, warm water to higher ground. She asked Carla again if she had heard children singing, making it clear this time. The woman smiled again and shook her head. There were no children now at the villa, she said. Not for many years. And for fear of being misunderstood, as well as finding the language problem difficult, Pippa said no more. She swam back to her rock, wondering perhaps if it were some kind of audible mirage she'd experienced, something only apparent from there, a focus of sound caused by the concave reflector of the surrounding rocks maybe. Like the Whispering Gallery of St Paul's. It had come from the other side of the bay; could that be it? But whatever the explanation, there was no sound to be heard now. The voices were gone. Yet she had heard them; she felt sure of that. The fact that this was the second odd thing of this kind to have happened—first the guitar and now this—gave her a feeling, not of apprehension exactly, but certainly of unease. There must be a rational explanation, she told herself; there must be. Raffaele had tried to justify the other with psychology, but she wasn't so sure. It wasn't just imagination. Not that alone. Of course the dreamy atmosphere of the place might have helped. She could see it was conducive to self-deception. You could imagine yourself a princess in a withdrawn place like this.

When she mentioned it to d'Anza later, a little self-consciously, he only smiled.

'It certainly came from the gardens,' he said. 'Your own explanation was probably correct. The rocks echo sounds in a very peculiar way. On a still evening I have heard people talking quite distinctly in the fishing boats out on the lake.' He did not seem perturbed. But then he made a remark which absolutely froze her. 'Don't worry, the island is full of strange noises that won't hurt you.'

It was so apt a near-quotation that she looked at him sharply to see from his expression if he intended any significance, but apparently not—it was quite innocent. Yet all the rest of that afternoon she thought about it. It was like a free translation into Italian and back again. A deliberate paraphrase? She could certainly have gone on with the quotation from memory.

'Sometimes a thousand twangling instruments
 Will hum about mine ears, and sometimes voices ...'

Left alone again she wandered into the music-room which she had seen opening off the large dining-room. She wanted to see if there was a guitar there. It was a cold place. Its emptiness spoke of shut windows and lack of use, the musty odour of a church—not very good for the instruments, one would have thought. But then there seemed to be a general lack of music in d'Anza's haven of culture. It was a notable gap. There were books and paintings and ceramics, marbles, tapestries, casts, wrought metal; but apart from his one reference to Beethoven she'd heard nothing about music. Perhaps it was his artistic blind spot. Even the most cultivated could have one.

Unused now perhaps but the room must have been busy at one time. There were two violins in cases, a 'cello, a set of bows, a bass clarinet, a harp (covered with a tea-cosy of figured silk) and a grand piano. But no guitar. Nor was there a record-player or radiogram. Something here had stopped for over thirty years, from the time d'Anza had gone away to join the colours. A pity. She would have liked to hear a record or two. The house got so quiet when she was on her own, as though it had gone to sleep. Not pop records necessarily. Something in keeping. Nicky had one, a favourite for when he was feeling languid. Respighi. 'The Fountains of Rome' on one side; 'The Pines' on the other. That would have done.

She lifted the lid of the piano and picked out random notes, then chords. A musical education had been largely wasted on her; she had not practised. All she could manage with any fluency was 'Für Elise'. She sat on the duet stool and played that. It took her back rather.

Things might have been different.

She might have stayed in France. In Vittel, to avoid a torrential shower, everyone had dashed for shelter and she had found herself in a kind of Second Empire summerhouse with a lot of other people who had been walking in the gardens. Old hatchet-faced hypochondriacs taking the régime, drinking the foul spa water. But the family who squashed in with her were different. They were nice. They had three boys, the eldest thirteen. M. Desault was a metallurgical chemist, head of a research laboratory at Epinal. He tested things for Peugeot. Stresses and strains. Metal fatigue. His wife was a journalist, darkly good-looking, forty. They needed an *au pair*. She could have stayed with them. They took her home to change her wet things. In two days everyone was gaily using the familiar pronoun. She could have stayed. But that would have been a different story, she sensed. Not so much from the way he looked at her as the way he tried *not* to look at her. *Tristesse*. His name was Alain. A sad affaire of the heart, caught on the rebound, and it would have ended bitterly, not with a bang but a whimper. A man twice her age and with everything to lose, his life. The French, how susceptible they are to youth. She moved on.

There are novels all around us.

Pippa stumbled at the twiddly bit, where she always did, broke off, closed the lid of the piano and went out into the fierce light which was scuffled with sparrows. She went in search of the dog, whose name she had discovered was Iago.

What she needed in this Eden was a playmate.

*   *   *

She wasn't a fool.

She knew herself to be as quick-witted as most and, physically vigorous, had turned the tables before now on some. The incident on the Brenner, for instance. She hadn't told d'Anza the outcome of that blocked carburettor.

A third of the way up on the new road, accelerating to take one of the straightened loops, the motor-cycle had started to cough and lose power. Not far ahead there was a refuge in the form of a lay-by, a viewpoint beneath dark green firs, and here she had run the machine off the motorway to rest. She got out her tool kit, dismantled a plug and examined it. She was no mechanic but she knew that plugs sometimes got sooted up. This one seemed to be all right. Then, still squatting, she became conscious that she was being watched by the driver of a big Siemens closed truck drawn in under the trees. As she went on working he detached himself from the nearside wheel against which he'd been leaning, smoking a cigarette, and came over to her. In German he had offered to help. She had caught the gist of it. She replied in English that he was very kind.

'No gas,' was his verdict after stripping down part of the engine. '*Es ist der Vergaser, ich glaube.* The carb. You know?' He tapped it to explain.

'Can it be put right?'

'It is not so good on this model. I will give you lift over the pass. You can get it checked in Vitipeno.'

'I think I'd rather try to get it going.'

With a grunt the man dismantled some more, blew through a small part and then put it together again. The machine fired after the third attempt. It sounded all right.

'Not so good,' the German declared. 'May go again. Long stretch. You know?' He pointed up to the col with its wild clouds forming and dispersing alarmingly. '*Steil*,' he said. For one extraordinary moment she thought from the expression and the angle of his arm that he was giving the Nazi salute; then she realized he was trying to indicate the gradient. 'Not good to stop up there. Nowhere. I will take you over.'

She was quite glad to help the man lift the machine into the van and travel with him in the cab, watching the spring scenery opening up more and more magnificently as they climbed until they were among the snow peaks. There had been a recent fall and ice rutted the roads. Sitting here was better than skidding about over those bumps. She wasn't particularly concerned at the way he snatched quick impatient looks at her, nor when once or twice, changing gear, his hand fumbled with her left knee. She knew that on that road and manhandling that big truck he would need both hands on the wheel and all his attention. And there was nowhere to stop. It was when, leaving the motorway for the loop road just outside Vitipeno, and he drew up in a convenient spot that she became more alert. Together they had gone into the back of the van to lift out her motor-cycle from its cushion of wood shavings on the floor. But instead of helping her he closed the rear doors and stood with his back against them.

'Now you are nice with me,' he said firmly. 'You know?'

She might have guessed this would happen. She ought to have stayed outside and insisted on his handing the bike out to her. Too late now. She watched him closely, judging her time. It wasn't the rape she was afraid of, though she didn't fancy this thick-necked brute. It was the murder afterwards if she lost her head.

Try to make him be gentle. Not to scratch. He was the sort who would hurt.

With her back to the bulkhead she faced him as he approached, and knew that she had the advantage in one particular. He was uncertain of her. A principle of judo is not to resist, but rather to encourage your opponent's self-confidence until he oversteps himself. His eyes, watching her carefully, lowered for a moment to the zip of her trousers and back again. She took her hands away from them and put them behind her, offering no defence. Smiling, she raised one foot.

'No. Boots off first,' she invited prettily.

Her hands, shoulders and buttocks were pressed against the bulkhead, ready for a good purchase. The man brightened. He was very willing to play this game. But as he bent to take the heel of her boot in his hands she suddenly thrust with all her strength, forward and upwards with the toe. With an exclamation of pain he doubled up, overbalanced and fell, clutching his groin. Pippa rushed past him, kicked open the doors and dragged her motor-cycle out roughly over the tail, bumping it down on to the road before jumping after it. It seemed to take ages. She could hear him scrambling up from the wood shavings. But with the doors open she felt better. There was traffic passing.

She hoped to God the bike would start. After the second attempt the motor spluttered to life. She let in the clutch and was away, down towards the cluster of red, white and green pennants flying from a distant garage.

She was in Italy and the customs checkpoint area.

* * *

Two days passed at the Villa Franceschini without incident and then a man arrived. D'Anza introduced him as a Tenente Maiello of the police department but welcomed him as a more personal friend. The *ispettore* had come to ask her about the accident and make a few notes. It was all very friendly. A report would have to be made —there was the question of the insurance—but he didn't think any charges would follow. He smiled respectfully at the Count and d'Anza nodded in return. Pippa had the impression that it would have been a bold man in this province who questioned d'Anza's authority.

Yesterday Raffaele had told her philosophically: 'One of these days the Communists will take everything over, the land will be nationalized, my vineyards will be part of a co-operative enterprise, the villa a state museum. Then I shall retire to Asolo and write my memoirs. I shall not be unhappy.'

Well, she thought, the Communists might be powerful in Rome, but here more than an element of feudalism still prevailed. The inspector was not only a public servant, he was a servant of the Count.

Testing the opportunity and watching Raffaele's reaction as she said it, Pippa suggested that she accompanied the officer back to the *Questura* and gave her account there. It was strange how this absurd feeling persisted that she was some kind of a prisoner. But she was still being dogged by Carla whenever she went beyond the confines of the house.

Maiello assured her that she was not to fatigue herself to such an extent. He looked towards the Count who nodded again, approvingly.

'It is not a question of giving formal evidence,' the lieutenant said. 'Merely a routine investigation for the report to the Department. I regret I must take your passport and driving licence for a day or so. But I will return them to you personally, Signorina Rowantree.' He bowed very gracefully and put both articles in his tunic pocket.

D'Anza chatted to him in Italian—about his wife and family, Pippa rather thought—showed him around the conservatory and the upper terrace, with an incidental complaint about the new electricity pylons going up the opposite hill, and sent him off with a bottle of *spumante*.

'I also need to go to the hospital sometime,' Pippa reminded the Count on his return. 'For a check up.'

He picked up his cigar which he had put down before seeing Maiello to the car. 'Patience, my dear. All in good time. They know you are here, the hospital people. They will send for you when they want you. Rossano will phone.'

She still had this feeling of uncertainty why she was here. Suddenly she knew what was bothering her; she remembered a book she had once read. She faced him. 'You are a collector,' she said in a direct challenge.

At first he looked puzzled by this apparent abrupt change of subject, then his frown cleared as he saw an explanation. 'That is a slang term?' he suggested. An English colloquialism too modern for his vocabulary.

He was innocent. Or he hadn't read the book. Or both. She looked up at him appealingly and in some desperation. 'Raf, it's difficult to explain. But why is everyone watching me, and stalling? Being nice, and saying no at the same time. You too.'

He studied her face. 'You want to go, is that it?' He said it quietly and factually. 'You want to leave?'

She was not afraid of him; he was so motionless and gentle and grave. 'No, not altogether. I mean I love this place, it's so beautiful. And you've been very kind. It's just that—I want to *feel* free to leave. Don't you see?'

Evidently he did not. He raised his eyebrows. 'You are free, Pippa. To do whatever you like—no one is preventing you. To leave if you wish.' He took her a few paces to the top of the steps. 'Look, there is the lodge entrance. The gates are open. You can walk out through them whenever you like.'

'No, I can't. That's just it. I'm not free, not inside. I don't know what it is exactly but there *is* something preventing me. Not physically. But something.' She meant there was a sort of invisible barrier, a glass curtain between her and her escape, only the preventive force was inside herself. It was very difficult to explain. It was as though she knew she was living in another dimension, or another time, and couldn't break out of it. She was a ghost looking through a window.

'Are you not happy here?'

'Yes, oh yes! Ecstatically....' They had come back into the house. She stood looking out. 'And no. Because I'm not sure. That's the odd thing.'

'Not sure?'

She put her head against the cool pane. 'I don't know what you expect of me. If I knew that I should be happier.'

Behind her, a long way behind her, he was silent. Then, minutes later it seemed, he said: 'I expect nothing.'

She knew, without turning round, that he was sitting down, still smoking, contemplating her back. She was conscious of the rich aroma of the cigar smoke, but she couldn't see him, not even a reflection in the window glass. But she could imagine him, legs crossed, sitting there inscrutably like a smoking Chinese sage, so wise and motionless that he had become dehumanized.

'You must not worry,' he assured her. 'Everything will be all right. I promise you. You must just let things happen. Trying to shape events is a mistake. Think of yourself as an observer, not as a participant. That is the error that so many fall into. They want to participate in life all the time. The watcher in the skies, from his flying saucer, observing life from a distance, seeing all those earth shadows we are too close to see—that is better. Observation, retrenchment, withdrawal, and finally and ideally—isolation. That is the basis of a good philosophy.'

'Not for the young,' she said. 'And I doubt if isolation is very good for anybody.' She could have added: Anyway for me. I'm just a bit lonely. But that might have been misconstrued, so she didn't.

* * *

The threatened Alpine storm which had returned each evening to hang over the lake did not materialize and in a day or two the thundery weather gave way to a fiercer, clearer, less humid atmosphere. Having for once given Carla the slip, but taking the spaniel with her, Pippa went down to her favourite spot by the boathouse where she could read under the trees. It was just after lunch, too soon to swim and really too hot to sunbathe comfortably. Perhaps she'd do that later. In the meantime she would just laze.

She crouched on the disused quayside on her haunches, playing with the dog. All at once she heard the children's voices again, not singing this time but shouting distantly. She spun her head round in that direction, and there, beyond the boathouse and the marching Lombardy poplars, out among the rocks by her swimming cove, quite a distance away, she saw them. A boy and a girl. The girl was on the rock, the leaning one, the very same one she herself had lain out on. She was perhaps ten or twelve. The boy was in the water, swimming and splashing about. It was difficult to see much of him at first except his head, but then he climbed out on to the base of the rock and seized her foot and she yelled at him. He seemed a little older. They were either quarrelling or it was a game. He scooped up handfuls of water and splashed her and she screamed again. The sounds were distant but shrill, the words indistinguishable exactly, but incredibly they sounded like English. Then there was a great deal of laughter. The children were not fighting, or if they had been it was now over. Then the boy slipped back into the water, rolling over like a dolphin, and the girl, with her longer fair hair streaming, flung herself in after him. Plunge. She could almost feel the contact with the water herself. There was no doubt about their existence this time—there they were.

Pippa, standing, watched the two dark blobs threshing about in the shimmering water, sometimes disappearing in the mirror path of the sun but always appearing again somewhere else. She might have taken them for a pair of otters playing, or seals, if she hadn't known otherwise. And at once she felt that there was something familiar about them, as if she'd seen them before, but of course that wasn't so. It couldn't be so. She'd only heard them.

So there *were* children here. Then why had everyone denied it? Suddenly she decided she must find out more about them, see them at close quarters. With Iago at her heels she ran back up the path, along the other track, across the rustic bridge and down through the olives. Here she slowed down and, holding the dog by the collar, advanced more cautiously, from tree to tree, camouflaging herself with their dappled shade, moving very quietly, until she was on the edge of the copper-green shingle. She looked about her. But there was neither sight of them nor sound.

Whoever they were they had gone.

'It could only have been your imagination,' d'Anza said.
'No.'
'Children could not get down to the bay without my knowledge.'
'But I saw them, Raf. I tell you, I saw them—and heard them. It was very real. So real it almost seemed to be happening to me....' She looked at him desperately, seeking his understanding. 'What's more, I recognized them.' No comment from him. 'They were Nicky and me.'

He looked surprised but he didn't laugh as she'd thought he might. Instead he threw a stone for Iago to chase, both clattering together across the flags, and waited until the dog had retrieved it. Then he said: 'You are overwrought, my dear. And the sun is hot.'

'What's that got to do with it?'
'You dozed down there. You have been dreaming.'
'No.'

She put her hand up to her head, trying to think, and her fingers raked into her hair, discovering the little scar. Was that it? Hallucinations. Something to do with the accident. Was this the answer? She looked at d'Anza again but he was too detached to help. She must see Dr Rossano, get to the hospital. How?

She could phone. Why hadn't she thought of that?

The only telephone she'd seen in this house was in the Count's study, although there must be others surely—in Giulia's domain, in a guest room somewhere. She determined to keep her eyes open.

In fact she found her opportunity that evening. D'Anza had disappeared to his basement to continue with something, his microphotography presumably. Illustrations for his book perhaps? She didn't quite see how. But with the house conveniently still she waited outside the study door for a moment, listening, and then glancing round for any sign of Marco or Enrico she pushed it open and switched on the light. She felt guilty as she crossed to the littered desk full of his personality. Looking once more over her shoulder she picked up the receiver. She managed to make the operator understand that she wanted the hospital of San Bernardino in Riva. Good—at least her Italian was fair enough for that. A long pause. Then a woman's voice. (A receptionist?) Pippa asked haltingly if she could speak to Dr Rossano. Dr Rossano was not on duty, she was told. No, Signora, not until Tuesday now—it was his rest period. Pippa asked if she could speak to someone else. She had been a patient. A week ago. She gave her name.

'You cannot make an appointment except through your doctor,' the voice informed her.

'Dr Rossano is my doctor.'

'Then you must see him first.'

It was impossible, hopeless. Her command of the language was insufficient. She put the instrument down. It would have to wait until Tuesday. Three days. Uncertainly she stood there, with her thighs leaning against the great untidy desk. Half her mind was trying to make out one of his indecipherable notes on Byron. Then she noticed the rolled glossy plate-sized photographs in one of the pigeon holes. Some of his work? She thought she could distinguish a girl's mouth, darkly curved, and, intrigued, she drew them out. She unrolled them, spread them with her fingers. The top print was undoubtedly Valencia. There followed others of the same woman, in furs, a magnificent gown slashed to the waist, a gypsy costume, one on a palomino horse bareback. There was a young man—she recognized Angelino Franconi. One portrait all grin like a toothpaste advertisement, another romantically scowling. Others she did not know. Circus people. A clown in the rain, ribbed umbrella ineffectual beneath an overflowing gutter. A girl, almost naked, swinging by her teeth from a trapeze. Pippa raised her eyebrows. Another girl, with dishevelled fair hair, lying asleep in bed. She looked at this one more closely; it was so natural it was really quite beautiful. The girl, also nude apparently for the sheet had been half thrown back as if in turning, lay with her head twisted over and pillowed on the arm, the fingers lightly curled. The moulding of the thin sheet, their only covering, to her parted legs, the chiaroscuro of the folds, the pale biscuit colour of her flesh, the white of the linen, the suggestion of dark red elsewhere (a bed cover?), the delicate curved line of neck and chin, the soft relaxation of the breasts—the one only slightly rounded, the other side-slipped to an adolescent profile, all gave this picture something of the quality of a painting, as though it had been deliberately composed, yet the details were so accidental and natural and convincing Pippa felt sure that the model was indeed asleep. Then as she stared at it she suddenly stiffened. Something about it was familiar.

Anger and disbelief! The hair, the red bed cover, the oyster clock! The girl—it was herself!

D'Anza had somehow been snooping in her room. That first

extraordinary night of the heat and the nightingales. Somehow, despite all her precautions he had been there, with his camera. She had been right the first time—that foreboding. He was just an old peeping Tom after all, a dirty old man. No more than that. Disappointment embittered her anger. She felt like tearing the prints up, all of them.

'You are looking for something?'

She swung round guiltily (yet why should she feel guilty?) to face him, standing in the doorway watching her. In his hand he carried another roll of plates, white outside, the pictures concealed.

'How dare you!' she said quietly.

He said nothing. He seemed neither ashamed nor amused, a little discomfited perhaps as though she'd forestalled something before it was ready and so spoilt an effect, but not embarrassed in any other way.

'I hate you,' she told him.

That made him hold his head up. 'Please accept my sincere apology. I invaded your privacy.'

'You old hypocrite!' Words. He could stand there being courteous.

He came towards the desk. 'I am sorry. You should understand, Pippa, that...'

'Don't try to explain. I'm not interested. Except to know how you got in.' He stood over her, looking down at the prints rolled in her hands.

'Nevertheless you will listen to me!' It was extraordinary how authoritative the old man was. The remains of his feudal rights? 'I shall take the trouble to explain and you will listen.' He took the prints from her and put them back in their pigeon holes. 'I love beauty. You said so, in effect, yourself. You said: "You love Italy." Italy I suppose epitomizes beauty, if any one thing does. Beauty moves me, sometimes literally to tears. Not as a sentimentalist, but as one who receives a revelation. The recognition of perfection is like that. More than anything else, more than sweetness, more than pathos—perfection in anything moves me. Your Bernard Shaw once said the only thing that could make him weep was the recognition of "rightness". Truth. I too. I want to look at perfect things, while I still have time.'

'If you want to add me to your collection you're going to be disappointed. I'm not perfect. I'm slightly soiled.'

'No, no—I want nothing. I expect nothing. One cannot command circumstances. Did you ever have a toy kaleidoscope as a child? You shake up the fragments, turn the instrument and see what pattern emerges. It is not a matter of expectation beyond the pleasure of curiosity. All that one knows is that the pattern will be beautiful and different ... And I do not collect things. I cannot afford them. Neither am I a rapist. Otherwise I should not be content with a model of the David in my Gallery, but with the original—towering to the roof. I want to be reminded of beauty, not to possess it. Learning to overcome the desire of possession is the most difficult injunction in both Eastern and Western philosophies, although fortunately it becomes easier as one grows older.'

She looked up at his hooded eyes, wondering how far she could believe them.

'Here are some others,' he said, 'which I have just finished processing. Do not judge by one only.' And he held out the second roll of plates. She hesitated for a moment before taking them, wondering what to expect. They were all of herself. Pippa, poetic and thoughtful, in a Greek chiton, taking a lone breakfast on an empty terrace. Pippa, laughing, crouched on her haunches romping with the dog. Pippa grimacing, doing a half skip, concentrating on playing hop-scotch with herself on the flagstones, believing herself to be unobserved. Pippa in dreamy profile, standing at the lake edge; another, more energetic, of her throwing stones into it. Pippa on a rock, gleaming like a Copenhagen mermaid, about to pay homage to the sun. She handed them back.

'What are you, a spirit?' she said. 'You're everywhere, aren't you?'

'A telescopic lens—it is quite simple. Only that way can you ensure naturalness. I hate the pose.'

'And I hate snoopers. Tell me how you got into my room.' It was not being photographed half naked that had outraged her—she'd done plenty of that already. It was his doing it without her knowledge and permission.

'Yes, I am sorry.' For the first time he seemed actually concerned. 'You are right. That was an unpardonable deception of an innocent. But the result—that contains no deceit. See.' He showed her herself again. 'No one could fail to be touched by that. He must appraise it with feelings of the purest tenderness. To any man who cannot then the Botticelli Venus is pornography ... Now as to the method —come, I will show you.'

He led her upstairs to her room, neither of them saying a word the whole way, and there drew aside the green and brown tapestry, a hunting scene, on one wall. He felt the top and bottom of the panelling and a long thin section folded inwards. 'Go through,' he invited her.

A slight twist, the thickness of the wall only, and she found herself a metre to the right looking into another room, sparsely furnished. She stepped down into it. A similar panel had been folded back, like a shutter.

'It was constructed in the time of Marengo. A bloody campaign.' He had followed her. '1800. There were many refugees. This house became a refuge for patriots and an escape route—both ways, I fancy. It was used again for much the same purpose in 1945, but this time for Axis high-ranking officers. After the fall of Rome, you must understand, all this northern region set itself up as the "Fascist Republican Government". At least the urban parts were under such control; the surrounding mountainous area was largely dominated by partisans. The Villa Franceschini was in fact intended to be the way of escape for Mussolini, but by some quirk of fate the driver took the Como route instead. And of course you know what happened. At Dongo.'

'He was shot and strung up by the heels. So end all tyrants.'

'Quite so.'

'But you weren't here then. You were in Scotland. So you can't be blamed for anything.'

He was silent for a full minute. 'My wife was here then,' he said. 'She was at the mercy of powerful men. She suffered twice. At the hands of two tribunals—before and after the surrender.' His face had sagged and darkened; Pippa saw that he was brooding on something he wasn't prepared to talk about. Then he took a deep breath, as though cleansing his system. 'My grandfather at the turn of the century also put this secret door to use. His purpose was more carnal.'

'The eccentric Alessandro?'

'He had a passion for his niece, it appears—a young girl. It was a great scandal. As you can imagine, in those days. Servants were everywhere, eyes all over the place. So he came and went this way. No one but the family ever knows the secret of these connecting rooms. It is passed down as a confidence, father to son.'

'Really? I'm honoured ... Now you can find me somewhere else to sleep.'

He bowed his head and spread out his hands, a gesture of humility. 'I give you my word you will not be disturbed again. Look, I will show you. The partition has a catch which you can immobilize from your side. You can fasten yourself in.'

'Perhaps you have other magic boxes.'

'I give you my word, no.'

She looked up at him. He seemed rather a pathetic old man, a haughty elderly voyeur clinging doubtfully to the past as though he had already lost confidence in it, uncertain before the onslaught of an alien age. Frail and obsolete. By-passed by events. She was not scared of him, and her resentment subsided.

'Word of a Count?' she asked. 'Swear on your eagle?'

He smiled. He knew she held no rancour.

That night she lay for a long time unable to sleep, listening to the nightingales and the odd rustling sounds in the dry leaves of the hydrangeas. Sometimes a tiny pebble, which had been lodged on the tiles by some nesting bird during the day, would cascade down like a miniature avalanche in the velvet quiet of the small hours which would all too soon be greying into dawn. She had first secured the trick panel and then climbed on to the bed to inspect the ceiling rose which had a suspicious looking cavity in it. It was probably innocent, she decided, but on the other hand it could have been the eye of some hidden camera—she felt she couldn't even make love to herself when overcome with loneliness—and to be on the safe side she plugged the ornamentation with a bit of chewed paper, standing a chair on top of her wash-stand to do so. Then she examined the rococo mirror. It seemed solid enough when she tapped it, but then she didn't really know how these things worked, so she draped it completely with one of the towels. Then, since there seemed no longer much point in having them fastened, she opened both the shutters and the windows and enjoyed, English fashion, the fresh night air which caressed her face and arms as she lay there, trying to sleep, listening to the faint weird sounds of the Veronese hill country. Flutterings. Watery sighs—the fountains being blown. A hollow flute-like sound. A reed pipe? An owl? The breath of wind again like a whisper. Then more mundane things—a late car, travelling fast, changing gear; a dog barking; an aeroplane. She saw it traverse the window slowly, lit up like a ship, a port light ruby red —on its way to Milan?

As well as listening in vain for the repetition of the guitar, children's voices, she was also trying to puzzle out the meaning of things. Why was she here, and what was going to happen next? The guitar, the voices, these were effects that d'Anza could no doubt easily have arranged with the aid of his scientific paraphernalia down in the basement. (What *was* down there?) But the children she had seen swimming, and Carla and Iago apparently hadn't, the children who vanished—that was something that demanded a different explanation. All these colourful surprises—the guitar, the children, the Minotaur, the photographs, the secret panel, the Mussolini story—were they all connected with her skull fracture? Hallucinations. Was she going inexorably step-by-step mad? She felt frightened and yet, strangely, not paralysed by this thought. Why? She was alone; no friend at hand if you discounted d'Anza, which she did. No one like Nicky or even Tom—and she was slipping inevitably out of her mind. Why wasn't she terrified? Was it because, beneath the surface fear, she wasn't convinced of the truth of it? There was something else, another explanation, something much more extraordinary. A reason for her being here. She was here for a purpose.

* * *

'You've got it wrong, Pippy. The labyrinth, you know, wasn't a sort of garden maze like the one at Hampton Court. It was more like a basement which ran under the whole of the palace of Knossos. That's where he was kept, the Minotaur. Only who was he really? Ha ha, that's the star question! You beat the jackpot if you can guess, and remember two million viewers are watching.'

'I don't know. You tell me.'

'Surprise, folks, surprise! It was old Minos himself. He liked dressing up and having bare-breasted girls jump over him before he tossed them.'

'It wasn't like that in *The Heroes*.'

'Nor *Tanglewood Tales*. Now ask me another.'

'So it was an elaborate game. A ritual. But why?'

'I expect he just liked to see their little pointed tits bounce.'

'Why do you always have to be so coarse? It isn't funny.'

'Pow! "Honour with Dignity." The old school motto.'

'That's Roedean.'

'Isn't that where you went? The home of nobleness.'

'Sometimes a woman quite likes respect.'

'And the other thirty-nine sayings of little St Philippa. They'll canonize you, darling.'

Once after one of their rows (because he had called her a sham) she had said: 'What about you then? You're not really a hippy. You could never be. You're as much a sham. You're just a renegade, like me. Renegades sometimes return. But you make too many demands on life.'

She got up, lit a cigarette, and read some more about the extraordinary Gabriele d'Annunzio.
It was nearly three o'clock before she closed the book and shortly afterwards slept, with the light still on. And with the onset of the chilly lake dawn she awoke from a fitful dream about South Pool.

She had been nine when they first went there. They were still living then in the top half of the house in Putney.
South Pool was a hamlet—not even a village really—at the extremity of a silted tidal creek. Enfolded in soft Devon hills. A pub, a post-office stores, and cob cottages with steps barricading themselves against the floods of spring tides. A stream running through the village. A ford with ducks. Local children had scattered stepping stones, flat-topped rocks and bricks. It was hot (not always, later, but it was that day) and there were dragonflies. And it was so *quiet*.
Number 2 Flag Cottages actually lay just outside the village, farther along the creek on the other side of the ford. One of a pair, not really old or picturesque, stone and slate-roofed, its garden wall was lapped by the water at high tide which was only an hour or two every day. The rest of the time it looked out on to mud and the dense overhanging trees opposite. The only occupants next door were an old couple. When they died (her mother had said on buying the cottages later) they would be able to have both. Pippa had hoped that they would hurry up and die soon. But country longevity is notorious; they were still there. Now she wished them well of it.
Great days. They had kept a boat, a rowing dinghy at first, then sail. Mudlarking with Nicky. Yellow lifejackets compulsory within sight of authority. It was from the steps leading down to their own little hard that she had seen her first heron. A tallish grey bird standing motionless on the hard mud, looking like Terry Macdonald. An idyll. And a long time ago, it seemed.
When she had been in love with Tom she had considered taking him down there. She used to dream about it. Love in a cottage. Tom

upstairs writing, writing. Or among the nettles there was an old summerhouse they could convert. Only she had to make sure of him first. She would have his baby. Children with jammy faces. Stepping stones.

* * *

That day, being Sunday and the gardens unavailable to trippers, Pippa had them to herself and so, taking advantage of this, she decided to exorcise one ghost at least. Accompanied by the dog Iago she made her way again by the remembered path into the Minotaur Garden where she eventually found the figure and stood before it deliberately, contemplating its ugliness. By daylight it was very different—still repellent but no longer terrifying; smaller apparently too, less life-like, a comparatively crude effort by some local rustic mason, a mere ribald joke on the part of the eccentric Alessandro. She stared at it challengingly for some time until she felt herself to be dominant, slightly ashamed of her panic of the other night, partly amused by it. Then with the dog obediently close and nosing the bushes, she made her way down, unhindered now, by the zigzag walks towards the lake side. It was grey and misty, although warm. Moisture dripped from the acacia leaves. Later it would be sunny, but at the moment it was rather oppressive. On one of the terraces she passed a young man she hadn't noticed before. He stood indistinct in the dark cavern made by one of the pendulous trees, leaning indolently with his back against the divided trunk, and she was conscious without looking directly at him that he was watching her with interest as she skipped down the steps. Something about him was familiar but she'd caught no more than a glimpse before he withdrew into the camouflage of the tree, and now her back was to him. It wasn't the singing gardener anyhow.

She was surprised to see one or two people on the landing stage, another pair strolling the length of the promenade. Evidently although the public transport boats didn't call on Sundays it wasn't out of bounds to the exclusive few who had their own. This was undoubtedly how the young man now standing under the banyan tree, smoking a panatella, had arrived. It made her feel immediately less isolated. Joining the visitors down the gravel slope and mingling with them, hearing their voices, she laughed at herself for that fanciful notion about being deliberately prevented from doing just this, about being kept a prisoner. She was quite free. Of course she was. There were people walking within hailing distance. She could have touched them. She could have gone up to any of them and said: 'Listen, there's something very odd going on here! I don't know what it is, but I feel slightly drunk and I'm convinced that it's concerned with something remarkable in the basement.'

She could guess with what look of alarm and embarrassment, withdrawing themselves hurriedly, this would be greeted. They couldn't be blamed if their suspicions were the same as her own had been yesterday, that she was a little mad. But she was not. The fact that she could think about this possibility, clearly and rationally, proved that she was sane. On Tuesday she would phone Dr Rossano again, fix an appointment. The examination would confirm her faith in her own progress.

Descending the last flight of steps with the spaniel close at her ankles she was amused to hear a man say knowledgeably but *sotto voce*, nudging his wife: 'That undoubtedly is the young Countess.' Perhaps she and the dog looked equally well-bred, or perhaps it was just the Capucci dress. The woman stared at her as she passed—a mixture of snobbish awe and resentment. It did so much for Pippa's ego that she decided she would return to the villa; she no longer needed company, her self-confidence was restored. There had been a time, tossing on her bed last night, when she had imagined all kinds of fantasies—it was not a private villa, it was a mental clinic; a dangerous case, she had been sent here for observation; Rossano was in the plot too; Carla was her wardress; d'Anza was a specialist putting her under his photomicroscope. From there she went on to even more unlikely notions. Raffaele, who spoke English so well, was her lost father whom she couldn't remember. He had engineered it all, the accident, everything; would reveal himself in his own time. They were like the discarded plots of unusable stories.

The sun now blazing and the mists disappearing in wreaths up the hill slopes where the remnants were finally absorbed by the trees, she was tempted to take a swim. Carla had gone to Mass. With no wardress to keep an eye on her it was with a pleasant feeling of freedom that she leapt and ran down the stony slope to her favourite secluded place with the water lapping the clumped red roots of the pines. She slipped out of her clothes. She hadn't bothered to go all the way back to the house for a bathing costume. If Raffaele was lurking over there in the boathouse with his telescopic camera then good luck to him; she didn't care. She stood for a moment, the sun smiting her skin, and then, with the dog barking excitedly, she plunged from the rocks into the cold depths. Like the other, the little girl she had seen. The spaniel, true to its breed, delighted with water, swam around with her. After fifteen minutes of exploring the rock crevices, pretending she was a child again searching for lobsters in Lannacombe Bay, she hauled herself up and sat wetly on the slab, feeling the embrace of the sun again, raked back her dripping hair and brushed away the water from her face and eyes.

And a few moments later became aware of the young man watching her.

It was the same young man she'd seen before, only this time he was perched in the lower fork of a tree immediately above her on the little cliff, hugging one knee. She slid quickly off the rock and trod water.

'All this part of the island is private,' she shouted up to him. She was very conscious of the clarity of the water. She kept it moving. 'You've come too far round. You should have kept to the gardens.'

He said nothing but just sat there smiling, looking down at her, appreciatively she supposed—the perfect view of her back and bottom and undulating legs. She tried putting all this information into her limping Italian. 'Questa baia è privata....'

'I know.' In English.

'Then would you go away please?' She tried tucking herself in close to the rock, hanging on to it.

'Why? It is very nice here.' His English was excellent.

'I should like to come out and get dressed.'

'Certainly.' But he made no attempt to move from his branch; instead he went on smoking casually, looking down at her pleasantly. There was a long pause in which she remained clasping the rock, getting tired and trying to find a toe-hold, uncertain what to do next.

'Look, I want to come out.'

'Pray don't let me interrupt your exercise. You were quite happy just now until you noticed me. Please continue. What were you doing—looking for pearls?'

God, he had been watching her for ages!

'Would you please go away? If not I shall have to set the dog on you. You're trespassing.'

'Iago?' With a little avalanche of stones into the water the man slipped from the tree fork, holding on to the trunk, and looked round for the animal who was at that moment scratching at something interesting among the fallen sticks. 'He and I are acquainted. He would not terrify anyone, I think, that one.' Another pause. 'And I am probably less of a trespasser here than you.'

She had no wish to continue a conversation with him but his manner intrigued her. She looked up at him and, foreshortened though her view was, he reminded her again of someone. Tall, wide brows, black hair, distinguished looking, even handsome. 'I grew up here,' he said. 'This is where I spent my boyhood.'

She leaned her arms on the rock and rested her chin on them, drawing her shoulders out. There was no point in continuing to protest modesty now after the event. Her legs drifted away. 'Who are you?' she asked. He was related to the Count; that was whom he reminded her of. It was the same face, the same moist lips. He was very much like the photo of Raffaele as a young officer.

'My name is Vincente d'Anza,' he said. 'And yours?'

'Please, if you will just let me get dressed. I'm getting cold.'

'Of course, I'm sorry ... But you don't seem to have a towel. How do you propose to dry yourself?'

'I *was* going to lie in the sun, but ...'

'Ah, then I will go a long way off.' He turned, hesitated, then drew off the red silk square he wore as a muffler inside his open necked shirt and parachuted it down to the foot of the slope. 'Perhaps you could use that,' he suggested, and scrambled up the stony scree again and disappeared, the dog with him. After a minute or so Pippa emerged, found her clothes and, without waiting to do more than squeeze the surface water off her skin with her hands and rub herself with the inadequate square, she pulled her things on. Then she shouted: 'Okay, I'm ready!'

Silence. The trees rustled and a fish plopped in the deep water; that was all.

She began to climb the path, looking around her as she went. In an open glade at the top she stopped and called out 'Hullo!' several times. 'Signor d'Anza!' It was deserted except for the bees hanging on to the wild yellow antirrhinums. Even Iago had gone. She called the dog, thinking the direction of its return might give her a lead. 'Iago!... Iago! Here!... *Qua*!' Her voice, deadened by the trees, petered into emptiness and brought no response. Sitting on a fallen tree limb she listened to the silence. There weren't even any birds, it seemed. An English wood would have been full of them.

Vincente d'Anza. Who was he? Another ghost who disappeared on investigation, like the children? Another hallucination? Then she looked at the crimson silk square, still damp in her hands. It had in one corner the embroidered monogram 'D'A' with the tail of the last letter encircling the whole. She pulled it through the loop of her finger and thumb. That at any rate was real enough. There had been a man there, a young man, his name Vincente. A tall, rather attractive man who looked like the Count, obviously a relative. But he hadn't mentioned anyone called Vincente. Another mystery. Now the dog was gone too.

She waited for a few more minutes, called again without result, then made her way slowly back to the villa. Here she found Iago flopped under the shade of a wicker chair, nose between paws. The animal sat up and grinned at her as she passed, then, receiving no response, subsided again. There was no sign of anyone else. Following the patriarchal custom the Count had presumably led the entire household to church.

Pippa went up to her room, took a shower, changed and came downstairs again, but first she placed the square in one of the drawers of her wardrobe and locked it. She tried to read the newspapers in the guests' waiting-room, or at least the headlines and captions under the pictures, then took a pair of secateurs from the conservatory and went out and cut herself a bowl of roses. "That undoubtedly is the young *contessa*." Well, it was a suitably ladylike occupation. Anyway there were very few flowers in the rooms, so many in the gardens, it seemed a pity not to have them. That was largely what was wrong with the house—it was cold and masculine. D'Anza admired his works of art but he couldn't see the need for flowers, other than a few formal arrangements like the one in the Little Gallery. She amused herself hammering the ends and making them stand up. This took her up to just before lunch time when Carla appeared with the menu for the evening meal for her to approve. Over the last few days this little ritual had become a habit which Pippa, at first startled, soon came to accept as being a required compliment. Unable even to decipher the flowing writing, let alone the exotic sounding names ("Fregolada di Castelfranco"— what on earth was that?) she invariably gave it consideration for a moment and then nodded gravely. Undoubtedly the young *contessa*.

She chose her moment deliberately, in the middle of lunch with Enrico absent and Raffaele silent, to fire her broadside.

'Raf, who is Vincente?'

The Count looked up sharply. The shot had registered. Direct hit.

'Vincente?' He attended to his plate again. 'Vincente who?'

'Your Vincente.' She could play this evasive game too.

In silence Raffaele finished his course, looking grim, then characteristically replenished her glass. Finally he said: 'So you have been ransacking my desk again? You have discovered a drawer full of letters, I suppose.'

Pippa said nothing in her own defence. She'd opened her mouth to do so but had the presence of mind to wait, the wisdom of which self control was rewarded a minute later when the Count, his manifest displeasure cooling, looked at her again but this time less accusingly. 'Well, you are not altogether to blame,' he admitted. 'I should have realized. You are bored. There is not much to occupy you in this place. I am afraid I have given you little to entertain you except curiosity.'

And curiosity can be dangerous, she thought. Dutifully she waited for Prospero to speak, to explain the newcomer. But she had to sustain her patience a while longer, until the end of the meal, in fact, before he repaid it. Having taken his habitual cigar to a comfortable chair, he brooded there a moment and then told her: 'Vincente is my son.'

It explained everything; and nothing.

'You didn't mention you had a son.'

'I prefer not to think of him as one. We are not on good terms.'

'Why?'

His old fox-brown eyes hardened with anger again. 'I will not be catechized by you, signorina!'

The young *contessa*, put in her place, drank up the last of her wine. Then, perhaps because he found her proper silence undermining to his own, he added: 'Vincente and I see little of each other these days.'

'He no longer visits?'

'He has an apartment in Rome somewhere. But he spends much of his time in America, I believe, on business affairs. He is in industry. He lives his own life, which suits me very well. As far as I am concerned he does not exist.'

There was obviously strong emotional involvement here so she decided to say nothing more about her meeting with Vincente, who for some reason which she respected had clearly not yet made his presence known to his father, though he was about somewhere, and she changed the subject. They talked about water ski-ing. Valencia sometimes came up here to practise, at Salò. This led the Count naturally back to his absorbing interest—film photography. He began to talk about Fellini, Resnais, Visconti. He spoke of 'Morte a Venezia'. Praise for Dirk Bogarde. Pippa asked if he was only interested in Continental pictures—were there no British or American directors?

'Well, Hitchcock of course. Are you familiar with "Psycho"? No, perhaps a little before your time. Hitchcock's "little joke"—a brilliant if macabre one. The critics had accused him of being facile and predictable, so he annoyed them by killing off his heroine half way through, brutally—all that blood in the shower!—and stuck a clinical coda on the end, a piece of quasi-social-documentary to mock the serious-minded. They never forgave him.'

Pippa was thinking of something else. 'Did you ever see a film called "Days of Our Eden"?' she asked him.

But he shook his head. 'I think not. A Hollywood movie?'

'An inflated lyric western.' Nicky's expression. 'It doesn't matter.'

* * *

She spent the afternoon writing another letter to Nicholas, this one much longer and more detailed than the last because she intended to find an opportunity to post it herself in Riva when she went to the hospital, whenever that might be. Perhaps a few days yet, but at least she would have it ready. As it proceeded she found her literary hand rather running away with her and she had to cross out chains of adjectives for fear it read like some terrible old set-piece by Marie Corelli—but what could you do? Exotic gardens, a strangely beautiful house, a presiding influence with a title like Count Raffaele Alessandro d'Anza-Pianezze, even the evocative name of the island itself—they were all extravagant, rhetorical, the whole country was impossibly operatic. One couldn't help writing in the same vein. She described everything in detail with the exception of the Vincente episode. For some reason which she was not prepared to analyse she made no mention of this. When it was finished she left it unsealed so that she could add any relevant postscript and then wrote another, a short note to Tom, merely telling him where she was. Then, having read the last through, she tore it up.

It was beginning to thunder again distantly. The sultry conditions had returned and, going out for some air, she noticed from her landscaped vantage point (significantly it was called the English garden) that to the north the fjord-like end of the lake was blotted out with low cloud. The palms rasped and whispered in the rising breeze as she walked through the gardens, still open but deserted. The cypresses, a serried row of diminishing spearheads, had gone a livid black. She glanced to left and right hopefully, thinking she might see Vincente again, lurking somewhere as before, watching her progress—but he wasn't evident. Disappointed? Perhaps. He was certainly the most exciting thing she'd encountered since her arrival here—well, interesting anyway. She wondered, was this all part of the myth, the ritual? The experience she was being prepared for?... 'Oh Pippy, you've got to grow up!' What ritual? So it came to pass, Titania waked and straightway loved an ass.

She had reached the end of the promenade walk without encountering anyone and now stood before the iron gate barring her way to the gullied courtyard and the area steps going down to the cellars. There was a sloping ramp for wine barrels. The basement... Some time, sooner or later, she knew she had to go into that basement and satisfy herself that Vincente didn't live down there on a chain. She wondered if the gate was locked. Gingerly, as with the other, she stabbed at the handle very lightly with one finger and then grasped it, turned it with difficulty and tried to push the gate open, but it was stiff and only rattled in its wheeled socket. There was a movement behind her and she swung round to see Marco, in his shirt sleeves but still neat, standing a short distance away, watching her from an open doorway, one hand on the opposite jamb.

'*Desidera, signora?*'

Staring back for a second, Pippa shook her head, then turned and walked away, with dignity she hoped, deliberately not hurrying, but conscious all the time of the man's eyes on her back like fingers.

*   *   *

About Zillah.

She ought to have let it work itself out of his system, she could see that now. Whatever it was. Of course he was fascinated by Zillah's green-coffee-and-milk skin. Black skin against white. The intriguing notion of a black and white coitus, with all its age-old undertones of the illicit, tradition of his class. Another way to lose his identity, to reject that tradition. When he'd had his little schoolboy experiment he would have come back to her.

It was probably due to a mood of nervous frustration as much as anything. No successes. The play about the schoolmaster (it was nameless as yet) had been re-drafted twice. She felt that he was beginning to hate it. It had been tinkered with too much. All that she knew of the other, which was still in manuscript, was the title. It was called 'The Dresden Amen'. She guessed it was satirical.

Zillah would have been transitory. But she was right not to allow it, Pippa thought. (Surely she was right?) Not so soon.

Of course Tom would lead her a dance, be unfaithful. She was prepared for that. He was an artist. As such he drank experience as other men need water. Or alcohol. Love in a cottage would not be a continuous idyll. He would reject her many times, humiliate her, make her weep again and again, and eventually love would die. In middle age, himself accepted, he would reject her. Some younger woman. Yet it would all have been worth it. Heaven and hell.

But not so soon.

*   *   *

During dinner that evening the wind, which had been rising very gradually all day, suddenly billowed to a steady intensity, but without gusts, as though it was water and someone was pushing it down the length of the lake with a broom, so that it streamed the curtains inwards on constant pennants of warm air. Thunder continued to grumble and occasionally to break out into nearer whip cracks which then echoed round the basin of local hills. Lightning flashes were now discernible snakes' tongues, not just electric flashes somewhere vaguely over the Alps.

'No fishing on the Lago di Garda tonight,' Raffaele said. 'It gets mountainous on occasions like this, when the wind blows down from the north. Sometimes in minutes. It is a very treacherous lake.'

'It's still pretty sultry.'

'It will remain so until the rain. Then it will be very different. Quite cold. Perhaps hail. This has been building up for days.'

'I think I'll go and watch it from my room.'

'Yes, it can be positively Byronic. Very wild and magnificent. Have you ever read "The Prisoner of Chillon"? No, the castle is actually more memorable than the poem.... Yes, go on up. You get a good view from there.'

When she could reasonably slip away (she felt she had a social duty to stay and talk to her benefactor as long as his conversation indicated that he needed her) Pippa went upstairs and stood at her bedroom window, watching the strange and as yet distant lightning effects. She was glad they were distant. Electric storms held a slightly sick fascination for her, drawing her and terrifying her at the same time. There had been that other one, at South Pool.

Reflected on the opposite shore, bringing it suddenly nearer, was the unnatural glare of a green twilight too bright for that hour, while the lake itself, in between, was a dark plum colour flecked with white spear points of waves. She could see houses, spires, details she had never observed before. The Giudicarian highlands were obliterated in an alarming black mass of approaching night, or thunderclouds, she couldn't make out which, and so was the far end of the lake and the steeps into which it normally lost itself. A wall of dark fog seemed to lie across the end of it and to be slowly expanding, the whole scene better illuminated from time to time by a dance of lightning and tantalizingly revealed before disappearing into nothing but memory.

Dutifully she tried to remember her Byron—there had been some awful cod stuff for A Level.

> 'The sky is changed!—And such a change! Oh night,
> And storm, and darkness, ye are wondrous
>   something-or-other...'

Her memory was as fragmented as the view. She searched a bit deeper.

> '...Far along
> From peak to peak, the rattling crags among
> Leaps the live thunder! Not from one lone cloud
> But every mountain now hath found a tongue...'

She opened the door and stepped out on to her private terrazza. The best viewpoint being obviously from the stone bench and the evening still warm and dry before the oncoming slow tidal wave of black rainclouds, she stood there with her hand on the back of the seat and watched the lights dimming out one by one up the valley as they were overtaken. The wind tugged at her clothes and ran through her. Below she could just make out the cypresses writhing in a frenzied turbulence like fronds of green and black seaweed. Then the lightning came again and in its flash she saw Vincente, level with her on the patio but further along, leaning against the arch of the small gate. He too appeared to be watching the progress of the storm. She stared at him, indistinct in the twilight, and presently she saw his face turn towards her. He knew she was there. There was no surprise in his expression. He had been studying her all the time she'd been out there. Now he detached himself from the gate and came across to her.

'I am intruding?' he said. It was barely a question and she shrugged her indifference.

'I was wondering how you had got here, that's all. I thought I'd fastened that gate.'

'It would have made no matter—I have a key. But no, I did not need to use it. The gate was unfastened. You were expecting me, I think.'

She was about to protest, to refute that indignantly, but he continued: 'Soon it will pour. We shall have to move from here.' He was close enough now for her to make out his features clearly. He had the same intense brown eyes as his father, but darker; bear rather than fox.

Coming through the lake valley as all the trees strained at their roots was a hollow rushing sound like a train emerging from a tunnel. The wind moulded her dress and stranded her hair across her mouth. She raked it away with her fingers.

'Your name is Pippa.'

'How do you know that?'

'I have learnt it. Since this morning. You are very pretty.'

'Why are you here?'

'Because you are very pretty.'

'Here in the villa, I mean. Why doesn't Raffaele know?'

'We do not talk about each other, my father and I.'

It was a strange sort of conversation, but then the whole situation was a little uncanny. The light was deteriorating rapidly and they could barely see each other with any degree of clarity. Then a gust of cold air, and the first drops fell, great isolated splashes like dinner plates.

'You must go in,' Vincente told her. 'You will soak.'

She felt an icy wet poultice strike her shoulder; another stung her face.

'You too,' she said. 'You'd better come inside.'

> 'How the lit lake shines, a phosphoric sea,
> And the big rain comes dancing to the earth!'

(To think that in the exam she hadn't even had a question on it. All that crazy swot for nothing.)

The sudden onslaught of the rain like whiplashes sent them both pelting to the shelter of her room. Inside they brushed the drops from their clothes and hair, looked at each other and laughed. The storm was now all round them; lightning and thunder hammering it out continuously and simultaneously; the curtains had gone wild. Pippa crossed to the switch and put on the lights. In the past she had been nervous of thunderstorms (that one at Flag Cottages; the walk home from Frogmore) but this tonight somehow she didn't mind. It was a king. The whole house was engulfed in it, and appeared to rock. It was like being on a ship. The villa was riding before a hurricane. Next morning, when dawn broke, they would find the wreckage cast up on the shores of Sicily.

Still gazing out of the window she felt his hands on her upper arms as he stood close behind her. She twisted her head to look at him and then turned to face him properly. He appraised her intently at close quarters.

'Not only pretty,' he said. 'Beautiful with it too. And I suspect intelligent. That is nice. Piquant.'

She raised her arms to his neck and instantly she was being kissed. It was very pleasant. She felt the pressure of his mouth trying to force her lips apart but she kept them firm. Not yet, Vincente, not yet. I hate being rushed. His breath tasted of scented cigar smoke. That was pleasant too. She became aware of her own heartbeats and, as he kissed the soft part of her neck, below the ears, a tremor of sweetness and relaxation ran up happily through her. She'd found a playmate.

He had very likely noticed the relaxation, a certain lumpiness in her weight in his arms. She tried to compensate by stiffening her limbs; she didn't want to give him the impression of a swooning schoolgirl. But the movement brought her more firmly against him and her mouth opened under his. One arm enfolded her: with the other he explored her side gently (searching for a zip?) and then came up to her breast where, perhaps disappointed at the formality of what he discovered there, he let it pause for only a short while before sliding it to the middle of her back.

'You shouldn't be here,' she told him. 'I've an idea your father would be very angry.'

'Does he frighten you?'

'Not really.'

'You are afraid of this house perhaps?'
'No, not at all. It's enchanting.'
'Of me?'
'A bit.'
'Why?'
'Well, I know nothing about you—except that you've an apartment in Rome and business interests in America.'
'Very good. He told you that? And that is all that is worth knowing. The present is all that matters, not tedious explanations, justifications. This is all that matters.' On the word he undressed her expertly but gently, without ruining anything, the Italian technique.
'You are no longer afraid?'
'Just dazed slightly. That's all.'
But the catch in her voice betrayed her nervous excitement as she watched his deft hands at work. She was astonished to see that on his left wrist he had an encircling mark similar to his father's. It must have been a birthmark, of course; not a scar after all. A hereditary feature, recurring at intervals, indicative of a fairly inbred aristocracy. Like the Hapsburg nose. Even his voice was reminiscent of the other's, lighter and younger but still recognizably d'Anza in quality. Under his stare she sat awkwardly on the side of the bed, as tensely as that first time, a Sunday evening five years ago, with the grammar-school boy from up the road who had so persistently waylaid her every holiday on his moped and now, with her mother safely at church and a Guild meeting afterwards, was successful in penetrating her at the second attempt. Poor Nigel!

* * *

She came slowly out of her sleep to a pearl dawn on the ceiling and the consciousness that her shoulders and arms were cold. Vincente was dressing; a vague figure by the window. She turned, drew the bedclothes up over herself and watched him.

> *'Wilt thou be gone? It is not yet near day.*
> *It was the nightingale, and not the lark ...'*

All those quotations, going round in her head like a carousel, about night's candles being burnt out. She was still half asleep, but oddly not relaxed; dreamy with the short night's exquisite moments, yes—yet not happy as she should have been. Dissatisfied with something. Herself? The circumstances? It was extraordinary but when she had first woken up, dragging herself physically out of that heavy morass of sleep, it had at first been Tom she'd thought was standing there outlined against the grey of the window, tucking in his shirt. She could have sworn she'd heard a tin alarm clock, and she lay there now automatically listening for the rumble of traffic outside, the rapid clip-clop of somebody's feet on their way to work. She could almost smell the London sourness, that sort of perpetual body-odour of the city, composed of soot grime, diesel fumes, cabbage water and stale cigarettes.

Then when she opened her eyes again properly she saw it wasn't Tom, it was Vincente; it wasn't a poky room on the corner of Cornwall Road, but the airy boudoir of Alessandro's niece and mistress; the storm had spent itself and it was morning, a chilly water-like dawn with the long curtains faintly, damply stirring. And she was glad.

> 'Night's candles are burnt out and jocund day
> Stands tip-toe on the misty mountain tops:
> I must be gone and live, or stay and die ...'

'When shall I see you again?' she said. There was no reason at all why she should ever see him, of course. He could go back to Rome, fly to Kennedy, be in his downtown office tomorrow, surrounded by rapacious typewriters. Perhaps that was what he was preparing to do now. She had no right to expect otherwise. She had given in too easily; there was no longer any incentive for him to stay. She watched him buttoning his cuffs.

At her voice he turned round. 'You are awake?' He came over to her, sat on the side of the bed, bent and kissed her forehead. Then he drew aside the sheet, lay across her and kissed her properly, holding the knuckles of her shoulders. 'Tonight,' he promised. 'At the same time.'

The bristles of his cheek rasped her face; she could make out the brown eyes, slightly bloodshot at the corners. The thought in her mind, however, was: How cheap did he think her? And this, because it was a touch of morality which had never given her much concern before, unnerved her. She wasn't relaxed as she should have been. Love had always made her light hearted, frivolous even. Lying on this fairytale bed she felt insecure, as though it were perched on the steep roof of some fairytale castle, that impossible one of Ludwig II's at Neuschwanstein. Or on the roof at Putney. She had shut her eyes and clung to Nicky's tie when they'd done that famous dance. The prefect's tie, which seemed to be the tangible part of Nicky's domination (that badge of authority), had given her a certain sense of security. Here there was none; as well as naked she felt vulnerable. And, intolerably, she felt shy. It was ridiculous, maddening. To be shy after the event. He had taught her a new way of making love; at least it was new to her. She supposed it was permissible. Everything is permissible. But its immediate effect was to embarrass her. Even more extraordinary was the undeniable knowledge that if Nicky had been here now she would have clung to him, to prevent herself from falling; nude as she was she would have shut her eyes and clung like a vertiginous limpet. Her imagination, like her eyes, would be battened down against that drop below her; she would banish it all by gripping his tie and tensing herself; the wet slates would disappear, the street traffic wouldn't be heard, the force of gravity neutralized. They would be just two angels supporting each other, weightless, on Chartres Cathedral. Pippy, she would hear him say, you've got to grow up. And she would open her eyes and the boudoir would be gone, the princess-and-the-pea fantasy, Vincente would be gone, and Raffaele and Marco and the swimming children and the Minotaur in the basement would all be gone. It was all a peculiar dream. She would wake up and find herself in a front room in Bracknell with fussy crossover net curtains. And hate it.

Vincente had not gone. When she opened her eyes again he was standing looking down at her. 'I will go through the secret entrance,' he said. 'It is more discreet. Leave it open for me this evening.'

The face descended, hovered, kissed her eyes, blacking out the image. Then a movement and he was no longer there. This time in reality. She heard the soft click of the panel. He knew all about that, of course. The family secret. When did they learn, the sons? A ritual at eighteen, after supper and wine, to mark the heir's sexual majority? Fidelity sworn over candles and communion, a prie-dieu and Friar Lawrence in the shadowy corner? Oh, God, it was all that indigestible d'Annunzio.

She sprang up, put on her kimono and went to the window, tying the belt as she looked out. It was light now, the tops of the mountains stratified with a fresh fall of snow, white streaks already turning to salmon. The air was like pine needles, icicles. Birds were singing; no lark that she could distinguish, but there was a blackbird, and a raucous one that sounded a bit like a jay. For several minutes she watched the mountain summit warm into gold, an overflowing crucible with glinting streams, after the night's rain, catching the sun farther and farther down the slopes, the lower parts still in grey horizontal mists and darkness. Then she got back into bed, as she was, without taking off the wrap, and slept until Carla, with coffee and a boiled egg, tapped at her door.

* * *

'I have to go into Milan,' Raffaele told her later that morning, armed with a sheaf of letters. He never appeared before eleven. 'You are able to amuse yourself?'

'Thank you, yes. I'll think of something.'

She looked up to see him studying her with that contemplative stare of his. 'You have found enough to divert you, my dear?'

'Yes, plenty.' Why was she blushing? It infuriated her; she never blushed. He meant nothing, of course.

'Swimming and reading. Restful activities both. You will soon be recuperated.' He meant nothing. Why then did he look through her as though she were made of glass? He appeared fragile and tired, his hands skeletal as they held the letters. 'You were not disturbed last night?' he added.

Startled, she dropped her book.

'The storm,' he explained. He meant nothing; nothing at all.

'No ... Oh no! I slept through it.'

'Good.' He turned to go, then poked at a vein of ivy growing up a pedestal, finally stripping it away vigorously like a plaster. 'I will bring you back something from Milan.'

'Oh, no, Raf—please! You have been too kind to me already.'

'Nonsense. Some little thing. I am very fond of you ... It is all right, you need not look so dismayed. We understand each other. I want nothing in return. I have apologized for my behaviour and you were gracious enough to forgive me.'

'No more presents, please, Raf.' She was genuinely embarrassed.

'Something better than that.' It was said shyly, still picking at the ivy stem. Then he marched off, shoulders back, a military walk, pre-Sidi Omar pride, a springing step, the dog ambling behind him.

Pippa retrieved her book. She had finished with d'Annunzio and she wasn't sorry. Now she was starting *Il Gattopardo*. It occurred to her that it was indicative of the subtle change that had come over her since arriving here that this novel, that had once bored her in English when she'd had to read it for A level, now possessed her in Italian even though it meant ploughing through it with the aid of a dictionary. She passed the rest of the morning with it, absorbed. Yet, fascinating though it was, there were moments, turning a page or sprawling herself more comfortably in the chair, when she looked up, searching for movement among the trees, for a figure standing there, a man appraising her. Vincente dominated her thoughts.

If Raf had gone to Milan then why didn't Vincente come out of hiding, wherever he was? And what was all the mystery anyhow? To be not on speaking terms to such an extent was absurd. She read on. No shadow of a man's approach fell across the page, yet she looked over her shoulder from time to time. The house held its counsel, impassive in the sunlight, sprawled like a dog and watching her with one eye, aware that she was the foreigner, with strange habits and not altogether to be trusted. No Vincente, no smell of cigar smoke, no hand overlaid on hers nor gentle fingering of the coiled spring of hair in front of her ear, as though he were weighing it. He would come tonight as he'd said. She would wait for that.

So taken up with this thought was she indeed that it wasn't until well into the afternoon that she remembered it had been her intention to phone an appointment with Dr Rossano tomorrow. Well, she could do it now with complete freedom. She had lunched alone. Raf had gone, and Marco with him, driving the Ascona. She had watched its dignified departure. She could go to the desk and phone. She could get up and go now. There was nothing to stop her.

She stubbed out her cigarette and went into the study. The clutter on Raf's desk was much as before. She searched around for a directory—she had forgotten the hospital number again. The photograph of Raf as a young man stared at her seriously, and again she was struck by its resemblance to Vincente. They were so much alike apart from the years. In those days he must have been as exciting to some woman as Vincente, turning her head and making her gasp in the night too—an amazing thought, for she'd never really considered the old before as ever having had the attributes of the young.

Turning over the ornaments she discovered another portrait—this time a woman, hard-faced, shadowy-eyed, even plain, all polka-dot shoulder-flounced dress and 1930s permanent wave. His wife? Another cause for amazement. He could have loved that, all through the POW camp? This was what had sustained him through five years of isolation and alien food and boredom and sheer frustration at the passing of precious time? The haemorrhage of his youth and manhood in a cold climate, nostalgia for old saint's-day parties, confirmation parties, children playing hide-and-seek in the sun-drenched garden of the Minotaur?

She picked up the phone.

Then she thought of Vincente and that wonderful hard chest like a moulded breastplate, and she hesitated. Rossano and his check-up would mean a consequent return to normality, convalescence declared over, or more visits to hospital; either way the life of the commonplace. She wanted the unreal to continue; she wanted this particular fairytale to go on, if Vincente and her new *dolce vita* were part of it; she wanted to put things off, to find excuses. She could always ring the hospital later, not now, tomorrow, next week. Rossano wasn't due back until tomorrow. Let's see what's going to happen about Vincente first. She'd had enough of Notting Hill. She was going to make the most of this new situation.

The young *contessa* twice over replaced the receiver.

Dinner also was taken in solitary state. (Life at the villa had become a succession of meals, graduating the passage of time like beads on a rosary.) Enrico, who had no English, waited on her with a personal language of smiles and grunts, nodding encouragingly when he showed her the wine-bottle label, clicking reassurance when she spilt some and mopping it up like an understanding mother. The rest of the house was empty. Oh why didn't Vincente come? They could wander through the dovetailed rooms together, hand in hand, and talk, and find out more about each other, those delicious mysteries of early friendship, and then on to the terrace to kiss in the open air, flanked by erotic statues leaping under the evening star, white Venus, to the running accompaniment of a fountain. He was wasting time.

She strolled through the house, inspected the flowers (they needed fresh water), drew the tasselled curtains, climbed a library ladder to examine a leather-and-gilt monogram (the eagle again, but with legs straddling a bull's horns) and then on at random. Eventually she found herself in a part, more impoverished than the rest, which suggested the servants' wing. The walls, green painted, were blotched where the plaster had crumbled, leaving it pink. There was a smell of cooking and the clatter of dishes and female voices from the kitchen hard by.

Opposite was a door, thick-enamelled with generations of brown, governess paint. Something told her (her sense of direction? the calculation of her feet? an intuition merely?) that this was the door to the cellar, the wine vault, and therefore the way to the basement. She felt her heart give a single jerk of excitement. She paused, considered, and then tried the handle. The door opened, away from her, revealing a dark flight of steps dropping away into further shadow. At the head of the staircase was a switch, and she reached in and clicked it on, to discover the bottom to be a stone-flagged area. She hesitated for perhaps as much as a minute. This was undoubtedly the basement that Raf had tried to discourage her from visiting. Why? Curiosity helped her make up her mind to find out. The only person she was afraid of in this house was Marco, and knowing him to have gone with the car to Milan she felt bold enough to explore further. Leaving the door open she descended the stairs.

There was nothing. Only empty wine bottles, straw sheaths, old packing cases and junk. What had she expected to find? Mussolini's treasure, a quarter of a century old? Biggles, you've got to grow up. She began to walk down a passage, white-tiled, like an old Metropolitan Railway conduit.

'Once upon a time' (Tom had snapped the cupboard drawer shut on her inquisitive fingers) 'there was this old smoothy named Bluebeard—and that *was* Perrault—who had a silken harem full of little concubines all under legal age. Well, six of them actually; one for each day of the week except Sunday, which was a day of rest. And since in business hours he was a chartered accountant in the city with a brass-plated office on Wall Street he naturally didn't want it to get around, and one day his latest acquisition, a convent-bred child called Yasmin, went snooping in the attics ... Are you listening, Pippa?'

The short passage opened on to another room, containing stores. Onions hanging up. Plates, chipped, discarded. An old knife-grinder. A broken coffee machine. Pippa made her way through an avenue of household impedimenta. Lamps. A paraffin cooker. In one place mushrooms were being cultivated, white golf balls in black fibrous compost. At the end an arch without a door, and beyond that another room, larger than the first. There was a veritable honeycomb of vaults down here. The basements of all great houses were like this. Hessian-lagged pipes, from which she could hear metallic gurglings, ran parallel to the ceiling. The boiler was somewhere near by, she guessed; this was why it wasn't chilly—quite warm in fact. She passed on.

A long chamber full of exhibits on stands, black metal objects, made her think first of an agricultural show, then, on closer examination, a folk museum. She recollected having seen gins and mantraps in Exeter. Or perhaps it was the Tower of London. The levered device she was looking at, with sweaty leather thongs and a rope round a drum, was a rack. Of course! The eccentric Alessandro! These little things would be thumbscrews. On the wall, crossed like heraldic banners, a variety of whips. She had no idea what that spiked cartwheel was for.

So this was what Raf was ashamed of; because it was an obscene parody of his own museum above, the Little Gallery. The obverse of his quintessence of beauty. This was where the Pasiphäe should have been. She wasn't particularly shocked however, or disgusted —more reluctantly fascinated than anything, as she had been as a child in the basement of Madame Tussaud's. It wasn't until she found herself staring at a polished fretted gridiron as large as a mattress and she realized that this was where somebody, some human being, had once agonized until roasted that her stomach turned weak and she made her escape.

Shaken, she returned to the drawing-room, picked up two or three magazines and fingered them through, nervously unable to read them or even to concentrate on the illustrations for long. She kept listening for Vincente. She wanted his comfort. At least he was gentle, and skilled. She tried the discipline of translating another page of *Il Gattopardo*.

'*Una volta lei si era slascosta dietro un enorme quadro posato per terra* ... Once she had hidden behind an enormous picture propped on the floor; and for a short time *Arturo Corbera at the Siege of Antioch* formed a protection for the girl's hopeful anxiety; but when she was found, with her smile veined in cobwebs and her hands veiled in dust, she was clasped tight, and though she kept on saying again and again, "No, Tancredi, no," her denial was in fact an invitation, for all he was doing was to stare with his blue eyes into her green ones. One luminous cold morning she was trembling in a dress that was still summery; he squeezed her to him, to warm her, on a sofa covered in tattered silk; her scented breath moved the hair on his forehead; they were moments ecstatic and painful, during which desire became a torment, restraint upon it a delight...'

She kept thinking she heard non-existent nightingales (it was

Radio Secondo coming from the domestic block, through an open fanlight window) and she abandoned it. Nor could she bring herself to write a postscript to Nicky's letter, still unsealed. The black museum defied cool description—at least until she could take a more distant view of it. At last she went up to her room, taking the book and magazines with her. She had already, before dinner, unlatched the communicating panel. It was still closed behind the tapestry. Now she undressed and bathed. She had intended to take a shower but, with her hand on the chrome faucet, she paused, changed her mind. It was nothing to do with Raf's remarks about *Psycho*, she told herself. She ran the old-fashioned bath, placed the sponge behind her head as she always did, and soaked, letting her limbs float, determined to relax. Cooling pipes reverberated; a floorboard creaked. Had she bolted the door? She sat up suddenly with a swirl of water to crane her head to see ... All that blood in the shower ... Oh for God's sake, Pipistrelle, relax!

Why had she called herself that? That was a silly name. They hadn't used it since the house in Putney.

'You're throttling me, Pipistrelle.'

'What?'

'My tie. Grab something else. I can't breathe.'

'Sorry.'

'That's better ... Do you come here often?'

'What?'

'I said, you dance *divinely*. Like a little bat. Enjoying it?'

'Super.'

'You're a liar, Pipistrelle. Let yourself go more. Shall I hang you upside down, little bat?'

'Nicky, let's go down now. Please?'

'Twinkle, twinkle, little bat.'

'Please, Nicky. Let's go down now!' The gleaming slates ...

She dried herself, went back to her room and brushed her hair vigorously before the mirror. Her eyes looked a little dark, she thought, the pupils dilated, the blue of the irises turned to wild hyacinth. It was a trick of the light. She hadn't been taking any narcotics. She spent a little time with a brush, making up her lashes, of which she was secretly rather proud.

When she heard the click of the panel behind her she stiffened, her elbows still on the dressing table top, not turning round but watching the tapestry through the mirror. The heavy material bellied out; someone was struggling with it. Vincente? A hand showed, tugging gently at the woven stuff where it had caught on a corner of the panel. Gold cuff-links. At least it wasn't Marco. She turned on her stool, her heart beating, and watched the tapestry swung aside.

Vincente, in evening dress as though he had come from a formal dinner, stepped into the room, blinked for a moment at the crystal lights. Then Pippa ran to him.

'I have missed you,' he said, holding her. 'All day.'

'Me too.' She buried her face in his shirt front. Silk cravat and spicy deodorant. 'Where have you been?' Oh, the relief of it!

'Boring but essential business. Then a boring but useful function. What have you been doing?'

'Reading ... And exploring.' She didn't tell him about the black museum.

They hugged more and more passionately; then he pulled apart the tie-cord of her towelling wrap, but her raised arms round his neck kept it from falling. His hands crept round between it and her back. Then, characteristic of him perhaps as an inventive lover, he opened both doors of the great wardrobe to reveal the full length mirrors on the reverse and turned her slightly so that she might see herself being caressed. At least it showed them both from the neck down—the angle of the piers cut off their faces. As in the other experiment she felt a little confused, even foolish; he in full evening regalia and she with nothing, there was an absurdity about it. His hand purposefully at work under her breast, the fingers of the other exploring the still damp fluff above the division of her thighs, she became embarrassed again and turned herself away with a deprecating laugh and got into bed.

Some time after midnight, lying there talking now, her arms behind her head, the moonlight filtering in, she said: 'Vincente, why aren't you on speaking terms with your father? Why are you banned from the house?'

For answer he kissed her armpit. 'Tomorrow night,' he said, 'must be the last—for a short while at any rate, Pippa my darling.'

Alarmed, she turned towards him. 'What do you mean?'

'I have to go away.'

'To Rome?'

'Temporarily.'

She listened to the oyster clock ticking madly.

'You have someone there? ... I know so little about you, Vincente. You're married?'

'No, I assure you ... But you, Pippa, you have someone.'
'What?'
'Last night, in your sleep, you groaned and said "Tom!" Who is he?'
Leaning out, she retrieved a pillow from the floor. She said nothing.
'He is your lover?' he persisted.
'Not now. It is over.'
'How long over?'
'A long time.'
'Then why did you sigh his name with such fervour?'

* * *

Lieutenant Maiello called the next day to give her back her passport and, gallantly, a punnet of enormous cherries from his garden. He assured her there would be no more trouble about the insurance. It was just a question of time.

'You are looking better already,' he said, smiling. 'Our Trentino air agrees with you. Rossano will be pleased with your progress.'

'*Ispettore*,' she said, 'tell me something.' They were alone on the terrace; or almost alone—Raf was at the far end giving orders to Giulia. 'What do you know of Signor Vincente?'

'Signor Vincente, signorina?' He echoed the name without showing he understood it.

'Count d'Anza's son.'

Maiello looked blank but polite. '*Mi rincresce*, I did not know that the Count had a son. I have not been in this district very long, you understand. I had always assumed he was childless.'

'Signor Vincente d'Anza has business interests in Rome and America. I thought perhaps you would have heard of him.'

Maiello bowed. '*Mi rinscresce tanto*, Signorina Rowantree.' He was very polite. 'I do not know. But you could well be correct.'

There was no point in pursuing the matter. She returned to the drawing-room. More composed today, even if constantly thinking of Vincente's imminent departure, she finished her letter to Nicky, though she didn't know when it would get posted. She still didn't care to put it on the hall table with the other outgoing mail for Marco to take into town. The weather hadn't yet returned to conditions warm enough for swimming but she took the dog for a walk, down to the bay, where she found a sheltered spot among the rocks and sat, hoping that Vincente would appear again. But he did not. Neither did she hear any children, nor Iago show interest. He lolled at her feet asleep while she read *Oggi*'s version of a day in the life of Princess Anne.

Raf was particularly attentive to her all day—or at meal times, which was when he tended to see her most—but whatever the present was that he'd promised to bring back from Milan it wasn't forthcoming, nor did he speak of it, and she was glad. The day wore on. She wished she could listen to Radio Nazionale but she still hadn't found a wireless in this house, apart from the one she'd heard in the domestic quarters, and there was certainly no television. Somehow she had the idea that d'Anza disapproved of such commercially sponsored entertainment. She tried the piano again. 'Für Elise' and a garbled bit of Chopin. Music. The difference between Nicky and Tom. Nicky had always had a taste for the opulent—Mahler and Richard Strauss, Bruckner. Tom preferred the delicate. 'L'Après-Midi' and Benjamin Britten (the conclusion of *A Midsummer Night's Dream* with Oberon as an unearthly counter-tenor), a vocal line of Pergolesi (*Tre giorni son che Nina in letto se ne sta*) which he used to sing over and over again, turning his guitar into a lute.

After dinner Raf took his usual cigar and *grappa* with her in the alcove overlooking the glint of the lake between foliage. Perhaps sensing her edginess, or mistaking it for boredom, he seemed loath to leave her this evening and go back to his study.

'You are *distraite*, Pippina,' he said, watching her.

'Am I?'

'Like a swallow testing its wings.'

She considered the simile, then took it up. 'Well, I've been here a week. I can't impose on your hospitality for ever. I must soon leave. Fly away.'

'As you wish. When you have seen everything.'

'I have—now.' She was thinking of the museum in the basement.

'Almost everything.'

He was so inscrutable, sitting there like a priest; she had no idea whether he was profoundly wise or just obtuse and deliberately mystifying.

'Is there more to discover?' She felt that he knew more about her movements than she'd confessed; a shrewd priest, rather than an ascetic one, he looked into the heart.

'There is always more to discover, fortunately. You are learning about life. That, after all, is what life is—a medium for human learning. *Sbagliando s'impara.* Only—people have strange ideas about what living is. Living it up, living it down—your language is full of interesting idioms. Perhaps we are too concerned about finding answers to everything. Maybe we should be content merely to experience the question. Knowing life to be an illusion (for even this chair I'm sitting on consists of nothing more solid than whirling bits of electricity) it is all the same necessary to live it as though it were true. So the cause we know to be hopeless is one we must continue to pursue. And the omniscient, omnipotent God I do not believe in is the power to whom I turn in my extremity, because this is the way I am designed. We are all characters in somebody's book. Another of our authors you must study is Pirandello.... One day, when you are my age, you will begin to learn about death, as well as life. That is an interesting experience too.'

Holding herself patiently for another hour she waited for him to depart, but for some reason he didn't. Instead he sat there, legs crossed on knee, talking about Bernini (the significance of the *Anima Beata* and *Anima Dannata* in the Palazzo di Spagua), Teilhard de Chardin, the war, his friend Gian-Mario, Shakespeare, the weather, how to catch mullet, everything. At last she could stand it no longer; she excused herself—the inevitable migraine—and went up to her room convinced that he was not deceived.

She went out on to her *terrazza*, a fur fabric coat loose over her shoulders, and looked down at the trees. The moon would rise later; just now it was dark. She could hear the four-stroke chug of the motor launch, a shouted remark and its echo, and then, as though to a timetable, the nightingale started up again. A strange presentiment grew within her that this was the last time she would stand here being happy. An unreasonable conviction, superstitious, no substance in it. She turned away, let herself into her room again, and found that Vincente was already there, waiting.

This time he was in casual clothes, a turtle neck cashmere sweater.

'Why do you have to go away?' she said.

'It is unavoidable. Don't worry. I shall return.'

'When?... I can't stay on here in your father's house indefinitely.'

'Do not distress yourself, mia Pippina. Everything is to be all right.'

'Take me with you.'

'Alas, I cannot.'

'I want to escape from here.'

'You shall. But not yet.'

She was conscious that at no time, even when making love, had he said that he loved her. Now he was going away, to Rome, New York, somewhere unspecified where she was not to follow, or couldn't. 'I love you,' she told him.

He kissed her. 'No, you do not, Pippina. You are a restless child. But I love you. Now let us make the most of our last evening.'

She clung to him and to her surprise found that she was crying. She never wept. She rarely wept. Well, only sometimes. She had cried when she'd left Tom. It was untrue what she'd told herself before.

The bout over, she felt better and relaxed with him happily. They got into bed but did nothing more than hold each other close. She felt she just wanted to cling to someone solid. Presently the moon came out silvering the edge of the curtains, and Vincente tugged the cord of the reading lamp, the only one left on, and they lay in the white lunar glimmer. Tenderly Pippa fingered the snake-like birthmark on his other wrist, under her cheek, close to her eyes. Then, feeling generous and hoping to please him, remembering his little predilection—or one of them—she slipped out and opened the wardrobe mirrors so that he could watch her reactions in the next ten minutes. That he should be an epicurean lover didn't worry her unduly now. Returning, she began to play, alternately eager and submissive. The nightingales throbbed. By now the moon was clear of the clouds.

Her head turning away from a gentle bite, she saw herself large-eyed in the glass. And then she screamed. For the man who enfolded her was not Vincente; it was Raffaele. The high priest, not the young one. His face in the mirror was old, his hands veined, the birth-mark common to both.

It was a trick of the light. It had to be. Or her nerves. A trick of the light, no more.

* * *

'Nicky, I can't tell you how good it is to see you!... Oh, it's pretty awful here sometimes when the Hell-Cats get really beastly, but one gets used to it. It can't be the same at a boys' school. You don't live all the time at an emotional pitch, do you?... Yes, I have one friend —Isobel. That's the one with the glasses and freckles. No, she's not very pretty. But she's nice ... Oh, that one's Amanda. Yes, she is rather. No brains though. Daddy's a colonel. She thinks she would quite like to live in South Africa. Probably would too ... The dark one? Oh, the *very* dark one with the enormous eyes? That's Delvi. She's from Iraq. She's all right. A bit wet. She reckons she's betrothed to some awful old man of forty. At least, a ceremony took place when she was nine. She doesn't have to marry him if she doesn't want to—it was just a ceremony—but she probably will because he's rich in oil and she says what does it matter as long as he's kind. Of course, she may have to share the house with three others ... Why do we have to keep talking about them? Let's talk about you ... The one with the husky voice? You mean Les. You wouldn't like her. I used to think it was short for Lesley until they warned me. You see now why I can't wait to get away from this place, Nicky?'

* * *

Vincente's departure at first light and her fitful sleep after the shock of last night (stupid scream! fortunately he had misconstrued it as a compliment to his technique) left her listless. As to Raf, more than a little ashamed of her false judgement of him (it was a natural distortion of the mirror, of course, or her own mind) she didn't feel able to face the Count and so spent most of the day in the open air, even going so far as to send in a simplified message *via* Carla to the effect that she didn't want any lunch. The maid returned a little later with a basket of cold chicken and a milk loaf—a sort of *brioche*—all wrapped up in a tablecloth with a bottle of their standard Franceschini, two glasses and forks, and they sat down together under the twisted grey olives and had a picnic. It was not by the bay. Pippa was avoiding that spot this morning because of its associations.

Although the two girls had little conversation they sat happily side by side throwing the last of the crumbs to the pigeons, Carla a little below the other and always deferential to her position. What *was* her position, Pippa wondered, or what did Carla imagine it was? She noticed the woman was always careful to call her 'signora'. What scandal did they fabricate in the servants' quarters? It would have been nice to know. Pippa, glad of her company today, longed to lay her head on her capable shoulder and have it all out. But she had never been given to showing her feelings, except rage. Honour with Dignity. You're thinking of Roedean. Why, isn't that where you went?

'Carla, have you ever been in love?'

The maid giggled. 'Many times, signora.'

'Deeply?'

'Signora?'

A cul-de-sac. She tried another path. 'When you marry—is there someone?'

'Oh, si! Many!' She grinned.

'But when the time comes—Is it someone you have known a long while? What is he like? Tell me.'

'Oh, that. There is Luigi Ricco. He is a boatman. He fishes. He is ardent, but I do not want him. I look for an American.'

'Why?'

'They are all rich, the Americans. He will take me away.'

'From here? This beautiful place?'

'I have lived here all my life, signora. So how do I know it is so? ... A big house, a car, a magnificent kitchen, everything automatic. A black servant maybe. These things are important ... An American, or perhaps a German. They are rich too.'

That afternoon, quite by chance, she met Raf on the stairs. Thinking he was busy at his work she was engaged in play-acting, amusing herself by coming down the grand staircase, as she used to do at school, in a variety of character guises. Her favourite was Valencia. This was the second time she had come down the great sweep, slowly, to imagined music. Respighi. 'The Fountains.' Head up, hand on the rail, haughty expression. A pity she was wearing a short skirt. The dress should mould to the knee.

On the mezzanine level she discovered Raffaele. He took up a previous conversation as though it had only just been broken off.

'Of course, Gian-Mario's greatest triumph in *O Paolo, O Francesca!* was getting Tosi to design the costumes. They were really the only things in the picture worth looking at in my opinion. The sheer authenticity of them forced Valencia to attempt, at least, to act the part. I'm told that Piero Tosi is the actor's demon, a perfectionist. Almost as hard a taskmaster as Visconti. Did you know that for *Il Gattopardo* Claudia Cardinale had to waltz for a month in a wasp-waisted corset he designed from contemporary records, but unfortunately for her her waist wasn't statistically the same as those of 1861 and she was skinned raw. The young lady suffered in silence. *La moda va e viene.* But "nothing stirs the imagination like the truth"—Tosi's own words ...'

Raffaele's own words continued in an unending stream. And she had to listen, politely. She had the impression that he was preparing the next revelation. It made her feel like a girl in a knife-throwing act. She wanted to bolt but knew that she had to keep very still while the Great Prospero took careful aim to a roll of drums. Tomorrow she would cable home for some money. She wanted to go. Back to the London grime. Suddenly she'd had enough. With the departure of Vincente she was unsettled again.

Raf had stopped talking. Now, with the batch of spent magazines from her room tucked under her arm, she wandered down into the drawing-room, thinking to change them and while away the time until dinner.

Entering by way of the open door she paused, half way in. The room was not empty. There was a woman sitting there at a table in the alcove, her back three-quarters towards her. She was contemplating a typewriter; not typing anything, just looking at the written sheet critically; that was why Pippa had heard nothing on coming in. The woman's face was turned away yet there was something familiar about the way she sat. A grey sleeveless pinafore dress, wool, lightweight but English, a silk shirt, paisley pattern, smart but business-like. Everything familiar. Where had they met before?

As Pippa stood there, just inside the doorway, wondering whether to go out again without making her presence known (disconcerted to find her priority as the only lady of the house withdrawn) she began, as she continued to look at the other woman, to feel an extraordinary sense of unease, a coldness, a conviction that something ghastly was about to happen, inexorably, in the way she'd had just before the accident. She was about to go into a second disaster. She was sliding towards it, unable to stop the momentum, just like the other time. She was going to get hurt.

Hearing her the woman turned her head, took off her glasses.

It was her mother.

'Hullo, darling,' she said casually. 'You've been a long time.' She pulled the page out of the typewriter and screwed it up. 'Pippa, I wish you wouldn't leave your things hanging up all over the bathroom. Terry Macdonald ran his face into your knickers. I think he was embarrassed.'

Pippa could hear a slithering sound. She was dimly conscious that it was caused by the magazines falling from her grasp, one by one, to the tiled floor. She felt weak, suspended, weightless, her mouth dry, her stomach turned to liquid. She was going to faint. She grasped the back of the chair and drew in a staggered breath, fragmented with hysteria, as though she were drowning.

'They've given Terry a new department,' her mother said. 'Did I tell you?'

Pippa tried to speak but her throat was strictured. It was so impossible, her mother sitting there surrounded by Italian marble, a black cherub on a pedestal at her side offering the air perpetual fruit. Someone walked across the ceiling heavily. (Carla above preparing beds?) A door slammed. It was absurd, impossible.

'Mummy.' She heard her own voice, as strange as a tape recording, hardly recognizable. 'What are you doing here?'

Her mother got up. Pippa recalled the dress. It was still in the wardrobe at home.

'Waiting for you, darling—what else?'

Pippa stared at her, the familiar face. She knew everything now. This was what she had been waiting for, the revelation. What d'Anza had been preparing her for. It was really all quite simple. Everything accounted for. She knew now and understood.

She was dead.

It was both extraordinary and yet so obvious; it explained everything. She ought to have realized it before. She had died in the crash. Life for her was over the moment her head had struck the petrol tanker. This was not herself standing here. Her body was in some mortuary or like her mother, buried. This was another part of her and it was experiencing some sort of purgatory in which she could still witness and think, observe everything with the senses and be conscious of rational thought, and yet not be part of it. She was as much a visitant as this shell of her mother, or the strange children, the guitar player or Vincente, all of whom at one time or another, to tell the truth, she had suspected as being insubstantial, however wild and quickly rejected the notion had been. She, or rather the conscious remaining part of her, was here for a purpose, as she had all along felt convinced, except that the ritual wasn't at all that which she'd imagined.... I have seen everything. Almost everything ... You are learning about life.... But too late, Raffaele, too late! I am dead!

She didn't want to be dead. Oh, God, she didn't want to be parted from life, from the world, the body, youth, living, feeling, the future, the sheer joy of it. She'd never counted it up before, never thought about it, but she should have had another fifty years at least.

She closed her eyes. She felt herself falling.

There was an orange-red glow, amorphous at first, which slowly drew itself in and concentrated to a rectangle, focusing itself as it did so. Her first belief was that it was the gas fire into the heart of which her mother had once welcomed her, and this seemed very natural since she lived there in the corolla of a deathless tulip, unconsumed. But as her senses quickened and hardened, giving her thoughts shape, she realized that it was a two-bar electric radiator, not a gas fire, she was looking at. On either side of it were polished glints of dark mahogany panels, a gilt picture frame, crimson upholstered chairs. She moved her face. Her cheek was against a dusty-smelling cushion. She was lying on a couch, a light feather quilt over her. Warm, comfortable, nice.

Suddenly she hurled it off, sat up wildly. Where was she now? What room was this? It was all so dark.

Her movements brought a sound from behind her, the scraping of a chair. A woman moved into view. Someone in black. It was Carla, looking wide-eyed and alarmed. She bent over the near-by table and there was a click and the room was suffused with a golden shadowless light. Her eyes dark as melted chocolate, she looked down at Pippa for a moment, then fled from the room. Voices. Pippa sat on the edge of the couch, her head in her hands, feeling sick. Then footsteps and voices together. Two men appeared, with Carla hovering behind them. One was Raffaele; the other she thought for a second, madly, was Vincente; but it wasn't. It was Dr Rossano in a belted sports jacket.

'Hullo!' he said reassuringly and came over and took her pulse, holding her wrist casually while he talked, as though it were unimportant but routine and courteous to do so. 'What happened to you? What were you doing on the floor, mm? Trip over the bearskin or something?'

She said nothing; it didn't seem to require an answer, a facetious question almost, or one designed to relieve tension. It succeeded. There was something gratefully reassuring about its ordinariness. Her head ached, but through it she was able to concentrate on one tremendous thing—she was alive. The man who was balancing her wrist was a man, not a figment of her imagination; he had bones and flesh, a wrist-watch with a sweep hand, Swiss make, Tissot. Sitting beside her, he turned the shade of the table lamp and probed very gently and skilfully the back of her head, parting her hair.

'Well, you don't seem to have done yourself any harm,' he said. Then he took a pencil-like instrument from his pocket and by its light examined each of her eyes in turn. She found herself looking up and down as she was told, into a soft beam.

'Nothing exceptional,' he told her. He seemed puzzled. 'A little nervous debility, very slight anaemia. Not enough to worry about.'

'Yes, I had it as a child.' She felt like a child now, answering.

'Well, eat up your spinach. It'll make you grow strong.' He was nice. Rossano put his gadget away, took her chin and scrutinized her tongue. 'Lie down again and keep warm. You can have a vermouth if you like.'

Raffaele gave orders to Carla, still hovering, to bring a bottle of Cinzano, but Pippa shook her head. Her throat was dry, yet she didn't want to drink. Silent, not caring to speak for fear of being discredited, she watched Rossano's movements; and perhaps her eyes sought out his diagnosis—she certainly didn't ask for it—for he smiled at her frankly. 'Well, you're not on drugs, which was my first thought, so you can safely take alcohol ... No? Well if you will excuse me, I will.'

When he had drunk it, she said: 'Dr Rossano, what's wrong with me?'

He raised his eyebrows politely and waited. So she went on. 'I thought I saw my dead mother. I was convinced of it.'

He didn't seem as astonished as she'd thought. He merely studied her with more interest. His face was open, pleasant.

'It's the concussion, isn't it?' She sought explanations; he merely examined the evidence. It is easy to be a scientist if one is cool by nature. 'That could be the reason, couldn't it. Hallucinations?'

'It could be, Miss Rowantree.'

'Am I going mad?'

'Certainly not.'

'Schizophrenia then?'

'You read too many journalistic articles. There ought to be a law against them. Now stop worrying.'

She lay back under the eiderdown. Someone had removed her shoes.

'When can I go home?' she inquired.

'Soon. You must come in for that X-ray first. Next Wednesday?

Morning? That will have given time, I should think, for any splinter displacement to become measurable. After that you can take the next plane from Milan if you like ... Until then the best thing you can do is to curl up with a good book.' His idiomatic English was impeccable.

Picking up the magazines still scattered near the door where she had dropped them, he placed them tidily at her feet, then turned over the d'Annunzio biography and the Lampedusa. 'You are studious, Miss Rowantree.' He looked surprised, as though seeing her in an unexpected light. 'Do you not find these two strange bedfellows?'

'A bit. I don't really know ... I don't read very well. Some of the constructions beat me, even with a dictionary. I skip. But I manage to get some of it.'

'Well done! Then you must try this.' He left the room and came back with his macintosh, from the pocket of which he extracted a paperback. It was Elio Vittorini's *Il Garofano Rossi*. 'This one is nice. You will find it interesting, after d'Annunzio.' He grinned, pleasant white teeth, crows'-feet of humour creasing his eyes. 'Stay at the Villa long enough and we shall have you a student, like the Count Raffaele here. But do not seek to escape into romance. It is so easy to live on an ivory tower. There is plenty of poverty on the other side of the village. The greatest element in Italian culture has always been its realism.' He caught Raffaele's eye and smiled. 'My friend does not agree with me. This is where we differ. Only in this.' He dropped the shiny book into her hands. 'When you have mastered that you must try *Erica*. That is nice too ... Not yet. When you have got over your depression. It will make you suffer, but you will feel better afterwards. Always a good test of a book ... Yes, that is better than d'Annunzio. Better than *Il Fuoco*. Anything could be better than that ridiculous obscenity.'

Pippa felt tired. She didn't want to talk about Italian literature. She closed her eyes and lay with her headache, under the quilt.

'I will send you in some supper,' Raf said. 'Then perhaps you had better go to bed.'

Her eyes opened again. 'I should like Carla to stay with me tonight. Or in the next room perhaps—you know, the one which communicates. Could she have a bed there?'

Raffaele gave orders to the girl who nodded and said '*Si, si!*' readily; then he turned back to Pippa. 'But do not retire for a little while yet.' He looked at his pocket watch. 'I am expecting a visitor.' It meant nothing to her and she didn't respond. She didn't feel like playing hostess. 'One who concerns you,' he added. 'A pleasant surprise. Marco has gone in to Brescia to meet the train.'

'Train?' She narrowed her eyes, curtaining off the pain of her headache.

'From Rome.'

The curtain was drawn aside, swept back, the migraine forgotten. Vincente? Was this the surprise?... Oddly enough she didn't know whether she wanted to see Vincente now. She had already said goodbye to him. Meeting someone again whom you've steeled yourself to do without can be a harrowing experience. Her life had been full of people she'd learnt to do without. 'Rome?' she said.

He was in one of his thoughtful, uncommunicative moods and went off to organize supper. At least his taciturnity was undemanding; it left her in peace. Usually he talked. Tonight it was Rossano. The doctor, over his second drink, had been studying her again.

'You are so English,' he said. 'Afraid to have a good cry in public. A good cry never did anyone any harm. It is therapeutically needful sometimes. Homo sapiens is the only animal that weeps. Or laughs. I wonder why. There must be a reason. A psychological function perhaps.'

'Dr Rossano, would you do something for me?' She searched through the leaves of Il Gattopardo and extracted the letter to Nicky. 'Would you post that for me?'

He glanced at the name and address and then smiled. 'Are you sure you need me to?'

She did not understand. Turning it over and over by the corners, he continued, choosing his words: 'It will take a long time to get to Canada. You may see him before then.'

She still did not understand, so he said more explicitly: 'Prepare yourself—but this is the one who is coming tonight.'

Pippa stared at him. 'Nicky?'

'Now I've spoilt the Count Raffaele's little surprise. You must pretend you did not know. He will be hurt.'

'Nicky? My brother Nicholas? Are you sure? Here?' It was impossible. 'He is in Alberta. Miles away.'

'No, he is in Rome on business. Or was until this afternoon. A World Health conference, I believe. Is he not a lawyer? It is to do with that. He represents his firm, their interests are at stake. The Count Raffaele found out by chance, and was able to telephone him. He told him of your accident and your whereabouts.'

'Why?'

'It was on my advice. We felt someone ought to know. He was the only relative you had mentioned ...'

'You make it sound serious.'

'No, it's just that someone ought to be caring for you. I am old fashioned. Square. Is that the term? Young girls on motor-cycles easy-riding all over Europe—I cannot say I approve. My own daughter is not allowed to travel without a chaperon, even by train. That is the difference between Italy and London. Or Los Angeles.'

'It sounds like a very unequal world. Can't she stand on her own two feet? Or does she prefer life in the seraglio?' She wasn't really interested. She was thinking about Nicky. But it served to cover her emotions. She went on: 'Who was talking about ivory towers just now? And the other side of the village? How's she going to learn?' Nicky was coming! Could it be true?

'It is not quite the same argument. I am simply concerned that someone I love should not suffer lasting hurt. One can discover the squalor of those alleys without actually bedding down there.'

'You think so? How else do you find out about the bugs?'

Looking down at her, he spread his hands in a gesture that conceded a fencing point, foreign and charming at the same time. 'You have a philosophy of compassion,' he said. 'That is good. So have the majority of the young. But they suffer from a conviction of impotence, making their protests more like cries of despair. They need to channel their intuitive morality into a positive faith—oh, not necesarily Christian but a constructive ethic—without the erosions of self pity or bitterness ... I think you are now ready to read Elio Vittorini.'

'What time will my brother be here?'

'Within an hour, very likely. Have something to eat now.'

* * *

South Pool. It would be nice down there now. May. Hawthorn blossom turning pink and dropping into the water. Too early for dragonflies.

They had rowed into a backwater to watch them, and moored among the drooping overhanging branches of trees. She had taken her sketch book to catch up on some holiday work.

'Tessie' (this was Sister Theresa) 'says I haven't nearly enough in my file. Because I'm lazy. The ugly bitch. Do you think I'll get "O" level? I can't see it.' Sitting in the stern she began to draw him leaning on the shipped oars. 'Why don't you take your shirt off? I want a lot of muscles and things.'

'Because I shall get burnt. My back's bad enough already. It's all right for you in the shade.'

'Change over then. I adore the sun. Lovely, gorgeous, burning sun. I should like to go to Italy, wouldn't you? Tessie's been there. She did Florence.'

'Good for Florence.'

'Sit still. Don't keep shifting about, I can't get you. You can read your book ...' The lapping of water under the thin hull. 'Do you like this bikini I got in Salcombe? It's very chic.'

'A waste of money. I don't know why you bother. You've got nothing to put in it.'

'I've gone brown already, I think. I've got white bands to prove it. You're *terribly* brown. Except for the peely bits. I won't put them in ... Do you know, you've got *massive* arm muscles. What's that from—cricket?'

'No, rowing. I'm in the college eight.'

'Oh, bugger! I've done it wrong.'

*   *   *

Left alone she stared at the electric fire and thence to the softly lit corners of the room filled with moving green oblong shapes occasioned by it, because of the accommodation of her retinae. An optical illusion.

But her mother had not been one. Nor a delusion? She had been as real as the typewriter still sitting there on its table with the paper curled in it. Pippa got up and examined it, to see if anything was written there. It was blank. There had been no one then. It was all imagination. Like the guitar and the children. And Vincente? How could that be? She had felt his weight. Was that nothing? A fantasy? Was imagination more concrete than tissue? Raf and his whirling bits of electricity. Patterns and kaleidoscopes. How far then was anything material, anything at all? This book she had in her hand, if she looked at it under Raf's microscope the printed word would disappear into a primeval forest of fibres. What then would happen to all the ideas, the author's communication, his voice—

would they not exist? Death and annihilation to them, never to return? Were they not both material and immaterial, those signs on the paper. The palace at Donnafugata, and the people in it, existed through Lampedusa's invention; were they any the less material than the paper it was written on? Angelica, surprised among the cobwebs, would go on whispering 'No, Tancredi, no!' surely? They lived, just as Leonardo's Gioconda lived. She had come to the point of doubting the very nature of reality, the existence of anything whatever absolute. Everything surely was relative, dependent upon something else? Why then shouldn't her mother live and speak to her, Tom play his guitar, she and Nicholas continue to gambol, ten years younger, in a lake they had never visited? She was confused; but the images were getting clearer.

Raffaele returned and presently Enrico brought in supper on a tray. The Count took nothing—presumably he'd had dinner alone—but sat and watched her from a distance, too well bred to fuss, but gravely considerate as always nonetheless, clicking his fingers to Enrico the moment she had finished her plate. On the outer edge of the muted lights his grey hair was just a steely gleam, unobtrusive, yet she was tensely conscious of him. The birthmark on his wrist, hidden by his shirt cuff, seemed to scream at her. She wanted to get up and verify that it was still there, she hadn't imagined it. (Faustus as well as Prospero?—it couldn't be. Could it?) What made the next half hour so tautly unbearable was that she couldn't mention Nicholas; she had to sit there and let him have his surprise, for which he had worked so earnestly. It was obviously going to give him pleasure. From time to time he stole a complacent glance at her, reminding her of Uncle Barney. That knowing mixture of affection and anticipation, that was how he used to look at them on Christmas Eve, with the presents still in the back of the old Wolseley. They had to pretend they didn't know. And each time for them was the aching fear that perhaps this year he hadn't brought anything, this year he had decided they were now too grown up—it was to be money instead. Money wasn't the same. And so they sat and waited (as she was waiting now) she and Nicky, and played games, and looked at each other and made secret sign language, and agonized. At least when she was seven and Nicky eleven they had agonized, together. Three years later it was only she. Nicky, having broken through the barrier of adolescence, was a man of the world. Home for the holidays, he tortured her known fear of heights, on the roof, smiling as he felt for the beating of her heart. That Christmas and thereafter from Uncle Barney, until his death, it was only money, not the heavenly grocery box. These two events—the roof and the abrogation of Santa Claus—marked the end of her childhood. Now, in the same way, she had to pretend for Uncle Raf. She didn't know about his present. And there was always the possibility it was a myth anyway ...

She heard the car draw up on the gravel.

Raffaele looked up—'Please excuse me, my dear'—and went out. Pippa threw off her eiderdown and searched around for her shoes. She felt inadequate in her nylon feet, vulnerable, smaller than she should have been. Somebody had taken them away. She was still looking for them irritably when d'Anza returned, a long time later it seemed, and fidgeted in the doorway, tall, spare and pleased with himself.

'My dear Pippina' (the name was a smile), 'will you prepare yourself for something unexpected, a little shock maybe, but enjoyable I think. Do not look so worried. Sit down, child. There is nothing to worry about.... It is your brother, Nicholas ...'

He was already standing behind the Count. A Maxwell Reed suit she recognized, the striped shirt he had worn that evening of his homecoming, when they had later gone out together and been taken for lovers by her friend the head waiter, which had made her laugh, but not Nicky, the old sobersides. It was all in the wardrobe at home, or on the other side of the Atlantic. Oh, God, it was like her mother. He was not really there. This was a delusion too. Nothing was real. Nothing, nothing!

'Hullo, Pippy,' he said quietly. 'What have you been doing with yourself?' A casual remark, like her mother's.

A pause, tottering on her shoeless feet, then she rushed into his arms. He was solid. His jacket smelt of the cleaners', and beneath it of travel, trains, cigarette smoke and male sweat. He was real. She heard herself sob his name with relief as she closed her eyes and shuddered as though she were suddenly cold. She couldn't stop. Convulsions of shivering.

*   *   *

The long walk home from Frogmore, where they'd got off the Dartmouth bus.

'It's simply *miles* to the cottage, Nick. I wish I could have a piggy-back.'

'I'm not going to hump a perfectly healthy thirteen-year-old, if that's what you're asking. Use your long legs.'

'I'm using them. And they ache.' The hill an agony, then the down gradient. 'Wasn't it a super film?'

'It was all right.'

'I think it was great ... When Jed asked her to marry him, and she said no. Because of the others ... I cried a bit.'

'I know.'

'You couldn't see.'

'During the bright moments. Wet streaks down your face. You sat there looking wide-eyed and glum.'

'I'm sorry.'

'And rather sweet really.'

'Is that why you bought me the Neapolitan tub?'

'To take your mind off it, yes ... What's that sickly smell?'

'Wild honeysuckle. It's everywhere. Isn't it *gorgeous*? And look at that moon!'

'We're going to have a storm. It's too heavy, and close. I thought I heard a rumble. Did you?'

'Oh God, I hope not. I hate storms. I shan't sleep ... I wish Mummy was here. Chasing back to London just because of that board meeting or whatever. It's no holiday for her ... Yes, *that* was lightning just then! Come on, we'd better step it out. Oh, hell, I hope it's not going to be a bad one. I shall come in with you if it is.'

'You'd better not.'

* * *

He was real. As they sat in the *ristorante* gardens by the boats drinking *espresso* froth which went by the name of coffee but which tasted like burnt rusks she kept coming back to this obvious fact. He tapped the ash of his cigarette into a thick glass object which purported to come from Venice and glinted in the hot sun almost as dazzlingly as the lake. They both wore dark glasses bought at the kiosk. He was in a casual shirt, open neck, light trousers—a typically English professional class mid-roader; he couldn't have been anything else. Earnestly and safely dressed, according to majority tastes, even on holiday. Real enough.

'This is all you needed, you know.' He indicated the café, the crowds, the sun winking on the spent glasses with red and green straws, the sparrows helping themselves to crumbs on the next table. 'All you wanted was to get away from that place for a while. I don't know why you didn't. You should have walked out.'

'I couldn't,' she told him. 'There was always some obstacle. I felt he was keeping me there.'

'All your imagination, Pippa.'

All her imagination. It had to be, of course. She had told him everything—almost everything, not the Vincente visits—and he had listened to her gravely until the small hours, knitting his brows sometimes and looking at her curiously. Then he'd told her to go to bed. And obediently she'd found it easy to sleep. Now for the first time in ten days she was not on the island but looking back at it from the point from which she'd first seen it. They had come across the causeway and wandered, like any other tourists, through the bric-à-brac shops of the little town, buying unneeded postcards and souvenirs, and were now sitting on wicker chairs at a glass-topped table, not opposite each other but adjacent so that they could watch the boats.

'He frightens me, Nicky ... He didn't at first. He was so kind. And wise, I thought. Like some old guru. Remote and pacific and kind. A mystic. You know, really gentle. But then I began to wonder ... There's something horribly odd about him.'

'Oh, nonsense!' She couldn't see his expression for the tinted glasses, only that they were directed at her steadily. 'What do you mean—"odd"?'

'I don't know ... He had a wardrobe of clothes, all my size.'

'Oh, that sort of odd. Yes, I think he might be. We'll get you home as soon as possible.'

'No, you still don't understand. God, do try! I was never really scared of *him*—until now, since you've come. Now I am. That's what I mean by odd. He once promised no harm would come to me in his house as long as he lived. I believed him ... It was the other things. Not Raffaele. They sort of revolved around him but he was still, in the centre. A pivot. He was reliable. I felt quite confident. Even when he took those stupid photos. But I wasn't confident about the other things.' She meant the children and the guitar playing, but she couldn't bring herself to name them.

Nicholas was silent for quite a long time. Then he said: 'Pippy, it was your imagination,' in the same tone that he'd once said, 'You've got to grow up.'

She took another cigarette from his packet, her fingers unsteady. It had to be said. 'I saw Mummy, I tell you. She spoke. In character. You know, in that maddeningly superior way. As though she was aware that one was a moron but was resigned to it. She always made me feel so inadequate.'

'Pippy, come off it!' His voice quiet and pained. Middle tenor.

'She was there. I saw here ... And I saw us too. Swimming in Lannacombe Bay. You remember that day we dived for lobsters, and I gashed my leg and you carried me up the beach to the car?' And all the time, when she wasn't worrying about the blood, she'd thought how nice it was to be carried, limp against his wet chest.

Nicholas arranged the things on the table in a neat symmetrical pattern, ashtray in the centre. 'Listen, Pippy, you've got to understand something. Don't get mad and don't be scared—it's all right. But you ought to know. You've got to face up to it. I've been talking to Dr Rossano. He thinks it may be your concussion. That's what's causing the hallucinations.'

'I know. I suggested that.'

'Well, then ... They will pass. It will get better.'

She blew a stream of smoke. 'Or worse. There could be more. They could get more frequent.

'No, he thinks not.'

She searched his face, what she could see of it against the sunlight, trying to read comfort, unsure as to his sincerity. You kept unpleasant things from people you loved. 'Nicky,' she said, 'I'm afraid still. I've thought all that out ... I don't want to go mad.'

'No one's going mad, darling. Don't be stupid.'

'Or blackouts. Or delusions. Or anything. I just want to be normal.'

Nicholas stretched out his hand, covered hers briefly, just long enough to feel the small bones of her knuckles, then withdrew it and took out his pocketbook. He seemed to be totting up expenses. 'You are ... Anyway, I'm here now. So you can relax. We'll go home soon.'

'When?' She watched a man on a pair of steps changing spent fairy light bulbs on one of the trees. It was all too beautiful to leave.

'Soon. When you're fit. I've got a week's leave of absence to sort things out. I must say Acetylan were very good about it.'

'We could go to Verona. I haven't been there. Or to Padua.' Not to Asolo, she thought suddenly. Raf had said she must go to Asolo before she left. Before she passed. What was there in Asolo? Another Pippa?

The man in the tree was enveloped in red blossom. Petals and curled leaves, twigs, came sprinkling down.

'We ought to start walking back,' he decided. He caught the waitress's attention and paid the bill, then stood up. Pippa followed.

'Buy me one of those,' she pleaded at a stall selling coloured spiky straw hats with dangling spun-glass ornaments like magnified plankton. She wanted the right to be silly. It was a barricade against darkness. Nicholas, without demur, put his hand in his pocket and sorted through his grubby lire. The hat was only cheap. The stall woman, nodding with approving smiles, placed it on her head for her carefully. It was vulgar and fun. A group of *capelloni*—not the youths who had followed her before—watched the movement of her brief shorts from a vantage point of a table under an arch, but she took Nicky's arm and walked past them, rendering them silent. No one this time tried to crowd her.

They crossed the road, separated again now the need for protection was over, and made their way along the causeway. At the lodge gate they rang the bell and waited. They rang again. Two small boys, bold as sparrows, glided round them on bicycles with cardboard rattles in the spokes, doing figures of eight at alarming angles. At the third press of the bell-push Marco appeared. He looked more alarmed than surly, not as neat as he usually was. He opened the gate and stood back, his expression blank but wide-eyed, as though he had just received some shock. He mumbled something inaudible. Then he repeated it.

'Egli è morte,' he said, 'il conte!'

Pippa stared at him. She couldn't believe it. He must have said something else.

'The Count, he is dead. Dr Rossano, he is up there now.'

'How?' All sorts of ideas came crowding into her mind, all impossible. He had committed suicide, shot himself, collapsed on the stairs. All discarded novels.

'Is dead the Count. Is all I know!' The man was himself again, hostile and truculent. 'You see for yourself.'

Leaving him they began to walk quickly up the slope. When they had gone a few steps he called out, to their backs, 'He is dead from the heart!' It had a chilling effect, the ambiguity of the phrase in his thick accent; something missing about it, like a bar of music unfixed in key because it lacked the deciding note. Did he mean that Raffaele was broken hearted? Or just that he'd had a heart attack? God, it couldn't have been suicide after all, could it? Something to do with her? Somehow she had killed him. It couldn't be, could it?

Neither she nor Nicholas spoke as they raced up the cobbled rampart leading to the terrace and the front of the house. It seemed incongruous that the day should be full of hot sunshine, still beneficent even now with the evening coming on and the shadows thrusting out across the lake towards them from the opposite side. The myrtles, as she passed them, rattled dry and aromatic, full of hover flies. The room with the clocks was open and they used this as a short cut, skirting the steps of the main entrance. Everything buzzed, swung, flashed, clicked and chattered in the silence, as it had done on that first day. The Count was dead, but the clocks were still alive, and would remain so, somehow charged with a bit of his spirit, until they ran down, one by one; unless somebody remembered to wind them. Was that a fanciful idea? She was being neurotic.

In the hall Giulia in tears bundled past them, screwing up her parchment face and her head-kerchief, donned hastily for the last rites, both together in her peasant grief, clawing the material across her mouth as though she was going to vomit. Carla and another servant followed her. The mahogany door of the study opened and Rossano came out to meet them. He led them away from it.

'You have heard.' He understood. '*Il conte Raffaele è deceduto!*' Moved, he said it to himself rather than to them. Then he went on, in English: 'He had collapsed at his desk. Enrico found him. It was almost certainly a heart attack. He'd had many before. I attended him for the last year. I have given instructions for the police to be informed, of course—this is usual—but their surgeon will undoubtedly confirm my finding for the certificate. Everything will be taken care of. You need not worry.'

Pippa continued to feel stunned. She leant against her brother.

'Poor Raf!' she murmured. 'I can't believe it.'

'Indeed he was my friend too.'

'May I see him?' Why had she said that? She was appalled by death; she'd been sickened by her mother's burial. Raffaele's husk would be merely obscene, or even funny perhaps, as grotesquely ridiculous as a puppet with the strings cut. She had no morbid wish to carry his death mask about in her memory like some old ghoul from Coronation Street, like Auntie Mavis, like Mrs Morgan from next door, like Giulia.

'The priest is with him. Padre Mazzola. It is better to leave them alone together.' Even Rossano, who struck her as being a rational man, a scientist, still fairly young in middle age, spoke as though d'Anza had immortality. Not just a pathetic husk? It was his Catholic indoctrination.

'I should like to see him.'

Rossano opened the double doors, led them into the brown room. It smelt untypically of flowers; there had never been flowers in this study before. Enrico was there, on guard before a shape stretched out on the long table which had been cleared of books and ornaments and now covered with a sheet. Two candles, guttering as they entered, burned at head and foot. Enrico turned. The priest, standing at the other end, reading to himself, looked up, frowned at the impropriety of Pippa's bare arms and legs, her loose uncovered hair. She was still carrying in her hand the garish straw hat dangling with gewgaws. Under the man's scrutiny she felt she had to put it on, and did so, but the frivolities swung and jingled round her face. She knew she looked cheap. And silly.

Rossano, speaking first to the priest, drew back one end of the sheet carefully and Pippa looked down at a handsome face, composed and comparatively unlined. If it hadn't been for the grey hair, thick against the glassy surface of the walnut veneer, she might have taken him for Vincente. Death had rewarded him with an age somewhere in between. She stood motionless for a while, staring. Raf, she said inwardly, I'm sorry if it was me. I'm sorry. I'm sorry.

'Thank you,' she said aloud, and turned away.

* * *

Standing at that revolting sink of Tom's she'd already many times furnished the cottage in her imagination. Ercol furniture in the big living-room downstairs which they would make by knocking out the dividing wall. Their bedroom would be the one overlooking the creek. Nick, whenever he came, could have the small one facing the lane. And the landing room over the stairs would do for the baby. Until he began to walk. Then they'd have to build on. Planning permission. You had to think ahead. Or perhaps the old couple next door would be gone by then....

*   *   *

Routine having been broken by Raffaele's death, everything was chaotic at the villa that evening. A meal of sorts eventually arrived in the small dining-room where they were left to look after themselves, she and Nicholas alone and opposite each other. She wore the dress which had been chosen for her that first evening. She didn't know why. An unconscious tribute? They didn't talk much. Afterwards she went upstairs to pack her few things. They were pathetically austere, almost unfamiliar, reminding her of another life. The jeans had been washed and neatly darned, the leather jacket sponged free of oil and road grime. She wondered whether, before she went, it would be possible to extract the misleading photographs from the desk downstairs in the room where Raf lay guarded by his watchdog. Not that it really mattered. Tomorrow they would catch the train to Milan, Nicholas going on south, herself for London. The scandal of the English *civetta* with the bare legs, young enough to be the old man's granddaughter but who had evidently become his mistress, would be remembered only by Giulia and Padre Mazzola.

But later that evening Nicholas called for her to come down. The police had arrived with their own doctor and Rossano again. She was glad that Inspector Maiello appeared to be in charge.

'I understand from Signor Rowantree, your brother,' he inclined his head, 'that you wish to return to England. I think I must ask you to remain at least for another day. No, no—there is not difficulty. Everything is in order. The death was from natural cause. This we confirm. But there is something for you to hear. It will be good, this I promise. Tomorrow I will return in the morning. The funeral is for the day after, at the church of Santa Maria Maggiore in Pianezze. You will attend? It would be nice—' The word 'gesture' escaped him, but she nodded her understanding, then glanced at Nicholas. Surely she could find something sombre to wear in the cupboard upstairs, or Carla would lend her her black.

She lay a little restless that night, smoking too much, listening to the crickets, wondering if Enrico were still on guard downstairs. She imagined him in his old uniform, corporal in olive drill, Veronese Light Infantry, stiffly remembering Sidi Omar, like some old Victorian Academy picture.... 'Semper Fidelis' ... About two o'clock a dog began to howl and kept it up pitifully. It was Iago. Mourning for the Count? Anyway she couldn't stand it, it was too unearthly. Something would have to be done about it. She got up and went to look for Nicholas. The room next to hers, which for one night had been fixed up for Carla, was now empty again. Too empty. She tapped on her brother's door, farther down the corridor.

'Nicky! You awake?... Nicky!' She thought how absurd these stage whispers sounded in the night, but the door was thick and he probably couldn't hear her, so she pushed it open and spoke again. A bedside lamp came on. Nicholas was half sitting up, squinting at his watch, eyes screwed up against the light.

'What's up?'

'Iago's howling—the dog. I don't know where it is. Come into the room next to me, Nicky. Please! It's all made up. If you don't fancy Carla's sheets you can bring your own.'

I have been here before, some part of her mind said. She even knew exactly what he was going to say in reply.

'Oh, God, Pippy, go back to bed! Go to sleep. Do you know what time it is? Nearly time to get up.' The two voices echoed, not quite in unison; the one his, the other *déjà vu*. It was a trick of memory, of course. It was the night of the walk back from Frogmore. *Days of Our Eden*. The thunderstorm, revolving round the estuary, had broken at last. Nicky, can I come in with you? It's the lightning. It does something to me, makes my tummy sour. *Oh, God, Pippy, go back to bed, girl!* It's the lightning, Nicky; I can't stand it. I wish Mummy hadn't gone back to London. She used to give me something. *Well, now you're here, go to sleep!* I can't. The bed isn't very big, is it? And you're hot. Do we need that quilt thing on? *Go to sleep, Pipistrelle. Do you know what time it is? Nearly time to get up.* I'm hot too now. All sweaty. Do you think it would be all right if I took my nightie off?

'Never mind,' Pippa said, and turned away. 'I can put up with the howling. No, it doesn't matter. I think it's stopped now anyway ... Sorry I disturbed you. Night!'

* * *

Oh, God, they're all impossible. Yes, that's Susan. She has a lisp which some people find amusing. She was once selected to present a

bouquet to Mr Heath and she's never got over it....
   The one next to her is Sarah. Her boyfriend tied her up and scratched his initials on the top of her leg with a pin. So she says. She showed me. Probably did it herself. Why are we talking about them? Aren't you glad to see me?... Oh, Christ, I shall be happy when I leave! Three more years!...

*   *   *

Ispettore Maiello returned next morning as he promised. He brought with him Dr Rossano and another man whom he introduced as Avocato Luigi Masi, the Count's family lawyer, who had travelled up from Milan. They met in the drawing-room. Enrico brought coffee and vermouth. It seemed to be a formal occasion. The solicitor wore his professional black with a shoestring tie.
   'This is going to come as a great surprise to you,' Rossano warned them. 'You had better sit down, Signor Rowantree. If you would be so kind,' he added. There was a faint note of deference in his voice which was impossible to analyse. Ironical? Or genuine?
   Her brother continued to stand behind the tall-backed carved chair where Pippa was already seated.
   Avocato Masi put on his glasses. He laid spread out on the table a document which crackled when he unfolded it from its pink ribbon. 'Do I understand you know nothing of this?' he inquired, Rossano translating.
   'Nothing.'
   'So the Count insisted when he came to see me last week. I had thought perhaps he was exaggerating. Or being naïve—he was at heart a very simple man. But as you assure me you knew nothing of what was in his mind we must accept the truth of that. It will certainly, therefore, as Dr Rossano says, come as a pleasant surprise to you....'
   He had left her something in his will, another of his little gifts; it flashed upon her before Rossano had finished repeating it. I will bring you back a little something from Milan. This was it. Money for clothes. For services rendered, Lawyer Masi was thinking behind those pebble glasses ... Or the Correggio! Could it be? She'd much rather have that. Waiting, she felt confused, excited and not very happy.
   'It is a complicated testament as far as administrative details are

concerned.' Everything was slowed down by the translation process. It was maddening. 'I will not elaborate upon them. But to put it concisely ... in effect, Mr Rowantree, you and your sister are the sole residual legatees ... after some bequests to the servants and elsewhere ... of the entire estate....'

Pippa sat uncomprehending in the hard upright chair. She felt it move as Nicky's hands gripped the back of it. Masi had finished speaking. It seemed to be all.

'This is ridiculous,' she heard Nicholas say.

Pippa continued to sit there, waiting for an explanation. When none came she said: 'What does it mean?'

'It means simply that, with the exception of a few thousand pounds, everything comes to you two. The villa, its contents, the estate, the island, the woods at Ledro, the vineyards at Brecchio and Negrar, the business—everything is yours to be divided and held equally.'

It was absurd, grotesque, horrifying. Almost obscene in its unnaturalness.

'It can't be.' She refused to believe it. 'It's not possible.'

'On the contrary, it is perfectly in order ... Drawn up by me, ratified and witnessed.'

'He must have been mad. He knew nothing about us. Why didn't you persuade him against it?'

Lawyer Masi shrugged. 'It is not for me to dissuade my clients... especially those of the order of Count Raffaele Alessandro d'Anza ... He seemed to know what he was doing ... He was a grown man. It was his affair.' He looked away from her while Rossano went over it. 'You should be delighted. You will be very comfortably off. As the Count was. The estate runs itself. My advice, if you need it, would be to keep on all the staff at Negrar and Brecchio. There is a very good manager there ... If you wish me to continue to act for you, as I did for the late Count, I shall be most happy to do so.'

Nicholas's hands had come down from the chair back to her shoulders, gripping them.

'But his family—' she protested. His death coming so soon after their arrival and the extraordinary will, wouldn't everyone be interested in that? The police? She looked at Maiello. He was interested, but inscrutable. He was studying her; that was all.

'He had no family, Miss Rowantree. A distant cousin was the last. He died recently in Los Angeles. I suppose there might be claims from *his* heirs. But he was a wealthy man, long domiciled in

America. No, it is unlikely that they would contest.'

Pippa stared at him. 'But Vincente,' she said. 'There is a son, Vincente.'

The lawyer knitted his brows, questioning Rossano to see if he'd got the translation right.

'There *was* a son, Vincente,' he corrected. 'He was killed several years ago in a plane crash, taking off for Amsterdam, I think, or New York.'

* * *

... Hullo, darling, you've been a long time. I wish you wouldn't leave your things hanging up all over the bathroom....

... Your name is Pippa. I have learnt it since this morning. You are very pretty. The present is all that matters, not tedious explanations, justifications. *This* is all that matters....

... Una volta una povera ragazzina di nome la Cenerentola....

... Once upon a time there was this little girl who didn't like school, and she used to wander about in the attics in her nightie reading Henry James and all fifteen volumes of Proust, because I forgot to tell you she was really very well educated. And one day up there she met Lewis Carroll with his camera. And he said: 'You are very beautiful. I shall write a best seller about you and call it *Lolita*....'

* * *

They attended the funeral.

A requiem Mass with full religious and military honours. Black drapes, plain vestments. Soloists, chorus, orchestra, wind band. *Tuba mirum* from Verdi. The little gold-and-white church packed. Black, black everywhere. The congregation (audience?) in their civic regalia, wearing orders. *Cavalieri* and *commendatori*. A splash of red from a colonel. Members of the local *comuno* looking stiff. Someone from the *Camera dei Deputati* who carried a briefcase and kept consulting his watch. Solemn, solemn candles. Fortissimo singing like the edge of a knife. 'Death in Pianezze.'

Afterwards the burial service in a gusty geometrical cemetery with rocketing cypresses and marble white-clothed angels (clothing what?). True to the theatricality of the occasion it rained, and everyone put up umbrellas.

As soon as it was over Pippa had wanted to go home, to England; but Nicholas had insisted that they should stay for at least a few days, to see things started in the way of organization. Besides, to leave at once might be construed as suspicious; Maiello, they felt, was still watching. The running of the place, as it turned out, hardly needed further organization. Lawyer Masi had explained everything to the staff and they accepted the situation, apparently without resentment. When Pippa, testing the ground apprehensively, gave an order about flowers it was obeyed, not immediately, it is true, but satisfactorily to the letter. It was a peculiar experience. The young *contessa*. She noticed that among themselves—not to his face—the servants called Nicholas *Sua Signoria*. Ironically, she imagined.

They walked together on the upper terrace. It was the next day. 'One of the first things I am going to do,' she declared, 'is to have those electric fences taken down. Horrible! Open up everything to the public. Up as far as here anyway.' She swept her hand across the foreground. 'We might even invite them inside. Say once a week for a start. I want to see some faces about.' Already she was talking as though she was established here, and was going to remain.

'You'll get to see plenty of people,' Nicholas said morosely, looking at her. 'When they find out. Journalists, touts, quacks. They won't leave you alone when they see you.'

* * *

'Who is that greaser you're going around with, Pip? I don't care for the look of him much.'

Buzz Gregory? Oh, he's all right.

'What exactly do you see in him?'

He's got a super six-fifty.

'That's what I mean. We don't want you all smashed up.'

Oh, knickers!

'You're only sixteen, Pippy. Mother and I think you ought to stay in more.'

She put you up to saying that.

'No, it's true. You didn't do very well in your "O" levels, did you? You've got all that time to catch up.'

(*Form Mistress's Report*: Philippa is basically a very intelligent and sensitive girl who must nevertheless discipline herself to the needs of academic study. *Sister Clare Hell-Cat.*)

'And let's face it, what has this Buzz Gregory got to offer you?'

A way out of here. We can get to the coast in seventy minutes.

'He's immature, Pip. He's only a kid inside. He'll be tinkering with that motor-bike long after he's my age. Or flying model aeroplanes or something. You're years older than he is.'

Great! Perhaps I can teach him a couple of things.

'Pip, you haven't—'

Oh, God, if you could see your face!... No, darling, not yet. He's a bit slow. Except on his bike.

Later, walking down one of the corridors. 'We could do with some more lights here, don't you think, Nick? Concealed wall lights up there, I fancy. I don't much like that dangly thing in the middle. It looks as though it's been specially dropped from the flies....

Why should I write about life? Life, darling Pipit, is some sardonic old magician's idea of a joke—grotesque and beautiful and tragic and absurd all at once. Listen (are you lying comfortably?)—Johann Wolfgang Goethe, the personification of the great Romantics whom he fathered, more handsome even than Byron, loftier than Hugo; Goethe at seventy, philosopher and author of *Faust*, fell in love with a child of seventeen. It was perhaps the profoundest experience of his life. He would have married her, but not unnaturally her parents refused. It broke the old man's heart and noble spirit. Laugh that one off ... Have we set the alarm clock?

On another occasion, 'I don't see why we can't have more bathrooms, do you? One built in for each of the main bedrooms—we could convert the dressing rooms. And at least a shower in the others. It shouldn't be difficult.'

As the next few days passed it seemed that Pippa, who had originally been so anxious to leave, grew more reluctant to do so as her interests and enthusiasm increased, while Nicholas, at first clearly excited by their good luck, became slowly more withdrawn. The effect of the place, or the responsibility perhaps, on him was strange. He grew more and more grim, edgy, quick-tempered. He telephoned Rome to clear up matters there and was infuriated when there were delays through the departments, caused partly by a bad line and partly by his refusal, or inability, to speak in anything but English. When she offered to help he was cutting. She might have a better command of the language (thanks to Rocky's Genoese conversation lessons) but he thought he had a better knowledge of law, which was what was wanted at the moment and more to the point. Perhaps he was just jealous of her ease of movement into this new situation (though after all she'd been here long enough to get acquainted with it more) but he watched her relationship with the staff critically. Carla came to her willingly; Giulia had to be flattered (one visit to the kitchen, full of praise, and then left alone to mature in a culture of self-confidence); Enrico was impossible, he took orders from no one but retired to his parlour and his grief. Thinking that perhaps this was because he was used to a man's command, Nicholas stepped in, unsuccessfully. The old man took orders from no one. All these things clearly irritated Nicholas. Little things. Once the lights went out. The power supply had failed; the engineers of the *municipo* were on strike. D'Anza had said this sometimes happened. There were plenty of candles, which made the rooms look even more romantic, and bigger and eerier, but Nicholas must needs search the basement with Marco for oil lamps. By the time they were cleaned, trimmed and filled with paraffin the lights came on again. This also piqued him. He liked his organization to be successful always.

But one result of this expedition was that he discovered the black museum—for some reason she hadn't mentioned it; another fact which irked him when he found out.

'You mean you know about that collection? You've seen it?'

'Oh, God, I've seen everything. More than that. But you won't believe me. Nobody will ... Yes, we'll get rid of it. Block it up, dump them all in the lake or something.'

He laughed wryly. 'Open it to your public. Make them pay extra. It might be profitable ... That's not a bad idea! Tie it in with the secret panel in your room. Conduct them through in small groups, organized tour with a guide like all the best places.'

He sounded just then so much like Tom. Her heart syncopated as she glanced across at him, rolling down his shirt sleeves. He even *looked* like Tom for a moment, except that he was clean shaven, a little slighter in build. She didn't want anyone or anything to remind her of Tom. All that was in a different life, years ago, a previous incarnation. She had enough to cope with in this new one.

'I'm going to invite Dr Rossano over to dinner,' she said. 'And his wife. He also has a teen-age daughter. I want to meet people. You think of somebody too.'

'Director of the Lombardy Bank. We need an immediate loan. We've got to pay everybody.'

'Avocato Masi said we could have something on probate. You take him up on that. That's your province.'

It was then that they heard the children's voices.

Two of them, a boy and a girl, laughing. Footsteps running down the corridor outside, towards them. Someone playing hide-and-seek. Laughter and protestations 'which were an invitation'. Silvery, breathless, charming. 'No, Paolo, no!' Quite clearly, just outside the door. A scandalized whisper; then muffled, deliciously, on an intake of breath: '*Ma non più, Paolo—no!*'

Pippa stared at her brother, but it was clear that he'd heard it too —which was what she was wondering. For a second he stared back at her, then whipped round, strode to the door and pulled it open. There was no one there. He stepped into the corridor, but it was empty and silent. Giulia crossing stolidly at the other end with an armful of sheets, that was all.

'You heard it,' Pippa said evenly when he returned. She hadn't moved. 'It wasn't a hallucination. It's not just me, I mean. You heard it too.'

Vindicated, she felt a great sense of relief which was akin to happiness. She was not going mad. She was sane. It was like the moment when the realism of Rossano's watch had discovered for her that she wasn't dead.

'Two of the servants,' Nicky decided. 'A couple you don't know about. It must have been.' He was a rationalist a law man, not prepared to admit of any other explanation. But Pippa didn't care; to her it came as a reprieve, like a new lease of life. She was no longer alone.

* * *

But where are we going to bury her, Nicky?
'I don't know. Does it matter?'
Somewhere where people won't dig her up by accident in years to come.
'There won't be anything left then, stupid.'
What about under the pear tree? That would be appropriate. She used to sit there and watch the sparrows....
Pippa standing with the stiff little bundle wrapped up in newspaper. The traffic noises beyond the small yard which served for garden, slightly muffled by the line of terrace houses. A radio disc jockey, loud with exuberant bonhomie, forcing the June evening.
I'll get the spade then, shall I?... Nicky, how much do you reckon you feel if you're only a cat? Pain, I mean?...
My brother is not really interested; he is listening to the jokes on the radio. But to me—I shall always remember this occasion. It will be branded into my memory. I am burying part of me out there, along with Dinah, in this black London soil. One day someone will dig it up, quite by accident. Here is a girl's heart. How odd—it is still living! You can feel it beating in your hands, quiescent like a captured pigeon.

* * *

The dinner next evening was not exactly successful, she thought. Rossano's daughter couldn't come, his wife spoke no English and so was cut off for the most part from Nicholas next to her; he remained aloof at the head of the table in the carved chair with the eagle, dispensing the wine, in a mood of distraction which gave him an air of superciliousness. He looked at Pippa from time to time when she smiled at something Rossano said, as though he thought she was enjoying herself too much. Perhaps he merely resented not being able to share it. He looked solemn, staring down the length of the table. Wine, she remembered, had the effect of making him become introspective.

'Ask them about—you know, that incident,' he said. 'Ask them if there are any more servants around. One named Paolo.'

But she frowned and shook her head. She didn't care about explanations, justifications. "The present is all that matters."

'Servants?' Rossano had caught most of it, looked smilingly puzzled.

'My brother thinks he has an explanation for my eccentricity. He believes the villa may be haunted.'

Rossano laughed. 'All places are haunted,' he said, 'by memories. But as you mean it, I think not ... Although it could well be—it has seen enough history.' He spoke to his wife in Italian, explaining the joke, and laughed again. 'As for the other thing, Miss Rowantree, eccentricity in beauty can be an asset.' He was being gallant, or facetious, she wasn't sure which. His wife began to speak rapidly in a deep animated voice, r's rolling like a kettle drum. He nodded and translated.

'The villa itself has had a history of eccentricity. It was like a retreat in the Count Raffaele's time, but earlier, before the war, there were some wild parties. So I'm told.'

'That was Vittoriale.'

'Perhaps. Gossip is vague. Of course there are rumours of unspeakable orgies during the Nazi occupation—there always are. Romantically exaggerated, I would think, and fostered by the extreme left.'

'Dr Rossano, you knew the Count as well as anyone. Why did he make us his heirs?'

The meal over, he accompanied her from the room.

'He was a great man, but he was a sentimentalist. He was affected by beauty. And he was always interested in the English. Once he advertised for a secretary; she had to be young, British and attractive. He meant no harm. He was an innocent. But it caused something of a scandal at the time. Ask Giulia.'

Nicholas was behind them.

She said: 'I can't help thinking it was something more than that, more complicated. He had something else at the back of his mind.'

'He liked young people, although he was inclined to be shy in their company. He evidently found you and your brother attractive. Generosity always gave him pleasure.'

That was true; yet it didn't satisfy her. 'There was some other reason. He had an unfathomable sense of humour. Somehow it was a joke.' Hitchcock's little joke. All that blood in the shower. Laugh that one off ... How well did he really love the British? Five years in captivity ... Cold and isolation ... Gabriele d'Annunzio was not a Fascist, he simply lived on into an unfortunate period of our history ... Our revels now are ended. These our actors, as I foretold you, were all spirits, and are melted into air, into thin air ... This is from Act IV, after the Masque. Credit will be given for close reference to the text.

'You must visit us next,' Mrs Rossano said. Even before the doctor translated, Pippa answered: '*Grazie*, Signora Rossano.'

* * *

... What d'you mean, I'm like a boy? I don't think I care for that much ...

The storm had passed inland, was now somewhere over Exeter, only an occasional flicker, a faint grumble.

Nicky, it's enormous! I didn't know it could grow like that! Is that because of me? It can't be. I'm not like a boy then, am I? ... Is it nice when I touch it? I *am* being gentle. Like that? Is that nice? Shall I go on? ... But isn't it supposed to be wicked? ...

... Tell me, you crazy girl, why it is that despite the fact I love you to distraction I can't write you satisfactory poetry. Tell me that! It should be pouring out in a bloody great gusher of oil. But with you I'm dry. I can turn out at a moment's notice a poem about Zillah's orange eyes, or kids' paintings seen from outside a school window, or an old man eating chips—but I can't write anything worth while about you. Nothing but rhetoric and sentimentality. Trivial. I'm suffering from an emotional blockage. Creative impotence. Isn't that a bitter cup for a writer? Can you understand that particular gall? No, of course you can't. Well, I'll tell you—you should be releasing in me great orgasms of spiritual energy. I ought to be writing you verses with the white-hot facility of Keats and Shakespeare and Hardy when they were in love with whatever girl or boy it was drove them to distraction ... And all you do is to make me despair. You make me doubt myself, my capacity. Because I know that if ever you were to leave me then it would come. Yards of immortal self-pity. And what's the good of that? Bugger you, you witch! ...

At school when she had to listen to all that stupid boasting about the fabulous men in their lives—the ski instructor at Davos who gave private lessons, the ride with Trevor into the New Forest and endless love among the bracken—she sat there and thought and kept silent. She could have said: 'You remember the bronzed brother of mine you all stared at? Well, I slept with him all one night when Mummy was away. It's something I've been longing to do for months. And it was beautiful. The comfort of it. I could have cried.'

Dumbfounded silly faces. Silent with horror, disbelief. Details, please, details—they would only be interested in details.

'What do you mean, you *played* together?'

Well, we loved each other without actually making love.

'Why not? If you were in bed?' (Suspicion. It was all a boast. Like Hans-Peter and Trevor and the pin scratcher.)

Well, have some sense. I didn't want a baby, did I? No, I know I'm not very well developed, but I'm thirteen, and you can. If you do it with your brother it comes out a monster. Sister Mercy said so. (All those limbless thalidomides in the sociology film. She would die if one was hers.) Besides, it was so nice to be with him, really with him, I went to sleep. The best part was waking up in the morning, before he did, and lying there and remembering it. The green light of leaves reflected on the ceiling. Then I got up and put on my nightie and made us both a cup of tea.

When I leave school I'm going to be his housekeeper. And let him make love to me if he wants to. Because he's the most super person and I adore him. Only I shall have to have something always to stop babies coming.

They wouldn't have believed any of that, not a word. So that term she talked of nothing but the picture *Days of Our Eden*.

* * *

They watched the departure of Rossano's car from the curve of the front steps, and then, almost before it had gone out of sight, all the twinkling lights of Pianezze suddenly went off, leaving only the stars and the aromatic wind in the pines. When they looked back they saw that the house lights had blacked out too. It was another power cut. Pippa drew the trailing silk lace wrap up over her shoulders and glanced at her brother who had been so uncharacteristically quiet all the evening. Now he seemed more cheerful.

'I'll find the lamps,' he said. Perhaps this vindication of his practical foresight renewed his confidence in himself as master of this foreign establishment, for he ran up the steps decisively, two at a stride. She lingered in the portico, unwilling to go in yet, listening to the watery cadence of a fountain which was barely visible below her, and the muffled barking somewhere of Iago. Of the two the dog was the only sound which had reality. Everything else was fantasy. Was she still only twenty? So much had happened in the last months, since Christmas, so many lifetimes; she felt twice that age. Perhaps when everything was settled, all the legal stuff, they could lock the place up, or leave it in the hands of a good steward, and go off somewhere. St-Tropez—how about that? Then she heard the nightingales again and she knew at once she would never be able to leave here. She was trapped like the sleeping princess in the Perrault story, surrounded by an impenetrable thicket of dead lovers for a hundred years ... Pippy, you've got to wake up. The answer was to open up the place. Flood it with life. And lights. A heated swimming pool. And people. Young people, not all these shades. Way-out parties. Gorgeous sun-burnt men and beautiful (well, not too beautiful) girls. Water sports on the lake, a red speed-boat, horse riding through the pines, music for dancing, ski-ing up there near Cortina. Holy Christ, it could be marvellous!... And talk—wonderful shimmering, *frivolous* talk. Not all those lectures about Michelangelo and the Florentine explosion; Verdi and Cavour and *Risorgimento* and the events of '45. Forget all that crap, Pip! Get out the wine, let it flow, dance all night. To hell with justifications, explanations, universal truths. The present is all that matters.

Through the wide windows she could see a luminous yellow globe, disembodied like a will-o'-the-wisp, moving about in the drawing-room. Presently it came to rest and was joined by another. Nicholas was flooding the place with lamps. Reluctantly she left the sighing and tinkling enchantment of the night outside and went in, to join her brother. She knew she was hooked on this particular drug, just as surely as Raffaele had been; and she understood now the meaning of that shelf of Italiana planted in her room. It represented the love–hate affairs of all those others who, at some time or another, had been subjugated by the country, enslaved to it, resented it and adored it, tried to break free and returned; permanent addiction.

'I'm going to bed,' she said, and took one of the lamps.

'We'd better just see that everything is switched off.'
'That's Marco's job.'
'Marco has left. You told him he could go. Remember?'
'At the end of the month, I said. Quite distinctly. Why has he gone already?'
'I don't know. It was your idea. Now we haven't got anybody. You don't think, do you?'
'Well then, Enrico can take charge.'
'He's senile. Impossible, we'll have to have somebody else.'
'All right, get somebody else then. You're the man. You see to it.'

Oh, Nicky, why are we quarrelling? This is how it always was. It always started like this, and then—wham! She could feel the tension between them building up like static electricity. 'Where's Carla? She's supposed to come and help me.'

'Undress? Can't you do that for yourself? You poor thing.'

She ignored him for a moment. They were walking through the Little Gallery, each carrying a light, making sure that everything was in order. Then she said coldly: 'To do my hair, I mean.'

It was when they reached the staircase that she thought of Raffaele. 'It consisted mainly of walking about from one room to another holding hands and carrying lamps ...' Well, they weren't holding hands.

'Nicky, you can remember Daddy, can't you? Before he left? What was he like?'

'Like? I don't know. Just a man. With a loud laugh and a big voice. That's all I remember.'

'Not reserved, and quiet? I thought he was ... How tall was he?'

'God, I don't know. Pretty tall. Why?'

She considered how she might tell him of her irrational conviction earlier, when she had first tried to puzzle it all out, that Raf was more than a stranger. But to put it into words it would have sounded such nonsense. A terribly childish fantasy. 'It doesn't matter,' she said. She hadn't the courage. A year or two ago they would have been close enough for her to try; she used to confide practically everything. Now they had drifted apart; there was a widening gap between them, a gulf of incommunicability. It was like another parting.

'Good night, Nicky,' she said and mounted the stairs, slowly because of the bouncing flame in the lamp, leaving him below. At the first turn she looked down at him, over the balustrade, and repeated: 'Don't let's quarrel.'

Then she went on up. She heard him moving about down below, securing bolts, shutters, talking to someone, Enrico presumably or Carla. She wondered whose job it was to wind the clocks.

'So then Henry Gibson, the great film director—'
Last time it was Henrik Ibsen.
'They were the same person. Brother to Virginia Woolf. You don't listen ... So then Henry Gibson took his hand-held camera to Italy and made a simple documentary about a confirmation. White lace and black peasants, sunlight and shadow, dust, a donkey-cart patient in the rip tide of traffic. All to an old and haunting theme tune. *Tre giorni son che Nina in letto se ne sta.* Attributed to Pergolesi, but which is in fact by Ciampi. (Advantage Mr Pleydell.) It was called *Pippa Passes*, and nobody liked it because it wasn't a proper story, just bits and pieces. But old man Gibson wasn't aware of it. He'd fallen in love with the country, not to mention the little girl and her proudest hour. Okay, print that!

She removed her earrings and laid them in the porcelain tray. She had closed the shutters but left her windows open to get a little air, and now, having undressed and returned from the expedition by lamplight to wash and brush her teeth (a novel adventure which by reason of the softer illumination rendered even that commonplace duty a romantic experience) she opened them again, despite the threat of visitations of moths lured from the honeysuckle. Though she had other, grander rooms to choose from now, she hadn't changed from this little princess boudoir, for which she had come to feel an affection. Sitting at her dressing-table she studied her face in the mirror. Eyes wide and abnormally dark, hair translucent, every strand glistening. Lamplight was more than becoming; it told lies. Darkness behind. Hands without a ring, cupped, supporting her chin. Thoughtful. A white nightdress. Demure. Except for the broderie anglaise——that was pretty. (Confirmation dress?) Tom, where are you and your bedtime stories? What are you doing at this moment? Making it sweatily with

Zillah? Or sitting aloof at some party, head bent, tuning a guitar for confidence? Where are you?

She clenched her teeth, covered her eyes with her hands. Thus she didn't see who it was who entered; she only heard the door. Looking up, expecting Carla, she saw in the mirror Nicholas holding his lamp aloft like a Flemish painting, soft luminous egg-yolk, white chimney, ruby glass base, pale earnest face, everything else fading into dark sepia, a picture without edges.

'Well?' She spoke to the mirror, without turning round.

'I thought you might like some help. Carla's not available.'

'You might have knocked.'

'Sorry. We never used to bother.'

'As kids. That was a long time ago.'

'Not so long, Pipistrelle.'

'Don't call me that!'

'Pippy, then.' He picked up the silver hairbrush. 'Like me to do it for you?'

She shrugged her indifference. She couldn't see his face from this close angle, only his hands. 'If you like. It always makes my arms ache.' Quickly she took out the last two or three grips and shook her hair free. She felt his hands at the nape of her neck, fingers lifting the long hair, then the gentle pull of the brush.

'You can do it harder than that,' she told him. The softness of his touch unnerved her slightly.

'Why were you such a little bitch tonight? At dinner, and after?... Yes, you were. You know very well what I mean. Putting on the grand manner for Rossano. And all that wide-eyed charm. Do you have to do that with every man you come into contact with? Can't you help it? You made him act like a fool, as though he suddenly felt young again. I suppose that's what you wanted.'

'Don't be stupid!'

'And another thing. I don't want this place filled with trippers. I've been thinking about that. Nor a lot of whacky houseparties for that matter. Let's enjoy it just as it is, by ourselves.'

Hair drawn back brom the brows, she watched her other face. 'Now you're tugging. Oh, leave me alone, Nicky! Why don't you go away?'

'Because you like it. You like having your hair done. You always did. When I do it.'

She closed her eyes.

* * *

... Nicky, let me go now. Please! I don't want to be a captive any longer. You're always the Indian, Nicky. It isn't fair ... You've tied me up too tight. It hurts ... Well, I know you're a Mohican, but you don't have to *be* so savage. Just pretend ... What are you doing to my hair? Be careful! Nicky, you're burning me! God, Nicky, no! Mummy will be in soon ...

A pinkness through her eyelids told her that the lights had come on again. Opening them, she looked at the room in the mirror, now brightly revealed and different, the lamp suddenly pale. Nicholas had stopped brushing, was resting one hand on her shoulder without really thinking about it, fingering the white lace decoration, anemones, as though he were absorbed in something else. He was miles away, perhaps back in the same childhood memory. The last of the Mohicans. Object: to frighten her and then go off laughing. When at last she managed to undo the knots and sought him out and thumped him he would hold her off with one hand, laugh again, and then buy her a Neapolitan tub.

She wanted to put her hand up to cover his, to tuck her chin against it, in a sudden yearning for affection, the need for both receiving it and giving it. We're all that we have now that Mummy's dead. If Mummy *is* dead. Until we start up a new life, each of us. So let's not quarrel ... But for some reason she didn't. Anyhow he'd only have walked away.

A dog barking below penetrated her consciousness slowly.

'It's Iago again,' she said. 'He's got shut in somewhere while we were doing the rounds.' She listened to the irritating sound for several minutes. 'One of us will have to go down and see.'

'Somebody will sort it out in a minute.' Nicholas sat on the edge of the bed behind her. 'You're too soft about that animal.'

Jealous of a dog too? Wasn't she allowed *anything*?

She got up. 'I'll have to go down and find out, do something.'

She searched for slippers, hooked them on, her mind full of strange rushing thoughts, impressions, like reflections of Underground train lights seen on the tunnel wall; disconnected flashes of illumination, each having meaning but not in their relationship, their juxtaposition. Raffaele, a petrol tanker, her mother, umbrellas in the rain; snaking electric cables, BAYSWATER, white tiles, advertisements, WAY OUT. She had the sensation that she was moving, moving towards something, no longer in control, racing forward in a dark capsule under London towards a predestined assignation, at some place and with some person she'd forgotten. Whom had she forgotten?

Nicholas watched her as she stood in the open doorway, listening, getting her direction. 'Want me to come with you?'

'It's *my* dog,' she answered. 'Go to bed.' She shook back her hair and set out.

All the same he followed her and they descended the staircase together, clicking on lights as they went. The carpet was thick under her feet, the night still mild for it wasn't until near dawn here in these parts that chill suddenly descended, and she felt cool and buoyant almost as though she were floating down in slow motion. She looked up at the chandelier festooned with new cobwebs, the pinkish-brown marble pilasters, the gilt-framed pictures (*Arturo Corbèra, all'assiedo di Antiocha?*) and was amazed once again to think that this was all hers. Or rather hers and Nicky's. It was fantastic, magnificent, unbelievable. She felt her brother take her hand, keeping pace with her but not in step, hers being a tripping broken rhythm, his a long stride, but both fitting the wide treads with the shallow risers. Gripping her fingers he pulled her faster until she was almost running headlong. Breathless, trying to hold on to the banister rail, she began to laugh.

'What's the hurry? He's my dog.'

His mouth twitched into a quirky smile as he looked at her. 'I just like to see your hair swinging out. You look a bit Renaissance. It's all this background. It goes.'

She slowed down, dragging at his hand, and her hair ceased to bounce and her clothing to mould itself Pre-Raphaelite fashion. They walked more sedately down the last flight and then suddenly, almost at the bottom, he picked her up and ran down the remaining steps and swung round with her. It was an expression of exuberance, outgrown and almost forgotten, which took her back about eight years. Before he'd started being a lawyer.

'Nicky!' she remonstrated. 'Honestly—Giulia will have a fit!'

Nevertheless she was glad his sober mood had been broken and he was more like his old self. This was how she remembered him.

He put her down carefully. One of her mules had come off in the gyration and lay on the stairs. She hopped now on one foot, trying to retrieve it.

'On the way back,' he said, gripping her wrists. 'You don't need slippers. Bare feet are good for you.' It made her dance like a trapped quail. This was more like the Nicholas she wanted to remember. Dominant, teasing, frightening, affectionate. It was like coming home. She kicked off the other slipper and surrendered. They were both laughing.

Iago barked again, hollow sounding and close.

'Down here,' she said and tugged herself away, running down the corridor towards the domestic block. Everywhere confirmed the impression that all the staff had gone to bed—lights out, no clatter, no radio, emptiness. At the end of the passage she stopped. The barking had ceased as unaccountably as it had begun, and though they both waited for a considerable time it was not repeated. 'He's settled down,' Pippa said, relieved.

'He'll start up again. Better go and look. He's probably in one of the basement store rooms.'

'I don't think we'd be able to hear that, all the way up there.'

'We'd better look all the same.'

He opened the brown door and darkness came up from below with the warm damp and the smell of garlic. There had been a basement area in the old house in Putney. Why had she suddenly just remembered that? It wasn't the same smell, for the damp which welled up from that cavern had been chill, conducive to the horned snails which nightly emerged from under a disused sink to forage in the dark and whose silvery paths continually meandered over the flagstones. This was different; warm, all wine lees and mushrooms.

Nicholas had already gone down ahead of her, having put on the light, and was waiting for her at the bottom, looking up. She descended the rough, slightly hollowed stone steps which cradled the light in concave pools round her bare feet. She stood listening.

'He's not down here. Iago!' She said it not very loudly.

But Nicholas drew her on. 'You never know,' he said.

Past the racks of wine bottles, straw husks, wooden vat, vinegary smell; past the domestic junk laid out like lots at an auction; stacked and dusty plates, flowered chamber pot, fish kettle; past the boiler; past the sweet smelling mushrooms. Something moved, squeaked, scuttled, was gone. A mouse. Not a rat. She didn't mind mice.

They had come to the black museum.

'He's not here,' she said.

She looked at the iron contraptions, casting shadows, more calmly with Nicholas beside her than before, yet still with distaste.

(That wire-mesh corselet hanging up on a nail—how was that supposed to work?)

'Nicky, let's get rid of all these things,' she said. 'Tomorrow! I hate them! They're obscene.' He said nothing, and when she glanced at him for some kind of affirmation she noticed he was smiling at her, amused she supposed by the escaped shiver in her voice. She had just realized that the untidy looking apparatus on the table, consisting of a dog collar and coils of insulated wire emerging from a black box must be for administering electric shocks. She wondered about the other electrode, like a brass ballpoint pen—where did that go? And what kind of person could want to amass such a pornographic collection of beastliness?

'He's not here,' she said again. 'Let's go.' And turned her back on it.

Nicholas, facing her, looked her directly in the eyes for a moment, still smiling; then he kissed her. For a second she was glad of his affection, which was comforting here in this macabre place; then immediately following she was filled with unease at the way he held her, hard against him with one arm round her back, the fingers of his other hand bunching the thin material of the nightdress in the small of her back. He had first kissed her lightly; now he thrust at her mouth, gripping her hard. She tried to push him away, levering her arms against his chest and twisting her head. His mouth now close to her ear, he whispered into it: 'Pipistrelle.'

He was teasing again, of course. The quiet sibilant, close into her ear, insinuated itself mockingly like an ironical caress. Twinkle, twinkle, little bat, how I wonder what you're at.

... Are you frightened, Pipistrelle? Close your eyes while I lead you through the churchyard. Don't open them until I say. I won't walk you into anything horrible ... I promise ... No, I mean it this time, honestly ...

'It's been a long day, Pippy,' he said. His voice no longer a whisper. Bright and hard. 'Let me take you up to bed.' An incorrigible tease and practical joker, when he wasn't being solemn.

'Don't be an idiot,' she said. In the old days, before she was a countess, it would have been: 'Stop arsing about Nick—do!' and they would both have laughed. It was a measure of the way things had changed.

'I mean it,' he said, and kissed her cheekbone. 'Come to bed with me.'

She didn't answer but concentrated on trying to force herself out of his lock. Suddenly she succeeded; it gave way and she was almost free, but he caught her by the wrists and held on to them with a grip which hurt her bones when she tugged.

'Don't be stupid!' she said. She was angry now. 'Let me go! Stop playing about!... Nicky!' As he held on she tried to bring up her knee—her usual defensive tactic in horseplay—but the long nightdress was inhibiting and bare feet were useless for kicking with. Nicholas grinned at her. It was maddening. Knowing dark eyes, teasing, cynical, warm, amused and exasperating. God, how well she remembered them! They'd broken her heart regularly every school holiday, making a recurring fool of her. She'd never learnt.

Looking past her, over her shoulder, he let her draw herself by her tugging farther into the room, then with the grin broadening he manoeuvred her sideways, tapping her ankle with the side of his shoe when she held firm, and digging his fingernails into her wrists until she winced. Back a little, further to one side. She didn't realize he was working towards an objective until he suddenly jerked her round, let go one of her hands and clamped it into a manacle which hung from a chain. She heard the locking click and knew that she had been tricked, yet tried desperately with her free hand to tug at the iron circlet, hoping somehow to get it off. Her attention distracted by this effort, she was unable to prevent him grasping it and forcing the other wrist into the second manacle. She was secured. Helpless.

Now he stood back and laughed, and laughed. How well she recollected that laugh too. Nicholas triumphant, rowing away from his small sister marooned on a rock ... She looked up at the chains, jerking at them, hoping something would give way, but they went up to a pulley block screwed securely to a beam.

'Night, Pippy!' he said, still laughing, and turned away towards the door in the arch.

'You're not going to leave me here?' she cried out. Not in this place, in the dark, all night. He couldn't! Not even Nicholas. He wasn't that sort of cruel. He always came back, when he'd had his laugh, to rescue her from the rock before the tide came up too far and she'd just about made up her mind to chance swimming for it. He wouldn't leave her there indefinitely.

He paused in the archway. 'Not if you're nice to me.'

'Oh, stop playing about! How do you get these things undone? Is there a key?'

He came back. 'On that bit of string,' he told her. And as she looked round for it he put his hand to another loop of chain and pulled it, once, twice. Her arms rose above her head, in front of her face, in two corresponding movements as the pulley clicked.

'Now you can't reach it,' he grinned.

'Oh, Nicky, please! Come on, do! You're the one who's got to grow up. Let me go!'

His eyes were serious now, rather large and fixed, a little wild.

'We've got to talk,' he said.

'What about?'

'This place.' His voice was hard again, but level. 'All this nonsense you've been talking. About ghosts. And headaches. And dear old Raffaele. It won't wash, Pipistrelle. You know it won't. You're not fooling anyone ... You're simply trying to get attention. What have you been up to, mm? I'll tell you. You're just a little gold-digger. Aren't you? That's it, isn't it? You're just a little tart. Basically.'

... A little Fascist whore. Tom could say that, because he was Tom, but not Nicholas. From him it was unacceptable because it was indecent.

'I hate you!' she said.

'A little dancing go-go scrubber. Anybody's bit. That's it, isn't it? All right then, let's see you dance!'

He jerked the loose chain again, once, twice, three times, and she felt her arms pulled. Her heels had left the ground and her weight was taken entirely on her toes. It was very uncomfortable.

'Nicky, you're hurting me! Let's talk about it in the morning. Get me down now.' The position was becoming increasingly painful to her arms as she shifted about, trying to find a better place to stand on tip-toe, the chains grating together above her. Looking upwards she tried to grasp the links, to haul on them and so prevent the manacles cutting into her wrists.

He stood watching her, as though she were performing something tricky in a gymnasium. Or she was a string puppet.

'Nicky, please!' There was pain in her wrists and shoulders. 'My shoulder, Nicky! You'll dislocate it again!' If it continued she felt she might faint. She took a deep breath and bit her lip.

'Be nice to me then.'

'Of course. Just hurry up, will you?' It always used to end like this, defeat and humiliation for Pippa, another victory for her maddening brother. He slackened the chain a little and she felt her weight on the floor again, her arms still above her head but relieved of their agony. He was still staring at her fixedly. 'Unlock these things now, Nick. Please!' He would make her beg, of course. She was prepared for that. But she was also beginning to be afraid. There was something so odd about him.

'Confess you're a little tart.' His mouth was thin and he looked pale. She had never seen him like this before. My God, she thought, he *is* crazy! He's the one who is mad. He's just a sadist after all!

'Confess it, Pipistrelle. You've been anybody's bit. Go on, confess it! Say: "Basically I'm just a little bed-hopping tart."'

She had to get away from him. 'All right,' she said. She had to humour him, to get out of these manacles. Say anything.

He took down the little key from the hook and swung it from its string in front of her face. 'Say it.'

She closed her eyes and repeated the words. Humiliation complete.

Silence. He made no move to release her. Then he said: 'I'm the only one who's ever loved you, Pippy. Really cared for you. You know that, don't you? In your heart you know that.'

'Yes, Nick, if you say so.' She was trying not to be mesmerized by the key, still swinging. Behind him and above was the bull mask.

'Trouble is, you're weak. Now we've got this place to ourselves I'm going to look after you more. You need someone. You can't be trusted on your own. You're headstrong and a bit wild and you attract the wrong sort of man. You'll be through the money in no time. Let me take care of you. Do you understand?'

'We'll talk about it in the morning.'

'No, now. We'll talk about it now. You've got to trust me.'

'Just unlock these things. Please. I want to go up to my room. I'm tired.'

He unfastened her left hand and she withdrew it quickly from the ring and rubbed it against her thigh. Nicholas took her fingers, examined the red mark thoughtfully, pushing back the lace edge of her cuff to do so, and then kissed the inside of her wrist where it had chafed.

'You're coming to bed with me,' he said. 'You promised.'

Her eyes widened, staring at him. Suddenly for the first time she realized he was not joking. He meant it.

She didn't know why it should horrify her so much now. A few years ago it would have been different. If he'd put it to her at sixteen, one wet holiday perhaps, she'd have been excited by the idea; amused but excited too, this challenge of something forbidden, even more clandestine than the cinema gropings in the back row with poor Nigel, the boy on the moped. Of the two Nicholas was easily the more attractive. It would have scared her deliciously, but she would probably have gone in the end. Now it was different, all different. Everything was different. She hated Nicholas, he terrified her and she wanted to get away from him.

'All right,' she heard herself say. Anything, promise anything. She had to get out of that other handcuff. He let go of her wrist and she put it behind her back. She tried to think. When she was free she would make a dash for it, up to her room. There would be storms outside but there was nothing he could do, except rouse the whole house, and he'd see reason in the morning and try to pretend it had never happened. She felt the click of the other lock. She had shut her eyes while she was thinking; now she pulled her hand down and opened them at the same time.

What she saw paralysed her.

It was not Nicholas standing in front of her. Or at least she thought not. It was a complete stranger, somebody she had never seen in her life before, a man in an open-necked shirt, sleeves like a blouse, full at the wrists. And on his head he wore the bull mask, wide horns, increasing his height, concealing his eyes.

It was mad. Not a trick of the light. Everything was mad. She was mad. Or dead. Nicholas was dead, coming over from Canada, a plane crash. Nothing existed but her imagination.

Too shocked to scream, she watched the anonymous creature begin to come towards her. Backing away from it at the same pace she continued until she felt her retreat blocked by a table behind her. She looked round. She was against one of the exhibit stands. From it she snatched up something with which to defend herself. It was a sort of bill-hook, with a spike and a blade to it, like a cut-down halberd. She grasped the instrument ready before her in both hands, gripping it firmly and steeling her muscles and her will; and when the man tried to take it from her she suddenly jerked it back, raised it fully above her head and brought it down with all her force on the headpiece.

The Minotaur, and the room, reeled back together; then the man inside stumbled and fell. There was blood. Great gushing spurts of it. Hitchcock's little joke. All that blood in the shower. The mask was shattered. The face beneath, under all the blood, was Nicholas's. She had killed Nicky. He lay on the floor, dead.

She was running, running, running.

She was outside, in the gardens, pelting through the maze of dark bushes. How had she got here?

Not keeping to the paths, just going on headlong down the slope in a straight line, crashing through the plantations, she heard her own breath panting from her open mouth. She was saying something, gasping it out as she ran, but she couldn't make out what—only that her entire being was calling out in misery. The night sky seemed to be lit up and though she dreaded to look back she did so at last, to see the whole villa going up in flames.

They had left the oil lamps alight and unguarded in her bedroom, that was it.

Götterdämmerung ...

* * *

Her shoulder was still hurting. This was because someone was holding her firmly by the upper arms. Gradually the formless interplay of lights and moving shadows began to focus and identify themselves as meaningful objects—a chromium electric fan, flowers in a vase, a white painted radiator, a plain curtained window with two horizontal bars. She appeared to be in bed, one which was too narrow and too tight for comfort, and the woman who was holding her had brown sleeves, but everything else was as yet confused. There were voices, but they were sounds only; they had no meaning. Someone was talking, someone else answered; that was all. A cold sensation appeared on her brow which was pleasant, very soothing and nice. A hand was wiping her forehead gently and she was conscious of a smell like a dentist's surgery, sweet and fresh, clinical. The two women, it suddenly occurred to her, were nurses. She was pleased with this deduction. It had a rationality in relationship to the other things which gave her confidence, discovering amid all this nebulous confusion the existence of some kind of cosmic order which was deeply and strangely, if inexplicably, heartening. It confirmed one's faith in the meaning of meaning. She even recognized the flowers. They were the same ones; they had not been changed. A pyramid of red and white and pink and yellow roses. But that was stupid, impossible; they could not have remained precisely the same like that, with the identical greetings card still propped up in front of it, all that time. It worried her, breaking the cosmos again.

'*Torna in vita*,' she heard someone say, and there was movement again. A figure loomed into view, someone she half recognized. It was Dr Rossano looking different. He appeared to be fatter than she had thought, his face coarser, fleshier, his hair thinner and wisped back over a balding scalp. He looked down at her, head at an angle, and smiled. Then he sat on the edge of the bed.

'All right now?' He held up his forefinger in front of her and watched her eyes focus upon it. 'Good! You are through. All over!'

She knit her brows and squinted at him painfully. Who was this person? Some other mirage, a false Rossano, another meaningless impersonation. She had been here before. This was the second time she had woken up to find Rossano taking her pulse, the third time he had told her everything was all right now. Her orbit had brought her back to the same point. There was no progression.

'You have had a nightmare, no? I think so. I also think that at some time you have been on one of the hallucinogens—LSD perhaps, am I right?... They can stay in the bloodstream for months, did you know? And then, triggered off by something reactive—another drug possibly—suddenly emerge, especially if you've had a bad trip once before, to give a recurrence. I think the sedative we gave you to ease you and help you sleep may have clashed with your old one to produce a condition of hypersensitivity. You certainly had an *incubo* from which we could not awaken you ... The fan is not bothering you?'

'How long?' She was still dazed.

'How long have you been asleep? Oh, maybe a couple of hours.'

Two hours, No more? She couldn't believe it. Nicky—he wasn't dead! A flood of relief, followed by doubt, confusion, disbelief. She could no longer believe anything. This was another layer of the onion, inside which would be found more lies, more confusion, layer within layer.

'Nicky?' she said.

'Your husband?'

'My brother.' Her own voice sounded weak. 'I didn't kill him?'

Rossano shook his head. 'A bad trip. Is that what you imagined?

Do not worry, it is all over now. You have killed no one, I assure you.'

And Raf—then it followed he wasn't dead either. This was incredible.

'Raffaele?' she murmured. How far could she trust this apparition in the white housecoat sitting heavily on her bed? Was this a real experience?

The familiarity of the Christian name caused Rossano to smile.

'You may be certain the Count and Countess d'Anza are both alive and well, if the contrary is what you are afraid of. And they are still most desirous to meet you.'

Pippa stared at the man studying her case history card.

'There was no Countess,' she said.

'Indeed I assure you, Miss Rowantree.' He slotted the buff card back into its folder and took a magazine from the top of the pile on the bedside cabinet below the flowers, flicked over the pages backwards and then, finding what he wanted, held it out to her. It showed a picture of a man and woman, both somewhere in their forties perhaps, sitting on a red brocade sofa in a stiff domestic attitude of celebrities being interviewed. The caption below stated that the Count Raffaele Alessandro d'Anza-Pianezze, with the Countess (formerly Signora Teresa Bucci, wife of ex-racing driver Eugenio Bucci) having returned from Rome to their summer residence on Lake Garda, the Villa Franceschini, were proposing to enlarge the premises to include a school of water sports and aqualung training. The man was square-faced with glasses, shortish, heavy-featured, with thick, dark, glossy hair—nothing like Raf at all. In another photograph, adjacent, the fourteen-year-old son of the Countess, Nino Bucci, home for the holidays, stood squinting at the sun in striped swimming briefs, a smiling likeness of the unsmiling, overdressed woman.

Pippa shook her head. 'But this is not the man. The man who spoke to me.' She went on to describe that first encounter in the grounds of the villa, and as she built up a picture of the tall man who had warned her of the danger of the gate Rossano looked at her with interest.

'Ah, that would be Lamotta, the Count's *fattore*—a retired army officer, I believe.... But to return to your disturbance, your bad dream, whatever it was, Miss Rowantree, you must tell me about it sometime. Soon, before you forget the details. Try to recall it now. Everything will rapidly slip into your subconscious memory within minutes. I find the whole subject interesting.'

But Pippa didn't want to talk.

'Very well. It is something you wish to forget. You are quite right. Do not worry about it. But if you think back you will probably find that everything, every single detail, is in some measure a reflection of some experience or some thought in your waking life, distorted perhaps by anxieties, enlarged by suppressed wishes, but originating in your memory, nowhere else. This is the nature of all dreams. The brain is a highly complex computer which has to programme itself in sleep from all the mass of data fed into it. Perhaps because we are used to, and therefore prefer, a logical world of cause and effect we expect this operation to perform some kind of sequence giving the effect of narrative. We are then surprised that this does not seem to follow the rules of our familiar life, that the narrative is apparently irrational, meaningless even. But why should it be otherwise? A dream is a collection of second experiences. A real incident, a wish, a fear, something you've read —all carry equal weight. If in your dream you murdered your brother then it is because at some time you did it in your thoughts. Most of us have, I suppose, if the truth were told.... Now, are you feeling better?'

'I don't know.'

'Because if you are now sufficiently composed we might consider letting you see your husband.' He watched her reaction. It was one of bewilderment again.

'Husband?' Why did he keep using that term? 'I'm not married. I have a brother. That's all.'

'He said he was your husband. He's been waiting here for some time, but we would not let him see you while you were under sedation. Now I think you are well enough. If you wish it.'

'I haven't got a husband.' The rational world was slipping away again just when she had come within sight of it.

Rossano glanced down at her ringless hand fumbling with the throat of her nightdress. Somebody had removed the green scarab for safety. 'Perhaps you don't agree with the institution of marriage,' he said. 'One is not concerned with technicalities ... Do you wish to see him?... I should if I were you. Even if you've quarrelled. He's come a long way.'

A pause. And then, as she didn't answer, he nodded to one of the nurses who left the room and then returned.

The rational world was receding, spinning away outwards, out into space at the speed of light. Tom stood there; and the cosmic particles of meaning finally disintegrated around him, exploding into the infinite as a corpuscular bloodstream, taking her life with it. Another apparition. This is the way the world ends. You peel an onion until you come to the centre, expecting to find the truth, and there you discover another onion for you to start all over again. And the heart breaks.

She felt her throat too dry to gasp, let alone articulate. She was dumb. The gridiron, how long can it be endured?

He was sitting beside her, on the chair provided, looking at her intensely, eyes strained, as though he had been out searching for her all night in some thick fog. Then he said: 'Are you all right, Pip?' Just that.

She sat up and clung to him desperately.

* * *

It was really Pippa.

I could scarcely believe it. After all that headlong chase across Europe on Dad's telegraphed cash. Twenty hours. It seemed like a week. Trains screaming in the night. Being sick in the lurching loo. Thinking of her. Time on bloody leaden wings. Change at Basle. Being frisked for drugs. They didn't like my face, or my appearance. The French at Calais were more interested in subversive literature. Their man didn't care too much for the little book of essays until he discovered they were by Montaigne. Then it was all right.

And there she was, sitting up in bed in a plain cotton nightdress, looking lost, anxious, searching me. Like someone staring through a fog. Is that you out there? Say something.

Wide grey cartwheel eyes with blue spokes. Lovely, innocent Pippa eyes, so easily hurt. The times I'd made them cloud over and then turn away. That was the image that had haunted me all the time she was lost. Remorse, you useless fool, won't bring back the dead; nor will it ever uncommit an act of cruelty. Find her, find her!

Her cheek against mine, I said: 'Forgive me.'

She had put up her arms; now she closed her eyes and wept, clinging to my shirt. I could feel the wet of her eyes although they were shut.

'Tell me you're all right,' I said.

And tight against my face she whispered: 'Tom?' It was a sort of question, I think. The first word I'd heard her say for seven weeks. Then she added, dutifully: 'I'm all right.' Her voice.

We held each other. I think the others had gone out of the room. It was just a double. No one in the other bed. We were alone.

'Listen,' I said, 'I've had a sort of reconciliation with my father. When you left I did some desperate things, including that. I told him about you—I had to tell someone—and he said: "Then why the hell aren't you out looking for her?" Which is about the most sympathetic thing he's said for years ... As though I hadn't! Been looking for you, I mean. I scoured the whole country for you. Went down to your hide-out in Devon. Found it through your solicitor. The cheques continued to turn up and I kept worrying him. At first he didn't know anything, or he wasn't prepared to say. Then I had you listed as a missing person and they co-operated. I was called to a mortuary once. The police. They'd found a girl in Epping Forest—you know, the usual. Awful strangulation marks, eyes open. Some poor kid. It nearly did for me. At night I kept seeing her eyes. Your eyes. I couldn't sleep. I thought it might have been you. It could still be you, somewhere, somewhere. I couldn't sleep. I just sat in the bloody kitchen. And I prayed. Don't know who to. Never done it before. Then the police called again. They'd spotted that "News in Brief" bit. Some Italian Count with a news-worthy wife—her first husband had been killed racing—had been involved in a spill. Your name on the passport. English girl—I suppose somebody thought it was worth a flash to Fleet Street.'

I had to keep on talking. It seemed to comfort her, like a night-light. 'You'd better come back and meet my father,' I said. 'I'm not going to give up writing but I don't want things to go on like this between us. When he hears your little deb accent his stony heart is going to melt. "Boy, you could have done worse after all." I can hear him saying it.'

I talked because I sensed that there was another name which kept forming itself in her mind.

'Zillah?' she said at last.

I kissed her wet cheek and held her. I suppose you could call that an act of contrition. Her convent would have had a name for it. But I meant it.

'That? Oh, that never got off the ground. Truly, Pipit. We

didn't even get to bed.' I don't know whether she believed me. It was all unnaturally quiet for a time, but she didn't move. Then I said: 'Listen, I'll tell you a story. If you're sitting comfortably, are you?... Once upon a time there was this young prince. His father, who was getting on a bit in years, wanted him to marry and take over the kingdom. But the lad didn't like ruling, nor had he met anyone he considered beautiful enough. So he said rudely: "Push off, Dad!" and left home. Thus he wandered about the world, earning his living as a minstrel, and getting thinner and hungrier and older until one day he arrived at this castle in St John's Wood where he was kindly offered hospitality. And there, floating down the stairs, was a lovely fairy girl who said her name was Morgan le Fay. And he knew she was his destiny. Unfortunately ...'

Suddenly, firmly, she tightened her arms round my neck. And laughed.